Oliver St. John Gogarty (1878–1957) was
educated at Stonyhurst, Oxford and Trinity
College, Dublin. Gogarty was a Fellow of the
Royal College of Surgeons of Ireland and, like
W.B. Yeats, became one of the first Senators of
the Irish Free State.

Tumbling in the Hay

OLIVER ST. JOHN GOGARTY

The lark, that tirra-lirra chants,
*   With heigh! with heigh! the thrush and the jay,*
Are summer songs for me and my aunts,
*   While we lie tumbling in the hay.*

SHAKESPEARE

SPHERE BOOKS LIMITED
30–32 Gray's Inn Road, London WC1X 8JL

First published in Great Britain by
Constable and Company Ltd 1939
Copyright © The Estate of Oliver St. John Gogarty 1939

Published by Sphere Books Ltd 1982

Set in Intertype Baskerville

Printed and bound in Great Britain by
Cox & Wyman Ltd, Reading

'They are likewise in modern language called balancing women, or tymbesteres, players upon the timbrel, which they also balanced occasionally, as we shall find a little farther on. It is almost needless to add, that the ancient usage of introducing females for the performance of these difficult specimens of art and agility, has been successfully continued to the present day.'

(From *The Sports and Pastimes of the People of England*, by Joseph Strutt.)

'Were such things here, as we doe speake about?
Or have we eaten on the insane Root,
That takes the Reason Prisoner?'

Macbeth.

CONTENTS

Chapter I

MANNERS MAKYTH MAN

Crazily the cab came slithering – Wiseman up – away from the Medical School, sideways across the greasy setts until immediately it took a turn to the left, then to the right up Fownes Street, past Golly's, and so on to the left again into Dame Street. Within it sat a lady upright and tight-lipped and a youth beside her who gesticulated suddenly as the vehicle passed the two myrtle bushes which, in tubs, stood to ornament with their dark-green pyramids Mr Golly's licensed premises. He gesticulated, holding his cuff tight with the fingers of his left hand, to distract his mother's attention from two young men of about his own age who stood at either side of the myrtled entrance, busily engaged in not noticing the cab or its occupants. Nevertheless, the youth thought it necessary to distract his mother's attention, if not from those about it, at least from the legend above the door which told in gold letters that the owner of the house was licensed to sell beer, wine or spirits for consumption on the premises. His precaution was superfluous, for his mother looked neither to right nor left. Her mind was preoccupied and rankling by the treatment she had just received from the Registrar of the Medical School.

What hurt her pride was this. After some delay in a bare room off the hall, she was admitted to the presence of a stout, squat, bearded figure, who glanced up without rising from his chair and queried sharply:

'Name?'

1

'I am Mrs Ouseley. You have probably heard of my late husband?'

'It's your son's name I want. I take it that this is your son?'

'Yes.'

'His name?'

'Gideon.'

He took a note. 'There are seven letters in Ouseley, I suppose? What school?'

'Stonyhurst.'

He took a note. 'A good school. Any others?'

'Clongowes.'

'Better still: nearer home.' He pointed his pen-handle at the youth. 'Your age, young man?'

'Twenty.'

He took a note.

'You want to enter the School of Anatomy. What have you got? Have you got First and Second Arts? It would be better if you took your hands out of your pockets.'

'He has passed Matriculation and First and Second Arts, and taken out his lectures in Botany, Biology, Chemistry and Physics.'

'All right, all right! That will be twelve guineas. It will be to your advantage and to mine if you will read this little brochure, for it will answer all your questions. Any intelligent boy can get qualified in Medicine provided he attends to his work. Osteology in the morning at nine o'clock sharp.'

He extended a small, red, paper-bound booklet with his left hand whilst scribbling notes with his right. But there was no-one to take it when he looked up. The last words he might have heard had he not been so business-like or rude, if you do not think that one term implies the other, were: 'You will open the door for your mother, Gideon.' He was alone.

The little man ran to the window. He had been so

2

accustomed to cut short what would have been the endless histories of country women giving the reasons for making their sons doctors, that he was quite astonished to find himself for once in his life cut short. What did she mean by flouncing out like that without as much as 'Good-day'? Was she mad enough to throw away two years of fees, lectures, not to mention exams passed? She had informed him that he had got First and Second Arts – that, of course, included Matriculation fees – Botany, Zoology, Chemistry and Physics. Was she going to throw them all away and to set her precious son back by years? Or, worse still, was she taking him somewhere else? As he could not lift the window, seized as it was with coats of paint that, though few, nevertheless, when spread over half a century, served to make it immovable, he could not hear the short direction Wiseman the cabby heard, 'To Trinity College at once.'

Wiseman closed the door, mounted the box, and removed first an old yellow blanket from the kidneys of his mare, then from its socket an ivy whip with rounded, polished knobs, a gift from the estate of his late employer – for Wiseman was the Ouseleys' coachman in the days when there were carriages and horses in Rutland Square. He had succeeded Durkin and Maria Edgeworth, the cook – we called her Edgeworth because her first name was Maria – and these were the founders of the Hay Hotel.

The Hay was symbolised for those with an eye to see by the hay with which one window, that to the left of the doorway, was stuffed and by the Chester cake, sugarsticks, squibs, matches and pipes; fireside gear, which furnished the other window and promised fuller fare within, independent of the hours of night or even morning. Here birds that sang darkling were refreshed, as were the jaded steeds which brought hither cabs belated in the dawn – refreshment, in a word, for man

3

and horse : which things go to prove, if proof indeed were needed, that out of evil cometh good.

The mare seemed to know so well that a direct drive-off was more in keeping with the offended dignity of her passenger that it was hard to turn her right-about in front of the School; but Wiseman coaxed her, and, with her tail pointed at the Registrar, she made off in a huff. That is why the cab came up Fownes Street, angrily rattling as if it bore Boadicea, on its way to Trinity College. It passed Golly's going well, and turned with majesty into Dame Street. And why shouldn't it? Wiseman's wife had been young Ouseley's wet-nurse. It was a respectable cab, and it looked it with its ivory knobs and handles within, silver without, and its silken-braided window straps. It had evidently been a brougham once. Perhaps it had been thrown in with the whip, 'the property of the late owner'. Like the door-handles, the lamps were silver; and if they had been permitted to become somewhat black, it was not from any considerations of mourning, but rather from a desire not to be obtrusive and so invite, maybe, the envy of other cabbies. It was, as I said, a respectable cab, not, for instance, one like Lucas's, whose owner would ask, as he drove chance lovers slowly round St Stephen's Green at night, 'Let me know when yez want me to put in the plank.' It was a most respectable cab, for Wiseman was a most respectable man. He never went to funerals when the boys would be playing a four-hand game on an overcoat stretched across their knees after the interment (when spades were trumps) as they drifted back from the 'Cross Guns' or Brian Boru's. He never drove lovers round the Green or along the quays to Ringsend and back. Never. Nor did he stoop to take toll of any Ariadne left by a retreating lover on the wharf. He with great constancy refused to share in borrowed bliss. When pressed to wait and promised that if he waited there

4

would be 'great gas' he would whip up and drive off, remarking as he drove, 'It's a great thing to have it in the house.' Domestic was his bliss: he had been blessed eleven times. He was enabled, with his well-plied cab and a little help from his wife's wet-nursing (for Providence will provide for the suckling), to rear his elevenfold family. Even the fact that, too young to go out to service and to help with the housekeeping, his family were still all about him caused him no misgivings. 'It's a great thing to have it in the house.'

'He wasn't long,' said Weary.

'Ho, she's taking him home!' said Silly Barney.

Now Weary had got his name from Barney because of a certain slowness or serenity of manner that admitted no rush nor permitted precipitation in solving any question which might arise regarding whose round it was — 'Weary with a weariness that doth not weary.' And Barney got his nickname from Weary because of a song he composed beginning 'Arrah, Barney, Silly Barney'.

Weary pointed out that the house of their friend was in the opposite direction. That was so; it was a spacious and copious house in Rutland Square which looked out upon Hengler's Circus, by which that old pleasant square was transformed into a slum. Not to go home only went to prove that there was something up. Curiosity led them to the corner. There it was. They could see the cab's back shining as it steered through the traffic behind Grattan's statue. It required a little manoeuvring to keep it in sight. It did not turn yet. Instead of turning it crossed the stream of traffic going north and south and went right on. Two halves of the great gate of Trinity College opened simultaneously at a signal from Wiseman. The porters in black velvet hunting caps (a joke from the days when there were Fellow Commoners in College?) closed them again.

Barney looked at Weary.

'In the name of God?'

'And of the Holy and Undivided Trinity,' said Weary Mac. There was nothing to do but to return to Mr Golly's licensed house.

Mr Golly was a corpulent, quick-moving, good-natured man with rolling chins and a pair of rolling brown eyes. His head was nested between two tufts of hair. Time had tonsured him prematurely. He had a way of leaning over to you confidentially from his side of the counter with 'D'ye know what I heard lately?' He would glance rapidly from side to side before dropping his voice to inaudibility. 'Listen here now.' You always felt deaf when listening there.

In spite of his proximity to the Medical School he had the greatest respect for the Faculty of Medicine, which even the 'medicals' themselves could not shake. On the contrary, it was they who gave it an interest that was almost mystical in its devotion, and this in spite of the fact that what was called the Medical School was only a School of Anatomy where dissections were carried on. Instruction in Medicine proper did not commence until the medicals began to walk the hospitals. All this was well known to Mr Golly, yet he believed in medicals even before they left the School of Anatomy to attend more advanced studies. The reason for his belief was inseparable from an idea that the younger the medical the more likely was he to be in possession of knowledge which would be fresh and unspoilt and all the more powerful, like nascent hydrogen before it was dissipated; and before the medicals themselves were dissipated, while each was still in the first flush of his enthusiasm – 'with the dew still on him,' as Brindsley said of a certain poet in his morning thirst. Thus it will be seen that there was something mystical in the nature of Mr Golly's

6

belief, something associated with the early traditions of the healing art when cures were transmitted through the agency of dreams. He wanted knowledge as fresh as it was when first imparted; he preferred the well on the mountain side to the river by the road. He preferred it 'first shot' before it became reduced by the routine of general practice to a mere rule of thumb. He believed that some time and somewhere in the evolution of a medical student a moment came when the great secret of life was handed down. All were sworn not to reveal it, but only to put this knowledge into practice. 'The practice of Medicine!' A window in his imagination opened on a scene where the oldest physician – Dr Little, shall we say? – took the youngest apart, pointed to a patient, whispered something which was followed by the solemn nodding of two heads and a finger on the lips of one. And then the writing in Latin with the sign of Zeus, one of those old pagan gods, in the top left-hand corner!

It was good to see the term beginning. It would bring a number of new medicals along. For some reason Garratty, the pathology porter, who had also charge of the dissecting-room, had been rather remiss of late. Between terms it was all right to talk things over, but he only knew from what people died. He had charge of their livers and lights and all that kind of thing. But he couldn't compare with a medical.

Mr Golly was neither an invalid nor an hypochondriac. On the contrary, he knew that 'medicine would do him a power of good', and, as he believed in it, he believed in almost unattainable heights, festivals, orgies and excesses of Health – supernatural and only to be achieved by some elixir as yet undiscovered or undisclosed. Himself apart, it would be a great thing to have his premises associated with medicals, dedicated as it were to Æsculapius, and he an authority and a consultant both for his customers and the rest of the Licensed Trade.

When the two-year students returned to wait for their friend, he buffered himself gently against the marble and leant across it. He looked quickly from one to the other, and then past Barney to the door. They had the place all to themselves. He could consult them in confidence, if not with it.

'It's like this,' he said solemnly. 'I suffer something shocking from flatulence.'

Weary became pensive with embarrassment. Barney hung his head and then shot a glance from his small, deep blue eyes somewhat furtively at Weary. Weary saved their faces by covering the consultation, for they undoubtedly were being consulted, and being consulted on a question of medicine in their second year filled them with consternation. Nevertheless, they represented the profession. They couldn't let it down or they would let themselves down and lose credit with Mr Golly.

'The wife, a merry woman in her day, often called out, "Another balloon gone, Gus!" as if I was one of them ould cods swapping balloons for rags and bones with the chisellers, "Another balloon gone, Gus!" I used to be getting to be a trial to her. Now if either of you gentlemen . . . ?' Having implied the question, he looked hopefully for a moment at each in turn and then gave the marble counter an unnecessary swipe of a glass-cloth to hide his embarrassment or his anxiety about the answer.

With only Botany, Zoology, Chemistry and Physics behind them, it was a more embarrassing moment for the two. Botany could not avail, and as for Zoology — surely they could not fit Golly into that *galère*. Their only hope was with the chemists and the men who expounded Physics.

Weary recovered first. His short acquaintance with

doctors had not gone for nothing. If he couldn't keep talking about disease without giving away anything, there would be little use in going on for Medicine at all. Besides, half of every cure consists in letting the patient talk and purge the stuffed bosom, so to speak. The doctor should turn himself into a clout into which the patient might clap all his slings and arrows. But all should be invested with an air of science. And the first of the sciences is Physics. He took a preliminary sip at his pint and put it down with deliberation.

'Do you believe in first principles, Mr Golly?' ⇒ opening the thesis.

Mr Golly bowed an egg that was as brown and speckled as that of a turkey, in assent.

'And would you say that your flatulence was worse in the morning?'

Mr Golly was confirmed in his conviction. Out of the mouths of babes! Encouragingly he testified to his physician : 'Ye'd make me think you had it yourself!'

Weary received the tribute in silence, then proceeded to carry the war farther into Mr Golly's constitution.

'So I thought,' he said. 'So I thought.'

Uncanny as it was to have some of his symptoms diagnosed prematurely, the repetition added something ominous to Mr Golly's complaint. What did 'So I thought' mean? Did it mean anything serious now? In spite of growing apprehension, he supplied an instance which was intended to bear Weary out.

'Worse in the morning, did ye say? There was a coursing match coming on early one morning at the Ninth Lock, and me and Jem Plant was up to meet Jack Lalor the barber at about half five. I declare to God!' He threw up his hands because there were sounds which words could not convey, not noticing that he held a match-box which, being half empty, rattled providentially, because music comes in where words leave off.

'I might have known it,' Weary remarked, nodding.

'But in the name of God how do you explain it?' Mr Golly asked in a voice far above a whisper. Unable to sustain the tension, he followed up anxiously: 'Is there any explanation at all?'

'A very simple one, as it seems to me. Weren't you drawing in a lot of night air that hadn't completely been aired by the sun? You said you believed in first principles. Now,' said Weary, quoting from Professor Campbell, the man with the round cuffs, 'let us proceed to inquire into the nature of air. Air, that is the atmosphere which surrounds the earth, is composed of many gaseous constituents. Of these nitrogen and oxygen are the principal; they are usually found in the proportion of 79.16 to 21.80 – roughly one to four.'

'When I was a chiseller,' Mr Golly interrupted, 'I always remembered that by "four to one on".' In his relief he laughed. Weary went on: 'There are many other gases in the air.'

'Four to one bar two,' Silly Barney observed.

In an even voice, Weary continued: 'I have not finished yet. There was an old Dublin doctor, Dr David McBride, who observed that carbon dioxide gas increased – increased,' said Weary sternly, shaking a tobacco-stained forefinger at Golly, 'increased at night. And you know what night air can be.'

'I get you now,' Mr Golly nodded.

'Causative factor number one – but what about the newly discovered argon? What about argon?'

'What about it?' Golly asked. 'When did it come in?'

'Are you codding?' Barney interjected. 'It was always there.'

'Why weren't we told about it?'

'Because it wasn't discovered.'

'And it was there all the time? And what was it doing?

There must be a shockin' lot of things in this world of which we know nothing,' said Mr Golly. 'Glory be to God!'

Mr Golly was called aside to serve a pint. They could hear him commenting on its excellence to the unseen customer. 'Here's me snowy-breasted pearl,' he remarked, referring to its foam. This gave Barney an opportunity to ask when he was coming into the consultation. It wasn't fair of Weary to get all the credit metaphorically and actually from Golly's cure. Weary was about to hand over his patient when that patient returned with : 'What does it do to you, anyway, this argon?'

'It's called argon, that is, "alpha", privative, and "ergon", work, because it does nothing,' Weary answered.

'Begorra,' said Golly, 'that is the very thing for me! Where can ye get it? And why does it do nothing?'

'Because it's an inert gas.'

'Because it's too weary to work,' Barney interjected, but Weary ignored him.

'According to the experiments of Kundt — ' that worthy continued.

'Oh, ho, ho!' roared Silly Barney.

'In mercurial vapour,' Weary added.

'Worse still!' remarked Barney, on whom the drink was beginning to tell, and laughed disconcertingly.

'Give us a chance, Mister!' Mr Golly intervened. Then he whispered hastily, fearing to be called away without being prescribed for, 'Eh, can you tell us what I am to do for it?'

'I was coming to that when Barney here interrupted. He can prescribe for you now, since he won't let me.' Mac appeared to resent Barney's interruption, but he was inwardly much relieved. He could not have continued the dissimulating dissertation much longer. It was Barney's turn. Barney took out a pencil and a pocket-book and said that it was like this. He drew a circle and what looked like a cannon ball with a little lightning conductor sticking out from beneath.

'Mr Golly,' he said, 'before undertaking anything, you must know where to get off.'

'There I am with you!' said Mr Golly.

'Now the greatest scientist the world ever saw, or one of them, was Foucault – Foucault the Frenchman, and he said before witnessing an experiment, "Tell me what to expect." '

'And wasn't he quite right?' said Mr Golly, fully approving. 'How did he know what they might put into it?'

'Now if you take medicine – and the taking of medicine is always something of an experiment – you must know what to expect. Is not that so?'

Mr Golly felt that too much was given to him to decide. He saw chances of a prescription for a bottle, or even a pill, receding, but he would not despair yet.

'What happened to this Fookoo in the end?' he inquired, not unconcerned, for his idea of an experiment was an explosion.

Weary looked at Silly Barney approvingly. He was saving the reputation of Medicine by putting the onus for the disease on the patient, to whom rightly it belonged. But Barney, knowing his own limitations, was not so sure that he could make Foucault cure flatulence by the pendulum experiment. A picture of Golly swinging slowly across the Pantheon with an inverted lightning conductor fixed fundamentally rose before his mind.

Mr Golly responded to a tapping in the front of the shop. At that moment, when the boys were nearly at the end of their tether, a sprightly figure rushed in, clapped both of them on the back.

'Gideon !' they welcomed.

'How much did you get on the links?' I asked, for it was I.

'We saw you in the cab being taken into Trinity. What happened in Cecilia Street?'

'The Registrar never offered my mother a chair, but left her standing. She walked out.'

'She couldn't stand it any longer,' Barney ventured and hummed a laugh.

'But I bet he offered her his little red book,' said Weary quietly.

'That bloody little book is the ruination of me,' Barney said. 'Ever since my mother got it, I can never cod her out of a penny. She knows how much every lecture costs and sends the cheque direct. All I can make anything out of is money for medical books, and Jimmy only lends five bob on a thirty-shilling edition.'

'Jimmy knows so much about medical books that he ought to be well qualified by this,' Weary suggested.

'Couldn't you pretend that you had to take out a grind?' I suggested.

'But she would want to know the name of the grinder, and she would make out the cheque in his name.'

'Well, let Weary be the grinder and we'll split the fees.'

'No, no,' said Barney, 'I'll grind Weary and let him touch his Da.'

'I'll grind the pair of you,' I volunteered.

'Trinity swank already,' Silly Barney said.

'You'd be in a nice stew if his mother wrote to Bermingham for your character,' Weary cogitated, meaning me.

'But I can imagine a letter to myself,' said Barney " "With all his cycling and all his athletics, he can still find time to teach you." '

'If between the three of us we can cure Golly we won't want any money, for we will get perpetual tick,' Mac opined.

'Our wants are few: a packet of Player's and a few

pints,' Barney realised modestly.

'There was no little red book in Trinity,' I boasted.

'Tell us what happened,' said Weary Mac.

'In Trinity the Registrar was Dr Anthony Traill, and the first thing he did – yet they all say he is uncouth – was to walk over and meet my mother halfway with a chair. The second thing he did – and it clinched it – was to remember my father, a most important point. I am now where it seems he intended that I should be placed. I am to prepare myself and endeavour to become worthy of a great profession, which contains men of the nobility of mind and the urbanity of manners of Sir Philip Smyly – who when my mother said that her case must be a trouble to him replied that he failed to find it so – see? So I'm entered on the books, and I got leave to go up for my Matric. next week even though I couldn't give them the usual notice. This was to make up for the fact that Dublin University doesn't recognise the Royal and so there are no *ad eundems*.'

'That's a nasty one on you, Barney,' Weary said. Barney was student of the Royal.

'He's lost two years all the same.'

'But I need not do anything but cycle and play football for two years. No more travelling twenty miles to and fro to play in a Cup Match. You should just see College Park from inside the railings.'

'More swank,' said Barney. ' "From inside the railings." '

'T.C.D. is not half as complicated as the Royal. In Trinity they called Botany and Zoology "Bugs and Weeds". I'll pass them on my ears. I didn't miss them with Bermingham, but I missed them with Traill.'

'Missed what?'

'My cuff links, of course. Bermingham asked me to take my hands out of my pockets and nearly spilt the beans before my mother. In Trinity I had to hold the

14

lapels of my coat to keep my cuffs out of sight. I was afraid she'd notice. How much did you get?'

'Eighteen-and-six in Cuffe Street,' said Barney, who was an expert at pawning and proud of it. At the thought of cuffs in Cuffe Street he went off into one of his murmuring fits of laughter. 'And we were trying not to spend it till you'd come.'

'Your uncle's moss agates are now with your "uncle",' Weary added.

I felt a sense of degradation. My friends repelled me. If my mother knew! The very thought of a pawn office! They saw nothing bad in it. They took it as a joke, a grim one at the worst, inseparable from the life of a 'medical'. So this was poverty. The feeling of humiliation and frustration brought about by poverty was such as she must have felt at the insolence to which poverty had subjected her an hour ago. But it was not her fault. It was mine, to degrade a family heirloom. Eighteen-and-six! That made it worse. She had prized them so much. I was yet to learn the difference between sentimental and 'business' values, between humanity and all the inhumanity that is concealed or excused by that thrice-accursed word 'business'.

'I have the ticket here if I can find it,' said Barney.

At that moment the Four Inseparables — Dolan, Hegarty, McCluskey and Roowan — appeared. They were always combined. Now one of the advantages of a pub over a club is that you never know who may come into it. In a club you know only too well. You can leave a pub without resigning; so we left, because, while there was no chance of our joining in the monosyllabic conversation of the Four, they could overhear ours, and that made us feel constrained. You have often seen two friends who know each other so well that they could drink in silence, but four without exchanging a word was rare this side of Somerset. The only thing to be done

15

with them was to send John the Citizen in. He was enough to break up any silence with his ejaculatory news – always the latest, always exciting. If he couldn't break their silence he would break up the group. But the Citizen, where was he?

Chapter II

IN COLLEGE PARK

I was watching Larry Oswald's calves very carefully as
we circled in a bicycle race round the College Park.
Larry, who was one of the best all-round athletes in
Ireland, was leading. I lay next behind him, waiting for
the least increase in the tension of the muscles in his
long, shapely calves. Then I'd be off. It was the third
round, and we were coming to the bell which rings to
announce the last lap. I had been floating along half
mesmerised by muscular fitness which made it possible
to move along the grass at twenty miles an hour as in a
dream. The grass ⚊ what is this the Professor of Weeds
called the grass in his last lecture? Yes, *Poa pratensis,*
meadow grass, that was it. I was doing twenty on *Poa
pratensis.*

'Gramineæ are sharply defined from all other plants,
and there are no genera as to which it is possible to feel
a doubt whether they should be referred to it or not.'
That was comforting and reassuring ⚊ no mistake, though
'referred to them or not' would be more correct. But
who had a doubt about grass? If I fell on *Poa pratensis*
I would be 'tumbling in the hay' prematurely, for it was
not hay-time and we were not in a meadow, but on a
clean-shaven lawn. 'Fertile glume and hyaline : spikelets
bisexual, or male and bisexual, each male standing close
to a bisexual.' The worst thought of all is that the sweet
odour of new-mown grass depends on cumarin, a chemi-
cal, of course. Why can't chemists keep their hands off

the scent of new-mown hay? It isn't as if they hadn't stinks enough.

Though I was full of Botany and Zoology from my lectures in the Royal, it would never do to treat those subjects lightly just because they called them Bugs and Weeds in Trinity College. The very fact that the professor happened to lecture on such a common thing as grass was a tip in time. He might knock a fellow out with a simple question, 'What is grass?' And what good would a knowledge of the seventy orders of Linnæus, the bird who knelt down and praised God when he saw a gorse bush in bloom, be to you if you couldn't tell the Professor of Botany what was grass? Why, the thing was everywhere, and that was enough to put you off your guard. It is the simplest things that are the hardest to define. Parker, who is the grinder in Astronomy, says: 'The simpler the statement, the harder and more complicated the Mathematics are which have to be employed to warrant it.' Don't think that these medical professors don't know it. Don't they? That is why I was tumbled completely by Purser in the physiology exam when he shot out, 'What is blood?' Now that was the very thing you would never think about. You would read up all about the corpuscles in the bleeding thing, but you'd never think of asking what it was. Too late you got the answer : 'Blood is a fluid medium,' etc. I would not be caught out that way again. That is why I know all about grass. And what is more, I know what it is. All flesh is grass, but grass isn't all flesh — by no means.

As we circled, my eye caught sight of a tall, red-headed man in knickerbockers with grey stockings. He stood under a tree smoking a pipe. Slow-burning tobacco! It was McNought, the Professor of Anatomy. He was watching the race with the greatest disapproval. Larry didn't care who was watching, for he was a Fellow Commoner and had independent means, which means that his money made him independent of a profession and professors. He also had a private cycling track in his grounds somewhere out in Bray. But my case was far different. I was dependent on professors; and the Professor of Anatomy was anything but a sport. He did not like the spectacle of muscle in action. He preferred still life. I knew the moment he saw me that I had lost my next 'Half', my anatomy exam, before it was held. I was wasting my time in the College Park when I should have been behind it in his one-storeyed building, picking with a forceps and displaying with a knife the nerves or the arteries, filled with red lead, of some unclaimed pauper's well-flayed, dark-red corpse. On a day like this with cumarin coming up from the grass!

Suddenly Larry, who was watching me through his ear over his left shoulder, missed a black figure, upright, with nodding head on his cycle, florid-faced and golden-haired. I heard the challenging roar of his half-inch pitch chain. I drew up on Larry. He could not see our challenger until too late. The bell went, and with it, lengths ahead, in the odour of cumarin, went Alfred Emerson Reynolds, son of the Professor of Chemistry.

Cumarin! I pulled the handle-bars almost out of my machine, forcing myself down to crush the pedals. The machine bounded forward. Larry too was astir. But it takes some riding to recover from a comparative lethargy wherein you are caught napping and to catch up three lengths on a fellow who has jumped you and who is still grassant – that is, going strong. Doubled up, turning the 75 gear as hard as I could, fearing to think lest thought destroy the mechanical rhythm of the body and interfere with the current of energy flowing instinctively into the limbs, I gained on him until I could see his back wheel-spokes of blue bright steel glistening in the sun. They made a disc transparent, so great was their speed. The scent of the grass was lost. I was beginning to see as in a spectrum; my ears grew cold — I could no longer hear our bicycles' musical hum. Suddenly the whitewash of the winning-line flashed up at me from the ground. It was all I could do to take off speed enough round the unbanked corner. Too late, Alfred had won! Good old Alfred E.! I rode a lap to cool off slowly and save the strain on the heart. I had missed the Mile Championship of Dublin University.

I might have known it with the professor standing there hoodoo-ing me from under a tree. Why couldn't he stay in his dead-house and leave me to look after my duties when it suits me? That is, about three weeks before any of their exams! I like to think of the little Japanese who asked permission to study and to pass in twelve months the three years' course in philosophy or whatever it was ordained for a doctorate by professors in Berlin.

There was nothing to be done about it but to take care that I would win the ten-miles in Belfast. Lady Jaffe's prize was a gold watch. Geordie Robinson, the plumber, who had won it last year, told me that a fellow can sledge it easily for ten. That will be better than wasting entrance fees for an exam the result of which is a foregone conclusion.

But if he only knew that I spent the early morning up at the Scalp pacing and training with Charlie Pease!

It would look like a swelled head if I congratulated Alfred. It would look as if beating me were a thing deserving congratulations. Let Larry do it. There was no doubt that anyone who could beat Larry was worthy of congratulations. What beat me was that — what do you call the opposite of a mascot? — that hoodoo with his pipe under the tree. All anatomists smoke when dissecting; probably they are so old-fashioned, ignorant and removed from life as to imagine that smoke is an antiseptic and a preservative of their beastly health and that it helps in their ghoulish job. I wonder, is there anything in the theory that slow-burning tobacco produces coal-tar products in the lower bowel? Compared to his predecessor, old Cunningham – but you couldn't compare anything to Cunningham. He took an interest in anatomy, I must admit; but he took such a great interest that it afforded comic relief. In his blue suit he would stand lecturing in the theatre, with a skull in his hand, before the class, and lose himself in rhapsodies. If I could only recall the verses which appeared in the Edinburgh University on his return as Professor to that city after long years in Trinity College, Dublin! Who was the writer? Why didn't I send him congratulations? Here are a few of the excellently descriptive lines :

> I saw him cross the dingy quad.
> > His clothes were plain. I shall not cease
> To muse on that impression odd :
> > An active sergeant of police !
>
> With skull in hand he held me thrall,
> > Astonishment enlarged his eyes,
> His attitude, his gestures all
> > Evinced a wild, intense surprise.
>
> 'And what is this low ridge here shown?'
> > Oh, what? I inly, all intense –
> 'Above the orbit on this bone?
> > It is the frontal eminence !'
>
> Oh, how relieved I was, how glad
> > The horrid thing was nothing worse !
> That night I dreamt and wished I had
> > A wife, a mother or a nurse,

He left T.C.D. after a long and successful career as a Scotsman. By the time he was invited to take the Chair of Anatomy in his native city he had enlisted all the schools of Dublin University into his anatomy lectures. Even those who were preparing to become parsons had to 'take out' something anatomical. And lecture fees and re-entrance fees for exams plus your salary mounted up. He was wise enough to let such a source of income as me alone.

His successor, McNought, must have been only a Scotsman very far removed, because, instead of rejoicing in my many failures to take his hobby seriously, he resented my hobby in the College Park. All he had convinced himself that I did not know would have been sufficient to give me the half Fellowship in the College of Surgeons.

Any exams I ever manage to pass are due to bad weather. For who in his senses would waste his days in a dead-house when the sun is shining outside, and when the whole subject of Anatomy is not a mind-full for a moron?

I found out what was wrong with Anatomy; it lacked humour. Also it amounted to a bastard language, because to learn the terms used in Anatomy is tantamount to learning a language, a mixture of Latin and Greek and remnants from the days before English was heard and Latin was the language of all wise men, and the history and names which enshrine the long descent of the science. The dry style of the textbooks is relieved but once in the three volumes of Cunningham, where his enthusiasm carries him away and he calls it the 'huge' Great Sciatic Nerve. I loved him for his enthusiasm. Being a romantic myself I would be the last to change, with a view to simplification, the terms and names of Anatomy with their long tradition and sometimes their magnificent sounds. 'The long pudendal nerve of Soemmering' always appeals to me. Who was Soemmering, who gave his name to the long pudendal? What a nerve he had! What a stir it would make if you went as the nerve to a fancy-dress ball; or if it could be personified to address a great meeting of medicals of both sexes! Where the major-domo would shout, 'I crave silence for the long pudendal nerve of Soemmering. Ladies and Gentlemen, the Long Pudendal!' What interest and excitement not unmixed with embarrassment would run through the assembly! But speech does not, thank goodness, reside in the Long Pudendal; that is reserved for the lingual nerve, and the wanderings of the lingual are hard to envisage and to memorise. Mnemonics are necessary. What doctor would be practising to-day were it not for mnemonics? – were it not for the Muses, if not sacred, profane, but yet Muses, with the light Wordsworth grudgingly admitted illumined Burns – 'the light that led astray was light from Heaven.' We must bring the Muse into Medicine, or, rather, bring Medicine, which has wandered, back to Phœbus, back to the god in whom all music and song and blood are pure. It is an awful task, but it has to be done. I must take the onus of it on my back, ably helped by a merry blade or two, and rewrite Anatomy in rhyme. It has to be done. It should have been done long ago. The Irish ollaves would have called in their poets to put the whole dull subject on a ballad basis as they put pedigrees and the Law:

> 'Begin, then, sisters of the sacred well
> That from beneath the seat of Jove doth spring.'

I was dissecting with Birrell, who wrote the adventures of the lingual nerve; if you read about it in Cunningham you would never realise its high destiny and all that it did, does and can do. The lingual nerve! The lingual nerve! What history has it not made! It has lifted man above the beasts and given him speech, and speech created thought. It has roused crowds and razed empires; it has enchanted the ear in song and poetry; it has wooed and won, thereby taking precedence over the Long Pudendal Nerve of Soemmering.

I was on the head and neck. Birrell was on the arm. He was digging into the antecubital fossa in front of the elbow. I was telling him about the glories and importance of the lingual nerve. The professor blew along suddenly and interrupted us.

'If there were less talk there would be more concentration. It is better to dissect in silence. There is nothing more distracting than talk. You, Ouseley, should try to expose the lingual nerve without cutting Wharton's duct. Be careful just there. Use the handle of the knife.'

'That nerve is mightier than the sword,' Birrell ventured.

'What do you mean?'

It was my turn. I didn't want to let Birrell in for all the irreverence.

'I was just telling Birrell when you came along, sir, that the lingual can move masses and can make wars and found cities.'

'By wagging the tongue it wags the world, so Ouseley says.'

The professor grew silent so suddenly that it amounted to a gasp.

'Do you believe that, Birrell?'

'Well, sir, allowing for Ouseley's poetic imagination.'

'The lingual nerve is *entirely* sensory,' said the professor with emphasis, as he somewhat abruptly went away.

'Now we're boiled,' said Birrell sadly.

'Yes,' I agreed. 'It was a bad break. I'm sorry for letting you in for it. What nerve does move the tongue, anyway? One would think from its name that it was the lingual.'

'Names in anatomy are put into mislead us,' Birrell thought. 'Let us ask Williams when he comes in for the foot.'

Instead of lifting man above the beasts as I thought, the lingual nerve has filled him up with wine, spirits and beer for consumption on the premises, so to speak, and brought him down at times. Store Street and Vine Street can witness to its being 'entirely sensory'. A nerve of taste indeed !

'I bet a bob that I will get the blooming nerve in the next exam. McNought never forgets. Read the book to me, Birrell. And for heaven's sake don't re-light that pipe. Remember what the Professor of Physiology says about slow-burning tobacco.' McNought may be a great anatomist, but he never noticed the mistake in his print of Rembrandt's 'Anatomy Lesson' where the flexors of the hand are painted as if they originated from the external condyle of the humerus. And yet I, bad as I am, won two quid from Billy Orpen, who is full of artistic anatomy.

Birrell opened Cunningham's *Anatomy*.

' "The nerve has been seen passing downwards between the ramus of the mandible and the internal pterygoid . . ." '

'Hold on a minute till I get that. Ramus is branch and mandible is your jaw-bone, the bone that carries the "point", in the language of Tommy Monk.'

' "It now inclines forward to reach the side of the tongue, and, passing over the constrictor of the pharynx, it lies below the last molar tooth, between the mucous membrane and the body of the mandible." '

'Body and ramus must be different parts of the same bone,' I remarked, but Birrell kept on reading :

' "In its further course the nerve keeps close to the side of the tongue, crossing the upper part of the hypoglossus and beyond the duct of Wharton. It is placed immediately under the mucous membrane of the tongue . . ." '

'Sure; if it wasn't, who could taste with it?'

' ". . . and can be traced as far as the tip." '

'Thanks, old chap. But I can't even see Wharton's duct, much less expose it. Was there ever such unnecessary meandering? Why can't the blooming nerve go straight and get on with its work without inclining, passing, lying, and exposing itself to the first drunken dentist that comes along and takes out your back tooth?' I let go the grapnel hook that held the tongue. 'Now that I have exposed as much as I can see of the beastly thing, give us that mnemonic you wrote on the lingual nerve. I am convinced that I'll be up against it on the paper. Wait a minute until I take it down.'

Birrell, who was master of mnemonics, recited the following, which I found I could remember better than the dead-house prose.

'Birrell, break into song!' And Birrell recited, his cheery face brightening as he beat time with his dissecting knife :

> ' "I'm going to swerve,"
> Said the lingual nerve.
> "Well, be sure you avoid,"
> Said the pterygoid,
> "Myself and the ramus
> When passing between us."
> "Oh, you'll be bucked,"
> Said Wharton's duct,
> "When you land in the kip
> At the tongue's top tip." '

'Well, it's damned well exposed, anyway, and you never injured the duct,' said Birrell, taking a look at my morning's work.

Suddenly I had a misgiving. 'Help me to turn the lady over,' I said, 'till I take a look at the Long Pudendal.'

'Better look it up in the male over there,' Birrell said, 'for it's not dissected in this. But what do you want to look at it for?'

'I'm perfectly convinced that there's a snag in it. Instead of presiding at every wedding and being a cause of mirth in others, as I had imagined, I bet a bob that it's not a motor but another "entirely sensory" nerve.'

'The Long Pudendal,' said Birrell, 'is a sensory nerve.

It only makes you scratch yourself.'

'Just my luck! I'm out of luck this morning. One might think that I had met McConkey.' McConkey was Birrell's pet aversion and mine, a hoodoo if ever there was one. One sight of him on your way to an exam and you were sure to be stuck. That is why Birrell and I took the small-pox cab, which has wooden windows, until we reached the examination hall, for one of our early attempts at the Half, while we were still amateurs. The professors had an edge on Birrell, either because he was my pal or because he filled the school with disrespectful rhymes. They may have heard of his invention. Perhaps it was that we were only amateur anatomists like friend Freyer, son of the great surgeon, who, much to his father's annoyance, put himself down in *Who's Who* : 'Hobbies: Half M.B. examinations.'

It was disappointing to hear that the Long Pudendal was only sensory. What did Soemmering mean by calling the thing the 'Long Shame-Faced nerve' when all it did was to feel? 'I'm hanged if I'll look up Soemmering's grave in Frankfort-on-Main after that,' said I.

I was beginning to lose interest in anatomy. There was no doubt about it : that wholly unsolicited interruption of McNought's cast a gloom over the dissecting-room.

'McNought has got a life sentence from Science or, rather, to it. He is surrounded by frozen, dead and inelastic words that have only one meaning. Stone walls do not a prison make, but scientific terms do. Now, Birrell, a word should be like a Chinese ideogram admitting of hundreds of interpretations, permitting full play to the imagination, adumbrating Truth in its every shade and meaning . . .'

'If you don't shut up, you'll find yourself and your Chinese anatomy bloody well adumbrated when McNought gets busy.'

It was time for our grind in Astronomy with Parker in

27

Botany Bay. Unlike most courses for B.A., Trinity College insists on a knowledge of Astronomy amongst, of course, other things. Now how can a fellow get the time, between Bugs and Weeds, Chemistry and Physics, not to mention Anatomy and Physiology, Latin, Greek and Trigonometry, to learn Astronomy? But it must be done if you are to get your double degree, B.A. and M.B. The short-cut is through the grinder. According to Birrell:

'Now Parker's a jolly good soul
And he keeps mercury in a bowl
Since the transit of Venus . . .
Affected . . .'

The Mercury alluded to was used to find the nadir in Botany Bay, though the place itself was the opposite of the zenith as far as houses and appearances went. As we proceeded merrily across the College Park an awful thought struck me. 'Birrell, come back a moment. It's not the lingual we'll get in the next exam, but the nerve that really moves the tongue.'

Birrell's face lost its shine for a second as he meditated. 'I think you're right,' he said slowly, as the dodge dawned on him too. 'It's more like his form to give us the one we should have known. Very like his form. What's to be done about it?'

'Let me tell you,' I said. 'It's out of the question to go back now and dissect it. If he saw us doing that we might not be asked about it at all. We might get a worse question. I suggest that we go to some of the boys up in the College of Surgeons and quietly dissect it there an hour or two before the exam, and we will know all about it fresh and pat.'

'But we must first see Williams. I wouldn't like to ask a Surgeon's man what it was,' said Birrell, an outdoor man like myself to whom it never occurred to look it up in the book. Of all the students who got through in astronomy I don't suppose one of them ever visited the Observatory at Dunsink. It was far nearer and easier to go to Parker in Botany Bay. Parker had a moustache and a bald head, and he seemed never to have left his ground-floor room in a house to the east of the Bay. You could take out grinds with him in almost any part of the B.A. Trigonometry, Astronomy, Algebra, almost anything. Trigonometry and Astronomy were enough for me. They hadn't it in the Royal, so I had to do star-gazing as an extra.

In a way it was interesting. You could find out where you were if you were at sea, by taking the altitude of the Pole, and when you knew that you had the latitude of the place, for the altitude of the Pole is equal to the latitude of the place. And you could find out how far east or west you were by a chronometer, and if the chronometer fell overboard, or was forgotten, or was sledged by the first mate, you could tell it by the moon. This process was harder than timing yourself, but, as Parker says, we must regard the heavens as the face of a great clock.

Then, as for eclipses, there were two kinds. One which could be seen from half the Earth; the other was rather local and could only be seen from certain spots, hence the expedition of savants or men of science who always choose the most distant islands and places to do their observations in. Those were usually solar eclipses. Birrell had a rhyme by which you could distinguish the kinds of eclipses, the local and the semi, or the hemispherical. I am a little shaky about the terms used in astronomy, but the principle is as clear as daylight to me, and that is the chief thing. You get rather sick about exactness in scientific terms. Why complicate things with a special lingo for each science? As Birrell recited his lines for recognising and differentiating between the eclipses, I realised that it would not be necessary to go to Parker's that afternoon.

That was the great advantage of Birrell's rhymes. At the same time, I could hardly ask Birrell, who was never in the Royal, to meet Weary Mac and Silly Barney. Birrell was well brought up, so was I; but he was a Protestant and he might think that my friends were low. Being a Catholic, I didn't, so I got more value out of life. I may be a bit of a snob, but you cannot mix 'Varsities.

Chapter III

THE FINDING OF THE ELIXIR

One morning Weary Mac had great luck. He was down at the School talking about horses to Garratty, the pathology porter, when the postman began to stuff the letter-box with the usual dozens of medical circulars. The porter scanned them with an experienced eye and selected a few letters from the bundle of halfpenny-stamped Cure-alls.

'If a fellow could find out what to do with this kind of stuff, he'd make a fortune,' said Garratty. 'They won't even light the stove.' He tore off an outer envelope and selected a more or less combustible page to light his pipe. The cover caught Weary's eye. It depicted a most depressing sight. The colour scheme was dark blue, but not so dark that you couldn't see a window half open, and through it half an individual with a livid countenance, peering into what was meant to be the ambrosial night, for a crescent moon swam in the top right-hand corner. Under the friendly silence of the moon all was calm save the face at the window. What was the man or woman doing at an open window at that hour of night? What secret scenes produced that look of insufferable terror? None could say without reading within the pamphlet. Weary read within:

' "Nothing is more distressing than air-hunger, the awful feeling that you are suffocating for the want of air, drowning on dry land in full daylight. Nay; for Asthma attacks its victims at an hour when help is hard to summon, when it is not immediately at hand. Asthma is worse at night. This explains what is happening on the illustrated cover of this brochure. The poor sufferer from this hitherto intractable disease has been awakened by a feeling of air-hunger. He feels as if he were choking. He draws a deep breath. It is unavailing. He gasps for air. He cannot breathe. He is seized with a terrible dread of impending dissolution. A fear principally due to the fact that he is unaware that Boreo has been discovered. He rushes to the window. He throws it open. See him at it now, hanging on his elbows in the typical position of the asthmatic starved for air."'

'Starved for air': just the very thing!

'You don't want this?' asked Weary of Garratty, the pathology porter.

'Arrah, for God's sake!' said Garratty with an assumption of scorn. 'I wish to God that you'd tell me what to do with them. The whole place is litthered with things like that. I could show you worse. Yesterday I seen one that would have made you laugh. It was of a fellow you'd think was shot dead in the street. All that was wrong with him was that he had a pain in his back and no pills. I declare to God some of them would give you a pain in the neck. But the ones about the ould ones is something terrible.' Garratty retained a Turkish prejudice against seeing women in the nude. He had long since given up opening gynaecological advertisements or those from the makers of trusses, reducing mixtures and abdominal supports.

Weary was thinking hard. 'Air-hunger.' If he put Golly on something that was the opposite of wind? If he treated him for asthma? But hold on! That would never do. The cure for air-hunger was more air, and it was less that Golly wanted. It might cure any little remission of his trouble and so make him worse. One would have thought that a man who wanted air would be different from one who had too much of it. There must be some way out.

What could it be? Hold hard! There was a great principle employed on his aunt by Dr Swan. 'Homo'-something or other; but it came to a case of a hair of the dog that bit you, in the end. What was that story Gideon told him? 'Like cures like,' as Dr Tyrrell remarked when he handed the bore at dinner an extra helping of tongue. Homeopathy! Had he been more experienced he would have known a most encouraging fact which has always been more or less a puzzle to me : that in Medicine as in Politics contradictory procedures are often practised with equal conviction and equal results. 'There is a divinity that doth shape our ends!' Weary carefully folded the pages and left Garratty to his work, a work which was relieved towards midday by attention to some of the larger pathological specimens which were preserved in square jars full of alcohol and ranged, labelled in order, on the shelves. Garratty's teeth were close set. He could strain the stuff between them. It was all right if you didn't shake the jars. Whoever shook a good vintage? He had already stranded a spleen and was now gradually reducing the level of a liver's preservative fluid. The great thing about it was that it kept you out of Golly's. 'Be jabers, it wasn't the only liver it preserved!'

Inappropriate as it was to the prescription, Weary had to copy it out legibly before presenting it to the apothecary, because he knew nothing about the pharmacopœia, and so he did not want to be asked to interpret his handwriting or explain what he wanted. The prescription was all right. He had signed it with Silly's name.

'You might add,' he said as he handed it over the counter, 'something out of Dr Sigerson's and Magee Finny's prescriptions if you have them here.'

The apothecary gasped, then looked hard at Weary. 'But how do you know that that might not make it incompatible?' he asked, surprised. 'What has the patient got?'

33

'I don't know,' said Weary. 'I was only asked to hand it in. The address is on the top.'

'I can see that. How many pills do you want? There is no mention of the amount.'

So it was pills, was it?

'I'd give her a dozen to begin with,' he said, confused. 'That's what she had before.'

'Then the name is wrong?'

'That's the husband,' said Weary. 'If you can't make them up, I'll have to go to the Apothecaries' Hall.'

Now the chemist was the last to be impatient with the ignorance of the public. On the contrary, he sympathised with it. How many times had he not to prescribe for them himself or to ring up their medical advisers to know what they meant by ordering certain mixtures? What did the doctors know about medicines anyway? They were dependent on apothecaries and on the great wholesale chemists. Where would half of them be without Burroughs and Wellcome's diary?

'There's hardly a drug in this bunch known to the British Pharmacopœia,' he said. 'Where did you get it? And who is Dr S. Barney Bulstrode? He's not in this town. Wait until I look him up in the Medical Directory. Somebody's been codding you.'

Consternation seized Weary Mac. Had he been guilty of forgery or anything? Would he be run in for writing a prescription without being qualified? The sooner he escaped from the shop the better.

'I got it from a fellow in a black suit in a public house.'

'Take it back and forget about it. And keep out of public houses.'

So Weary left the shop.

Going down Nassau Street he had to cross over to the Provost's corner: a heap of ordure was moving into Grafton Street. Why don't they put clay over it, or put a lid on it for the sake of public health? thought Weary,

34

as he walked through the polluted air. Chemists or apothecaries or whatever they called themselves never went into a public house. He liked that. If that were true, it was only because they were at home doping themselves. He would go to Paddy Hoey's and put the problem before him candidly – no names mentioned, of course. When he entered the premises Paddy was engaged in prescribing for a lady and in giving her advice.

'Now take skin food; the skin has no stomach, so how can you feed it?' asked Paddy Hoey.

'But the label says that it can absorb . . .' the lady protested.

'Soap and water and a good rub with a rough towel. The only way the complexion can be altered is either by keeping fit or drinking the nose off yer face until it shines like a cigar. Do you get me?' asked Paddy Hoey.

'But many ladies have red noses who are quite abstemious,' she protested. 'They have to use powder. How do you account for that?'

'Constipation plain and simple,' said Paddy Hoey. 'Starvation, exercise and a dose of castor oil, if you want an antidote.'

When the lady had left, on Weary's entry, Paddy shouted: 'And how's Mister Me-Bloody-Friend? And how is the *"Adsunt artes"*?' He quoted somewhat irreverently from an hexameter on the front of his shop, which read: *'Et medicæ adsunt artes herbarumque potestas.'* He extended his hand in greeting. 'Do you know what it is?' he continued. 'This place would drive you mad: nothing but ould ones coming in for beauty treatment with faces on them that u'd crack a coffin lid. A fellow here can't click with a decent tart at all.' He looked at the clock when he heard Mac's invitation. 'I'll be in Martin Brennan's in Fleet Street in two twos. That'll be Game Ball.'

While Mac was waiting in Martin Brennan's, Tommy

Monk, the Brummagem Bantam, one time Champion of the Midlands, hero of a hundred fights, deaf from the impact of a thousand punches, was explaining to Martin Brennan how he put away Chambers in the third round – towards the end of it – with Ditto Repeato, or the Postman's knock. Did he think he'd let him go on till he got his second wind? Not half! Wot ho! He held in his left hand an imaginary watch, while he worked his right up and down to represent the Count.

'How did it end?'

''ow did who end? Chambers? He came to a bad end. He went up at eight and came down at nine. Lehmann, my manager, absconded with the purse. Absconded is roight. That's what 'e did all roight. He was a wrong 'un all roight. But I'll meet him some day. The world is very small all roight.'

Weary Mac had an anxious time waiting for Paddy Hoey. After all, Martin was the proprietor and, as such, he couldn't be expected to give drink away to his visitors. There was no use calling them customers, for there would be no custom if they all got free drinks. Soon Martin would be called away and Weary would be left with Tommy, whose auditory infirmity did not extend to invitations. Like to those who can hear best in vibrating places such as a railway carriage or an omnibus, Tommy could always hear well in a pub.

In came Paddy, and Mac ordered a ball of malt, Tommy advanced and shook Paddy's hand. He might as well be shaking hands with me before a fight, thought Mac; and ordered a drink for Tommy, who sipped it in silence to give the youngsters a chance. There was no excluding him.

While Paddy's stomach was rejoicing in its treasure trove, he confided to Weary: 'No. The grand passion was never my forte. I'd rather have a bottle of stout.' Weary produced his prescription and handed it to Paddy, who presently exclaimed aloud: 'Well now, be the Roost of the Dead, I never saw the likes of this! Who's this Barney Bulstrode? He ought to get a clatter on the jaw.'

'Wot he ought to get is Ditto Repeato,' said Tommy Monk. The time had evidently come when Mac could go no further. There wasn't a chemist in Dublin who would or could compound the stuff. Therefore the time had come to make a clean breast of it. Weary explained the situation, names apart.

He had not concealed the name for more than a sentence when Paddy said: 'If you don't mean Golly, I'm the Whores' Bank.'

How Paddy could be the Whores' Bank beat Mac, for she was a hoarse old woman who ostensibly sold boot laces and matches after dark on O'Connell Bridge.

'He has me so pestered that as long as I have half a dollar in me pocket I keep away from his pub. I started him on a mixture, but he has no faith in an apothecary once a medical comes on the scene; besides, he has more faith in a pill.'

'Can't you help a fellow at all, at all?' asked Mac.

'Sure. But what he really wants is to stop sipping pints all day and then going to bed on gin and ginger beer.'

A sudden flash of generosity struck Paddy.

'Hold on a minute while I run round to the shop.'

In his corner Tommy prolonged his drink.

' 'Ere, Martin,' called Tommy; but if Mac entertained a hope it was dashed, for all Tommy wanted to know was what Martin thought of his own chances for the Biscuit Cup at the coming Grocers' Sports at Jones's Road. When Martin came, Tommy publicly laid aside his empty glass.

'Here they are,' said Paddy, who was soon back. 'They are a patent founded on peppermint. If they don't make him worse they'll leave him as he is, and that's what he wants. It's the worst turn you ever did to take a disease away from a fellow, provided it keeps him occupied and takes his mind off himself. There's some people who have nothing else left to live for but their own death. Give him no more than half a dozen at a time. You'll find that he'll give most of them away doing good to others.' Paddy sang a stave of a sea shanty, 'Blow the man up! Blow the man down!' as he handed over the box of patent pills.

Mac thanked his friend. Had it not been for Tommy in his neutral corner he was sure that Paddy would have put up a round. He decided to accompany him from the shop. There was a lunch counter in Bowes, and Paddy had to lunch somewhere. Perhaps he would ask him in.

Chapter IV

BACK TO THE BOYS

'Citizen!' It was the Citizen's voice. We called him 'Citizen' because he called all of us citizens. Where he got his Socialism from it is hard to tell. Probably he got it in South America. We all saw him off for ever to South America, and stood him drinks and gave him what amounted to an American wake, when he was going away for ever, but he came back like Paddy Hoey at the end of the term. It was behind King Billy's statue of the famous horse that faces towards Dublin Castle – with its bent leg longer than its straight one, for the bent leg touches the ground too – that the 'Citizen' shouted, before he came over and gazed at me with that strange, enigmatical, quizzical smile on his beautiful mouth, while his bright eyes watched alertly. He always began half inaudibly in the middle of a sentence, smiling and watching you.

'In a bad way, begob. The Citizens are in a bad way.'

'Where are they?' I inquired. I knew that he was referring to Weary and Barney and the four-combine that consisted of Dolan, Hegarty, McCluskey and Roowan.

'All but Hegarty,' the Citizen added.

From that I deduced that the results of the exam. in the Royal were unfavourable to my friends.

'Were they all stuck?' I asked, to confirm my suspicions.

The Citizen smiled brightly and mischievously, though he must have been included in the *débâcle*.

'And where are the boys?'

He looked towards Golly's and joined me who was going there. 'I was stuck myself,' he volunteered, so cheerfully that it seemed an achievement to have failed in a medical exam. I felt that I was being left out of this perverse distinction.

'I'll be stuck next week in the Half,' I explained.

'You're in Trinity now? But it's much easier than the Royal.'

'You deceive yourself, Citizen,' I said. 'I thought that too until I entered; it is much simpler, but it's not easier for all that. Besides, there's no Astronomy in the Royal.'

'Astronomy, be Jaysus!' the Citizen yelled. 'In the name of God, for what?'

I was disappointed at the impression I was making, or, rather, failing to make. So I told him rather primly that you couldn't get your B.A. in T.C.D. without Astronomy. He smiled to himself, and I felt that I was a fool to be trying to impress such a mercurial temperament as that of the Citizen. Yet I went on, fascinated in a strange sort of way.

'It's very useful, John,' I said. 'For instance, suppose you are in a boat at sea and the chronometer and sextant are lost, how are you to know where you are without Astronomy?'

'Who wants to know, anyway?' asked the Citizen.

* * *

Barney was singing in Golly's 'back'. Weary was beating time in mockery.

'Too looral, Too looral, Too looral, lai Ay!
We're happy and merry, contented and gay.
With pigs in our parlours and drakes that won't lay,
Too looral, Too looral, Too looral, lai Ay!'

'Gentlemen, the Provost!' shouted Barney, stopping singing when he sighted me.

They were all right in Botany and Physics. It seems that it was that useless Chemistry and Zoology that brought Barney and Weary down; also a grudge against Barney and Weary for upsetting the class.

It appeared that Professor Campbell, the old gentleman with the round cuffs, was lecturing on the four Halogens. 'Bromine, Fluorine, Chlorine and Iodine, never found free in Nature, always combined.' He continued : 'They are called Halogens, from *als*, "salt", and *gennao*, "I produce" – in allusion to common salt, the chief source of the chlorine compounds. Bromine is called from *Bromos*, "a stench" ' ('Hah, Hegarty !' someone shouted.) 'Fluorine from *fluor*, "spar"; Iodine from *ioeides*, "violet-coloured"; and Chlorine from *chloros*, "greenish-yellow". Again, Bromine, Fluorine, Chlorine, and Iodine.' Then suddenly, to Weary, who was yawning and inattentive, the Professor put the question, 'What are the four Halogens?'

'Dolan, Hegarty, McCluskey and Roowan, never found free in Nature, always combined !' Barney answered for him. It was enough to make any professor have a down on a fellow, but we called the four friends the Halogens from that day.

Three of them now were entertaining Hegarty in silence at the back of the shop. It was so irritating that Barney, who could stand it no longer, shouted, 'Hah, Hegarty.' A call he used to chivvy that inoffensive, small-skulled, studious little man by shouting it out *à propos* of nothing whenever a spell of silence threatened to settle on the class. It drew attention which was quite unwelcome to retiring little Hegarty, implying as it did that Hegarty was under constant observation and had to be constantly reminded to attend to his work. It may have seemed a bullying thing to do with the four of them together, but 'always combined' the Halogens were enough to irritate any decent man with their obtrusive rejoicing and entertainment of Hegarty. It looked as if it was meant to annoy us, entertaining the only fellow who had achieved a pass out of a class of thirty-three. As if the other remaining Halogens would have passed too only for us. If they meant to imply that – and I don't see how they could imply much by sitting silently with a pal – they would have been perfectly right.

The Citizen took out a crumpled examination paper and quoted out very loud : 'Question 3. Describe the skull of an Elasmobranch." '

'Hah! Hegarty!' Barney interjected.

Now the Elasmobranchs are sharks and skates, and they don't have much brains. In fact John's professor of anatomy, Fraser, in the College of Surgeons, when he was training me to get my own back on McNought, used to assure me – 'There's mony a beastie in the Indian Ocean who has nothing more in the way of brains than his lumbar enlargement. And that's half way down his tail.' It was hardly fair to direct remarks like that at Hegarty merely because he had a small head and was twice as old as anyone in the class. I think there was another reason and that was that, whether he knew it or not, the Citizen was jealous. Hegarty had been a chemist in a small country town, and to escape after years of boredom and pulling the devil by the tail he tried to qualify himself and become a doctor, even though that might leave his position unchanged more or less. Anyway he worked hard, and, so far from being spiteful at the poor fellow's success, both Barney and Weary should have been apologetic for the way they made a cod of the whole Zoology class by having constitutional representatives for all the animals in Thomson's *Zoology*, and that has 813 pages. They elected members of the various groups of animals, reptiles, insects and fishes and then they subdivided that again by appointing representatives for the different systems of these birds and beasts. There are about half a dozen systems in every thing alive, or there can be if they get the proper professor. There are the Respiratory System, the Alimentary System, the Muscular System, the Nervous System, the Reproductive System and the Excretory System. There may be others, but these are quite enough. Broderick elected me to represent the Snail, among others, on account of my prowess on the race-track, and I had to know all about the love affairs of snails or their Reproductive System by heart. And what made the professor have a down on me and on the whole class except Hegarty – who he knew couldn't help it but had to come in with us or we wouldn't let him into the class – was that, no matter who was asked a question about an animal, the member who stood for that animal had to reply. That is how it happened that when Christian was asked about the Reproductory System of Lumbricus, which, as everyone knows, is the common or garden Earthworm, Christian couldn't answer, for that would be an invasion of O'Keeffe's bailiwick, for he was the member for Worms, who, as Thompson says, 'form a heterogeneous mob including about a dozen classes whose relationship are imperfectly known.' That is why, when the professor said, 'Christian, describe the reproductive system of Lumbricus,' O'Keeffe had to stand up and recite as fast as he could – for the further you got before being ordered out gave you kudos with the boys – that history of earthly love.

'When two worms unite sexually they lie opposed in opposite directions, the head of one towards the tail of the other, and what happens is . . .' O'Keeffe pattered out for all he was worth. But Blaney the professor said dryly, 'What happens is that you leave this class in a direction opposite to that by which you entered and do not reappear in it for a week.' It was very hard lines in a way, for O'Keeffe was a well-meaning fellow and inoffensive, and he had spent a lot of time learning the system by rote, for he had a poor understanding. But it might have stood to him, as Barney says, in the end. All he had to do was to have the luck, as I had, to be asked about his heterogeneous mob in his *viva voce* and he would have got a scholarship. Instead of that he got chucked out. But O'Keeffe took it like a sportsman, for he knew he had all our sympathy. It would have gone hard with Hegarty had he been chucked out. It would have gone hard with me had I been asked about fishes for instance, or gastropods, that's things that walk on their belly – but not quite the way an army marches – and I standing for snails, when Blaney called out : 'Tell me and the class how two snails pair; and do not recite it at a gallop but enumerate slowly and distinctly.' So I told him all about the harpoon they have for anchoring one another, 'which is called, cynically enough, Cupid's dart.' He listened patiently to the end of their marvellous marriage, for each is male and female in turn. 'Why "cynically enough"?' was all he said. It is my opinion that if he had asked the class any of the other systems, they would have spoken more slowly but indistinctly – that is, if they answered at all.

But though the boys were comforting themselves very nicely, and Golly left them more or less to themselves to work it off, signs were not wanting of something more than jealousy, which after all was within our control. There was the feeling of what was brewing for the morrow and that was 'Hardwicke Street', which Barney uses as an equivalent for being hard up; and danger of a visit of his mother to town. He looked down into his chest and said out of some deep memory, 'God blast Bermingham's little red book.' Weary, who was very cunning, whispered to me, 'His Ma will be up by the first train when she reads the results.' This may or may not have been true, but there was no doubt at all of a prolonged residence in Hardwicke Street and of all the boys being hard up for at least a month. I found myself beginning to doubt very much if it would be all right about the ten miles at Ballinafeigh next week, so much that I refused a pint in the next round. Barney lived in a little two-storey house one window wide in the actual Hardwicke Street off North Frederick Street. This was for reasons which were obvious to us all, but he was supposed to be living in Heytesbury Street, where the lodgings were more respectable and expensive. His allowance was equated to the rent of his presumed abode. His allowance was also equated to his clothing. He was supposed to be *respectfully* attired at all times. Respectfully attired meant to Barney's mother the garb of a young curate or clerical student. That is why Barney could never get out of black and dress in brown like Weary, or in any colour like me. But though McSweeney's was paid quarterly to issue ecclesiastical raiment to her medical son, there were two compensations. One of these was the umbrella which went with the costume, for which seven-and-sixpence was set aside; the other was an overcoat. Everyone knew where his overcoat had gone. Jimmy had it neatly folded on a shelf behind the Bank with other 'soft goods'. But the umbrella lost long ago, was lost long enough to be replaced. What we were discussing, now that we were forced to take thought for the morrow, was whether the nice conduct of an umbrella when Barney went to meet his mother at Kingsbridge would distract that lady's attention from the absence of his overcoat and lull her curiosity. Would she not reason thus, as Barney hoped: If he has an umbrella, which can be done without more easily than an overcoat, is it not evident that he also has the coat? 'True, the umbrella would be the first to go,' I ventured.

'Begob, you're right!' the Citizen agreed enthusiastically.

'Wait awhile,' said the cautious Weary. 'The umbrella has already gone first.'

'He is thinking of a new one,' I replied.

'He can get clothes from McSweeney's on tick,' Weary said.

'Jayshus!' said the Citizen.

Barney was resenting the discussion on the limitations of his *ménage* when I had a brain wave.

'It would be easier to borrow an umbrella from Golly than an overcoat. You can be going to a funeral.'

'It's his own funeral,' the Citizen said.

'Would a lady's brolly be any use?' I inquired, mentioning my aunt's.

'No,' said Weary. 'It's light brown.'

'Jayshus!' exclaimed the Citizen.

'His mother has not written to announce her coming yet,' I said, not wanting to ford a stream until we came to it.

'Ah,' Weary informed us – and it did not improve Barney's temper to have his trails so well known – 'she is not given to announcing her visits. She arrives suddenly at the most awkward times.'

'But he's living in Hardwicke Street and she doesn't know his address,' the Citizen remarked.

'It means that he has to spend an hour, after every train, in Heytesbury Street, with O'Keeffe who digs there.'

'Leave it to me,' I said at last, overcome by the awful aftermath of Barney's getting stuck in a medical exam. I remembered an old umbrella up in the loft above what used to be the coachman's room at home.

'Good old boy!' said Barney, wakened up from a brown study. 'Let's all have another drink.'

'I'm afraid I can't,' I excused.

'Oh, ho! What's happened now?'

'It affects the muscles,' I explained.

'He's learning astronomy,' the Citizen shrieked.

'Is he learning it with his backside? Like Socrates in Second Arts?' Silly Barney inquired.

Now they were just in the mood to make me drink and break my training, so I preferred to be codded about astronomy than athletics.

'I'm learning it all right. It is necessary in Trinity.'

'When you're at sea and have thrown all the instruments overboard it's very useful,' the Citizen volunteered.

'What instruments are these?' asked Weary Mac, seeing a ray of hope.

'There aren't any instruments,' I said regretfully. 'If there were I'd be only too pleased.'

'You mentioned a chronometer,' John reminded me.

'There's no such thing as a chronometer,' said I, meaning that they did not serve them out to you or charge your parents up with them in the Astronomy class. As Barney was eyeing me suspiciously, Golly made it worse by coming back and breaking in with his show of knowledge :

'Of course there is, me son. Here's one I won at a coursing match with Jack Lalor the barber,' he said, producing a gold watch – one of those that Jimmy calls 'a full hunter'.

'Ho! Ho!' Barney muttered.

Now none of us had watches. We all knew that. The very suspicion of having such an unnecessary machine when the whole town was full of clocks, going or stopped, not to mention every public house with them five minutes fast – and of withholding it from the common pool was the act, to say the least of it, unworthy of a sportsman. I hastened to explain.

'We all have microscopes provided at the exams, but you can't take them out and pawn them,' I said. 'And chronometers are not even served out in Astronomy. They are hypothetical. And besides, there's no Astronomy class. You are supposed to make it up for yourself. That means a grinder. And my grinder's Parker, if you want to know.'

'Have you Astronomy too?' Golly inquired.

'I have indeed.'

'All about the stars?'

I nodded and went on: 'It's not so simple as it sounds. Yet you could be knocked out by the simplest question.'

'For instance, what?' asked Mr Golly.

'They might ask you "What's Space?"'

'Easy enough. Couldn't you tell them it was Nothing?'

'But then they would ask you what was Nothing.'

'Easy enough,' said Mr Golly. 'You could tell them it was a bung-hole without a barrel.' He gave a laugh and kicked an imaginary cork. 'Have they any way of telling your fortune?' He inquired seriously, wondering if he could put astronomy to any use, have his horoscope read, and 'all that sort of a thing'.

'We are supposed not to be ignorant of any science on the earth. I was warned by Parker that the Rev Mr Roberts once asked a fellow in the B.A. examination in Astronomy, "What are the co-seismic lines?" and then to explain what earthly influence led to the formation of the Giant's Causeway.'

Mr Golly was greatly impressed. Two more students arrived. Five was an audience he could not resist. Realising that geology was outside all our subjects, he adopted it. He stood up for the Giant's Causeway. He took it to himself.

'Isn't it one of the Wonders of the World, anyway?' he asked indignantly. 'And what more do they want?'

'It's the forces that led to its strange formation he was after when he asked the question,' I explained. 'Why is it formed of hexagons of basalt? How were they shaped with six sides, as if they were put in a mould and set all together, even the ones that are nearly round with hardly a space between them?'

'Look it here now,' said Mr Golly. He turned his back on us for a moment, and then faced us, holding a little pewter tea measure. 'Look it here. This should be round but it isn't. It's dinged. You might think that it was done

48

on purpose. It has five or six sides. Well' — he raised it above his shoulder and brought it down on a glass cloth with a bang — 'the hand of God came down on it like that, punched it bloody well out. And there you are.'

'It may have been an accident,' said the Citizen.

'Ah, go to God!' said Mr Golly contemptuously. 'There's no accidents in Heaven, except marriages.'

'Nor any of that kind of a thing,' John interjected.

'Nor in astronomy, worse luck,' I said.

The Halogens were slipping away. It would soon be time for us all to go.

'Hah, Hegarty!' Barney remarked as the little fellow passed.

'Now take an eclipse of the Moon,' said Weary Mac. He tried to get a shadow from his cigarette-case to fall on the counter, but there were too many lights.

'Can I assist you?' asked Golly, mystified.

'We're all eclipsed,' the Citizen said.

'I've seen a few of them myself,' Golly informed us. 'You have to look at them through a bit of black glass.'

'Those would be solar eclipses,' I explained.

'Begorra, you're right. And they're rare enough in these parts,' said Mr Golly. 'Now that I come to think of it, I've only seen one or two.'

'Have you not seen an eclipse of the Moon?' Barney asked, wakening up.

'I saw one,' Weary said. 'And as it invaded the moon's disc it made a crescent. Then the shadow passed and left another crescent behind; then the moon was clear again. It took about twenty minutes.'

'That was a quick one,' said Mr Golly. 'What would happen if it hit half a moon?'

Now I was strong on eclipses and I knew the difference between solar and lunar eclipses well, thanks to Birrell's rhyme which told you that the solar sort was local.

'There once was a solar eclipse
Which could only be seen from the Kips.
  As the daylight grew darker
  I thought I saw Parker
Astride on a . . .'

I was only waiting for an opportunity to come out strong when they made a howler, but so far they were talking intelligently enough. It was always hard to get in a word when Weary was in possession, for he had a way of holding the house and of keeping interrupters at bay. That, strangely enough, was due to his slowness and deliberateness of speech.

Suddenly Mr Golly inquired: 'Did yez ever see an Hunter's Moon? I seen one when I was out ratting one evening with Jack Lalor the barber. A grand sight it was entirely.'

There was no chance for me now for the conversation was off eclipses. I told the Citizen Birrell's rhyme. The pleasant mouth smiled. I could see him turning the limerick over in his mind. Suddenly he exploded with admiration. 'Who was this huer Parker? Whurrup! He must have been a great huer anyway.'

Barney shrank into himself, for he was sensitive and modest, which qualities Mac asserted came to him from his clothes. Seeing his attitude the Citizen explained, 'Huers means those who paint the town red or any hue.'

And now the boys had to hear the rhyme.

'Trinity swank,' said Barney, but he said it good-naturedly.

'That reminds me,' Golly volunteered.

'Jayshus! Of what?' the Citizen inquired.

'There was a cattle-dealer here one night with five hundred pounds on him, and he went down there and got lost for a week, and when Moriarty with two other detectives went to find him, they went into all the houses and were pulling the bedclothes off all the whores and the artists in the beds. Moriarty told me he got the fright of his life. He had to straighten up suddenly and stand to attention. He had just pulled the bedclothes off a High Court judge. And now, gentlemen, don't you think it's about time we were getting home?'

Weary put his stained fingers in his left waistcoat-pocket and extracted a few sixpences and some coppers which he carefully counted, for it was his round. He paid up for it conscientiously, and we started for home. They were all coming my way except Weary.

While Barney was detaching himself from the counter, the Citizen stood up. His dancing eyes regarded me, while his beautiful mouth was hardly touched by his slow enigmatical smile. A companionable hour with him was impossible, not to mention a continuous or even coherent conversation. He appeared to think in flashes from some deep, uncommunicable life. He had a way of shooting out a word as if it contained a significant message or revealed to you some secret with which he held you to be concerned in some mysterious way of which he had a quizzical knowledge. It had the effect of implying guilt to you past, present or to come.

The Citizen regarded me with his riddling eyes and said: 'Piano Mary.'

Chapter V

I DO WELL IN ASTRONOMY

That Queen who founded the College was looking down upon me from the wall. What a place to put such a picture! In an examination hall it's enough to make you lose your head. I began to think of the little girl who, like myself, was up for an examination and wrote: 'Queen Elizabeth was the Virgin Queen. As a queen she was a great success.' She succeeded in handing the Irish People (whoever they were at that time) this establishment. You could read it on the frame of the portrait: '*Elizabeth Regina hujusce Collegii Fondatrix.*' There was a print of her in the library too – in fact, several prints. One had a longer inscription: '*Elizabet D. G. Angliae, Franciae, Hiberniae et Verginiae Regina fidei Christianiæ propugnatrix acerrima.*' I liked '*propugnatrix acerrima*'. It 'took the words out of my mouth', as Golly says when he is pretending that he already knew what you are telling him. But here I was under the picture, and I had been so for three days. It seems that I am being pursued by red-headed hoodoos of both sexes. I was doing well until the Virgin Queen caught my eye or I caught hers. And yet that lady for all her appearance composed and sang:

> 'Some gentle passions steal into my mind,
> For I am soft and made of melting snow.
> O be more cruel, love, and so be kind,
> Let me or float or sink, be high or low.'

My eyes had cause to wander, for it was no use keeping them on the examination paper in an effort to 'answer any five of the given questions'. Dr Tyrrell, who had set the English paper, held that 'virgin' is derived from *vir* and *egeo*. Professor McNeill, on the other hand, derives it not from *vir* and *egeo,* but from *vir* and *ago*. Not from the want of a man, but from the action of a man somewhat in the same way as lumbago acts. Thus he gets 'virago'. Once a thing becomes a matter for professors there is no knowing where the truth lies. But McNeill's derivation seems more worthy of the Virgin Queen.

I was up for the last subject in the B.A. examination – Astronomy. As I said, all was going well until I caught sight of the red-head who let me in for all my troubles by founding this bloody College *juxta Dublinensem.* Everyone knows that I know all about Astronomy – that is, all the answers to the ordinary sensible questions such as Parker tells you to look out for; but when it comes to the eccentric questions, well – 'there I leave you,' as Golly says. Luckily I got the solar eclipse and I saw it from the viewpoint of the examiner, which is the better viewpoint than Birrell's, seeing that the examiner is the Rev Mr Roberts, who is a splendid-looking man with a bearing that makes you feel when you are saluting him that you are forcing your existence on the attention of the Duke of Wellington. I even was able to answer 'Kepler's Problem'. And when a thing becomes a problem to a professional astronomer like Kepler, it was hardly fair to ask a fellow who only wants his B.A. in order to get his M.D. to work the third law out which enables you to compute the time taken by the radius vector to sweep over the entire area of the orbit; this lands you with the problem of constructing successive radii vectores the angles of which are measured off from the radius vector of the body at the original given position. Thus it will be seen that a knowledge of Kepler the Astronomer would lead me to a licence as a doctor to prescribe Kepler's extract of malt. That was three; but there were two questions more. And look at the next question: 'What are the secular and periodic variations?' And Holy Heaven, Number Five! 'Since the elements and co-ordinates completely determine each other you can ignore one. Show how this principle was used by Lagrange in determining the variations of an oscillating ellipse.' Now that is what I call an eccentric question, for no one but an eccentric old cod would ever have thought of it. You would think that they were out to find out the things you didn't know and avoid asking you one thing that you did. Suppose you asked me to name the satellites of Uranus, I could have immediately come out with 'Oberon and Titania'. But why should anyone want to mix Algebra up with Astronomy? Thank God, I was over my Algebra on the first day. And I was trying to make up for a spot of bad luck in that paper as the days went on. But now I was oscillating between the Rev Mr Roberts and the Virgin Queen to 'float or sink, be high or low'. There was one faint hope: he was a parson and so a conscientious man, and he would sympathise with my scruples about Astronomy and with the awful suspicion I had that (as the Professor of Moral Philosophy whom we call 'The Master of Those Who Know', said of Life) 'the whole thing's a bloody cod'. After all, Astronomy dealt with the Origin of Things, and he would be sure to sympathise with one who had difficulties in believing in the truth of a theory which was founded on an exception, so to speak. The scruple which would not have troubled me so much if nothing depended on it would make the Rev Mr Roberts feel that he was another Galileo if he explained it. He could explain mostly everything about Astronomy and I couldn't. He would at least realise that I was a conscientious kind of bloke who liked to have his reason satisfied as he went on. I could see him

54

on the dais reading a little book. It couldn't be a prayer
book – that is, it needn't be a prayer book. Parsons don't
have to read prayer books all day long like priests. I wish
I had read more in my book, but, after all, I had gone
to Parker, and he gets everyone through if they read his
notes and don't lend them to fellows who don't join his
class; that is, almost everyone through. I knew of only
one exception, and he was a fellow who had read too
much at home after attending Parker. I rarely read at
home except when it is too wet to go out, for if a fellow
reads too much at home, especially Astronomy, he might
find himself like Ryan, who was a very hard-working student, off his chump and up in the Asylum, for that's
where they put Ryan when he found out too late his
mistake in confusing the celestial with the terrestial globe.
It never occurred to him that anyone could be so base
as to represent for the sake of simplicity all the stars as
level, ignoring the difference in their distances from the
earth and putting them all at the same level on the surface of a globe – a globe which you were supposed to look
at from the outside, though everyone knew that we were
inside it and under the dome of stars. He could see
Scorpio written on it, he told me, and a lot of dragons :
puzzling enough, but he knew that it meant the tropics,
or one of the tropics, Capricorn or something like that,
but there wasn't even a bloody North Pole.

'That's not on the level anyway, a dodge like that!'
he complained to Parker, who in his turn strongly advised him not to present himself for examination during
the Hilary term anyway, in which it was well known
examiners were subject to hallucinations.

Indignation and disappointment and an outraged sense
of fair play sent him off his chump for the term, which
did not sound so badly if you called it a nervous break-
down. What was the limerick Emerson E. wrote about
him?

'If in Richmond Asylum we probe,
We find, clad in fantastic robe,
   Ryan tracing ellipses
   And making eclipses,
While he murmurs, "That bloody ould globe!"' [1]

I like the 'fantastic robe' with its suggestion of a high conical hat and astrologers' signs. Ryan would have found Astrology less exacting; he would have had more scope for his imagination. Astronomy, on the other hand, leaves little room for individuality, as Ryan's case proved. But it shows what it can do to a fellow if he studies it too hard.

Now that was a mistake I never made. Not that I was beginning to regret it. No; I was getting somewhat anxious as to why I was being left to the last by Roberts for my *viva voce*. I hoped there was nothing of an omen in being left to the last. I was wondering what he would ask me and if he would take a glance over my paper before deciding whether it was worth while to put me to the question, so to speak. Some examiners were like that, particularly medical examiners. These codded themselves that 'they had a duty to the public', but it will be a bit too thick if there turns out to be another 'duty to the public' in Astronomy. As a rule people who think they have duties to the public give me a pain in the neck. If they confined themselves to their own business they would find that the public is quite capable of looking after itself.

I don't see how I can be stuck if he listens to my plea, that even though the Algebra paper was over, I find this kind of thing in the Astronomy paper:

> Consider an equation of the form
> $U = a \sin (nt + L_0)$

that *a sin* looks suspiciously like trigonometry, which

made it still worse. 'Brought sin into the world and all our woe.' I will complain to Roberts if I find that I am being sunk. It would be fine if I could remember that tag about eternity. It might get his mind off me and on to our mortal lot and to the transience of life compared with eternity, and then he wouldn't think it worth while to stick a fellow who was just a pilgrim of eternity passing for a moment through College, the shadow of a bird flying, so to speak, and all that sort of thing. I have it! 'Great clocks.' It's about the planets, it must be. It can hardly be about the fixed stars.

'Great clocks of eternity which beat ages as ours beat seconds.' If I can stuff him with that it will bring a secular variation, so to speak, and, I may say, make it hardly worth his while to deal with a poor mortal as if he were an immortal bloody fixed star.

What were the little things Parker represented by two pins, when he put a loop of string round them and tightened it with a pencil and attempted to describe a circle, only to find that it came out an ellipse? Why couldn't he tell us the names of what the pins represented and never mind the circle that became an oval because it had two centres? I'm 'game ball', as Golly says, if I can remember what the little pins were. I am sure to get something about our planet in an Astronomy exam = after all, we have to live upon it.

I was right.

'What is the ecliptic?'

Sure I had it by heart. 'A great circle in the heavens.'

He did not seem satisfied. 'Is your great circle relative to anything?'

'It's not a great circle at all. It's an ellipse.'

'If I heard you rightly, you just told me that the ecliptic was a great circle in the heavens.'

'What I meant to say was that it should be a great circle but it turns out to be an ellipse.'

'Can you define an ellipse?'

'Certainly. It's a flattened circle like an oval because it runs round two points instead of one.'

'What are the two points in the ecliptic?'

Steady on! 'That's just the puzzle. That's what made me disheartened.'

Now this shows how the brain works in an emergency. If only I could enlist his sympathy for a fellow who had to go on with a thing that was founded on a fallacy. No, 'fallacy' would never do. I scented a dignified bit of a jag if I said that Astronomy was founded on a fallacy. He might ask me, Was that my reason for adding to its fallacies by my paper? No, 'fallacy' was out. But was it not enough to give a fellow a bit of conscientious scruple because he had to study a subject, believe in a subject which was – what shall I call it? – 'largely conjectural'. He was sure to cotton to a fellow with a conscience and resolve 'largely conjectural'. He seemed a bit sympathetic already. I thought his voice is softened a bit. Now he asks, 'What was it made you disheartened with the subject of our study?'

'That business about the ecliptic going round in an ellipse when it should be a circle. That filled me with misgivings. It made me think that perhaps the whole thing was a ——— conjectural, was largely conjectural, and yet we have to take it for gospel truth.'

He regarded me sympathetically for an intolerable time. Then he slowly took a fistful of foolscap and produced a golden pencil. It seems that in his youth he had had misgivings too, but the thing was explained thus, if I would follow him for a moment. I was so attentive to his explanation that I could not understand it. I found myself playing marbles with the seven bones of the wrist which Fraser recommended me to carry always in my pocket, at least until I had got my own back on McNought. Seven bones, seven planets. Seven? There had to be seven, as Hegel pointed out.

'You understand now the cause of the form of the path the ecliptic takes although the sun is its single focus.' 'Focus!' He took the word out of my mouth. 'Focus.' Of course. If there were two, they were 'foci', the things Parker put the string round. 'Yes, Sir. And why, the ecliptic has not two foci.' ('Foci' is good!)

'Few students have studied the subject without submitting themselves to grinders, who by a series of unworthy mnemonics or rules of thumb take all the interest out of it. You have approached it apparently yourself. If your interest survives your medical studies, I can recommend the pursuit of Astronomy as one which will take you out of yourself and fill you with awe and with a vivid realisation of the wondrous architecture of the world and the omnipotence of its Creator. I will give you five.'

'Leslie is quite right,' I said to myself as I descended the dais, 'when he says that the English idea of a Church is to put a gentleman in every parish.' Now Roberts is a great gentleman! He hasn't got a parish, but he is a Fellow of Trinity College, which is nearly the same thing. He is a great gentleman, for what is a gentleman but one with sympathy and understanding for others? He tumbled to my difficulty and sympathised with my conscientious scruples about Astronomy, and explained them away. A great gentleman! If he was like the bunch on the other side of the Park he would have asked me 'What is Space?' You might as well ask a chap 'What is Nothing?' A thing no one could tell except a mathematician, because it isn't. But, as Dr Tyrell is reported to have said of somebody, 'For a mathematician he was *almost* a gentleman.' It shows he knew the difference. I would give a lot to meet the doctor. From what I hear of him he must be a great gentleman like Mr Roberts, who has just given me five, thereby co-operating with me in keeping up the University's reputation for learning. I am probably saved.

And now: 'Some gentler passions steal into my mind.'

I wish that the Church had more to say to the Medical School, which would be all the better if they packed a few gentlemen into it, a few sportsmen like the Rev Mr Roberts.

And the little book he was reading was Plato's *Symposium*. A great gentleman! For he treated me as if I were one. Anyone who would try to cod him would be worthy of contempt. He took it for granted that I was a gentleman, for he lives in a region where there is no question but that all therein are gentlemen. He took it for granted that because of that trivial difficulty about foci I thought things out for myself without submitting my mind to grinders and such like. When I see Yandell Birrell with his

> '. . . solar eclipse
> Which could only be seen from the kips' etc.

I will tell him what I think of him. It may be all very well for people of a weak kind of intellect to depend on unworthy mnemonics, but the kind of intellect I have does not need them. I may not have as good an intellect as Sir Isaac Newton—he was a bit of a genius in his spare time. When I say 'not as good an intellect' I don't mean that he had necessarily a better intellect than mine, but a different kind of one, if you see what I mean. Every genius has a different kind of intellect. I have not the same kind of genius; every genius is different in his own way. But I do not need to have my memory depending on unworthy mnemonic limericks and rules of thumb such as Birrell depends on, not alone for Astronomy, but for Medicine. It is not so bad to use a few limericks to enable you to get past McNought and that bunch in the Medical School who are distinctly not gentlemen like the

Rev Mr Roberts, but it is beneath one's self-respect to
try them on a gentleman, a great gentleman, like the
Rev Mr Roberts.

Chapter VI

THE BENIGN DOCTOR

As I was leaving the examination hall, the last man out, in came Marshall, the splendid fellow who bears the mace in front of the Provost and bails the undergraduates out of Store Street. He is bigger and taller than Alfred, Lord Tennyson, with the same sort of beard but better-looking and a finer figure of a man. He came along and inquired if I was I. As a matter of fact I was not so sure who I was at the moment. It was nothing to be too positive about. My mind was running round oscillating ellipses with only one focus. If only I had known that the Rev Mr Roberts was taking the *viva voce.* I should have come into the room wearing a velvet gown like Tycho Brahe to show my respect for the heavens. I deserve to be presented with a pedigree hound for all I have gone through. Tycho's tyke was given him by the King of Denmark. One of Mahaffy's hounds would be good enough for me. I took what I hoped would be a last look at the Queen, who had only her father to blame if she did happen to be her sister's daughter, which was enough to make anyone self-centred.

'Dr Tyrrell would like to see you in the Hall,' said Marshall.

Now it was Dr Tyrrell, the Regius Professor of Greek, who had set the English paper. What had I done? I was being carpeted for what? Thank heaven I have read his verse translation of Aristophanes and could quote some of it :

'How oft have I been vexed to the very soul,
How seldom had a treat! A brace, perhaps;
Two brace, at most – and then my disappointments –
Oh, they were millions, billions – sea-sand-dillions.'

'Sea-sand-dillions' was a good one.

And then that bit near the end of the *Acharnaians* about Peace :

'Dear me, but her breast
  Is as firm as a quince!
Come, kiss me your best,
  O my sweet jewel, since
It was I drained the first flask and foremost, with never
  a wink or a wince.'

We cross the cobbled quad, Marshall leading and I about four yards behind. It's a pity that he is not carrying his mace and that Weary and Barney are not here to see us now, I thought. The sight would set them revolving round the two of us with Marshall for focus ('focus' was the word Roberts took out of my mouth) like the satellites of Uranus. It would stop them from making a cod of my astronomy and fill them with respect for Dublin University.

On my way I caught sight of Birrell and a few friends who were looking at a paper under the Campanile : poor devils, wondering if they had passed.

His gown flying out behind him, his grey striped trousers gone at the knees from much sitting, my Tutor crossed in front of the Chapel, blear-eyed, rushing into the Past. He was blear-eyed from staring at old papyri on which he doubtless considered me to be a nasty little palimpsest. It was an ill omen to see him. I had only seen him once, when I was being handed over to him on entering. He avoided me. And I – 'needless to say, and all that kind of thing.' But I didn't like the way he was carrying a bundle of papers : a list of names of those who had passed? Was my name missing, so that he blinked himself rejoicing across the Quad? Or had I passed for ever beyond his neglect? I would have preferred to meet a magpie.

Why was I being taken to the dining-hall and not to the Professor's room in the Front? It seemed a bit odd at twelve noon. Now what had I done on that English paper? Written too much, perhaps. I have a habit of writing too much when I like a thing, and that English paper was the only fair one of the whole series and the only one that I liked. One thing was certain and reassuring, and that was that I was not up for sprinting round the College Park, for the learned doctor was a sport and he seldom missed an athletic meeting or a match. No, I couldn't be up for training in the Park.

He sat in a room off the Hall, a full-browed figure with a prominent forehead, 'rich-crowned with memory': light blue eyes in a clear pink countenance. This was the renowned Professor Tyrrell, the greatest Greek and *diseur* of his day, a 'worthy', if ever there was one, *kalos k'agathos,* which, as everyone knows, means comely and worthy, and is the Greek for a gentleman. His knowledge of the structure of the metres of classical poetry was equalled only by his knowledge and love of English poetry. The inhuman and superhuman examination for Fellowship had not broken the elasticity of his intellect, and it had undoubtedly broken that of nearly all the Fellows except Mahaffy, Palmer and Macran, and left them solitaries or eccentrics fit for nothing but to be tutors, palæographists, mathematicians or musicians, a brow-beaten, banished race, sending out by night furtive notes from quad-surrounded flutes, all but inaudible but fairy-like music in the silence under the moon when the College was supposed to be asleep. For this reason, and not because I had small Latin and less Greek, and also because I had no wish to sit in Hall with a stuffed head for the rest of my unnatural life, I never presented myself for Fellowship. And there was no Fellowship in Astronomy.

He received me, when Marshall drew his attention, with a kindly murmur, put out his shapely hand and motioned me into a chair. I admired the grey full-skirted frock-coat he wore, and the ring with the quadriga through which his dark-red tie was drawn.

'So you are the young man who admires Tennyson and remembers so many lines?'

Saved!

'It may interest you to know that I awarded you ten for that paper of yours.' He sighed happily and rang a little bell.

'I am extremely grateful, sir. It will be a very great help.'

'You have been kept very late. I forget what the subject was – I asked to set the paper in English Literature. What was the subject for which you were up just now?'

'Astronomy.'

'That is hardly a subject for one to revel in. I am afraid that it has fallen among mathematicians. By the way, how did you get on with those people?'

'When I scrambled through the Trigonometry paper and looked up to find Mr Beare waiting to take me in a *viva* on Virgil, I thought that I was in the Seventh Heaven.'

'Instead of which you found yourself in the Sixth Eclogue. But I meant, how did you get on with the Astronomers who think that by adopting that subject they will strike their heads against the stars? I hope you did as well with them in their subject as you did with me?'

'Hardly, sir. I am afraid that the nebulosity of my mind was the only contribution I made to it. My ideas of Astronomy are like the nebula in Andromeda or "Like a storm of fireflies tangled in a silver braid".'

He smiled reminiscently. He seemed pleased at something; probably it was that I was not addicted to Mathematics.

'Yes. You were the only one to point out the line in "Locksley Hall" where it might be said that Tennyson's exquisite ear failed him:

> ' "Many a night from yonder ivied casement, ere I went to rest,
> Did I gaze on great Orion sloping slowly to the west." '

Now the diæresis after the fifth foot, after "casement"... Of course you noticed it? I wonder that he did not realise how foreign it is to the trochaic metre. You, as I say, noticed it. And the other example – let me see.' He inclined his great forehead, and closed his eyes and murmured metrically, recalling the verse. The butler appeared, stood expectant for a moment and emitted a little 'Sir?' At last the doctor, who was thinking of another diæresis, noticed him. 'Oh, Watchorn, my young friend must be tired. I think the occasion calls for a little light refreshment. A glass of port, for instance, would not be inexcusable under the circumstances. He has been sitting for his degree examination for hours. Bring us – let me see – a bottle of your oldest vintage, something that cannot be said to be too young for the day. Something revealing the bee's wing. As for me, I will take another whiskey drink.'

I was greatly impressed. It must be wonderful to be a Fellow and to be able to order port with such assurance and to have such a dependable butler. In our house, on the rare occasions we gave dinners, port was a matter of the gravest concern. Nobody could satisfy my father, except my mother, on its choice. There was always an impressive argument about vintages, bottles and binns, which she usually concluded, and cured his fastidiousness by sending out for a few bottles to Findlater's. I never heard of a bee in a bottle before. It must be a metaphor;

66

but the only metaphorical bees of which I had heard were not in bottles of port.

So I was being rewarded for remembering Tennyson just as Sir Hugh Lane, according to Sickert, was knighted for admiring Manet. It was all very delightful. I hoped that the doctor would remember the line, for the heaven I had just been trying to scale was not 'the highest heaven of invention'. He produced an oblong snuff-box of some dull metal, saying, after a pinch of snuff : 'Dear me, is it not extraordinary how hard it is to recall a lonely line without the context! Our ideas, or at least our memory, depends to a great extent upon association. There ought to be some credit given for the inconsequent. It would make a new form of humour, while not perhaps carrying one very far in an examination where the tendency is biased in favour of association and coherence of ideas.'

He smiled pleasantly in his own vein. He looked out upon the world from a sustained viewpoint of lofty irony and agreeable disdain born of a classical self-sufficiency, a kind of Epicurean stoicism before which the common and undistinguished ways of men appeared as hardly to be borne, and the ways of the pretentious and the self-righteous not to be borne at all, but to be encountered by ridicule. But even his sarcasm was benign.

'What suggested Medicine to you as a career?'

'It is more or less congenital in our family. Nobody ever thought of anything else for me.'

He pondered as if he were considering a way of escape. Then he asked : 'Where did you get your interest in literature?'

'That, such as it is, sir, came as a reaction against the Royal University, that bodiless examination booth to which I was attached for two years.'

'But what brought you to us?'

'The Registrar, Dr Traill. He was so polite to my mother, who was rather hurt after the scant courtesy she found in the Medical School of Cecilia Street, that she decided to cut my two years as a loss and to begin afresh where my father had intended to send me.'

He murmured to himself, 'Traill – polite.'

I hastened to the defence of my benefactor.

'He was, as the saying goes, "The making of me"; and that in spite of stories we heard of his being rather bovine.'

His face brightened, as it would when he made an apt comparison from the poets.

'Likening his "maker" to a grazed ox,' he quoted. And he was so pleased with its appositeness that he forgave me for my championing of Traill. After a while he said, 'Once it was my lot to examine in the Royal University. I was examining in Greek; that may have been the reason why I was ushered into a bare room furnished in the Doric mode with all its severity. It was a perfectly bare room, except for a deal table in the middle and two bent-wood chairs. The only attempt at mural decoration was the word *Skatos*, scribbled in lead pencil over the mantelpiece, doubtless by a departing candidate.'

Without a smile he took a pinch of snuff, and continued: 'It had something of the terseness of that great unknown Comic poet of Athens who survives vigorously in one line.' He sipped his glass as he collected himself to deliver a short encomium on some old dead singer dear to his heart.

'You know,' he began, 'that the Athenians had a pestilential little Republic on their west flank. It was in the island of what is now Corfu but was then called Corcyra. To this every expelled ruffian and absconding undesirable of every class resorted, together with many piratical gangs. Now every Comic poet of Athens was a conservative and looked upon this republic of libertines with contempt. They must have been mouthing about Freedom, as those will do who have no culture of their own but see in Freedom an excuse for idleness. There is no line in the whole range of classical literature more devastating in its denunciation of the pretences of demagogues and politicians than that lonely line, "Corcyra is a free country; you can commit a nuisance wherever you please." Can you tell me another?'

I was taken aback under the compliment which implied a knowledge which was worthy of his attention.

'Licence, they mean,' he murmured reminiscently.

'It sounds like Aristophanes,' was all I could say.

'Aristophanes!' he exclaimed at once.

What have I fallen into now? I thought. I should have kept off Greek.

'What a poet that was! Was there ever such another? His genius is unique in the world's history. It is impossible to convey an adequate idea of him simply because there is no one with whom to compare him. We should have to take half a dozen, not excluding Shakespeare, but including Shelley for swiftness and Catullus for terseness and simplicity. Incomparable!' He seemed delighted that this was so.

'You know that lyric in the *Clouds*?'

I was on guard, so I left it alone.

'And then he can descend to the lewdest ribaldry without defiling his genius or lessening his power to charm.' I ventured to agree, adding that for that reason he was my favourite, and for the additional reason that he hated political dishonesty and humbug.

'Of course! You have read the *Clouds*?'

I confessed that the part where Socrates was being parodied with his nose on the earth learning geology while his backside was studying astronomy, was not unpleasing.

'For sheer control and verse flexibility, to what modern English lyrist would you compare him?'

It felt like a question on which much depended. With the doctor I could hazard a guess and take a wild leap with the assurance that he would forgive its boldness,

69

even welcome it, were it at all reasonable.

'Gilbert,' I said.

He hummed like a sunny hive. I had pleased him beyond words. 'Now there are very few,' he began. Suddenly he came to some decision. He looked at his watch.

'It is just time to go over to Jammet's and see Lewis about some prawns and sample some of that excellent ale. If you have not to yield yourself up just yet, as I shall have to yield myself up to my family at dinner-time, you might come along.'

Who could refuse? I summoned my courage – the port had gone to my head – and accepted with the diffidence that was due from, for all I knew, an undergraduate still.

'Ah, that eleven-foot line of monosyllables! Who else could have approached its counterpart in English?

'"Expecting the sensation of a short, sharp shock
From a cheap and chippy chopper on a big black block!"'

Of course, it is Gilbert,' he said as we went down the steps.

I walked by his side, regretting that the little Greek I knew came from an attempt to translate the parts marked *Non Legitur* in my books at school.

He walked slowly – it was the sign of a Greek gentleman not to hurry – as he received the evidences of his popularity in the honour and love of all the students who saluted him with a smile. The porters at the gate were magnificent. Their salutes had the dignity of a tradition of three hundred years. We crossed the Green. He walked with his coat buttoned, holding his left hand behind him, palm outwards. His right held a cherry-wood stick. Of course there was no sign of either Barney or Weary; nor would there be – Jammet's was beyond their means, and though we all may have been said to be drinking beyond our means, we did not feel it as much in Golly's as we would have felt it in Jammet's. My aunt, of course, says that nobody can afford to drink at all; which is absurd, for it is obvious that in a little time nobody could afford to sell drinks to insolvents. But it would have made them sit up if they saw me with the Professor of Greek.

Lloyd Poch was in Jammet's. He was a great Welshman who came over to teach men how to live – that is, Trinity men – on interrupted means or none. He sat beside me at the marble counter. Kelly, and not Lewis, stood under the *Pereunt horæ*. It did a fellow good to see Kelly. He never grew old. He could persuade an oyster with two passes to yield itself up to be devoured alive. No one sat on the other side of the Professor. He was hedged by a zone of respect. It looked as if people were afraid of him and he did not like it. He said when the drinks were served : 'It saddens me for a moment to think that the men of Dublin are not worthy of their public houses. They are so brutalised that they require low bars, shebeens, kips and music-halls to amuse them. They have to be spoken to in a special argot which amounts to a special language, and they have sunk so low as to resent being treated equally.'

It was quite true. When a learned and urbane man like the doctor gives them the lead, as it were, they fight shy of him – all but Willie Wallis. And even he thinks it necessary to remember his public-school accent, which makes him self-conscious and shows that even he distrusts his public house. But were they as much unworthy of their pubs as the company of the doctor?

'Now if the editor of the *Irish Times* were to dive into this bar for half-an-hour on his way to the office, what a difference it would make – not indeed to us' (very decently he included Poch and me) – 'but to the public at large ! It would tend to terminate the regrettable severance which exists between the amusements of the masses. The town would not be divided as it is at the present into: No pubs; clubs; hotels; restaurants and graded pubs. If there were

71

no separation between high and low in their amusements, there would be no high and low: there would be no low haunts, and no Dan Lowry's. They should be all members of the one pub. But the Editor, instead of drinking, spends his spare time in trying to be Mahaffy; and Mahaffy, as everyone knows, only drinks claret in private houses. But what is one to say when you hear of a counsel trying to make capital out of the fact that the defendant said he was going down town to a public house, and actually succeeding with this humbug before a Dublin jury? He enlisted their prejudice. Are we a nation of hypocrites, or is a Dublin jury the most easily humbugged assembly of humbugs that ever existed? I cannot understand it, especially as I am convinced that every member of that jury went out for a drink the very minute the case was over.' He lifted his tankard while I turned to Poch.

Now Poch was a man after my own heart. He was in the Medical School, and he could not see any more than myself why we should be referred to books when we paid for lectures, demonstrations and performances on the dead and the quick. 'Will you bring that lobster, quick?' some host of Oscar Wilde said to the waiter. 'May I have mine dead?' Oscar tentatively inquired. It's in that sense and because of that story that I remembered that 'quick' really means 'alive'. It was no use telling it to the doctor, who probably had invented it, so I told it to Poch. But Poch, though he showed us, both by precept and more frequently by example, how to be carefree, was somewhat concerned this afternoon. It seemed that there was an accident at Hengler's. And he was concerned lest he should impress nobody with his importance, as the Messenger who bears the bad news in Greek tragedies.

Hengler's is a circus in Rutland Square. By means of it, the authorities of the Rotunda Gardens are enabled to introduce the appropriate amount of slumdom into the grandest of all the Dublin squares. To them it seems necessary to introduce a certain amount of decay into the heart of the city, as if it could only commend itself to the citizens by decomposition, as if they took the town for a cheese – and they must have taken their tastes from gorgonzola, which commends itself to those who like decay. However, Hengler's circus was the chief romance of my youth. By peeping through a knot-hole in its side, you could sometimes see the clown preparing himself, or a horse going round, and when you were pushed away you knew that the Square bully was gazing at the acrobat putting on her tights.

'And she fell from the top of the thirty-foot pole and smashed her face.' The doctor, who liked all forms of athletics, overheard, and asked for details.

'It was a show given by Le Greco – a strong man in Hengler's circus.'

'In Hengler's circus? He must have called himself Le Greco to distinguish himself from El Greco, lest the inhabitants of Dublin find themselves taken in by a picture exhibition and not an exhibition of clowns. But what happened?'

'He was dressed up in his lion-skin and holding two acrobats and his wife on the top of a pole stuck in his belt, when suddenly he dropped dead. His wife was spinning on the top of the pole and she had the farthest to fall. The pole rebounded and broke her nose and knocked her senseless.'

'What a strange place to be spinning! She must have been already senseless before she ascended. Now, Penelope – '

'I should have said "revolving", sir. She had a brass boss on her belt and she used to revolve herself on the top of the pole till her husband dropped dead.'

'But surely, if you are using the imperfect tense, it was her habitual practice to revolve as that of her husband consisted in dropping dead.'

'The others may have been rehearsals,' I suggested.

73

'This must have been the real thing.'

Seeing that Poch was disconcerted, the kindly doctor included him in the round. 'A quart of ale is a dish for a king. We must give these prawns something to swim in.' It was for acts such as this the young men loved the benign doctor.

Now prawns are like little lobsters or 'the animal provided' whose guts I used to get to 'expose' in the Royal. They are only found in Dublin Bay. The next place for them, I hear, is Plymouth. But they would be no use there for they only go well with beer. I refused the lemon sole which was to follow when I thought of over-eating and Ballinafeigh.

'What hospital is the contortionist in?' I asked Poch. I think he said Mercer's, but the doctor was telling us about the fellow whose eye was caught by the legend over Jammet's clock and who made an immortal translation. The clock, a square of metal painted blue, with a circular face picked out in gold was set into the wall of the bar in front of the counter. In gold the legend *Pereunt horæ et notantur* was inscribed above the dial. Whether he had heard my question or only the word 'contortionist', I cannot tell. It was strange that he should have thought of the quaint translation at the moment: I wish I could remember whom he named as the author. The real author probably was himself. He was so full of wit and humour that he had to invent others to help him to carry the overplus.

'*Pereunt horæ et notantur:* The whores pass by and are spotted,' he murmured audibly, much amused.

'It's a good rendering if not exactly a translation, for it conveys the warning. There would be no meaning in telling us that our hours were numbered if we spent them well. And whoever wrote that knew there were certain things that led to hours misspent. The very place for that motto is in an oyster bar.'

He acquiesced, and presumptuously I went on :

'It adds a pleasant tang to life to know that it's fleeting. If I may be forgiven for employing a medical term: Death is Life's astringent.'

'That reminds me,' said the doctor. 'I would like a little *sauce à la tartare* with this sole.'

Chapter VII

BACCALAUREUS IN ARTIBUS

I lounged about the front gates waiting for results like another chronic medical who used to 'lounge about the College courts on the wait for misery and ill-luck' one hundred and fifty odd years ago; but he now stands immortal as bronze, in bronze, with his contemporary Burke, before the University which treated him so scurvily. His tutor was a savage bully; mine is a mild palæographist who thinks more of rescuing papyri from cameldung than me from McNought. I am glad to think that Oliver Goldsmith was a chronic medical and that, like the poet Gray, he hated mathematics, and that, like Swift and his companion in bronze, Burke, he barely got a B.A. degree. Barely will do well enough for me, I thought. If I do scrape through I will be in the company of the great whose greatness seemingly went in inverse ratio to the approbation of their professors. Modesty will, of course, forbid me from going too much into detail, but I will mention their records to my Aunt, having first got Birrell to address half-a-dozen letters in different hands to my house, with B.A., T.C.D., in large type after my name. I will give them time to work before turning up at home, and they will more than counteract any little misunderstanding that may ensue in my Half M.B. exam next time with McNought. It is an extraordinary thing that Trinity's greatest sons were in her eyes her greatest dunces. I would put up with being a dunce 'so were I equalled with them in renown'.

It takes a long time, it seems, to post the results up in the front gate. I have heard rumours enough already, and the porter who has just come from the direction of the Senior Lecturer's room looked as if he expected a tip – that is, he looked with interest at me not unmixed with sympathy at the way I have been treated hitherto. But until they post you up you never can be sure that you have passed. It's better to see the results in the glass case before going off to see the boys and allow myself to relax, perhaps only to wake up after, say, half-a-dozen pints to find that I was stuck. It will be time to rejoice and to react to all the midnight oil and Parker thraldom when the results are out. Meanwhile, I sit on the rail and see who is going in and out.

The sculptor Foley, who was our best sculptor, gave, I see, the same set of calves to his three masterpieces, Grattan, Goldsmith and Burke. Now, obviously, they all could not have had Herculean calves like those. The older men's would have shrunken, but Goldsmith's would not, for he died youngest of the three. He had a low-sized, thick, robust, ungainly body fit to withstand all kinds of fatigue; and he won a contest at throwing the hammer, which was a sledge in those days, at the fair of Ballymahon. Now, next to Ballahadereen, in which they say every house is a pub except the convent and the police barracks, and you can never be sure of a police barracks, Ballymahon is the drunkenest town in Ireland, and there must have been great challenging and great stimulation, as well as great emulation, when the poet swung and slung the sledge so well and beat all the warty boys. He must have thrown a hammer or something on College Park and have been seen by a prototype of McNought, for he never passed through the Medical School.

I have the greatest sympathy with Oliver, who, because he never put on side, was never rightly appreciated – particularly in England, where even poets have to conform.

77

He preferred friendship to fame. Like Charles J. Fox, he 'subdued ambition'. Locke, the *Human Understanding* fellow, must have been a bit of an athlete in Oxford, for he was refused admission into their Medical School, the McNoughts of the time being Dean Fell and Dr Allestree, who are only remembered now as obstructions. I wish someone would pass this bit of history with its moral on to McNought. I am too reserved to do it myself, but Birrell might bring the subject up, and suggest that it is taking a great risk with your repute in the eyes of posterity to stick a fellow just because he happens to have a little too much energy to be absorbed by the Half.

I notice that there is no statue of Dean Swift. He didn't pass the B.A., at all, but got it *speciali gratia*, by special favour.

'Physics – *male;* Greek and Latin – *bene;* Thema – *negligenter.*'

That may be said of my Half; but where is the *speciali gratia*? Nowhere. Its place is taken by a special grudge.

It is enough to put a fellow off studiousness. I wouldn't be at all surprised if it were that that put me off too close attention to work. And, conversely, when you think of what success in College exams might mean, when you think of how Oscar Wilde ended, it is better to be with the dunces, beginning with Dun Scotus, the Irish born, himself.

Dr Salmon, the Provost, only swore once in his life, and that was when he said: 'Damn exams!' And, by Dean Swift, he was quite right.

'"Talk of the Devil!" I was just thinking of you, Birrell, old man.'

'Yandell Birrell, if *you* please.'

'Why, what's up?'

'Your swelled head. It's swelled up.'

'But upon my word! I'm sitting here waiting for the results.'

'Oh, you are, are you? You cut me in the quad, when you were going off behind Marshall to see Dr Tyrrell, who took you out to lunch. Do you think I have never met Lloyd Poch?'

'But that has not swelled my head. I think you must have met McConkey.'

'No; but you know bloody well, or you ought to know, that you would not have been honoured by the professor if you were a "failed B.A." like a Babu barrister. And you who – '

'Honestly, I never knew – '

'And you who passed chiefly on account of my mnemonics hadn't the decency to recognise me when you went swanking across the quad.'

'As a matter of fact, Birrell, Yandell – as a matter of fact – ' But what was the use of telling him that I was done with his childish limericks and that, the very opposite to what he thought, was the reason why the Rev Mr Roberts congratulated me? Besides, I didn't want to break with Yandell Birrell, who evidently was stuck and was naturally in an awful wax and had to wreak it on somebody. I couldn't even tell him what Mr Roberts said. This awfully unjust and groundless allegation of having a swelled head put me in such a false position, that to explain anything just now would only make it worse.

'I can't believe that I am through,' I said, with disarming modesty and implied solicitude for himself.

'If you would look in the Front Hall instead of watching for the Doctor to come out of Jammet's, you would have seen what ought to make you ashamed of yourself.' And he went angrily through the front gate.

It would never do to be seen trying to get a look at the results. I gave the porter two-and-sixpence and asked him to bring me a copy of the list. Meanwhile, I tried to resume my soliloquy on Art. Why should a fellow like Birrell divert my train of thought? I will dismiss him from my mind. Foley was quite right to idealise the subjects of his statues whom he had never met, just as Michael Angelo did Moses and the Sybil whom he had never met. The aim of Art is spiritual expression, and it would be the very contradiction of Art were it not to detach itself from the material and the factual. That is where American poets go astray. Rather it is where they keep earthbound and think that things significant in the daily round are therefore themes fit for . . . Blast it! If I don't put things right with Birrell before Monday he'll not help me in the Half, and his being stuck in the B.A. may have come from concentrating on the Half. And I depending on his lyrics for the pelvis and the head and neck!

What the hell is Goldsmith writing in that little book? Jack Lalor the barber told Golly that he was taking down Grattan's tick-tack; but Lalor's mind runs on racing. If Goldsmith were alive to-day and aware of all our environment and our thoughts, what would he tell us? We know what his opinion was of T.C.D. That it was 'no place for an ambitious man or one who was sensitive to contempt'. Now, goodness knows I am not ambitious, but I am bloody well sensitive to Mr Me-bloody-friend Yandell Birrell, 'failed B.A.'s', contempt and his efforts to put me in the wrong. But it's just as well that I didn't tell him what the Rev Mr Roberts thought. What would Mr McAnatomy think if he heard ' "We are going to new digs, said the Internal Pudics"?' One thing is certain – I am no longer a nuisance to my tutor, and I would cut him if he could see enough in the daylight to realise that I was ignoring him. Only for the Master of those who know and his lectures in philosophy, moral and otherwise – I suppose what isn't moral philosophy must be natural – I wouldn't have learnt a damn thing in this College. But then, as Mahaffy says, 'you are not supposed to learn, you are supposed to experience and to conduct yourself. You can go to Scotland for mere information if that appeals to you.' I'll have to stay on the books until I get an M.D. It may be for years. I hope that my tutor doesn't come into that part of the work. I will send the Master, who very kindly promised to intercede if the occasion arises, to McNought.

Now I know what Goldsmith is writing in his book. He is describing the death of his tutor who 'was killed in a discreditable brawl'. That's where Oliver got 'tattering a whore in a kip'.

'Thanks,' I said, as the porter produced the list. I began at the bottom so as not to lose time, and I saw my name at first glance. There I am, and content to be last with the old Alma Mater's most distinguished sons. And only slightly better than Dean Swift. I too have subdued ambition – swelled head, indeed !

I had better go home to dinner and see what value there is in my B.A. Not much, I think, seeing all the fees that were paid for this my tardy degree. My mother will doubtless point out the fact that I should have got it long ago. Early or late, it will knock Barney and Elwood out. Weary, of course, shall have read the results in the *Evening Mail* and be sadly and spitefully jealous in his own quiet way.

It's a fine thing to have the Western Front of Dublin University behind you. That's a wall you can put your back to when it comes to scholarship. 'B.A., T.C.D.' I could now get a job as usher in any school in the colonies, or even a job as reporter to the *Irish Times*. It is a great test of sound scholarship and all-round intellectual capacity.

What months of bad weather are represented by my B.A. !

Mr Beddy, 'who is really kind-hearted and conscientious,' and who met my mother at the Sodality, was helping her now in the business about a building loan. Some of our land apparently had to be developed by house property within a certain time, or the rental would increase out of all proportion to the value of the fields as fields. That meant that thousands had to be raised, and Mr Beddy, who, even though he was only for the moment at all events a solicitor's clerk, but later on, please God, he would be a fully qualified solicitor, knew where the money could be raised against the security of the houses he would build for us. So, as my mother was engaged, I dined alone with my aunt, who waited for me, worse luck.

'I know I'm very late, but I have had a most trying day. It is no easy task to get your B.A. from all the Professors and Scholars of Trinity College, and Dublin University — no easy task. If I could afford it now that it is all over, I would relax at an edifying opera if there was one; as there is not, a theatre will have to do.'

'You passed?'

I said 'Yes' as languidly as I could, for a 'theatre' was depending on my need for recuperation. 'If I had less knowledge and more influence I could have got a *speciali gratia* degree like Dean Swift.'

'Like Dean Swift?'

'Yes. He failed to pass. The B.A. exam of Trinity was too stiff for him. He failed to pass; so they gave him one by special favour.'

'But you passed? Oh, won't your poor mother be pleased! She has been praying for your success. Wait until I run in to tell her.'

'Aunt,' I called after her, 'don't disturb her, but you might tell her privately so that Mr Beddy, who doesn't understand drama and might think that a B.A. of Dublin University should not go even to a *good* play, doesn't hear it, that you think I deserve a pound to pay porters and for hiring gowns and that kind of thing. But I had rather have the pleasure of telling her to-morrow when her mind is free from business. Leave her alone.'

'Perhaps you are right. Just wait.'

Of course I was right. My mother would have remarked, 'Well, it's about time. Now stay in and read for your Medical degree.'

Before I go to see Barney I must look up that umbrella. It will show that I am not taken up with thinking of myself. It should be somewhere in the loft. It was. But it was useless – useless, that is so say, for Barney's purpose, which was to make it deputise for his overcoat when he should swank it at Kingsbridge for the edification of his Ma. The last time I used it was when I was about nine, and then it was as a parachute to enable me to jump from the loft down on a heap of sand. It could hold off the rain from people getting in or out of a brougham, but it could not hold off the force of gravity. And as for holding off the suspicions of Barney's mother : she would see a livery in the place of an overcoat on her beloved son. No; the two-handed umbrella was no use. It should have been given to Wiseman with the assortment of whips, but Wiseman probably refused it. The other cabbies would have codded him. And the boys would make a nice cod of me if I were to produce it in Golly's. It might do for an apple woman, they would say, or to roof the Whores' Bank.

But they never cod anybody who has a quid. And they won't cod me, for have I not just passed one of the greatest intelligence tests in the world? Let Barney and Weary find it out for themselves. If I were to be the first to inform them, they would put it down to Trinity swank. I think, as it's nearly closing time, I'll take a turn to An Stad.

Chapter VIII

AN STAD

I was greatly impressed by Michael Cusack's legs. He was a very broad man, with a brown beard and great calves which bulged out under his dark knee-breeches. He was also a great Gael. He kept a school of athletics at 5, Philpott Place, and he usually walked about carrying a hurley stick bound with iron, which suggested Titanic hurling matches before the Sassenach softened and diminished the stature of the Gael. He looked like Hercules with his club. Now any form of athletics challenges and fascinates me. To win a word from him would be encouraging. But how could a great Gael pass a word of approval on such a form of new-fangled athletics—if athletics it could be called—as cycle-racing? At any rate, it couldn't be called anything, for the idea of Gaelic athletics was conveyed in Gaelic, and there was no tradition in Irish for cycle-racing. But I was allowed to look at him in the Stad. Now the Stad was half a shop, very nearly at the corner of North Frederick Street, where old Peebles lived, and Gardiner's Row. It was under the shadow of the steeple of a Presbyterian church. Every night the Gaelic revivers dropped in to see Cathal McGarvey. Cathal, as his name implies, was a great Gael because he knew Teigue O'Donoghue well, and Teigue was a Gaelic poet and a native speaker on whom almost everything depended for reviving the language and bringing back the nation once again.

I was attracted to Teigue. True, he was not as burly

84

as Michael Cusack. He was not burly at all, but slight, which did not matter because he was a poet, and all poets fascinate me as much as athletes, for one activity is an outward sign of the other. If only I knew enough Gaelic to appreciate him; or, if only I had not forgotten the Youthful Exploits of Finn and the Pursuit of Diarmuid and Grainne which I had learned at Richmond Street, when I was there with Tom Kettle and we were both about ten or eleven. But I did not know enough Gaelic, so I had to depend on Teigue's reputation, and to be more frustrated than ever because I could not commune with him in his own tongue—my tongue, too, though it wasn't literally my mother tongue. It was nobody's mother tongue in Dublin, nor had it ever been but for a month or two when the town was taken and the Danes driven out by the Gael. But it was mother tongue of the people in the part of the country where Teigue came from, and that was enough for anyone with the least pretensions to patriotism.

Cathal McGarvey, the owner of the Stud, wore his hair long on the top of his head (because he was a singer at smokers or concerts), and it curled at the sides as it fell down. He wore a very big black tie, because he composed his own songs. And one of these I must not forget. It was about a retired Civil Servant who used to go fishing in the canal to kill time, until Leech's opened, and he was looked down upon during all his weary vigil by Leech's clock. He made his reputation and he sang his songs in English; and in that language he sold his cigarettes. It was a pity that I was not strong enough to play hurley, and I began to regret it until it was borne in upon me that at the Stad nobody did anything except smoke cigarettes, but they all approved of it, and you knew they were ready to play it for the nation's sake. Michael Cusack did not play it either, but he had a big iron-bound club that did play it once upon a time; so that was all right. There was a great atmosphere of nationality gathered about the Stad. It was a good place to slip out to at night, for one who lived about fifteen doors away, and to talk about the revival of Gaelic. Even if few people talked to me there was always Cathal, who was too civil and too much of a business man not to talk to anyone while waiting for a revival of the nation.

Arthur Griffith talked to me, and so did Shaun T. and one or two of his friends, who were schoolmasters. And no one was as determined as Arthur to revive the Gael and make us a nation once again. But before this could be done we must bring back the Members from Westminster. I told this to Tom Kettle, and I will never forget his answer.

'Ireland politically is an invalid and is not yet strong enough for freedom.' But then Tom was in with Joe Devlin and Redmond, who had an interest in Westminster, and they knew nothing about the spirit that was stirring in the Stad.

Arthur Griffith was smaller in stature than the others. But he had more strength of will and more determination. And he said very little, except to jerk out an epigram by the way of keeping us right politically. He very rarely had to do this because, even when nobody talked, it was understood that we all stood for the Cause at the Stad. This silence and understanding kept us from being jealous about each other's zeal. So there was a united front at the Stad. Even if we had a misgiving about the whole-heartedness of our neighbour we could all believe in Arthur Griffith. And for anyone who preferred the athletic side of the Gael to the political side – for Arthur was short-sighted and wore pince-nez, which the ancient Gaels did not – there was always Michael Cusack.

Though Arthur, or Art, as it appears was his name in Irish, was short of stature, he had a fine head with a straight forehead, for which Lavater would give you more than for any other type of forehead, and Lavater knew more about faces and what they purported in character than anyone before or after his time. It is a pity that the rest of the body cannot be made as interesting as the face, then anatomy would become readable. It seems odd to make everything depend on the last of the vertebræ from which the head is developed, as Goethe discovered – and he was a poet and not a professor – and to ignore the rest. No one cared much about Michael Cusack's forehead. His personality was in his calves. But when you leave athletics and take up politics you must depend upon the head. This is hardly fair to politicians. It puts many of them at a disadvantage and shuts them out from the category of *mens sana in corpore sano*. Thus there is a disharmony at the outset once you let yourself concentrate on the brains of a man and forget his body. I don't suggest that there should be no brains in politics, nor do I propose that there should be nothing but brawn; but there should be a mixture of both. If there were nothing but Michael Cusacks in Ireland one might get a little bored; and if there were nothing but brains in Ireland there would be very little sport. Which things go to prove that it takes all the vertebræ to make a man with a backbone.

That is how I came to be a patriot from a mixture of admirations for Cusack's calves and Griffith's character; from the heroic tradition of the invincible athletic Gael, and the actual existence of one incorruptible modern statesman.

The 'pre-requisites', as the Citizen, the Revolutionary, would call them, for a movement in a nation are self-sacrifice, a newspaper and a public meeting. Obviously the newspaper is necessary to enlighten the people before they will come up for a public meeting, and there must be a lot of private friends at the meeting to keep it public. Otherwise it might be broken up. And meanwhile each friend has to work for the Cause. I worked for the Cause on Tom Kettle, only to be met with a rebuff. I was advised to ask him who made the country an invalid by draining it of its life blood in emigration and taxation, and if he thought that by walking into the enemy's parlour in Westminster he was likely to effect a change. I did not try the Cause on the Benign Doctor, because he knew all about causes from the days of Corcyra and Cleon down.

I wasn't much good at self-sacrifice. There was no need to be. So many people were sacrificing me at the moment that it would have seemed superfluous to try it on myself. But if you couldn't find anything in yourself that was in need of being sacrificed, at least you should take the whole thing seriously and not turn it into a laughing matter. That is why there was so little talk in the Stad, for fear anyone might laugh while the nation was being re-born. And yet midwives are cheery people. Besides, I wondered if we were not metamorphosing into English yokels. For I remembered Mahaffy telling McGurk that the English boor seldom laughs, and then only at very coarse fun : *'Is it not remarkable, my friend, that the savage and the ignorant laugh less and understand less of this great fund of enjoyment than civilised people?'* And I was very fond of laughter. In fact, I disliked and suspected anyone who could not join in a laugh. There is something wanting in anyone who is too serious. He is uncivilised, and therefore a potential menace to society. A good laugh at the right moment might have killed Calvin. That is why I love Barney and Weary and the Citizen, because they are always laughing or leading up to a laugh. That is why I spent so much time trying to amuse Arthur.

But the last and the first thing a patriot should do was to believe in the Irish people. Now the 'Irish People' were not supposed to be in Trinity College; they were somewhere in the country, especially in the parts where Teigue came from. And I was in Trinity College where Robert Emmet came from, and yet I was supposed not to be of the 'Irish People'. Therefore, to believe in them was to disbelieve in oneself. And being incapable of such sacrifice, I preferred belief in myself to belief in the 'Irish People'. I found that a lot of the Irish people do the same. It keeps them off the rates.

As Golly says:

> 'If each before his own door swept
> The village would be clean.'

Now Arthur Griffith believed in the 'Irish People', which would have been all right if the 'Irish People' believed in themselves or consisted of three million Arthur Griffiths; for then all the Irish People would believe in the same thing and themselves at the same time. But the Irish people believe only in that which they know to be untrue. There was only one Arthur Griffith, and he also believed in self-sacrifice, which, in view of Irish history, seemed to me to be superfluous, for you have only to become their Leader when the Irish People will start sacrificing you. Human sacrifice has never quite died out in Ireland. It is merely reserved for 'Leaders'.

Chapter IX

CROWNER'S QUEST

'Let us get everything quite clear,' said Friery the Coroner, whose head, as a rule, never began to clear until late in the afternoon. 'Let us get everything quite clear. Who was the deceased?'

There was no reply.

'Don't all speak at once,' said Friery the Coroner sarcastically to the witnesses and jury. And when the silence became ominous he turned to the Serjeant with: 'Have you no respect for the Court?'

On a slab outside lay a sad caricature of Hercules: toes and thumbs turned out, great chest and thighs relaxed. *Rigor mortis* had passed off. He appeared to be a man in his early forties. On a chair were placed his cupped belt and a leopard skin. Two buskins with tawdry gilt straps stood on the floor. This was Le Greco, the French Hercules of the circus bills.

Mercer's House-surgeon was the first to give evidence. He stated that death was due to a lesion of a bloodvessel in the brain.

'Why not more?' asked Friery the Coroner. 'Let us have precision at all costs.'

The doctor opined that the lesion of one vessel would be quite sufficient to cause death. It depended on its size and situation, but, of course, in deference to the Court, he would not rule out the possibility of more than one vessel having given way.

'So I thought,' said Friery the Coroner.

'In addition,' the House-surgeon went on, 'there were internal abdominal injuries which would have proved fatal had the subject rallied from the stroke.'

'So he would have died in any case?' said Friery the Coroner, who wanted precision at all costs. 'Can you describe the internal injuries?'

'The omentum and the intestines were torn, the bladder was ruptured, there was hæmorrhage and extravasation –'

'You have heard that,' said Friery the Coroner. 'The omentum was torn. I think that we may agree that he would have died in any case,' and he wrote down the word 'extravasation'.

The jury began to whisper among themselves.

'Stop that muttering and speak up.'

The foreman respectfully indicated that the corpse had not been identified. Nobody knew who suffered from the injuries described.

'I was coming to that,' said Friery the Coroner.

But actually it was the Serjeant who came to his aid. He winked portentously at the Coroner and twisted his wrist, revealing a notebook.

'Proceed, Serjeant Murtagh.' Then recollecting himself : 'That was the very first question I put, but I received no reply. Proceed, if you please, Serjeant.'

'In answer to inquiries made on the spot,' the Serjeant proceeded, 'I ascertained that the deceased corp was that of one Jules Brotonne, otherwise known by his trade or professional name as Le Greco, who dropped dead in Hengler's Circus while he was supporting his wife and two acrobats on a pole. He is said to have come of an aristocratic French family who fell on evil days during the Revolution. He leaves a broken-nosed widow in hospital, suffering from a fall and a dislocated shoulder, subjective noises and an intermittent pulse. I have a witness here who knew them in Birmingham.'

'I will hear the witness,' said Friery the Coroner.

The Serjeant made a motion of his left arm, and instead of being 'called', Tommy Monks, the Brummagem Bantam, was thrust forward, apparently from a fold in the Serjeant's greatcoat.

'This man knew them, your Worship.'

'Who was this Brotonne?' the Coroner asked.

Tommy Monks put his hand behind his ear, which action caused the Coroner to shout: 'Who was this Brotonne?'

' 'Ow was it brought on?' Tommy repeated. ' 'Ow, but by overtaxing hisself when he had a few over the oight. I often sez to him, I sez, "Jim, you'll bust up some foine doy sure as Fate." I warned him all right. I did so all right. No one should never put glasses of rum in his bottles of Guinness.'

'You knew him then?' Friery shouted, much interested.

'Oo, him? I should just think I did, and his woife too.'

'Who is his wife – or his widow, rather?'

'Oh, she's a beaut, all right,' affirmed Tommy Monks.

'She has a broken nose,' Friery remarked in no very loud tones.

Nevertheless, chivalrously Tommy Monks repeated, 'She's a beaut all right. About eighteen, and eight and a half. All right she is.'

'And now she lies in?' The Coroner pointed to the House-surgeon with the handle of his pen.

'Mercer's Hospital.'

'Injuries not serious, I hope?' said the Coroner cursorily.

'Not as bad as we have heard them described by the Serjeant, who must have been talking to a nurse. A fracture of the nasal bones, that's about all.'

'Will there be much disfigurement?'

'Undoubtedly there will be some.'

The Coroner hid his disappointment by making a note.
'But we have not yet heard from witness — who was this Brotonne?'

The Serjeant, who was beside him, passed the question closely in Tommy's ear, 'Who was this Brotonne?'

''E was what you might call a light 'eavy, outside welter weight, that is, but not clarss enough for 'eavy. 'E 'adn't the timber for a champion — that's wot made 'im take up this 'ere balancing business. The sawdust was more his loine; 'e wasn't made for the ring.'

'Now, now. Let us get "this balancing business" clearly. What did he do? What was his exhibition in Hengler's? Of what did his exhibition in the circus consist?'

The question was duly magnified.

'Ow, that? 'E 'ad his woife up the pole balancing on her belt and twirling round and round while two Frenchies 'eld on to it and spread thisselves out on each side underneath, 'olding on by a foot an' 'and for all the world like the double X on a bottle of stout.'

'Extraordinary!' exclaimed Friery, who was following the description closely. 'But I don't understand how any woman can balance and revolve on the top of a pole without injuring herself in some way.'

'It's easy enough if you 'ave a belt, for the top of the pole spins round on ball-bearings; but it's far more dangerous on 'er back. She couldn't manage it nohow. She couldn't get her 'ead back far enough, and there was no 'elping herself if she got dizzy. But it's easy enough if you 'ave a belt, kind of cup-shaped buckle. You has to be agile all right.'

'How did she break her nose?'

'If you arsks me, she broke it when she lept away from the pole. She landed on her feet orl roight, but she hit herself with 'er knee on the nose. The other two blokes fell 'eavier.'

'Where are the other acrobats?'

'In hospital still, but they have nothing to add to the evidence.'

'Gentlemen, you can view the corpse.'

''Oo wants to view 'im? I seen 'im take the count. I seen him all roight. I knows Jem Broughton's form. One over the oight 'e 'ad all roight.'

The Law was explained to the reluctant old pugilist.

While the corpse was being viewed, Friery said nonchalantly to the Serjeant, 'Tell Mrs Brotonne that I want to see her as soon as she gets out of Mercer's. And you might tell the boys that "Natural Causes" will do if they want to be in time for the first race at Leopardstown.'

Chapter X

BARNEY TAKES HONOURS

In the Bailey (first turn to your right) is a pleasant beer pump attached to the marble bar. Griffith was sitting at it one evening, facing the windows, sipping light ale and thinking of the Irish People. At least he was probably thinking of the Irish People, but I was thinking only of one of them, and I was beginning to feel a little uneasy. Soon it would be all right, for it was getting on towards eleven o'clock, and then the pubs would be shut, and this place would be shut and there would be no further fear of an intrusion. Hubert Murphy was telling him of a holiday he had spent in the Channel Islands where there was no Income Tax.

'There should be none here,' said Arthur with suppressed passion, striking the counter.

But, as Golly says, 'Call no man happy till he's rotten.' I could not feel secure until after eleven, for that afternoon Silly Barney had received the intelligence unofficially that he had passed in Biology with first-class honours. He had got three Reproductive Systems in succession – almost a Royal Flush. There was sure to be a celebration, with Weary and the Citizen helping him to rejoice. And celebration meant inebriation to most medicals, and that meant a deal of song. Now Silly was attracted by the unconverted and unmusical Arthur, who shrugged him off in no uncertain way whenever he tried to catch his ear or to butt in on him when he was thinking of the Irish People. Silly had thought about the Irish

People, but from a somewhat different angle from Arthur's; and the angles could never make a right-angle, for Silly's attitude appeared to Arthur to continue the tradition of the stage Irishman who, as everyone knows, never existed in real life but only in the imagination of enemies of the real Ireland. To treat the Irishman as a funny or contradictory character was to become an enemy of the Irish People. And I simply dreaded Barney's lyric, the lyric which caused Weary Mac to give him his nickname, fearing that he might sing it to Arthur in my presence.

It was all right so far. It was ten to. We were quite satisfied that there could not be a better name for the movement than SINN FEIN, which, meaning as it did not OURSELVES ALONE, which might exclude external aid and communications, but WE OURSELVES, would inculcate a sense of self-reliance and bring men's thoughts to dwell on Ireland and not to fly off to Westminster, where at best we were asking England to give us leave to give her a black eye. It would put an end to the demoralising effect which Westminster had on Irish Members who after a few years get themselves dug in with a host of other interests other than Ireland's, such as promoting Bills for private companies – witness Tim Healy – or they got themselves weakened by kowtowing to English prestige that made an Irishman so forgetful of his own heritage of culture as to be actually flattered if he came to be accepted as one of themselves. England was the only country that could make money and servile subjects out of selling snubs. That's what WE OURSELVES would stop. It sounded well. But another thing, which did not sound any too well, smote my outward ear. The swing door opened and a sober-suited figure topped by a glowing countenance took the stool beside me and broke into song :

'Arrah, Barney, Silly Barney!
The humour in the corner of your eye,
Wid your blarney, Silly Barney
Would kill the sparrows in the sky!
No aversion, rale diversion.
     Ho, Ho, Ha, Ha, Ho, Ho, He, He, Ho Ho!'

Arthur shrugged uneasily. I resolved under no circumstances to introduce my lyrical acquaintance. I was too embarrassed at the moment to consider him a friend. I sat in silence between Arthur and the Bard who knew the reproductive systems of all creation. If Weary would only come and remove him. But Weary's defection was to me an indication of the advanced state of Barney's exaltation. Weary had slipped home. Where was the Citizen? The Citizen had enough wits left to avoid being seen in such company by Arthur Griffith, who was intolerant of drunken men and suffered fools badly.

'Too-looral, and Too-looral, Too-looral, aye-eh!
We're happy and merry, contented and gay,
With pigs in our parlours and drakes that won't lay.
Too-looral, Too-looral, Too-looral, aye-eh!'

Awful! And the suggestion it implied that the natives were factors in their own low standard of living! Relief was not long in coming.

'Are ye the young men that passed up Grafton Street a while ago, singing? Are ye aware that ye fell through Switzer's window and it's broke?' a deep voice inquired in tones that contained the answer. Seeing Griffith, the Serjeant subdued his voice somewhat, which made Barney's chances of ever being on familiar terms with Arthur slenderer than ever.

'There's Regulations,' the Serjeant continued oracularly. 'And even if there was no Regulations, I'd still have to summon ye.' Which goes to show that a man can be an automaton of Justice or that sometimes in Ireland

Justice gets out of hand : *Ruat cœlum,* so to speak.

'Come across now to Harry Street.'

So the Bard of Love departed. As he went he sang, a little defiantly as I thought :

> 'Stone walls do not a prison make,
>   Nor iron bars . . .'

At the words 'iron bars' he began to laugh, doubtless thinking of Arthur averse at the bar.

' "Iron bars" ! – Ho, Ho, Ha, He,' he roared as he was borne away.

Silence.

'Hah, Helix!' was the last I heard of him, and that was meant for me.

It was eleven-thirty by the time I left Arthur at the Pillar. I must go back to see about Silly. I began to feel that it would not do to let a pal down even if he was a bit vindictive. That 'Hah, Helix!' was quite uncalled for. But he was in durance vile and he must be bailed out.

Streets look strange in the empty night. The flickering lamps seem to make them larger and emptier, as if to gain room for casting shadows in rivalry with one another. An old hoarse voice brayed suddenly from the middle of the bridge : 'Matches, boot-laces, matches.' The Whores' Bank !

I hurried along Westmoreland Street and up by Switzer's, and was relieved to see no window broken, and marvelled all the more at Barney, who was able to fall through a plate-glass window without breaking the glass.

In Harry Street Station only the Serjeant was on night duty. He recognised me, and this, coupled by the fact that he knew me for a companion of the law-abiding Mr Griffith, made things smooth. He threw his thumb over his shoulder in the direction of the cells. He whispered : 'You can hear him talking to himself. One word now and he'll start singing again.' He lifted the lid of the desk against which he was leaning. 'Here's the contents of his pockets. Did you ever? Where did he get the little green lobster? I can understand the two snails. But imagine going round with a tweezer and a knife; and the cork on the end of the corkscrew instead of the point of the knife! And look at all these notes.'

Amazed, I saw that with infinite labour Barney had copied out the greater part of Thomson's *Zoology*. Apparently it was his way of memorising. No examiner could say that *he* hadn't read the book. He could send out for his overcoat and prove it by his notes. But at the moment he had no overcoat. There was sevenpence in his waistcoat pocket, some cigarettes, no matches, and a latchkey attached to a ball of twine, and the morning's examination papers in Zoology.

My curiosity was great. I must see it.

'That's the cause of all his trouble,' I said as I pointed to it.

'Indeed now?' said the Serjeant.

It was headed:

FIRST EXAMINATION IN MEDICINE
Scheme A

(1) Remove the left valve and the left half of the mantle of the animal provided. Sketch and label all parts displayed.

(2) Remove the sternum and anterior abdominal wall of the animal provided. Sketch and label the various organs.

(3) Remove the appendages from one side of the animal provided. Sketch and arrange in order and label.

(4) Tease out the specimens of tissue provided; stain with hæmatoxylin; mount it in glycerine; identify it.

Well, I thought, if Barney could identify anything after he had 'teased' it and had stained himself and half his fingers with hæmatoxylin, he deserves to pass! But where were the three questions in succession about Reproductive Systems? Here they were. Page two.

What, I wondered, were the animals 'provided'? The Citizen had the luck of meeting a fishwoman with a perambulator bearing live prawns to the back of the laboratory. That, being interpreted, meant that for one thing at least there would be 'a freshwater crayfish', hard to obtain in quantities, to dissect: the 'little green lobster'.

Weary had spent the day preceding the examination making up to Joe Dunne of d'Olier Street so that he might be given the tip if rabbits were ordered for delivery in the morning to the University in Earlsfort Terrace. Barney had been making inquiries involving much dalliance in the various oyster bars. Question One looked like oysters. But where were the three questions in succession, 'the Royal Flush' he spoke of about the Reproductive Systems? Here was one:

(1) Give a description of the respiratory and reproductive system of Astacus.

Now that was a nasty one if a fellow had forgotten what Astacus was. That gives you an idea of the way examiners go on using a special language. Everybody knows – at least, that is to say, I do – that Astacus is a kind of freshwater lobster. It includes prawns. But why try to cod a fellow with prawns instead of freshwater crayfish? Simply because they couldn't catch enough crayfish, and an uncooked prawn which nobody ever sees uncooked looks much the same.

(2) Describe fully the renal and reproductive system of the Leech.

The Leech indeed! And we were all trying to become Leeches!

(3)   Give an account of the excretory and reproductive
      system of Balanoglossus.

I knew that one myself! I was a member for it when
I was in the Royal. I had it by heart; and one day I got
it all out before I was stopped by Blaney. Of course
there was a snag in it. The two systems are described
together. It begins with a negative. Let me see. Here
goes :

'No nephridia are known, but from the region of the
collar two ciliated funnels open to the exterior, and the
enigmatical proboscis gland is possibly excretory.

'The sexes are separate. A number of paired genital
organs lie dorsally in a series on each side of the body
cavity in and behind the region with gill slits.'

I always liked the sand eel for puzzling the professors
with its 'enigmatical proboscis'.

The purple-hearted fan of flame over the Serjeant's
desk whistled and blinked. I handed back the Zoology
paper.

'I suppose he was stuck?' the Serjeant inquired with
a hint of commiseration. 'The poor fellow!'

'No, indeed, Serjeant, but he passed with honour
marks. He knew all about every animal they gave him.
And he had to know about every animal in the world,
including things that were never in Noah's Ark.'

'Indeed now!' said the Serjeant, greatly impressed.

'Will the window cost him much?' I inquired.

'Window?'

'Switzer's window.'

'Oh, that! It was Brown Thomas's window he nearly
fell into. I took him in here to steady him a bit. I'll let
him out now that I know that he is only one of them
medicals. But if he'd only stop singing and codding me
about my feet!'

That was reassuring. For we were in no position to

101

pay for a plate-glass window. But compliance with the Serjeant's conditions on the part of the prisoner was not so reassuring.

'Leave him to me.'

'Well, since the place is empty to-night, try your hand with him.'

As I approached the cell my footsteps were unheard, for the recitation did not die down. He was orating in righteous tones. I stopped. The voice rose in oracular crescendo.

'And now the Reproductive System of Palinurus?' He put the question to himself, which he had evidently been asked, and was rehearsing his triumph.

'Ho, ho, sir! my crustacean friend Palinurus, the rock lobster. Reproductive System? Certainly.' Then, with an unnecessary assumption of righteous lover's wrath, he took the loving lobster's part and quoted from Thomson, adding fermata to fermata unnecessarily.

'The male seizes the female in his great claws, throws her on her back and deposits . . .' I could see him gesticulating like a wrestler as he acted the part. He must be daft.

I tapped the door of the cell. He listened. Then : 'Ho, ho, another gastropod, with his Reproductive System in the upper part of his foot! They propagate their species by giving each other the boot. That's why – Ho, ho!'

'Barney,' I said, 'shut up!'

'Hah, Helix!' he called, recognising my voice. 'Shut up, locked up, blocked up, mocked up. Why should I shut up? I am shut up!'

'In order to get out and to go home.'

'I have given my landlady notice this morning. And I'm getting free lodging for the night. Where's Arthur?'

'Now listen. You'll be fined if you stay here until morning, for falling through Switzer's window. If you shut up now the Serjeant will let you out. Why spoil the whole thing and lose the bonus from home for passing so well?'

'Bonus from home?'

His mind became sufficiently unpreoccupied to remember the three-pounds per pass he was promised and to see a way out of Jimmy's for his umbrella and topcoat.

'Get me out,' he said.

'Hold on till I get a cab.'

The Serjeant got us a cab, and between us we put Barney in with all his belongings, except the dissecting knife, which I presented to the Serjeant in case he had corns. As it was not mine, the ill-luck would not be on me. With great providence I pulled up the window on the side next to the station for fear that some last remark from my friend might undo the good work and land him back again.

'You have been more than decent, Serjeant, to help a poor medical who has been through so much and has passed such a hard examination. He has been studying very hard and he is a bit upset. Goodnight, and thanks.'

'Goodnight, fell Serjeant!' Barney shouted; but I had the window shut. As I opened the door to get into the cab, I heard the Serjeant exclaim to himself: 'There's nothing beatin' the mind of man barrin' the bees!'

On the way to Hardwicke Street he explained that his housing troubles were due to his landlady not being lady enough to keep a dog. He had always stayed the longest in those digs where the landlady kept a dog, for the dog kept his breakfasts from mouldering on the top of the wardrobe; but in this case she discovered by scent many mornings' ham and eggs.

'You nearly got yourself a week for referring to the Serjeant's feet. Don't you know that policemen are rather sensitive about their feet?'

But I was only bringing the whole business on myself over again.

'In Phylum mollusca there is no head. They are distinguished by the absence of a head. Distinguished, mark you!' and he roared with laughter. 'The reproductive organs lie in the upper part of the foot adjacent to the digestive gland.'

'We've had all that.'

'When mature, the male is easily known by a strange modification on his fifth left arm – Serjeant's stripes – and he wouldn't believe it till I offered to show it to him in my notes. He thought it was a note on the development of a policeman. Until I explained' – he began to quote – ' "As food and as bait many Gastropods are very useful; their shells have supplied tools, utensils and objects of delight . . ." "Objects of delight," ' Barney repeated, musing. 'The juices of Purpura and Murex furnished the Tyrian purple, more charming than all aniline.'

> ' "But he who fished the Murex up;
>   What porridge had John Keats?" '

I asked; for I had been thinking of the Murex when I was trying to get Gamage's to make me a racing vest that would be white, crossed diagonally by two stripes of the real purple, the Roman toga stuff, which must have been a kind of cross between cherry red and bright purple. I got it at last and was keeping it to spring across the Ulster cracks at Ballinafeigh.

'Don't talk to me of porridge,' Barney said, thinking of the morning. 'What about coming down to the Hay Hotel, or calling in on the Midwifery lads – Weary will be on night duty?'

'I have hardly enough to pay for the cab.'

Resigned, he pushed in the half-open door and called out 'Light Ho!' as he struck a match.

Presently a light appeared. His landlady was standing at the top of the ladder-like stairs, grasping her nightgown and a candle that flickered with indignation.

'Such are the advantages of electricity,' he remarked. 'And now the animal provided must clamber up to bed.'

Chapter XI

GOOD LUCK UP NORTH

'Perkins, I'm in agony. Get me something!'

Perkins, with his red waistcoat and brass buttons, was a porter in the Ballast Office, and he knew, when Mr Pease called for something, what was meant.

Mr Pease was the father of the renowned Charlie, who was the greatest cyclist of his time in Europe among amateurs.

While Perkins was on his way to the window-shutter which covered a small wine cellar, Mr Pease turned his large red face and curly white head to me and remarked, 'I hate eavesdroppers!'

I was puzzled a bit, for we had been saying nothing at the time.

Perkins, with a pleasant smile, returned instantly with a decanter and a syphon on a tray. There were two glasses.

'Nothing for me,' I implored.

Mr Pease drained his drink with the remark, 'Good luck up North.'

A burly man in his day the father of Charlie must have been, with sound heart and lungs. In shape, Charlie had taken after his mother, but no matter how good a figure one's mother was, if you have a crock for a father you can be no good: that is, as an athlete. And 'Old Pease', a scion of the great Yorkshire family, was a stout man in his day. He was a stout man now, but in another sense. He took a great interest in his son's victories, which he followed more or less accurately all over the kingdom, for Charlie was champion of England as well as of Ireland. And it is a much harder thing to be champion of Ireland, seeing that Ireland is a nest of cycling champions since the days that Harry Reynolds beat the world at Copenhagen.

'Good luck up North!' He knew I was on my way. 'We have time to go over to the Red Bank for a little lunch, and then we will call a cab.'

Perkins, with the dexterity of a keeper, handed him his 'gun' and hat. He called his malacca cane with the ivory top his gun, because it was made hollow like a barrel, and when you unscrewed the ivory knob a long test-tube-like arrangement that could hold about a noggin of brandy was uncorked. Sometimes excitement made its owner weak, and sometimes he got weak through the boredom of waiting in out-of-the-way stations for Charlie; and he always got weak on a Sunday morning, because his habit of going into town to get something in his office was interrupted. You can't interrupt the routine of a man's life without making him weak. So he kept weakness at bay with his 'gun'. One day, when he was cheering one of Charlie's spectacular victories, he inadvertently banged his 'gun' too hard on the floor of the Grand Stand. It took weeks to get the barrel rebored. 'And only for you boys calling on me every Sunday morning, I would have died. My wife could not keep the tantalus locked when you blew in – not with propriety.' And he snorted indignantly through his wide mahogany nose.

As I was one of those who had frequently saved his life I stood well with him. Besides, did I not race with his son? And now that his son was not going up North I made bold to go. There was no chance of a pot where Charlie was riding. And very decently he left Ballinafeigh to me.

The fact that Charlie indulged in such an unaristocratic game as cycling saved me. He looked so like an infantry officer, with his little sleek head and little moustache, and he dressed and behaved so mannerly and won such lovely cups on his shining bicycle that he was an exemplar and an excuse. Of course, there was Larry Oswald and Emerson E., but they were more or less enclosed in College, and did not display themselves all over the country, even in fields at country meetings which were little better than assemblies such as one might see at coursing matches with Jack Lalor the barber, and they had not to earn a livelihood later on.

For the rest, were they not all tradesmen? Could I point to one, with the exceptions mentioned, who was not engaged in some trade or other, and did I expect my aunt or my mother to recognise the plumber? It sounds like snobbery; and why shouldn't it? It was. But when a fellow has an aunt who knows all about the Royal Family and half the Almanach de Gotha by heart, and when we have turkey, goose or gurnard for dinner, calls the stuffing 'the concealment', what is a fellow to do?

That is where Charlie came in. He could come into our house 'all right', as old Tommy Monks, the trainer, would say. Charlie was trained for a room as well as for the arena, and he knew colonel's daughters and nice people like that. So was it any wonder that I was fond of Charlie? Besides, there was another reason. He was not greedy. He was not a pot-hunter by any means. When a fellow wanted to bring something really useful home, that would appease the family, like a cut-glass claret jug, or a set of fish-eaters, or a case of little coffee cups in silver open-work, he would stand down at the last moment; and that was all right for me, because opposition had already been frightened off or had to go to work. For instance, when he should have been racing at

Waterford, all he did was to mark my card with myself. And that is how I got a few firsts and £4 3s. od. from Jimmy for the fitted suitcase. I gave the lobster knives and the barometer to my aunt against her birthday, which otherwise was never mentioned.

It might have seemed slightly cynical to the sportsmen in Belfast if they could see us marking the programme for their cycle meeting. You would think that we were the only competitors and that we had arranged the wins before the pistol went. But be that as it may, they would have had cause for complaint, for disliking us, for no one likes a fellow or fellows who are always cocksure. Anyway, I wasn't cocksure, for I knew the sportsmen in the North, and I was still lumpy where I had got kicked by a sporting spectator as I was backing over the sideline to take a corner against Cliftonville last winter. How could anyone be sure? The North had done its own handicapping, and I saw myself with a crowd hanging on to my back wheel with a lap or two to spare on me, for the race was ten miles. I was not at all sure, even though those links simply had to come out of Cuffe Street, or my mater would go to the police and it would not be so easy getting Barney out then. Not that I would let him in for it, but you never know the procedure of the Law and what 'procedure' might mean. It might very well mean that Barney was to precede me to gaol.

When we crossed Westmoreland Street and rounded the corner, the Red Bank hove in sight.

'I always like this restaurant,' Old Pease remarked. 'The waiters are so respectful, and they seem to know what I want. I invariably lunch there if I am not away.' Like the simple Englishman that he was, it was only necessary to give him the least excuse and he would be pleased. He had the gift of relishing life. A gift long lost to us.

The waiters certainly gave us a welcome. They informed him with word and smiles that he was expected. Was he not a little late? He did not know if he was, till he remembered : 'Of course ! It was due to Perkins. But let us proceed. Some lobsters and the usual . . .'

'It does one good to come here. Now you see – "Yorkshire relish". They know that I'm from Yorkshire, and they put that out as a little compliment to me. Could anyone be more considerate or more thoughtful?'

If I don't get in my word now, I thought, it will be too late to change the devilled lobster which he has apparently ordered for me to a little beefsteak. Charlie always eats a little beefsteak slightly underdone.

'May I have a lunch such as Charlie takes?'

'Oh, dear me, of course. But what kind of a lunch does Charlie take? He tells me that everything agrees with him, as it certainly does with me. For the life of me I cannot see why men should quarrel with good whiskey and a devilled lobster.'

I could, if they had to ride ten miles on a strange track with the whole place hoping that you would break your neck and that the native favourite would win; and possibly they had to win a heat or get placed merely, if they had to spare themselves, for there would be heats if there were too many entrants for the track to hold, and there were sure to be, for the handicapping was in the hands of the judges, and if they were anything like the gentry in Jones's Road the limit men would have a mile. Devilled lobster and a large whiskey would be the last thing to give you your second wind.

'No sweet?'

'No, thanks.'

'I never take one either,' Mr Pease remarked, as he took his hat and gun. It would have been perfectly obvious that a sweet was out of the question for Mr Pease, to anyone who knew the theories of the Professor of

Physiology about what happens to sugar in the liver. I didn't take sugar, though it is supposed to turn into energy, for I wanted to keep round about eleven stone.

When we reached Amiens Street station I gazed anxiously into the train. No. The Workmen's Club was not represented, neither was the National Club, which made things so difficult for me by playing handball on Sundays at the rear of 11, Rutland Square, which was within sight and hearing of our house. I was thinking that Cocky Meade, whose stepfather was Professor Reynolds's laboratory porter, might have had a day off. Not that it really mattered, for Cocky Meade was a long-distance man, the fifty-miles champion, and he usually rode behind pace, but he could have made the going very fast. Emerson E. was absent. He was probably testing breaking-points with Alexander in the Engineering School. Needless to say, with McNought on the watch, no medicals raced except myself. My bicycle was safe in the guard's van. There was no name on its label. With Mr Pease I went along the train. He would not notice after lunch that I was travelling third class. I would not have been travelling at all had it not been for the fact that Barney lent me two-thirds of his bonus until I won. *Haud facile emergunt*, etc. But there was no use in springing that or even Dr Johnson's translation – 'This mournful truth is everywhere expressed, Slow rises worth by poverty oppressed' – on Mr Pease. I would keep it in reserve for Professor Tyrrell, on whom it would do all right. Mr Pease took no notice of anything until he came to the engine. He gazed in silence at the many gauges, clocks and things in the engine-driver's cab which were shimmering, seen through the heated air.

'Good old Charlie!' he remarked; and then, as an afterthought: 'They call me "Old Pease", if you please!'

He had taken the engine's instruments for prizes won by his son.

It's a very pleasant journey to Belfast, even though you have to travel third class. You can look out of the window at the many inlets that come under the train into the fields from the sea, and at the little rushy rivers that run out into long bays. Then the bridge at Drogheda gives you a view up the Boyne, which is one of the oldest rivers – that is, from an historical point of view – in Ireland. You could hear all about it at the Stad if they were in a legendary mood. There was a lot of farming going on, but whether it was Sir Horace's idea or not I couldn't say. My mind was not on the subject of farming, though, of course, I knew all about the chemistry of soil, silica, and beneficial microbes coming out of manure and all that sort of thing. If it was Sir Henry Robinson's idea it must have been all right, for my aunt knew Sir Henry Robinson, and he was a great friend of the Chief Secretary, whoever he might be.

I looked in my bag. If I had forgotten my red shoes with blocks made by Elley in Camden Street, with blocks to fit the pedals, I was dished. They were there all right. I felt the five-shilling piece I had sewn into the bottom of my jersey in front, at the edge. In case of a protest five shillings must be lodged. That is about the best place to carry holy medals as mascots if your aunt sews them in surreptitiously. If you fall they cannot go into you, whereas if they are sewn into the edge at the back they have to be dug out. That happened to me twice : oval medals are the worst.

There was a great crowd at Ballinafeigh. It is different up North. There is far more betting for one thing – you might think it was a Derby meeting; and for another, they take the whole thing very seriously as if it was a business affair, and the seriousness increases in direct ratio with the value of the prizes. And then there are sure to be people hanging about the dressing-tent who think more of winning a few shillings than of seeing a good race. These gougers would think nothing of letting some of the air out of your tyres just before a race. But there were good sportsmen too in the North: Geordie Robinson was the best of the bunch. He it was who was decent enough to put me on my guard. Then there was the actual race itself, on a track that slanted downwards, and was three laps to the mile and right hand in, which is unusual. Besides, it was edged with a cement kerb, and if your inside pedal touched that it was all up with you literally and no mistake, for the crowd behind you couldn't help riding over you, and you were sure to get a few rat-trap pedals across your head, no matter how low you pressed it down when you had stopped sliding along on the palms of your hands, elbows and knees. I had been skinned once or twice in my time, and had to spend the nights with my knees in band-boxes to keep the clothes off, and wear gloves to hide my hands, and stay away from meals. That's the reason I have white shiny knee-caps now, for Ballsbridge has nice clean sand. My blue elbows came from the cinders at Jones's Road. It's very easy to fall, for you cannot tell what the fellow in front of you is going to do. If you hang on to him and he is out for the lap prize you may catch your men all the quicker, but if he feels you behind he may pull up suddenly after a sprint when he thinks he has done his lap, and then one touch of your front wheel against his back wheel and you'd think you were going down a chute. Then there were rough fellows of the baser sort who were not beyond giving you a little unseen tip of the elbow on the end of your handle-bar, which was calculated to send you shooting over the banking into the crowd. This could only be done by a better man, who could catch up on you on the inside if you got too excited at the bell and went a bit wide at the corners from centrifugal force. And what made this so rotten was that the judges couldn't see it. They nearly always blamed you for swerving wide, and then trying to bore in on a man who was able to corner better and who couldn't be expected to follow you out to the edge of the track.

I stayed in the queerest hotel I was ever in. There were all sorts of unsporting quotations on the wall. One was :

> *'Be sure your sin will find you out.'*

And there was a Bible beside every bed, and the wall did not run quite up to the ceiling, and you could hear loud snores in the middle of the afternoon. These came from special constables who had been on duty all night. I didn't like to leave my bag there, but I took it along with me to the track. I had my racing things on under my clothes. And I kept them on when I rode round to have a look at the track. It was far too dangerous, slanting sideways as it was and hardly any banking to speak of; five feet perhaps, just up to the spectators' chins at the downhill corner. When I saw the little pyramids of black basalt instead of Poa pratensis, with which the course was paved, I was glad that Charlie had given me a pair of his old tyres, which were quite new – that is, newer than anything I could get.

I wouldn't dream of competing in the mile. But I had to compete in something to limber up; besides it would never do to compete only in one race, and, if I won it, to clear out. So I had a shot at the five miles, just to see how the wheels held on the corners and how fast a fellow might dive for the last corner without going into the ladies' hats. If I am fastest loser in a heat of the five will I be put into the final? That wouldn't do me much good, unless I won the five, and if I brought any more third prize salad bowls to Jimmy it would be just about the last straw, for Jimmy with his strong calves was always winning salad bowls himself. I'll let them all go ahead and then do some pioneering work trying to catch them. That is how to get an idea of the track. Then I can get a cup of tea, and hang about with my bag on the back of the bicycle until the ten miles comes on.

It seems that the people were sorry that I was beaten in my heat. But I put that down to the good effect a jersey made to order had on the crowd who knew all the cheap reds, whites and blacks of the ordinary competitors.

I picked up my bag, which I had left near the policeman who was on duty near the table which held all the prizes, and pulled on my flannels and coat.

It was almost impossible to get a cup of tea. If you hadn't the correct Northern accent the barmaid couldn't understand you. Besides, I was too near the door of the marquee to attract attention. They thought, perhaps, that I was waiting for someone to finish his meal. At last I got a cup which wasn't too bad; I could feel the blood getting into my legs, which were none too warm.

It's a bad thing not to have a friend to push you off. It would be worse if the race was half a mile, but it didn't matter much in ten. What did matter was the kind of row that broke out amongst the stewards. One of them ran up to me with a programme in his hand, and asked rather angrily:

'Are you Pease?'

'I wish I were,' I said.

'Well, you've bloody well got tae be Pease, for the crood want a scratch man and they're bloody well goin' tae hev it, or they'll tear the place doon.' He gesticulated wildly. Evidently he was more connected with the charity for which the meeting was held than with cycle-racing.

'But how can you blame me for not being Pease?'

'Ay! Jest a minit. Hold on jest a wee.' He waved his arm, and two men with tall hats and flying tails ran over to him. They had a long talk which, by the signs they made, presumably was critical. At last a decent-looking fellow came over and apologised and then asked me the same question. I shook my head.

'That is rather unfortunate. You see, the great attraction of the afternoon to the crowd was the opportunity of seeing the winner of the blue riband of Great Britain on the track. You are a short mark man, but you must understand – no offence – it is not quite the same.'

'But what has all this got to do with me?'

'It's got this to do with you. As we have no scratch man, ye'll have to go back to scratch.'

As if it were not bad enough to put me back to twenty-five yards from the champion of Ireland and England: he that could give me half a mile and lap me in ten!

'I'll go back to scratch, provided you bring back the field proportionately and put the man with the handicap of a lap on me at twenty-five yards behind me.'

'But they'll protest, and they'll have every right to, for the handicapper has given them a lap.'

'What about me? He has given me twenty-five yards, and I have a right to it if you don't put them back when you are putting me back.'

'But they'll lose twenty-five yards.'

'So will I. But I don't want them hanging on to my back wheel and perhaps bringing me down at the corners.'

The crowd began to indulge in cat-calls and loud whistles began to sound. Those must be the Orangemen, I thought; and I began to wish that I had come in my College black with its gold shield displaying the arms of T.C.D.

'You had better do as yer told: there's a heap of money on this race.' I knew that was probably right, for when Windy Way won the hundred-yards sprint (he had to win, even though it would shorten his odds for the Powderhall Handicap, for his pal Purdy Clegg was making a book) there was a most unholy uproar. And there was another uproar now at the delay. I tried to delay as long as I could. In the hurry the limit men would not realise that they were losing twenty-five yards.

'I'm virtual scratch, anyway. Is not that enough?'

But I had to go back to the starting-line 'for the sake of the time-keeping'. And there the fellow with the programme pushed me off.

Bad as the start was, I widened the gap a bit on the limit men, and when I caught up on the next group in the third lap they seemed to take fright, for they tried to join up with the men with a quarter of a mile start. This they did not do for three or four laps. But there was a group spread out half-way round the track. It would be all right to leave them there on the chance that I would be wafted along and catch them with the field. But with them, evidently, was one of those fellows who don't mind running themselves to death for the sake of a lap prize – a pair of carvers or an ink-bottle. Anyway, we were making no progress, and if I couldn't get our group to move, I would have to go after the leaders myself. If I saw the least chance of the field uniting before the bell I wouldn't have been so anxious, but there couldn't be more than three miles to go. Yes, a steward with a tall hat yelled, 'Three miles to go' – and we might never catch up. One of those stupid mass wants of movement might happen to a field, especially a field such as this, which was disgracefully over-crowded. There must be at least forty competitors on a twelve-foot track. I tried to pass, suggesting that the limit men were catching up. But they wouldn't let me out. I was only feinting at any rate, but I got alarmed now, realising that I was trapped more or less, and that I couldn't get out at will no matter how fast I could go. And, what made it worse, some of the riders were breaking up and slowing the whole show.

'We'll be lapped if we don't move on!' I remarked. But no one moved on. Suddenly it dawned on me that they hadn't got the pace, and the fellow out for the lap prize had only to ride about half the distance fast in order to be sure of a pot. That was a new handicap on me. It would have been all right, of course, if we had him in our group setting the pace for us, but we had not, and we, if anything, as a crowd were losing pace. I had so much in hand that I grew anxious, because I knew that you cannot win a race hands down without taking something out of yourself.

Suddenly, as I was determined to get out and leave them all behind until I caught the leaders whom, over my right shoulder, I could see circling, a strange thing happened. Two fellows gave up. That seemed to have the opposite effect on the rest, for they all made off panic-stricken like one man, shouting encouragement to each other. What was the idea? Perhaps they were nursing one of those crocks to win, and now he had cracked up and it was anybody's race; perhaps they thought that now was the time to drop me, for we were going so easily that anyone could have speeded matters up. Whatever was the reason, I found myself going as hard as I liked behind a bunch of about twenty that went as if they all were out for the lap prize. It may have been that that moved them when they saw no other chance of winning a pot. Some of them were sighing, and some of them looked as if they were dead. Anyway, I lay as far behind as was advisable, for this was the kind of rush that leads to a crash when some fellow collapses in the middle of a group and brings the whole show down and over him.

I was watching the kerb of cement with half an eye, and waiting to see when some of my obstructionists would touch. Suddenly, as we passed, the johnny in the tall hat yelled, 'One mile to go!'

God! Only three laps, and we were still fifty yards from the dozen or so in front.

My group spurted again. I hadn't a hope in heaven of getting past. What I must do now, I said to myself, is first to take it coldly; second, to wait till the bell and depend on the inclination downhill of the track. There will be just the faintest chance that, in their excitement, when they hear the bell the whole thirty or forty will go wide, for it takes a cool customer to go all out and yet to survive the bend. I may get through on the inside. I wasn't sorry now that it was three laps to the mile. But I was getting a bit too nervous waiting for the bell. A sudden slowing for an instant told me that we had caught the field. I couldn't see ahead; they must have been five ranks deep. But – what a rush, and the bell ringing and I last of all the field! Only the turn can save me now, I realised, and I grew calm with suppressed fear, for it was a matter for skill – nerves could keep till afterwards.

Three came down in a little group with a grinding noise – one of them gave the kind of grunt that a fellow knocked unconscious gives – but they were too far back to help me. That bell still ringing! Now we go downhill. If I don't hit that cursed cement border! Surely at this pace no one can corner, so there will have to be room to get through on the inside, and then my effort, hardly daring to put pressure on the right pedal as I hug the corner at well over twenty-five miles an hour. It was frozen work watching for the exact moment. It leaped to meet me. They all went wide. I knew it, but that can keep. With my head down very gingerly waiting for the least give from the back tyre, I slithered round the bend. Not one of them had recovered yet. I was just round it. Holy heaven, let me into the straight! But the tall fellow farthest on the outside was the first to recover; I was leading but for him and, perhaps, one of two or three on my left. The tall fellow closed in. He had the advantage of half a length. What would happen to me? I don't believe he saw me between himself and the cement edge. He was lying in over me. He intended to run me against the kerb. I spread my elbows in self-defence. As I was about to be killed, his handlebar hit my elbow, and he changed his mind as suddenly as his direction. He went like a human projectile into a sea of heads, for he left the track where the side was banked up to the spectators' chins. I heard a roar that nearly distracted me, for I was open to the least stimulus; but I am clear at last and alone in the straight, and good-bye to the mounting pyramid of flesh and steel far behind. I am in such a transport with motion that I cannot feel the machine. I am dawdling home at 35 m.p.h.

The roar did not stop, but I did. I didn't care how suddenly the strain crowded in on my heart from the sudden muscular relaxation. It would have been lunacy to circle round that track far away from the Royal Irish Constabulary and help. Someone was meant to win and it wasn't supposed to be me. I hadn't forgotten the supporters of Cliftonville and the kick that hamstrung me last Christmas. I didn't want a naggin thrown at me, or a stick stuck between the spokes. They were carrying in the fellow who had touched me on the elbow with his handle-bar. Judging by the sympathy of the crowd, he should have won. He had a handicap of about a third of a mile, and he was a fellow that, once he got on your back wheel, could never be shaken off. It was well for me that, in putting me back, they put him back too away from me.

Some of those who were gesticulating turned out to be asking friends in the crowd if they had five shillings. For, as I have said, you had to lodge five shillings before your protest could be heard. I had five shillings sewn in my jersey. That saved the time it took to go to the tents, so I turned back and handed it in, and told the committee in Lady Jaffe's hearing (and it was she who had presented a prize of 'a magnificent gold watch' to the committee) how I was hemmed in and nearly killed; and how surprised I was to find that a Trinity man could be so scurvily treated in Ulster, and how I had to get back for an examination in Anatomy at once.

The committee were not as sympathetic as one would have expected, but Lady Jaffe was, because she was a lady like my aunt and could sympathise with a young medical student who was up against such rough people as were competing at the meeting, even if she disapproved of his low taste in sport. She was sure that the committee would not mind if she herself presented me with the watch. They hardly could, seeing that she was the donor. And if I hurried, I might get the six-twenty.

Somebody plucked my elbow. A spare old man with a wizened face, dead but for its intelligent bright eyes, whispered loudly: 'Jest you roide 'ome if yer wants to keep in form all roight, and the start's now.' He winked and jerked his thumb. 'There wuz too many people to the acre on the last lap.'

I got the watch, but I did not get that train. For one thing, it stopped at Portadown, which might contain a few fellows of the baser sort who seemed disappointed with the day's sport, particularly at the pile-up that marred the finish of the ten miles. After I had slipped into my bags and coat and was in mufti, so to speak, I heard a small-sized but sturdy little fellow remark, 'He's got away with the watch, but he has yet to get past Portadown.' Now Portadown is regarded unfavourably by some, who would let their prejudice take them so far as to appeal to others to withhold at its station certain hygienic amenities recommended by the railway company. This prejudice has even found vent in writing – anonymous, I must confess. Somebody had scrawled under the official notice in the carriage, *'You are requested not to use the lavatory when the train is standing at a station,'* the words 'except at Portadown'.

On the whole, as the stop might be a long one, I had the watch, and was anxious not to put temptation in some poor fellow's way who might be the worse for drink and disappointment, I decided to cycle round Portadown and, if necessary, back to Dublin. After all, it was only a hundred miles and I would arrive comfortably in eight hours. That would bring me home about four in the morning, and I had often been up later than that. I could breakfast in The Hay. There would be plenty of time, for the examination was not till the afternoon.

And to think that Tommy Stoddard offered me only £9 for a bicycle like this!

McNought Proves Worthy of his Name

A nice gang of friends I have, anyway! Friends only in that there is something not altogether unpleasing to them in my misfortunes, as La Rochefoucauld, one of the French philosophers, remarks.

Don't think that I don't know all they were saying after my last round with McNought. I got most of it from Golly early this morning; some of it from the Citizen, who was too embarrassed at meeting me to be coherent – not that he is anything but a bunch of ejaculations when he's not embarrassed; some from Mac, who told me what Barney said; and the rest from Barney's commiserating account of Mac's lack of sympathy with me in my last shot at the Half. Not one of them realised that I had ridden in two races, heats and all, that I only narrowly escaped death, and that I had ridden a hundred miles through the night and had to put up with the awful coffee for breakfast in The Hay.

I pieced the whole thing together. As I see it, it was something like this: the Seventh proposition of Euclid — it couldn't have been any other way, for it's all on the same base.

In comes the Citizen, and as usual makes a sudden announcement *à propos* of nothing.

'Giddy's out!' he shouts.

The boys turn slowly. It's probably Weary's round. So he says nothing.

'How out?' Golly says.

'Out of what?' Barney asks.

'He must mean out of the Half,' Weary says, who was hoping for it.

'Stuck, staggered and shot out by McNought this morning,' said the Citizen.

'That would be the May Half,' Barney said. 'You don't mean to say that he is stuck so soon again in Anatomy?'

'Dished,' said John. 'And no wonder.'

Weary suppressed his pleasure with a smile.

'That will be about the tenth time,' he commented.

'Mebbe he's taking the Long Course,' Mr Golly suggested, who after all is a decent man.

'Why do you say "no wonder"?' Barney inquires.

'Do you know what he told McNought when Mac said "You don't seem to have applied yourself to your subject, Mr Ouseley"?'

'What?'

' "No, Sir," says Giddy. "I thought the exam was this afternoon!" '

'Jayshus! And it's a three-years' course!'

It will be some time before I'll drink with that bunch again. I like old Golly, and I don't want to be kept out;

but a fellow can always choose his time if he wants to avoid company.

But when I think of Barney getting honours simply because he met an old fishwife with a perambulator full of prawns, from which he guessed that he would get a crayfish to dissect on the afternoon of his exam, and of Mac, who is lectures ahead of his exams, it makes me sick. If they said it before one's face I would have been the first to laugh at it, because everyone knows that the result of the race came out before the exam in this morning's papers, and McNought saw it and put the exam on to 9 a.m., before I could get my second wind, so to speak.

But, after all, I have the watch.

The best way to punish them is to leave Mac and the Citizen out when Barney, who is not too bad, has seen Jimmy about the watch.

Nice bloody friends!

Chapter XII

A HOLD UP

If you could believe Weary, the Citizen was in the hell
of a stew. There seemed to be something in the story,
judging by the evident sly satisfaction the telling gave
to Weary. It appears that the Citizen, shortly after his
return from South America, from Buenos Aires, walked
into the dissecting-room with a brace of guns and held
up the whole room, including the Professor of Anatomy,
Dr Bermingham. He was a very good Professor of Anatomy, the Citizen acknowledged that: 'But why the
hell was he there?' Who the hell would have thought
that he would be in the dissecting-room, where
McLoughlin, the demonstrator of Anatomy, and not the
Professor, should have been? Mac would take the hold-
up as a joke. The Citizen was only trying the effect as a
disguise of his moustachios, as he called them, when
explaining the reason for the hold-up. He wanted to
give them a chance before shaving them off. 'Señor, be
gob,' shouted the Citizen, exalted by his dream of himself.

Weary knew something about the Law from hearing
his friends talking about it. Barney smiled superciliously.
He knew more. Had Weary ever spent half a night in a
cell? Well, he had, not once or twice in our rough
island's story. It would be all right for the Citizen if he
had passed his exams before going suddenly to Buenos
Aires with no excuse at all, in the middle of the term.
Besides, the Citizen was suspected of being a bit of a

boon companion of three or four students who had not the reputation of the school at heart. Idle fellows, drinking and gossiping even with the porter from the Pathological Museum. If you asked him, it would go hard with the Citizen, especially as one of the bunch had done a most disloyal and inexcusable thing – deserted to another Medical School, that of Trinity College. And the School in Cecilia Street only just struggling for recognition! And now this fellow glaring like a madman down two revolver barrels. So Barney summed up. According to Weary, the Citizen was dressed like an escaped cowboy from Hengler's, that's where he must have got the sheepskin trousers. But for a while he did actually impose on the Professor, chiefly because his scanning speech suggested G.P.I. Bermingham had to take steps to teach him and his friends a lesson, and teach them a sharp lesson if the reputation of the School was not to suffer from ridicule.

'I have no more to say to you. You had better get legal advice.'

'So that was what he said?' I remarked to Weary, when he had finished the eventful history of the Citizen's morning in the Medical School. 'They have summoned the Citizen?'

'Using firearms with intent to endanger life.'

'In a dissecting-room?'

'That's what the Citizen says. He says he only went in there to hold up the corpses. He never dreamt that Bermingham would be there as well.'

'But that won't account for the two revolvers.'

'He says they are curios he got on an estancia, his uncle's ranch in the Argentine. They are all decorated with silver.' Mac lingered on the word 'silver' and said that he couldn't feel sorry. He thought that the Citizen deserved his fate if, instead of lending the pistols to Barney to sledge for us, he employed them in the senseless foolery of trying the effect of his fierce moustachios on the boys who were dissecting. And now they were confiscated by the police.

'So now,' said Weary with mischievous relish, 'he has to get legal advice.'

'You might as well try to employ a boa constrictor as a tape-measure as to go to a lawyer for legal advice. If it is to be any use, you must go to a good lawyer, and he has to be a crook to learn the tricks of the trade. And in order that there may be trade, he has to plunge you deeper and deeper into the law and his maw.'

'What is the Citizen to do?'

'We had better ask Golly who is the best lawyer for John.'

'What about the fellow who is so kind to your Mother?'

'Oh, Beddy? But he is a high-class kind of bloke. Besides, he isn't qualified.'

'I don't see what's wrong with that,' Weary commented meditatively.

'Only that he can no more appear before a judge than we can practise.'

We consulted Golly, that man of the world. When he heard the story his eyes filled with suspicion and began to oscillate like the needle of a manometer. 'And I've only just come from trying to bail out Toucher Duff. I can't bail out the Citizen, if that's what you mean.'

On being assured that the Citizen was not 'in' yet, and that we would not trespass on his prerogative as a householder to bail a man out, Mr Golly brightened and gave a dramatic description of what happened to Duff. It appeared that that citizen was charged for being drunk and disorderly. He had resisted arrest so successfully that four policemen were injured and he himself was in a bad way.

'What is the charge?' the beak inquired; but before

the Serjeant could read it the Toucher volunteered, 'Sober, your Worship, and refusing to fight.' It was no use. He's put back for a week. But it's a solicitor you're after? Well, I always say 'Set a thief to catch a thief,' and the worst rogue for wriggling and twisting is old Friery. It was he got the Toucher's sister off when she sold margarine for butter. He's the boy that will explain to the judge that you can't shoot a dead man. And isn't that the charge against the Citizen?

'Will there be any need to explain to the judge that you cannot shoot a dead man?' I inquired, innocent of legal procedure.

'Ah, God help you. Need, is it? Why, it will have to be proved beyond Yea or Nay.'

'You would think that it was pretty obvious.'

'Obvious, is it? Why, it's the obvious that has to be be proved. Where would the Law be if anything was obvious? Nothing is there at all until it's proved. Why, I myself had to prove my identity if you please. Me that's – ' Words failed Mr Golly at the thought of his want of existence in the eyes of the Law. 'And the queer thing about it all was that the fellow I was supposed to be "known to", the fellow who identified me, I didn't know from Adam's race. I never served him with a drink and nobody identified him. As the saying is, "the Law's an ass", and the licensing laws – '

'Wait awhile,' Weary interjected, waving a stained forefinger. 'Wait awhile. There's a distinct difference between shooting and killing. I hold that you can shoot a dead man but that you can't kill him.'

'But nobody killed him,' said Mr Golly.

'Wait awhile. It doesn't matter who or what killed him. You can shoot him after someone else killed him, can't you? Or after he died?'

'I suppose you can,' said Mr Golly. 'But who'd hit a man when he's down?'

'That's not the point,' Weary insisted. 'The point is that the Citizen will be charged with shooting – '

'It must be with intent.'

'But he did not shoot at all,' I objected.

'He had the intention,' Weary persisted.

'That's what I sez,' Golly argued. 'There must be intent. You took the words – '

How long the confusion would have continued I cannot say; but Michael the curate, returning a roller towel to its roller, clicked it back sharply behind Golly. Fat men as a rule have good nerves. It may have been a familiar sound to Golly, but it made Weary, who could not see the source of the noise, jump as if he heard a revolver missing fire.

'I advise him anyway,' said Golly as he left the shop, 'to see Foxey Friery. He knows a lot about dead-houses and he's well up.'

As usual, it was hard to get a connected history out of the Citizen. As far as could be ascertained, between his exaltations and exclamations at the wonder of the world and his adventures in it, he had the surprise of his life when he visited Foxey Friery, the Coroner, at his offices at the Moore Street corner of Rutland Square, West.

'He listened for a minute. Then he stood up threatening me. Is it to me you're coming with a complaint? For the love of Mike do you know to whom yer talking? Is it coddin' me you are with your troubles? They're nothing, nothing at all compared to mine. (Jayshus!) Ye wouldn't have a monkey about you for costs, by any chance?'

'So there is no one representing you?'

'I'm representing myself to-night at the corner of the Square near Findlater's Church. On my way out through the waiting-room I picked up a lovely bit of stuff with a broken nose. I told her it was no use trying to see the solicitor; that he was in worse trouble than the pair of us.'

After watching us with his sparkling eyes, the Citizen repeated, smiling, 'Findlater's Church!'

'She really doesn't love him,' the Citizen continued, with a faintly mocking smile.

'What's she like?' I asked.

'Who does she like?' asked Silly.

'She has a lovely figure, be Jabers. And eyes with eyelashes in bundles of three.'

'Branching dendrically,' said Silly Barney.

'And I think – I think – ,' said the Citizen, 'that Rasher Doyle is her fancy man.'

'The greengrocer?'

The Citizen nodded.

When Barney had stopped chuckling, the Citizen, after a split second's reflection, suddenly exclaimed, 'He says it with cabbages and cucumbers! He says it with cabbages! I declare to God!'

'Who's Rasher Doyle?' asked Weary Mac.

'Did you ever hear of the Rasher?' I turned the question on to Golly, to whom everything and everybody were known.

'No,' said Golly, 'but I often heard tell of a pig's ear: first thing in the morning with a pint of buttermilk. There was a medical's pal who shall be nameless, as the saying is. A hard chaw if there ever was one. After a terrible night drinking shebeen poison and all that kind of a thing in the kips, he was feeling so bad that he was afraid to look in the morning paper for fear that he'd find his name in the Obituary Column. It was he who told me first about the pig's ear. Half toasted; but don't burn all the grizzle.'

'He had more reason to expect to find himself among the Births,' said Barney, 'for he was the fellow who sold himself as a corpse to Professor Frazer up in the Surgeons', and when he crawled out of the sack at night only to find that his pals had drunk all the proceeds, "It's the last time I'll die for you, you ungrateful huers," sez he.'

'Don't forget the buttermilk.'

And Golly looked at us for approbation of his homely prescription for those who, forgetful of the diversion of the ambrosial night, considered only the morning's melancholy.

'Did you ever try it yourself?' asked Weary, who as a rule never made a *gaffe*.

We felt slightly embarrassed, for it was rather too personal a question.

'No, but a pig's ear is better than a rasher with a pint of buttermilk in the morning.'

So that's how Rasher Doyle must have got his name, thought I.

'Many's the time Old Friery told me he had one fried in the Hay Hotel.'

Chapter XIII

A CONSULTATION WITH COUNSEL

Hosanna the Barrister was to meet Old Friery the Coroner in Golly's back at ten. It was getting on for eleven now. Christy Friery was called 'old', not exactly for his age, but for the length of time he had been before the public as City Coroner. He was just as often called Red Friery, on account of the red beard from under which his belly began, and into which his two long cheeks flowed like pink blubber from a pair of foxy eyes with yellow-white lashes, some of which were stubbed at the ends like the legs of a fly, as a result of his attempts to light a cigarette in a breeze. He always wore a black silk hat and a black frock-coat, with a black alpaca waistcoat to keep him cool and yet professional. It was said that the tailor who had taken his measure was out of pocket because he had not taken it as quickly as the bookmakers.

Hosanna the barrister was different. He was a tall, thin, low-shouldered man with a sudden stomach like the protuberance of a sea-horse, and a mangy moustache and eyebrows, which he used for concentrating or brow-beating, and full florid lips, purple and exuberant, suggesting a Moor or a pair of earthworms on their honeymoon. An unblinking glass eye gave his countenance a fixed regard which suggested unwavering loyalty and steadfastness. He was a ready barrister, with a voice which could rant like a street preacher or whisper as insinuatingly as a charwoman ordering a glass of plain.

When shouting he was at his best – *in excelsis,* in fact; that is why he was called Hosanna, though his family name was Bumleigh. Juniors called him when in full blast the Fog Horn, but it was a bad nickname, for a fog horn does not make a fog but is used in time of fog, whereas his roars and vapourings produced each other, and the result was confounded confusion. He was too easily seen through to be a hypocrite; but he was useful as a second-rate work of art is useful : it exemplifies the obstacles to perfection. 'Nobody can be superior to nothing,' as Barney says; but if the half failures were not there, it would be hard to know who were the better advocates.

For all the humbug which was inseparable from his profession, he was a man of upright life so far as conduct went, thanks to his having read on the barrows more second-hand smutty books than anyone in Dublin. Others held – but what did they know? – that his virtue was due to accompanying the four honest solicitors who were addicted to Art on their triennial trips to Paris. They may have come to this conclusion from a 'show me your company and I'll tell you what you are'. But this could not be right either, because he owed a considerable amount of his practice to his association with Lad Lane and other 'whereases'.

Now, instead of being supported by shady solicitors, he was supporting one, for Old Friery as a solicitor was about the shadiest in Dublin – a qualification which would have been more becoming to the rôle of Coroner among the unhouselled shades of the morgue than to the rôle of attorney.

Old Friery the Coroner came into Golly's snug and took his breakfast, which consisted of an aspirin and a naggin of malt.

'Go easy with the water,' he said, as Golly emptied the naggin into a half-pint tumbler. 'I wouldn't have to take this at all if it wasn't for the wind that gets congealed round me heart.'

Mr Golly stood back, halted, and surveyed him. He went back another little bit, to gather way as it were, and then came forward bravely like an engine preparing to shunt.

'Isn't it you that's in luck?' And he stared hard at Friery.

Friery, whose nerves were on edge, didn't relish the stare.

'I wouldn't have noticed it if you hadn't told me,' said the Coroner dryly. 'I'm up to-day in the Recorder's Court. Where is the luck?'

'It's here in me waistcoat pocket,' Golly replied. 'You spoke of the wind getting congealed round your heart?'

'If it wasn't round me heart it might be round worse. I'm moidered from this blasted flatulence. It takes a naggin to break it every morning.'

'I suffered something shocking from it myself until I got this. I haven't tried them yet. But they'll cure anything from lumbago to a smoking chimney. I have it from the horse's mouth, first shot.' He tapped a box of pills.

'The horse's mouth' was an unhappy metaphor. It jarred on Friery, who lost a race which he would have won (talking of horses' mouths) 'if the bastard had only put out his tongue'. Horse's mouth!

'I'll just stop two and give you four,' said the generous Mr Golly.

The Coroner took one and put the rest of the pills in an empty matchbox, which with difficulty he returned to his waistcoat pocket.

'Do you expect me to swallow this without a drink?' he asked.

Mr Golly, who was not prepared for the complication, slowly obliged.

'Why can't that bloody fellow Bumleigh keep his appointment? He should have been here hours ago. I'll have to be getting off.' As he displayed no haste, and as it was the third time in an hour that the Coroner 'had to be getting off', he had evidently used words which were not 'operative'.

'What do you take to open your stomach in the morning?' he asked to humour Golly, who had stood the drink.

'Anything at all,' said Golly, 'that will break the wind and let the food in. There was a chemist fellow called Hoey in here one day and he explained the whole thing to me. Of course I disagree with him – that is, I'd be sorry to go the whole way with him. He's only a chemist, not a doctor. He said it wasn't wind.'

'Then what did he explain?' asked the Coroner hopelessly.

'He explained why your heart goes rolling round in the morning and your stomach fills with air.'

'I wish to God he had my heart,' said the Coroner.

' "It's not wind at all," sez Hoey, "but it's your stomach that swells up like a pig's bladder. The minute it bulges up to hit the heart there's hell to pay," sez he.'

'He's not far wrong,' said Friery the Coroner.

' "Yer heart is like a bull-frog leppin' on a bladder. No wonder yer agitated in the mornings." Them's the very words he used.'

'Who's this fellow Hoey?' the Coroner asked, interested.

'He's a kind of chemist's assistant. Of course he's not a doctor. But I've two prime boys here now and they're coming on nicely in the curriculum and that sort of thing,' Mr Golly explained.

A tapping on the glass panel of the door announced Bumleigh.

To a question, he replied: 'A dry ginger ale.'

When Mr Golly reappeared Bumleigh spoke so confidentially to Friery that Golly, recognising 'legal stuff and all that kind of thing', felt himself constrained to withdraw.

'The ould huer comes along,' Friery explained. ' "I have just this lump sum that himself left me, and I'd like you to invest it for me, sir," sez she.'

'And the lady was?' Hosanna asked.

'The Toucher's relict, of course. I thought I told you.'

Bumleigh nodded sententiously and hummed. 'Invest?' he whispered equivocally.

'She might have meant me to put it into a brewery, but I would do no such thing. Not I. Why should I? Invest a poor woman's legacy in drink, is it?'

'To spend money on drink would have been highly reprehensible. What will you have?' asked Bumleigh the barrister.

The Coroner indicated his tumbler as if he resented the superfluous question. Everyone knew that he had to take whiskey because beer or porter made him fat.

Bumleigh threw back his Cantrell and Cochrane with a relish and reluctantly ordered a large Jameson for his companion.

' "I've something gilt-edged," sez I, "something that can't go wrong, something that will give you an interest as well as multiply your capital if we don't spoil the market," ' Friery continued. ' "Something that will leave you comfortable for your old age. Leave it to me," sez I. With that, she left the monkey and went out.'

'An organ-grinder's widow?'

Contemptuously Friery went on: 'I rang up a few of the boys to get it on in dribs and drabs on the course for the four-thirty at Baldoyle. None of these huers of bookmakers will take a bet from me lately, not even in honest cash. Well, after a hard morning's work on the telephone I got four ponies on.'

'On four ponies,' Bumleigh suggested. He was answered by a glance of contempt.

'Well, you know what happened? Jayshus, if the bastard had only put out his tongue!'

'And she is now taking proceedings?'

'Proceedings, is it? I'm proceeding to Green Street this morning, and I want you to defend me before that old goat, Falconer the Recorder.'

Hosanna nodded sententiously, and said 'Hum.'

'Stop that bumming or you'll drive me mad. Christ! To look at you one would think that I was for the Jug. You might think that I hadn't obeyed instructions or that I did something dishonest. Instead of helping me out, you are Job's comforter. Can't you work yourself into one of your righteous wraths and bloody well roar like Hell's blazes? Tell them where they get off; and the criminal scandal of suspecting the City Coroner. And then give them a squirt of tears, and say that never in your life did you hear of a more blackmailing attempt to get blood out of a most respected sportsman. Didn't I breed the Artful Dodger? Holy God, do you know who I am at all?'

'Is all the money gone?' asked Bumleigh the barrister noncommittally.

The Coroner raised his hands as if he were rising from the sea. He did not see why there should be fees between colleagues.

Hosanna whistled softly, pointed his eyebrows at the ceiling, and coming down to earth, gulped his mineral.

'Suppose we make a clean breast of it?'

'Clean breast me neck! Wasn't the horse pulled? How could anything be clean from that stable? I tell ye we're up against a gang of twisters and copers. There was trickery in it from the word "Go"!'

Bumleigh nodded sententiously.

137

'Honest to God, Bumleigh, you'd think I had done something dishonest. And I up against a gang of rogues! Who the hell is briefing you, anyway?'

'Tell me nothing, tell me nothing!' Bumleigh implored. 'The less I know, the better I am. But calm yourself, my friend. I was only wishing that your case was, shall we say, more difficult to defend. Had it been a straightforward case – that is' – he checked himself to choose a word that would be nearer, all things considered, to *le mot juste* than 'straightforward' – 'what I mean is, you know in Law, that the worse the case the better. I'm not sure that I have the forensic skill to deal with a simple and uncomplicated action; yet yours is not very far from one. But tell me no more, 'twould only complicate the brief. It is well that you happen to be a solicitor or I couldn't take instructions at all.' He sighed and placed his hand over his diaphragm. He groaned inaudibly and then raised his hand genteelly to his mouth.

'Those gaseous waters!'

'Coddin' apart, try one of these; they cured me. I know what's wrong with you.' The Coroner took the matchbox, after a struggle, from his waistcoat-pocket, which the protuberance of his belly kept closed. 'Try one of these.'

'What are they?'

'They are for the wind. I got them from Golly before you came in. He suffers from flatulence himself.'

'May I keep it until we are in Court?'

Friery nodded, using his belly for an ash-tray when his cigarette-ash fell.

'Have you got an empty matchbox?'

Bumleigh fumbled, for he did not smoke and a matchbox was not among his possessions.

'You can put it in your spectacle case.'

Chapter XIV

LUMEN CURIÆ

The Recorder, a white old man, was in his restless
dotage. You never knew what side he'd be on. If he
favoured you at the beginning of a case you might be
in gaol at the end.

'And who is this widow?' he asked.

'She isn't a widow, your Lordship,' Lad Lane, the
counsel for the plaintiff, said.

'Nonsense! I am distinctly under the impression that
she is the widow of Toucher Duff. You said so yourself.'

'I said "relict", your Lordship. She is a lady who lived
as his housekeeper with the lately departed sportsman.'

The Recorder sat up and glared over his spectacles at
the woman who, acting on instructions, was sobbing
quietly, for she had been told that when Counsel produced his handkerchief she was to break down. On a
second and emergency production she was to collapse.
This was round one.

'You mean that she was living with him?' the Recorder demanded.

Bumleigh groaned, disedified. His foot touched
Friery's under the table. Apparently all so far was going
well. A prostitute against a man of repute.

'Speak up, my good woman, and stop that sniffling.
Tell the court, were you living with this – this – what's
his name? – this Toucher person?'

'I was living with him, me Lord.'

Bumleigh saw victory in the offing.

'And now you are unprotected. It's a serious offence to rob the defenceless.' The Recorder was unaccountable!

'Your Lordship!'

'Sit down, Mr Bumleigh!'

Bumleigh groaned and rumbled internally. Friery tapped him over his spectacle case. Bumleigh took the hint.

'How came you to meet the defendant?'

'When he was holding an inquest on the Toucher.'

'Your – your paramour?'

Having not the faintest notion what 'paramour' meant, she answered: 'He always treated me well.'

'Continue.'

'The Toucher sez Old Friery was one of those – '

'Mr Friery!' the Recorder corrected.

The result of this was to confuse the plaintiff. She looked in vain for the handkerchief. The Recorder came to her aid.

'You have just told us that the Coroner here held an inquest on – on – Go on – and that you were favourably impressed.'

'Well, he let him be removed before the things got stale for the wake.'

'And that was enough to make you entrust him with all you possessed?'

'He often defended the Toucher when he got himself mixed up with the polis. And he defended me for the Margarine.'

The Recorder held up the court. 'Margurine,' he corrected, hardening the g.

'Margurine' brought back to mind one of Friery's forensic triumphs in the very court where now he found himself arraigned. The Recorder, who was given to endless irrelevant soliloquies, was trying the present plaintiff, who, months before, was accused of selling margarine as butter. She was defended by Friery.

'The pronunciation of this word must be settled before I can permit the hearing of this case to continue. After all, it is necessary to know what we are talking about – ' 'Hear, hear!' said a solitary voice in the gallery, but it was unsupported. 'It is a matter of first principles – pronunciation. There seems to be a difference of opinion about the value of the g. Is it soft as in "marjarine" or hard? – I confess that I myself incline to a hard g as in "margurine".'

Friery, who knew that this could go on for an hour, was growing impatient. He interrupted: 'My client has settled that question to her own satisfaction. She called it "butter". That's why she's here.'

But it was Christy Friery himself was here now.

'It is obvious that you trusted him,' the Recorder remarked.

'The defendant does not deny receiving this money and dissipating it – Mr Bumleigh?'

Bumleigh rose to address the court. He began on a low key. He used a well-known gambit.

'Never has it been my experience to defend so important a civic official from a more trivial charge, or one coming from a more unsavoury source. What have we here? We have a woman, a self-confessed prostitute, arraigning a most respectable solicitor. She charges him with having misappropriated monies—for that is what it amounts to. No, no, Mr Lane me Lad.'

'Your Worship?' Mr Lad Lane was motioned down. That raised the voice of Bumleigh to stentorian pitch. He roared: 'A goat-toothed woman against the City Coroner!' He flung his gown off his arm as he pointed dramatically to Friery, whom he nearly hit upon the head. 'And how, and from what, and from whom did she receive the money?'

'From the Toucher who once caused a scene at Bal-doyle with the Coroner, while he had occasion to conduct some members of the Vice-regal Party over the course.'

'It was only Lord Dudley's jockey, me Lord.'

'Silence!' roared Bumleigh in a voice that murdered silence.

'When he found himself accosted by the late Toucher, who seized him by the arms and whispered dramatically, "Don't let them see me." '

'Who were the people by whom he did not wish to be seen?' The Recorder inquired.

'The bookmakers, your Worship.'

'So this woman's paramour was not *persona grata* with bookmakers?'

'He was, your Worship. He was only pretending. He was attempting a confidence trick.'

'It is all very confusing. Proceed, Mr Bumleigh.'

' "Don't let them see me talking to you. Your bet would not be worth placing if they knew it was me gave you the tip. And they'd blame me for robbing them. Oh, don't let them see me!" While this confidence trick was being played – '

'Confidence trick!' Lad Lane echoed disconcertingly.

'I said confidence trick, for there is no other name for the means whereby this bookies' tout obtained the money which has now gone rightly back to those from whom it came. Every racegoer, every sportsman knows' – his voice fell to its insinuating semitone – 'in which category I have reason to include your Worship.'

'But not as a betting man, Mr Bumleigh. Not as a gambler!'

Bumleigh bowed, corrected. A bad break.

'We have here money from a contaminated source. We have a story of "instructions" to this conscientious solicitor. And what were those instructions? What were they? I ask Heaven.'

'You'll be on surer ground if you confine yourself to where you're known,' Lad Lane remarked. 'They were – and let this not be highly passed over – we have the plaintiff's own admission. What did she tell the Coroner? What were her instructions? "Invest it for me." ' He looked round the court and glared horribly at the door, through which a large policeman, who had slipped out for 'a small one', was just then returning. That worthy fell back concussed by the voice of conscience.

'She told him to invest.'

'That is admitted, Mr Bumleigh.'

This caused the air to lose some vibrations and, unstimulated by the echoes of his own production, the orator had to begin again.

' "Invest," I said. Now what does "invest" mean? What does it connote to bookmakers, touts of whom this unfortunate female's partner in sin was one! What does it mean but to put the money on a horse? I submit – I submit that this woman, impressed by the integrity of the Coroner exercising his solemn function and investigating the awful problem of death, tried to take advantage of his fair credit with those who accept bets (a sad practice, I regret to say; almost a reprehensible practice) and to get him to put her money on in his own name. What else does "invest" mean to the sporting fraternity? What did this lecherous leman mean?' He swung round with the centrifugal force of his own question and pointed his eyebrows like the ears of an alert horse at two maiden sisters whom Friery had done out of five hundred pounds at the beginning of the flat-racing season.

'I said lecherous leman, and I mean it. Who is this leman?' He roared, and wriggled his wrists high in the air. 'Who is this leman?'

At this moment a spare old man with a wizened face – dead but for its intelligent bright eyes – and a broken nose that appeared to have been tattooed on the bridge or stricken by a cinder clinker, stood up at the back of the court. It was Tommy Monks, the Brummagem Bantam, hero of a hundred fights, one time champion of the Midlands. He was half deaf from the impact of a thousand punches. He had never heard so clearly since he was a young man. He thought that Hosanna was asking him about his one-time manager, so he stood up to him and answered:

'He was a wrong 'un all right.'

Having spoken, he subsided with his head lowered to keep the shouting off his point. The fetid court-house retched and re-echoed. The Impeachment of Warren Hastings was as nothing compared with the invective of Bumleigh bombinating at his best. 'Who is this lech – '

Lad Lane threw in his handkerchief; his client took the count.

'I perceive that the lady has fainted. Revive her, constable.' The Recorder extended his water carafe and tumbler.

The plaintiff had the good fortune to awake just in time.

'It's a heart attack!' she whispered. 'Dr Nedley says, "When she gets them, bring her into Hedigan's and make her take a large brandy or a few balls of malt."' She swooned again. She was half restored by a 'Baby Power'.

The Recorder appeared to be relieved.

'Could you modulate your voice, Mr Bumleigh?' he said, and then, in tones of kindness, asked the convalescent – 'Tell me, how came you to be associated with Mr Duff, and how long did this – this liaison last?'

'His Worship is addressing you,' the police constable whispered.

'After me other sister died, your Worship.'

'Had he two – had you two – had you a sister?'

'I had. And when she died I was the only one he had left.'

The Recorder jerked his head swiftly from side to side

like a goalkeeper expecting a shot from dribbling forwards. Then he shouted reproachfully, 'She was his sister, Mr Bumleigh! Is not that so, my good woman?'

'But I never said I wasn't. I never told a lie.'

Now it was Bumleigh who was in distress; he appeared to have some of the symptoms of acute colic. He looked reproachfully at Friery. That worthy surreptitiously suggested that it was time for tears. Forget the flatulence.

'We have here,' continued Bumleigh in a voice that contained the immemorial woe of the world since Time began its human story, 'we have on the one side a woman associated with those racegoing gangs that infest the racecourses of England, and are about to begin their nefarious operations in our hitherto crimeless country. And on the other side, at my hand here, is one of the most respected and beloved citizens who ever held public office in any country. A friend of the poor, a general comforter of the distressed. When a body has been taken from the Liffey after long immersion, and the wife of the unfortunate human being who was "Found Drowned" approaches the Morgue to try to identify in death what had been in life her bread-winner, is she confronted with red tape or the corpse? No; but with the Coroner. This kindly man makes it his business – nay, his duty – to attend what has become the last home of the unfortunate or the suicide, and to meet there the distressed relatives of whosoever – pardon me – of whomsoever has been laid out on the Morgue's melancholy slate. Does he persecute the bereaved with questions? No. What does he do? He does all that a man may do, and let us hope it is not always in vain – he comforts the afflicted and releases the corpse in time for the wake and the sad, insolvent obsequies of the poor. That, your Lordship, is our City Coroner. What city on the broad surface of the earth has a coroner to compare to him? When I think of all the affliction with which it is his lot to be confronted, when I see in my mind's eye the widows in shawls dragging along their fatherless children, I think of Friery the Coroner, the Comforter. I see his kindly pat on the head for the bereaved and bereft' (still speaking, he leant sideways to indicate with flattened hand the height of the toddler's head), 'and I can hardly withhold a manly tear. I – ' He sobbed, griped with emotion and the pill that had as it appears been thoughtfully and propitiously administered, and a large tear was the result. It rolled down his gown. The Coroner bowed his head, overwhelmed by his own benevolence. A tear struck the back of his client's chubby hand. 'I am not ashamed of my feelings, your Lordship. You too have had experience in this court of much of the misery that exists among the poor. You have protected them by long sentences from the rascal and the rogue. Now I ask you to protect this benevolent citizen from the machinations of the race-gangs and the footpads and other ruffians who are at the back of this conspiracy of blackmail. I have done.' He sat down, snorting with emotion.

'Really, it seems to me that this is not a simple matter at all. It must be inquired into. I will remand the defendant for a week in protective custody. Of course, now that you have reminded me, you will understand that no stigma accrues to it. It is merely a measure for his own safety.'

Friery shook the tear from the back of his hand in disgust and scowled at Bumleigh. 'You overdid it,' he whispered. 'You hypocritical old hulk! Why the hell didn't you cut out that protection blather? Now you have me in Mountjoy, and there's not the least use in appealing to that old goat.'

Bumleigh, who was always dignified, forbore to reply rudely. 'You nearly poisoned me with your pill. It went the wrong way,' was all he said. He left the court with hastening steps. He was resigned to the ingratitude which marks the daily round. This time he was 'on the run' and no mistake!

Friery called after him, 'You must have taken the pill upside down,' which only made it worse because it showed a lack of sympathy; for who can tell when a pill is upside down? It was to the direction of its action he probably referred.

Chapter XV

'OH, MON!'

Here's to you, Professor Fraser, with your trim beard and your two pair of spectacles and the black leather sleeves of your dissecting-coat, and your lunch in a torn bit of brown paper between the knees of the corpse. I can see you reverently lifting an armful of intestines which you had freed from peritoneum and omentum and turning them round as you explained, 'contra-clockwise'. You were the greatest anatomist that ever came to Ireland from that land of science, Scotland. You loved the work and you infected others with your enthusiasm. Through my admiration and affection for you I managed to get past NcNought, who is merely a dead-house director compared to you.

'Oh, mon! see how the recurrent laryngeal has to elongate out with the neck as the neck grows and the arch of the aorta comes down – for a wee babbie has no neck.'

I'll not desert the College of Surgeons, but I will hang about it just to be near you. Though your interest ends in Anatomy, you can help me when I am practising surgery on the cadaver. Thanks to you, I knocked the concealment out of McNought.

And now I can and will circle fast or slowly round the College Park as scantily clad as possible and practise sprinting, though the grass rather slows one's pedalling – before and after as well as during the hours of Anatomy lectures. A few cheery shouts to Larry Oswald across the

Park will have an effect in the dissecting room somewhat similar to that of the Citizen's visit to another dissecting room with his brace of pistols.

And now I will walk to Richmond Hospital and meet Sir Thomas Myles.

Golly was the first to congratulate me. I was modest. 'It was more or less a fluke,' I confessed.

'Just by chance, as the cow said when she kicked the hare.' Golly improved the moment. 'You'll be doing, what, Medicine next?'

'Midwifery next. And it should be interesting if for nothing else but that it deals with birth, not death. I'm living in the Holles Street Lying-in Hospital. When I get Midwifery there remain only Surgery and Medicine. Then I'm qualified.'

'And then every puck a goal,' said Golly, prophesying a successful career for me, as he 'pucked' an imaginary ball with a hurley stick, also a 'false creation'.

I wish I had Midwifery over me. Then there would be only two subjects to get.

'You can't have them all at once, as the elephant said to the flea. Aren't you satisfied to have got as far as you have?' he asked.

A little time elapsed. Then Golly, overcome by curiosity, returned as one fascinated, and, lowering his voice to a whisper, inquired, 'This Midwifery? Have you to be going about with ould ones?' By which he meant the Sairey Gamps of the city. Evidently here was another source of mystery for that inquiring mind.

'There are young ones in it too.'

'D'ye tell me now? Young ones?'

'Yes, of course. It is not the old ones that you'd be expecting to bear the children.'

Mr Golly felt slightly embarrassed. Then he asked, 'Is there much of that kind of thing in it?'

'Before I can become a doctor I must do fourteen conductions myself.' I saw that he was puzzled, so I explained that conduction meant delivering children. In came Weary.

'Where's Barney? So you got through?'

'I was telling him,' said Mr Golly, 'that he should be contented and rest on his oars and take it easy and all that kind of a thing, but he wants to go on at once for Midwifery and do fourteen' – he paused – 'on young ones having children.'

'We all have to do that,' said Weary. 'We must get credit for fourteen conductions.'

'You took the very word out of my mouth!' said Mr Golly.

'Before we can get qualified.'

'It must be a terrible strain.'

Weary acknowledged that it was a terrible strain. For the young mothers at all events, I conceded; and that the severity of the strain was in inverse ratio to the skill of the attendant. He hoped soon to be resident in Holles Street himself. And the queer thing was that lady doctors were no good for attending to women in their confinement. Men were the best.

'A hair of the dog,' said Mr Golly authoritatively. Then, dropping his voice confidentially, he informed us, 'It was a lady doctor did in the poor Missus, Lord rest her.'

Weary evinced the greatest interest. Mr Golly, encouraged, went on, looking first over his shoulder and then from left to right.

'A lady doctor. It was largely the Missus's fault. She'd have no one near her except a couple of ould ones out of the Coombe and a lady doctor. She was called in when something went wrong with the Missus one night – '

'Ah,' said Weary solemnly, 'It's nearly always at night.'

'And she came in, anyway, punctual enough and all

that kind of thing. Sober too – not that I would have minded a few jars in a man and all that kind of a thing, if he was a woman's doctor. But if you see what I mean, she was sober and she left no margin, if you see what I mean, for mistake – '

'No margin of error that might be allowed for and corrected by a consultation afterwards?'

'You have taken the very words out of my mouth,' said Mr Golly abruptly, caught up by his narrative and not wishing to be interrupted again.

'Cocksure, you might call her. "It's Nature asserting herself," sez she.'

Mac nodded in sympathetic understanding. 'Nature asserting herself; just so.'

'I took her aside and confided to her my little trouble about the flatulence. "It's only wind," sez she. Think of her audacity! "It's only wind," sez she to *me*. "*Only* wind? *Only* wind?" sez I. "Have ye never heard of the Tay Bridge disaster?" '

'Well, whether it was or not, she left the poor Missus in a hell of a state and off she goes on her holidays. Now I just ask you, what do you make out of that! "I've got to take them now," sez she.'

'Nature asserting herself,' Mac whispered to me, not wishing to appear facetious to Golly, who had turned away to hide the effects of memory.

'Giddy,' said Barney, entering suddenly and wiping perspiration from his brow, 'you may order me a pint. I deserve it. Here's the ten pounds and here's the ticket, but it's in my name, so I'll keep it for you among the archives. I've had a terrible time with Jimmy over your watch. From the start he suspected that it was yours. For God's sake!'

'I'm drawing it,' said Golly with his back turned.

Refreshed, Barney told us the tale of the morning's diplomatic work. 'You know, if you want a quid from

Jimmy you must make it thirty bob. Now in higher finance, so to speak, in the region of ten pounds, it would never do to act so proportionately. Eleven pounds is about the limit over ten pounds. It conveys a sense of your knowledge of the value of money, for sometimes Jimmy takes upon himself to become conscientious out of consideration for your parents and to stop what he might think was a squandering of money. Therefore the question of motive arises. Now I went provided with excellent reason — '

We all listened to the master of finance.

'Not to break my mother's heart. Jimmy knew I got honours, and he knew what a bloody awful disappointment he would inflict on my parent if he failed me in making up a cheque that somehow went west when I should have paid my lecture fees. I could never pass an exam again if I failed to pay the fees.'

'Of course not,' Weary agreed, greatly edified.

'Jimmy took the watch and pretended not to look at it; but Jimmy can tell the value of a thing by the feel, without ever looking at it, except at the end of the leg of your trousers at the back where the mileage is recorded. "Where did you get this?" says he. "It's an heirloom," I told him. An heirloom! And he opened it and put that neck-of-a-bottle-like thing into his eye. Then after a close scrutiny he said to himself quietly, "Heirloom me arse! It's Hargraves of Liverpool."

' "Ours is a short-lived family," I said.

' "Of course, Giddy Ouseley wasn't up in the North lately at all at all by any chance? Oh, no! By no means. I don't think." '

'It's hard to cod Jimmy,' Mac meditated sadly.

Greatly interested, I implored Barney to go on. I could see the querulous, good-natured little man with his tawny eyes shot with spicules of gold, as it were, from all the watches, rings, etc., they had scrutinised, walking up and down disconcertingly behind the counter trying to compensate for his good nature by loud-voiced badinage and complaints. I could see the thick ball of his thumb as he brought his hand down with a bang on the counter to clinch as it were his final decision about the 'advance'. 'That'll do ye now. You might think we were made of money!'

'He kept staring into it with his magnifying glass. "There's no such thing as a date at all at all in a watch," said Jimmy. "This one is only five years old."

' "And I have only had it two days. I got it from my uncle for getting honours; and I had to let the lecture cheque go to pay the digs and do a little very parsimonious entertaining – as well as pay a few tips."

' "Nine pounds," said Jimmy. "Here," and he called to his clerk.'

'Oh,' Mac assured us, 'that was a good sign.'

' "Do you not appreciate the movement?" ' I asked.

' "English hunter, and nine pounds. And that's final." '

'That was a good sign,' Mac repeated, who appreciated the movement of Jimmy's mind.

Barney said, 'That stuff about the movements which are worthless in a watch is no good with Jimmy for, as you know, pawnbrokers think only of the case. Having failed, I tried another tack. "Are the resources of your establishment exhausted?" I asked.

' "It's not my establishment," Jimmy said as he walked into the trap.

' "I know that," I said. "But there would be precious little establishment if it weren't for you. And I for one wouldn't deal in it. But as manager, you are all-powerful and your word is law, and you can decide, not only the difference between nine pounds and eleven, but appreciate the exigencies of a student's life who has to live in an expensive city, according to the idea of people far down in the country. If it was anyone else but my mother,

I wouldn't trouble you at all." And I nearly broke down,' said Barney.

'Of course Jimmy wouldn't give in before his clerk.' Weary spoke with experience.

'No,' said Barney, 'but decently enough, when he shook the sand on the ticket there was ten quid marked on it instead of nine.'

'He's not so bad at all,' Weary said, adding, 'sometimes,' as an afterthought.

'He's a sportsman, and he knew all the time that that watch was a prize for cycling won by me.'

'All balls!' Silly Barney exclaimed.

'Barney refers to the crest of the Medici,' I explained to Weary Mac.

'He usually shouts something after you as you are going out. Did he let you depart in peace?' asked Weary.

'No,' Barney admitted.

'What did he say?' I asked.

'He told me,' Barney said smiling and somewhat crest-fallen, to "tell Giddy that I congratulate him on his uncle".'

Chapter XVI

GOOD BEER AND A CATHOLIC CHURCH

Part of the property which Mr Beddy was very kindly
saving for us (after office hours) consisted of an old
seventeenth-century house on the south bank of the Tolka,
near the Botanic Gardens. It was a grey old house facing
the distant hills, with its two storeys, a gable in the
middle, and a rounded tower-like structure at either end.
The hall door at ground level was in one tower; the
other, which was only half as high, had a door into
the garden; and a lovely old garden it was, at the back of
the house. A stair led down from the first landing to a path
between two propped-up mulberry trees, each on its little
square of lawn. They looked like banyan trees, so many
were the supports that held up their zinc-patched boughs
so that they might redden the ground with their abun-
dant berries for an extra score of years. The last tenant
was a Miss Hutton, who lived to ninety, for peace dwelt
in the old garden with its little lawns for each mulberry
tree, its circle of hazels, and its immense yew hedge that
walled it in from the orchard and kitchen garden on the
west and met the end of a semicircle of yew trees which
protected it with their close evergreen branches from the
winds out of the north. On the east side a stone wall,
topped with foxgloves, red and white, self-sown from the
herbarium beneath, let the level sun flood in from over
the Bay and stipple the dark yew hedge with points of
morning gold. The beds were marked out with boxwood
margins and contained simples: mullein, digitalis, lily of

the valley, bryony and thyme. There were two old green seats under the yews, and on one of these the Master and I used to sit in the evenings, talking, and drinking the new German beer that Davy Byrne introduced to Dublin from Nuremberg. Here the Master and I affirmed our philosophy; not that I affirmed much, for I was ignorant of logic, or, as the Master called it, 'the science of the Logos, the divine word or reason.' But I was imbibing it from him during the many happy hours we used to sit, until the dusty sunlight reddened the yew-boles and fringed with translucent green the heavy hedge of yew.

The sheltered dimness under the trees was conducive to meditation, for it provided the shade that seems to be necessary to all forms of contemplative pleasures, from drinking to discussing the science of pure thought, the ground plan of which was laid down by the mighty *maestro di color che sanno*, as that terse fellow Dante calls Aristotle, and as I call the Professor of Philosophy of Trinity College, Dublin – a gentler soul, a wiser or more lovable man than whom never lived.

' "Put me near good beer and a Catholic Church," Hegel exclaimed near the end of his days. And could there be anything better?' the Master asked me as he took his seat. He had a habit of uttering as an exclamation, by way of a jest, what was later on to become the text of an earnest and delightful discussion.

'You may consider yourself Hegel as far as the beer goes,' I said, 'for the good beer is here, and I stand for the Church.'

He smiled incredulously, then said, 'We were talking of Plato the other night.'

'It was the night before last. Last night we were in the greenhouse talking of Spinoza, because it was raining.'

'The rain accounted for our being in the greenhouse, not for our choice of subject.'

'I am sorry! My English is a little slipshod. This evening you promised to explain – No, no. You promised to explain this evening how Hegel excelled the Intellectualists.'

'Can you name them? Now, before we proceed, can you name them?'

'Certainly : Descartes, Spinoza, Leibnitz.'

'Good. You forget nothing. If you would only apply that memory of yours to the retention of certain facts that go to a knowledge of Anatomy, for instance, it would save me many uninspiring interviews with McNought.'

A sudden realisation of the trouble to which I was subjecting one of the gentlest and most generous of men, and the distaste and difficulties which met one who was not even my tutor in tackling my Professor of Anatomy, overwhelmed me. I stuttered out an apology and tried to express the profound gratitude which indeed I felt, all the more because such things were done with such unobtrusive good nature.

'I cannot tell you how very grateful I am. The best proof of it, I hope, will be to make such interviews on my behalf no longer necessary. Your kindness is very dear to me, and I will never forget it.'

It was true. For my mother's sake and mine, out of his kindness of heart the Master undertook the duties which were properly those of my tutor, and did his best for me with the professors of the Medical School. Seeing that the truth of this was soaking in, so to speak, he said: 'Don't take that as a reflection on you, my dear fellow; we remember best that which we are interested in. I must admit that I would find it very hard to summon up an interest in Anatomy.'

'Sir, the very thought of it makes me stupid.'

The Master, changing his voice, quoted: ' "When a youth therefore appears dull of apprehension and seems to derive no advantage from study and instruction, the tutor must exercise his sagacity in discovering whether the soil be absolutely barren or sown with seed repugnant to his nature, or of such quality as requires repeated culture and length of time to get its juices in fermentation." '

The most Goldsmith-like of men quoting Goldsmith! Did he think of Goldsmith because he was a chronic medical? I preferred to think that he took naturally to Goldsmith, who, like himself, thought nothing of academical fame and who suffered from the lack of self-assertion – just as the College will suffer yet, I thought, from the lack of recognition of the greatness of its greatest contemporary son, truly the mighty *maestro di color che sanno*. And he was exercising his sagacity on behalf of me.

'It is my prejudices which afflict me more than my distastes,' I confessed. 'But I am now interested in Anatomy because I have met a Scotsman to whom its study is all-absorbing and a complete philosophy of life. I have learnt a great deal from him; whether it will be accepted in another quarter remains to be seen.'

'A complete philosophy of life! No one had that but Hegel. He went farther than Plato and Aristotle. Plato's great discovery – By the way, what was Plato's great discovery, do you remember?'

'That the truth of things is thought.'

'Very good. And how did Aristotle advance on that?'

'Plato's thought was one-sided and undefined. He saw truth only in the universal in general without relating it to the particular. Aristotle supplied this second factor.'

'Very good.' The Master looked about him as if he thought he had missed his umbrella. I opened two bottles of 'good beer'.

After a little silence he put down his empty glass, with a sigh, and, gathering his mind, began : 'Hegel, let me tell you, outsoars them all by his dialectic. The interconnection of the universal and the particular, the immanent dialectic of their interdependence, the identity of their opposition, this was the *third factor* of thought which remained for Hegel to supply. Furthermore, from this identity of opposites he went on to show that truth is what falsehood has to become. He took it that falsehood itself bears witness to the truth. For truth is everywhere, even in what we call the false; and what we call the false has strugglings of dialectic within it, for the falsehood that contained no dialectic would be like the truth that contained no repudiation of error, an empty abstraction.'

'Hegel does not believe in personal immortality?'

'Why should he?' answered the Master of Those Who Know.

This was rather disconcerting. So I started as if aggrieved. 'But wasn't he a Christian?'

'Just a moment. Let us take things in order and get our definitions clear. Now tell me what you mean by personal immortality.'

I realised that I was not doing too well at all. I was stumped, flummoxed, so to speak (if you see what I mean), for an appreciable interval, because I had to ask myself and find out what I really did mean by personal immortality. I had a lot of undigested ideas and unexamined notions to clear away before going on with the discussion. That is the worst of philosophy : you have to know what you are talking about before you can get an answer, and by the time you clear your mind you don't want any answer. Did I mean, I asked myself, by 'personal immortality' that a fellow who died at say sixty or seventy years of age would go on being sixty or seventy for ever and ever? Would he stay at sixty or go on ageing for ever and ever till he reached a few million years, and then what would he look like? Obviously it would not do to go on surviving for ever and ever as we were at the hour of our death, or to go on being like Weary, always calculating and full of a grudging nature, or like the Citizen, swift and abrupt, or like my aunt, with an over-sensitive sense of smell – hyperosmia, they call it. Would she go on for

ever being a nuisance to me, herself, and to 'Dearie' the
dentist, who hasn't thanked me yet for sending her to
him, for he had to employ an invention of which he is
very proud to 'protect himself' from her power of observation through her nose. His invention consists in putting
a tiny drop of oil of cloves on the upper lip so that the
patient can go on smelling that instead of his breath.
Were these people and all their peculiarities to be inde-
finitely prolonged? Or should we all die in our heyday,
so as to have something left for Eternity?

'There are difficulties in my mind,' I said.

'Would your difficulties be resolved,' asked the greatest
of teachers, 'if I suggested that they arise from a consideration of entanglements in material conditions, stunted
developments and accidental finitudes? I do not wish to
intrude on your train of thought, but it occurs to me
that you are considering such things as a stumbling-block
to defining what you mean by "personal immortality".'

'Yes,' I said, my mind clearing. As a matter of fact, at
the moment he spoke I was wondering – Would 'Dearie's'
thirst be immortal in the next world as it was uninter-
mittent in this, and would he have to dodge my aunt for
ever, and would she disapprove of and distrust for ever
'those who smell of drink'? But I didn't like to put it so
unphilosophically to the Master, who took the thought
out of my head, so to speak; for you can be sure that a
thing that can be put plainly cannot be a proper subject
for philosophy, so I said that I was wondering how those
who were born maimed or who had a clouded intellect,
those whose minds (like Birrell's, for instance) weren't up
to the mark of 'the divine word or reason', would carry
on. Another example added itself which I forbore to mention : I was wondering how a poor devil of a doctor, say,
like Auchinleck, who lived by curing venereal diseases in
this world, would fare in heaven.

The Master said : 'Conditions such as those which are

present to your mind, including stupidity and all kinds of idiosyncrasies, make up a content which we wrongly call ourselves. Hegel would decline to see personality in such contingent and nugatory idiosyncrasies that make a person a particular *kind* of person – '

'Contingent and nugatory idiosyncrasies!' He took the words out of my mouth. I know a gang that consists of nothing else. I shall not mention names, for they have no personalities and they should not have names at all. But there is one 'accidental finitude' who spends his time passing his nugatory idiosyncrasy on to me. Fraser will fix him all right, and I'll apply my memory and then decline to see personality in him for the rest of his natural, or rather, unnatural life. And I know a lot of fellows who would need a good deal of education and backbone before they could be said to have a personality that could even be damned. But when a fellow is discussing philosophy, the first thing to do is to have an unruffled mind. So I dismissed the whole bunch and concentrated a bit, and began to remember that our mortal bodies would be purified and perfected and made fond of music and all that sort of thing, before being drawn into a kind of ego-less universal being. I might as well believe in Hegel's unidiosyncrasised personality, or however you like to put it; but you see what I mean? So I said, for I was getting the hang of the thing : 'Of course not. Why should he concede personality to cripples or cranks or nitwits? But of course he will concede immortality to our purified personalities?'

I no sooner spoke than I felt that my suggestion was wanting in something, for the Master looked extra tole-rant as he said : 'Let us not be vague. Hegel's conception permits no notion of a purified, universalised, dematerialised self. Such a notion is a monstrosity of the vulgar imagination; not an identity of opposites, but a confusion of contradictories.' (Holy Heaven! My notion is a monstrosity of vulgar imagination?) Death is appointed not to this, not to that class of existence, but to existence in general.'

There must be something wrong somewhere, for I could have told him that myself and added that 'Reproduction is the beginning of Death', as old Thompson says; but before he gets the idea that I have a vulgar imagination I must put up a bit of scrap, a philosophical resistance, if I express myself clearly, and develop an 'honest doubt' about Hegel.

'Does he allow immortality at all?'

'I will answer that, if I may, by asking you another question: Do you believe in the immortality of your earthly body?'

'I can't say I do.' I was a bit out of training, anyway, lately.

'And would it not be grotesque to suppose the everlasting continuance of the mentality which is determined by the physical characteristics of your earthly body? A personal preference, shall we say, for beer to wine?'

With my forefinger in the neck of an empty, very dexterously I flung it into the great hedge, which received it in silence and buried it among its many predecessors of happy evenings, far beyond all hope of discovery, and very silently I drew the corks from another brace. That hedge must be filling up. That is why I tried an outer ring with the last empty. It would never do to have the gardener come in with the news of a nest of bottles worth tuppence each jingling in the hedge.

'Existence is essentially finite and therefore essentially mortal. But the spirit no more belongs to the world of mortal things than does the harmony of the diapason to the mutability of the strings.'

'"The proud and careless notes live on,
But bless our hands that ebb away,"'

I quoted, hoping to get a little poetry into the argument, for when things begin to get too pressing and too definite there is always a hope of escape from reality for you in poetry.

'I understand it all now,' I said. 'If I have followed you correctly, I may take it that my reason, with its ideas of the good and the beautiful, is not to be swept away?'

'Reason is indeed never to be swept away, but you cannot say that your reason, or any particular person's reason for that matter, must remain, any more than your addiction to this excellent lager must remain. Now, my dear fellow, I'm not blaming you for it – but Reason is never to be swept away; it is the last word of Being; the Good and the Beautiful are its manifestations – manifestations of the Eternal Idea winning out in the world of immediate existence, and there is no way out of this entanglement except death.'

I am far too deeply in the world of immediate existence now to make, possibly and more than likely, a fool of myself by asking how does Hegel account for Death: couldn't he scrap that with the rest of his 'accidental finitudes and imperfections', for it looks like the worst of the lot to me?

But the Master began to dwell lovingly and sentimentally on his last sentence, as was his habit after a prolonged discussion where there was good beer. Holding his glass against the gilded fringe of the hedge in which a little of the setting sun lingered, he murmured : 'And, last of all, there is no way out of this entanglement except death.'

'Was the fellow, the philosopher, I mean, a Christian at all?'

'Who?'

'Hegel, I mean; was he a Christian?'

The Master finished his drink before replying.

'Now that is a question of more than speculative interest.'

You see how well I am coming on, I said to myself. I am now able to propound a question of more than speculative interest to the Master of Those Who Know.

'He was a Lutheran.'

'A Lutheran? Luther was the fellow who did more to change the physiognomy of England than any other people since the Jews.'

'How dare you!' exclaimed the Master. 'Let me explain Hegel's relation to Christianity. But before I take you up on your frivolous nonsense, open another bottle of beer.'

A translucent yew-berry fell on the Master's knee. Looking up against the light into the tree, he said : 'Do you see the light in that yew-berry? No. To illustrate it better, hand me that bottle of beer. Christianity is not merely a form in which to capture the light of Hegelianism just as that golden fluid captures the rays of – below they had all faded – captures the light of the evening. It is the inevitable expression of it. But a consideration such as this sounds like an apology to those who have not reached the philosophic standpoint.'

Ho, I said to myself, that is a very gentle jag, but a jag all the same, at you, my lad, for not having attained to the philosophic standpoint; even that other Nuremberger, Perkaio the dwarf, realised his artistic standpoint, his *kunstlicher standpunkt*, when he first stood before the great tun on which, when he had emptied it, they tolled him dead. If my mind were not so full I would ask him – 'What is the philosophic standpoint?'

'At that standpoint the whole aspect of the case is changed.'

It must be splendid to reach it, I thought.

'For Hegel, true philosophy and the religion of Christianity were one.' (And he a Lutheran!) 'But remember that the Hegelian conception of religion is diametrically opposed to the shallow liberalism that reduces religion to "mortality touched by emotion". Religion,' said the

Master, waxing alcoholically eloquent (the only sign of a little finitude and imperfection of personality he exhibited) – 'Religion!'

'Good beer, please!'

'Would it be prudent, Master?'

'Religion is not a matter of prudence for ourselves, or benevolence to others, but of the worship of that same God whom philosophy contemplates as the Absolute Truth!'

A light breeze coming with the first rareness of the night caused a movement in the great hedge, which was accompanied by a tinkling sound like that made by a lustre on the mantelpiece when the housemaid is dusting and you are trying to read.

'Oh, ah,' exclaimed the Master. 'Hearken! "The horns of elf-land faintly blowing."'

'No, no,' I said.

'Whist. What is it?'

'It is the struggling of the dialectic in the empty bottles towards the poison of the full.'

'You dirty brute! Is nothing immune from your mockery?'

'It is one of the imperfections of my personality, but it also has its dialectic in reverence, where it is due.'

In spite of the way we were guarded from interruption, solicitude for the Master who had no overcoat might have precipitated a message from my aunt. There was no fear of my mother, for Mr Beddy, who was very kindly saving our property for us (after office hours), had accompanied her to the sodality in Gardiner Street and would very kindly see her home; and though 'prudence for ourselves' should have closed the symposium, I asked: 'Why did Hegel want to live near a Catholic church?'

'To study Catholicism.'

I refrained from asking why he wanted to study it if he were a Lutheran. I suspected that he wanted absolution from the Absolute and all that kind of thing in his old age. Probably, like Newton before him, he recoiled from the results of his thinking and decided not to vary from the kindly race of men.

I did not want to appear narrow or bigoted, or to divulge the fact that I had a vulgar imagination, or to let the Medical School obtrude into the realms of pure reason, but I said : 'It is extraordinary what an influence Luther had on the physiognomy of England. Where did the English people get their expression of exaggerated concern and over-responsibility, as if they were all managers of an enormous store with no customers, but from Luther? What has pinched and darkened their faces had taken from them the Falstaffian fullness which was the face of Merrie England? And we all know that Falstaff was a typical Englishman until Luther treated him as scurvily as Prince Hal. What are the English people taking so seriously? Can they not find any more people to forgive for the wrongs they themselves have inflicted? Can it be that when Luther came in, mirth went out? The best thing we must give Hegel credit for (philosophy apart) is that he recognised this and wanted to get away from it all and to drink good beer beside a Catholic church, perhaps one like that at Nuremberg where Hans Sachs lived and Perkaio drank with a beerhouse built in between the buttresses. Your portrait of him in your rooms shows a decent, full-faced fellow like Beethoven, with a round nose that would redden nicely when he had achieved the philosophic standpoint which, as you say, "changes the whole aspect".'

'I forgive your nonsense; but you must admit that there were great abuses in the Church before Luther set out to reform them. You cannot blame him for that.'

'It is Hegel I am blaming, for calling himself a Lutheran and thus abetting Luther when, according to his own contention, anything that was wrong with the Church would have settled itself if left alone, without any Reformation.'

'He never said anything of the sort,' the Master affirmed.

'Oh, yes he did. He said, "truth is everywhere even in what we call the false," and according to you he taught that falsehood itself bears witness to the truth.'

'What has all this got to do with the Reformation?'

'This, that if Luther had left the Church alone without trying to reform it, it would have reformed itself. Even its mistakes would have borne witness to the truth. But instead of waiting, he has bequeathed to us the difficulty of reforming the Reformation. My hope is that Hegel is right, and that if left alone the Reformation will reform itself "because of the strugglings of dialectic within it," and that all Lutherans will end as Hegel did, "beside good beer and a Catholic church." '

To this the Master replied nothing. Instead of replying, he sighed gently as one suffering from a slight despair. I of course knew, as anyone in a position to judge would have known, that I had achieved the 'philosophical standpoint'. The aspect of everything had changed.

Night had fallen. Remembering Mr Murtagh's (of Irishtown) warning about the difficulty of getting 'the long-legged ones up once they fall', I took the Master's arm, for I knew the path. Suddenly, with melodramatic suddenness, he glared about him and said in a deep voice, solemnly gesturing caution, *Fafnir lagert in finstern walde.*

We went out by a side door so as to avoid Mr Beddy, who might be returning at any moment, full of grace with my mother, in a tuppenny tram. And, coming back, I went to get a dictionary to look up what the devil is meant by 'dialectic'. Here it is: 'According to Hegel, each concept in the development of thought by a primitive necessity develops its own diametric opposite, and to this reaction of thought against itself, regarded not as final, but as subject to a subsequent reconcilement in a higher order of thought, he gave the name of dialectic.'

'Well, it's never too late to know what you were talking

about,' I said to myself. And so to bed, to sleep, perchance to dream of something which is beyond my ken, but cannot be swept away. It is peculiarly unsatisfying. It is as if someone were to assure two love-sick lovers: 'Cheer up! You two may be swept away, but Reproduction shall never be swept away.'

Chapter XVII

MIDWIFERY

Dublin is a slum, an extensive and terrible slum hidden behind the shallow façades of the rarely painted shops, banks and shabby offices in its few principal streets. There are many reasons but no excuses for this state of things. One reason is that the class of citizen who ruled the city has changed and civic pride has given way to civic jobbery, and the old idea of what was proud and comely has gone with the city's ancient pride when, in its brick and granite, silver and rose, Dublin stood, the seventh city in Christendom. It is now a slum, and I am living in a particularly bad example of one in Holles Street which, though only a few yards behind the fashionable Merrion Square, is an awful slum. But here I must reside, for here dwell the proletariat, the people who bear the *proles*, which means the offspring on whom I have to officiate in person while they are being born, so that I may become skilled enough to deliver the more delicate – that is, the rare – children of the rich, who do not produce reserves in sufficient quantity to combat the city's infantile mortality successfully. Therefore they have all the more to cherish what they have got. The proletariat produce the slums and the slums produce the high death-rate; and the Corporation tolerates it all. This will go on until the day arrives when slums shall be no more, when rich and poor alike shall have equal families as they do in Stockholm, and when there shall be no Income Tax; but this will take twenty years before Sinn Fein comes into its own and the country shall be free, and we shall see the perfect hospital in Holles Street. Meanwhile, I will light a cigarette. Where did I put the *Irish Times* – the paper that puts the births before the marriages?

What is this?

MARRIAGES

GOLLY—NULTY.—August 17th, at the Cathedral, Naul (with nuptial mass), George Polycarp Golly, very quietly *in secundas nuces*, to Teresa (Teasy), widow of the late Festus Nagle of the Naul, and granddaughter of Thomas Pontey (Tom), also of the Naul.

Weary and Barney are in this! I can see it all as plain as plain. First they codded Golly that it was fashionable to put in 'a bit of French', and then they chanced that *nuces* would slip in in mistake for *noces* and pass the compositor, and so make a complete fool of poor Golly. They had an idea that it would fetch me, B.A., T.C.D., and bring me racing down to meet them in Golly's to enjoy the joke. But how did it pass the editor's Horatian eye? Probably Weary, with his most quietly innocuous air, handed it in languidly to 'Fash', which means 'Fashionable Intelligence', and the boy in the front of the office who says 'O.K.' accepted it and charged the usual fee. It's no harm to cod the editor, who is one of those self-important fellows who never take a joke. I will send him this copy marked, for he keeps the staff up until the small hours, waiting until he has finished giving himself writers' cramp, writing his leaders and thinking that he is Addison.

'I will take another cup of tea, thank you, Mrs Creeley. Last night was rather loquacious, to say the least of it.'

'Saving your presence, I never seen more empties in all me born days.'

The reference was to certain bottles of stout which

were consumed during the vigil of the preceding evening and the night. The consumption was not confined solely to the residents of the Lying-in Hospital, but was due in some not inconsiderable measure to their friends and to the acquaintances of their friends. Even a lying-in hospital is not without its traditions of hospitality. As gentlemen about to become qualified we have a large understanding of human nature, for we never know when we ourselves shall have to depend on the hospitality 'after hours' of some other hospital. (I wonder if it is not from this that the word 'hospitality' is derived.) So we became 'wondrous kind', etc. But Lame Murta was accountable for at least a quarter of the twelve dozen. You have only to send down to Kennedy's if you doubt me. 'We have only a few gross bottled, and then there's reserves for Mr Murta out of that.' I must admit that he always paid on the nail. So with three dozen accounted for beforehand, so to speak, and Medlicott on duty, and Vincent in residence, and Weary and Barney bringing in Kinch from The Hay long after midnight – I won't include myself, for I am rather abstemious – 7 into 144 isn't anything like two dozen a-piece; and with the Lame Lad demanding an extra drink from us after every 'peroration', as he calls his speeches, you might call it about a dozen and a quarter to a man; and this stretched out until five in the morning, when, as everybody knows, life parts from the body by preference at four in the morning – it's little; and we having to tide ourselves over the critical hour and keep our loins girded to pull out the reserves against death, 'it's little or nothing,' as the cabman said when he swallowed the pint.

Lame Murta, as you might have diagnosed, is a decent fellow, though of course not of the same class, so to speak, as Birrell, but Birrell was doing his midwifery in the Rotunda, which is too close to my house to be suitable. My Aunt might have asked what would have been so obvious as to be banal, 'Why don't you live here and walk over to the Rotunda if and when you are required?' That would never have done. First of all the public could not have got that attention with its unremitting supervision which is its due and which only residents in hospitals can supply; and, secondly, there was something I didn't like in 'if and when'. So I came to Holles Street and met Lame Murta, who suffered from – what would Connolly Norman, the Lunacy doctor, have called it? Polylallia – that is, ceaseless speechifying.

There is a high cupboard with no top in a recess of the wall of the Residents' Room. That is to say, it is not roofed, so that, if you open one of the doors and climb up, using the shelves as rungs of a ladder, you will find yourself on the top shelf with a barrier in front of you like the rail of a platform. This, Lame Murta could not resist. He went up every night when we were in session, and orated. When we locked the cupboard door he was fixed for the night. He had to be locked up, for, if we turned our backs, he would fish himself up a bottle or two out of his turn. He was such a politician and such a polylallist that he nearly straggled into John Redmond's party, and he might now be representing the fens of Leitrim with distinction in Westminster only that he once was unparliamentary, he put things plainly. This the Press called blaspheming. He told the truth. It was at a try-out and they put him up to speak to a lot of 'the backbones of our country' at Drumshambo, when he says, 'There's one thing certain, that whatever comes out of it it's ye that'll get nothing. When did the poor man ever get anything out of a lot of politicians? And if ye elect one of yourselves to power, you'll only make him and yourselves worse : for ye'll be jealous and he'll get a swelled head. That's how it goes,' said Lame Murta. So, after a reprimand from Joe Devlin, who warned him against saying anything clear and definite when serving the country, he developed a great voice and a good complicated style.

He had been speaking for some hours from the top shelf when a lull comes in the conversation, and if we heard him it was not our fault.

'On one fact you may rest assured,' said Lame Murta. 'The day is not far distant when the Green Flag shall be seen. That day is not far distant.'

'Begob, it's not!' the Citizen shouts. 'Here's the dawn.'

'The sunburst of Erin,' Lame Murta went on, and all that kind of a thing. It's hard to remember three hours' oratory, and your mind would be good for nothing if you did.

Vincent got in a nasty one on Medlicott, who was on duty, when he said that his mind was more on the Labour Ward where a tram-man's wife was to be conducted than on Murta's cheap oratory. Now Medlicott is a very decent chap, but he is too easily enticed, if you see what I mean. So much so, that one Sunday, when he thought that his old fellow had gone off for a week-end, he was caught in bed with two women by the old lad's returning — unexpectedly I need not say. 'I don't mind,' says his father, 'the fact that you are turning your ancestral abode into a common stews, my young man, so much as the want of a sense of proportion your conduct reveals in a painful degree to me, your afflicted da. One woman is enough for ten men. Look at the wreck your Mother made of me.' The Medlicotts are a queer family. I think they must be Quakers, for they stick together and there is no scandal. But it was very regrettable because it was enough to upset the mutual trust and confidence on which family life is founded, for his father to return like that.

Medlicott heard a scream and he jumped up from his chair.

'Don't be an idiot. It's only her first pains,' said Vincent, who had good hearing, 'and it'll be time enough, and it's only decent to wait until you are wanted. The sister in charge will send for you in time. Meanwhile, try to observe a little professional conduct and don't be too anxious to butt into women's affairs, for that Wertt of Hamburg was burned at the stake.'

I thought I heard a low moan.

'You forget, my good friend,' said Medlicott, somewhat stiffly, to Vincent, who was resident in the Coombe and had fifty conductions to his credit, so he knew what he was talking about. Vincent was one of those medicals who find residence in hospitals so enjoyable that they deliberately leave one exam of the Final unpassed so as to continue in residence. He was dresser to Sir Thomas Myles, and that would make him eligible later on for residence in the Richmond, though all he had to 'dress' this morning he told me was a housemaid's knee. Where the dressing came in I couldn't . . .

'You forget, my good man, that while I am on duty I have charge of the Labour Ward, and while on duty I am responsible.'

'I suppose you were irresponsible when you were in charge of the Conception Ward in Harcourt Street?'

'He had a consultation with his father, I understand,' said Barney. It was a bit hard. 'There is a dialectic of conception in every parturition, I believe,' said Vincent, referring to me in jest. But I took it patiently. After all, what is philosophy for if you can't take a joke?

But Medlicott did not look like taking all this codding as a joke. God knows what he mightn't have done, but a sudden piercing scream reached the room from the room overhead and silenced us all but Lame Murta, who was not supposed to be in a hospital at all but at the hustings :

'To rescue the farmers of Ireland from this dire condition the Wyndham Act was devised. I say devised advisedly because it was not prepared and thrust with a "take it or leave it" at our heads.' The ceiling began to shake. Medlicott got up, and in a half-friendly way, not chucking it until he had first caught his eye, he slung an empty across the table at Vincent's head. Vincent put his hand up, but the bottle flew up and got the orator in the waistcoat. The Lame Lad caught it and said, as if replying to a heckler, 'The emptiness of this contribution is only equalled by the emptiness of the skull of him who flung it at a representative of the Irish people.' We cheered the Lame Fellow and sent him up a full one.

Another scream startled the air.

'That must be one of those thick-ankled ones,' said Vincent. 'They are broken in pieces when it comes to childbirth.'

Nobody asked why. So I inquired.

'It's like this,' he said, and he drew an oval on the tablecloth. 'Thick ankles go with an androgynous pelvis, and an androgynous . . .'

Kinch emitted a loud guffaw.

Kinch had poor manners. His laughter was to disguise his ignorance of the medical term for a man-woman pair of hips, and to entice the hearer to placate him and to provide the information that, once obtained, he would pose as having known. He put you in the wrong with his laugh. But I knew Kinch to the bone, and it was not well covered; so I said, making it as difficult for him to cod medicals as I could (for he was only a medical student's pal, not a medical by any means), 'Vincent, let Kinch into this. He knows damn all about Greek, and he hasn't the guts to say so but he tries to laugh it off.'

Vincent said, 'Is that so?' Then he went on to explain that it was all very well for a male athlete to have legs which could hold a coin in four places, between the thighs, at the knees, calves and ankles, but that wouldn't do for a woman. If they wanted to make their bottoms (Vincent wasn't really coarse, but we were all together and there were no ladies present) look like men's they had better not go in for child-bearing as a hobby, so to speak. It was all wrong. There was no antero-posterior room for the head. The child has to be born as if you wanted to force one egg through another held sideways and not on end. Now the true female pelvis is circular and the *conjugata vera* . . .

'The thin-ankled ones for me,' John yelled, excited, looking through the neck of a bottle of stout.

'In the blazon of love, which Brantome learned from the laughing lips of a lady of Toledo,' said Kinch, who had a hell of a knowledge about literature, medieval and the rest of it, 'there are three things that should be small in a woman, and the ankles are included.' But I knew Kinch had been reading a certain masterpiece on the life of François Villon.

There was another sound audible from the so-called Labour Ward, which was what used to be a back drawing-room of some forgotten gentle family fifty years ago.

'It's going hard with her,' said Weary Mac.

'God,' said Cosgrove, 'she'll be lucky if she has the child before the afternoon!'

'God!' I exclaimed. 'Is it as bad as that?'

'In a primipara certainly.'

I didn't like to appear sentimental before the bunch, but I couldn't help asking what the hell was the meaning of the aimless agony of childbirth.

'It serves them bloody well right,' the Citizen said, 'for keeping us waiting, keeping us guessing and then not turning up.'

I thought of Findlater's Church.

'It's supposed to increase mother-love,' said Weary Mac.

'Bunk!' said Barney. 'When that great fellow in Boston gave anæsthetics to women in labour, it was not with a loss of mother-love he had to contend but with a bloody bunch of bigoted ignoramuses who quoted the Bible at him until he quoted it back at them, and gave girls a whiff of ether.'

'He quoted?' Kinch asked.

'They said that . . .' While Barney was cudgelling his brains, sufficient silence fell to permit the voice of the orator being heard.

'Deserted as I am by my colleagues, and left to thirst at the hour of my peroration, I commend to the perpetual contempt of the Irish people men who could be so forgetful of the immemorial traditions of hospitals of this country as to . . .'

'Pass him up two or three, for God's sake,' Cosgrove commanded.

We cheered the Lame Fellow and passed them up.

Barney quoted – and it had a clerical ring coming from him in his black clothes – ' "Unto the woman, he said, I will greatly multiply thy sorrow and thy conception; in sorrow shalt thou bring forth children." '

'But what did that great huer in Boston answer?' Elwood asked.

'He turned the tables on the hypocrites – '

'On the sadists,' Kinch remarked, correcting us as it were.

'All he said was, " 'In the sweat of thy face shalt thou eat bread.' " I have seen very few clergymen conforming to that,' says he. That was all. After a brave fight against humbug and prejudice he gave the girls ether and made Boston at once the most humane and civilised capital in the world. Adam got an anæsthetic when the Lord did a costatectomy and he had Eve,' Vincent said.

But it was high time for me to show my knowledge and to take a share in the conversation. I took an interest in Midwifery, that is, I read the curious old books about it. I even read or read about that mad monk Jacob Rueff's extraordinary booklet written in 1544 at a time when only monks were permitted to discuss a subject taboo to all males other, for their hearts were pure : *A Very Cheerful Booklet of Encouragement concerning the Conception and Birth of Man and its Frequent Accidents and Hindrances*. I knew something about the history of anæsthetics and also about humbug. I was not going to see Dublin which is the high place of humbug beaten and Boston getting away with it. 'It was the old cods in Dublin and not Boston who resisted the use of chloroform in childbirth,' I said authoritatively. The boys listened, all except the orator who was supposed by this time to be in Westminster. 'Aye, at first they said it would cause convulsions, hæmorrhage, pneumonia and paralysis. Then when Simpson quoted the statistics of their own Rotunda and suggested that pain killed more than chloroform ever would, they started the hypocritical racket. Some of them wrote to ask Simpson did he not think that nobody in Dublin had as yet used anæsthetics in Midwifery (they probably knew bloody well that nobody had done so). They said that the feeling was very strong against its use in the ordinary cases merely to avert the ordinary amount of pain which the Almighty had seen fit – and most wisely no doubt – (whenever you hear anyone talking about the Almighty 'seeing fit' and saying 'no doubt' put him down for an aggressive humbug) to allot to natural labour,' and all the rest of the usual mush. When it comes to pure sanctimonious humbug you can't beat our old city. Why, the word 'cod' has been coined in Dublin to fill a pressing want. The City of the Old Cods.'

'Balls !' said Kinch.

'Baile-ata-Claith,' I replied, 'where "the feeling is very strong"; but where is the man who will speak out and tell the truth? No. It's always some sneaking, subterranean "feeling" which is very strong. To hell with humbug !' I was somewhat heated apparently.

The thought of all the immemorial, unnecessary woe

that our mothers had to undergo saddened me with the realisation of its futility, but against this the thought of the golden opportunity Medicine gave to us to do the one thing necessary, to give the one inestimable gift to humanity, the abolition of pain, cheered me. And I resolved to study this branch of Medicine seriously, for something more than a snook at McNought. I swore to keep half a pint of chloroform and a leaded-handled mask in my bag from that moment. When she was unconscious the mask would fall off.

'A lady doctor who had a kid, told me,' said John, 'that it's only after you are exhausted and fainting with agony that the real pains come on.'

'What puzzles me,' said I, 'is why they ever look at any of us.'

'Sometimes they don't,' the Citizen volunteered.

'Did she not meet you, John?' I asked.

'Yes, after three-quarters of an hour.'

'What kept her?'

'Maybe she had to wait a few minutes till she forgot her dear husband,' said John, with his merry eyes laughing at the suggestion.

'Has she thin ankles?' asked Weary Mac.

It is strange that when the orator shouted loudest the conversation was most engrossing and the more inaudible he became. As I was thinking to myself of the hopeless woe of the young mothers who never got an anæsthetic – for you can't call a rope to bear down with an anæsthetic – but were allowed to suffer on provided they were healthy, and this chiefly owing to the custom of their elders, the 'auld ones', who had a child in agony thirty years ago perhaps, and so insisted that the young women should 'go through it' in their turn – man's inhumanity to Man is as nothing compared with the remorseless and relentless inhumanity of woman to woman, or man for that matter; and the holiest women are the worst – the sound of the orator grew into sense. He was shouting about bursting. At first I thought that it was Erin bursting from her toils or gyves, or whatever she is to burst from, but it wasn't. A natural necessity constrained him painfully and he was roaring to us to take him down.

I drew the attention of Vincent to the plight of our friend.

'But Medlicott has the key,' was all he said.

'Get him a nurse,' Barney suggested.

'But, damn it all!' said I. Help was urgently required. Not until someone pointed out that the under shelves of the cupboard contained all our provisions did Barney go up for the key. He came back without it, explaining that Medlicott was swinging a ten-pounder to make it breathe. We sent him up again. Gingerly we lifted poor Murta down, and he disappeared from the room rapidly.

'Retention,' said Vincent.

But Kinch recited solemnly, 'Diodorus reports that among the Corsicans, and this is true of primitive races all over the world, particularly in Malaya, it is customary after the birth of a child for the father to withdraw himself and take to his bed as if in the pains of parturition, and to receive all the attention and the delicacies that in civilised races are usually reserved for the mother. Even his wife has to commiserate with him. This custom is called couvade. So while Murta is lying-in, you will understand, Gentlemen, that it is merely as a gesture of disapproval that I drink his bottle of stout.'

'It was only by the merest fluke that I realised that the Lame Fellow was complaining of his own and not mouthing the immemorial woes of this cheery land of ours. At first I thought it was the usual

'Lamentation and an ancient tale of wrong,
Like a tale of little meaning though the words be strong,
Chanted from an ill-used race,'

that he was giving in his outburst. And it was not the

Voice of the People we were listening to but the Voice . . .'

'You saved the groceries, Giddy,' Vincent said, interrupting.

Barney was smiling to himself. 'Cough it up,' Vincent commanded.

When she came out dazed from the chloroform she said she had heard a voice giving her a name for her newborn girl.

'It's a lovely name.'

'Medlicott looked a bit embarrassed. But I said that it was not usual to designate a girl by that name or to call the whole by the part; but that if she called her Virginia it would have somewhat the same sound and the advantage of having two more letters; but oh, what a difference in the meaning *and* the name.' But Barney's mind was a conundrum in itself.

Chapter XVIII

SUPPER WITH THE GODS

TRINITY COLLEGE,
DUBLIN.

MY DEAR FASOLT,

Am I never to see you again? If you are free come in and see me on Tuesday after dinner.

Always yours,
FAFNIR.

It was an invitation from the dear Master of Those Who Know. I call him Fafnir because we were so often lagert in the evenings under the yews. And he called me Fasolt. It will be a welcome change from this *uncta popina* in which I live. There are some names which, the moment they are heard, you realise that the owners of them you will never meet. Jack Lalor the barber is certainly one. Never, I know intuitively, shall I meet that figure face to face, associated as he is in my mind with early morning, running dogs, and modern instances. He will always move as elusive on my horizon as summer lightning, incandescent, intangible.

Piano Mary is another who might be perceived as in a glass darkly but never *facie ad faciem*. Oh, no! And yet the name 'Piano Mary' intrigues me, as the antique dealers say when they mean 'interests'. Is she some governess gone astray, which means that she has reached the Kips and there got her name from jeering companions who, jealous of the lady-like accomplishments of music, mock her by that nickname? It is no good conjecturing.

To me she is airy nothing and nothing but a name and unsubstantial. But 'Mahaffy'! That is a substantial name. I know I shall meet Mahaffy, maybe this very night. When the Master asks his friends to wine in his rooms after dinner in the Hall it is, to use a meiosis, enjoyable.

I hope that that friend of mine, Jimmy, behind the Bank, has seen to it that my dress suit is properly valeted. I wonder what interest he will charge. I haven't seen the thing for three months, and if you leave it in a day longer with the interest unpaid, it is liable to be – 'Auch! Bosh. I've heard all that.' And with his voice rising and his manner becoming more martial, 'Out it goes! Auctioned out of hand! What do you take me for? That'll do ye, now. Going, going, gone!' But Jimmy's sentences are liable to be remitted, and I am sure that he has not sold my dinner jacket and dress suit. And the louder he expostulates the cheaper he'll let it out. Especially when I tell him whom I am going to meet. It will sink in deeply before he deprecates it with 'Mahaffy? I know all about Mahaffy. "Epic and Lyric Poets" – three bob! Published at twelve-and-six!' If I could only hire it for the evening. It 'locks up a bit of capital', as the stockbrokers say, to take it out. And you replace it *ex div.*

It will be good to meet the Master and to have to report to him, or rather to have to report that I met a gentleman in the Medical School who gave me a high pass in Midwifery. And be it recorded his name is Purefoy – Dr Purefoy, the Pure of Faith. What a noble title for a man, even though the faith he had at the moment was only faith in me! He knows how to examine in Midwifery. He brings out the best points of a man. 'Are you a son of my friend, the late owner of those magnificent red setters?'

The answer was in the affirmative.

'Tell me now, was Rufus a get of Garryowen? Had not your father a share in Garryowen with Giltrap, or did he send his bitches to be served by that great dog?'

'That I cannot say. He and Giltrap were great friends, and they used to go off shooting together.'

'Have you any dogs now?'

'We have one red setter, Rufina, but it has never been shot over. It is a bitch.'

That appealed to him. There is a dialectic of a litter in a bitch.

'Now if you take an old man's advice, get her covered by a get of Garryowen. I have the greatest admiration for that dog, and any blood of his is sure to have a perfect head and fine feather. Be careful that she doesn't get distemper. It is a pity to keep a setter as a carriage dog.' I refrained from telling him that we had no carriage, but I promised to look after the process of procreation and parturition. 'Now, coming to the matter before us. Suppose you were attending a woman in a mountainy dispensary and you were without help, and you ascertained it was a case of a breech presentation, what would you do?'

I dared not risk it. He had been so kind up to this. I would not have hesitated to tell McNought, had he been Professor of Midwifery (Oh, not the woman, Lord!), that I would have put out the cat. He would have been sure to fall for it and to ask severely, 'What has the cat got to do with it?' Then very blandly, for I would be stuck in any case, I would say, 'You know what to expect from a mountainy labour? *Nascitur ridiculus mus.*' But when I looked at the aristocratic face of the simple-mannered and simple-minded old gentleman with the little cyst beside his nose, and his tall hat which they say he wears while operating, beside his hands, and his scarf caught up in an old-world flat oval ring, I could not think of being facetious. Instead of ill-timed jocularity, I assumed a look of the utmost concern, put out an effort and did my best to 'satisfy the examiner'. I took no risk with words, however.

My experience with examiners teaches me that words are treacherous currency; and as this was a matter of handling, for a breech presentation calls for technique and not talk, I put myself in the attitude of a man about to trundle a barrel or a long-shoreman trying to revolve a bollard or a capstan with his hands. He nodded in complete understanding. My gesture was nearly as unavoidable as the automatic gesture one makes when asked what is a circular stair like. I maintained a felicitous silence, sighed a little and wiped imaginary 'drops of onset' from my brow, for version is apt to be an exhausting feat.

The fifteen minutes allowed for the *viva voce* were running out quite harmlessly – so far. Again he nodded, but asked, 'And then?' Wishing to keep Midwifery on as elevated a plane as possible, I said: 'And then I would render thanks to Providence for providing a sufficient quantity of amniotic fluid to enable me to bring down the head.' Being himself of a religious turn of mind, he forbore to probe further into the inscrutable ways of Providence. Greatly impressed, he said: 'I suppose you will adopt Midwifery as your speciality when you are qualified?' The last thing I thought of saying was that I would prefer any branch of the *praxis*, even the treatment of V.Ds., to Midwifery.

'I do not know yet. But I have spent a long time in residence in a lying-in hospital,' was all I said. The dialectic in that was evident. Long residence suggested short study as the one thing necessary fully to equip me to act on the body as Socrates acted on the mind. But 'when you are qualified' had a hopeful ring. It meant that he was not making himself an obstacle to that happy event. I looked at Dr Barry's certificate. It sounded magnificent when read aloud:

This is to certify that this student has attended the practice of the National Maternity Hospital from 20th April to 20th

October, and has attended forty cases, having personal charge of fourteen.

(*Signed*) P. J. BARRY,
Master.

That's enough to increase the birth-rate on Mount Athos. It's enough to set me up for life. If the women knew I had half a pint of chloroform in my little bag, they would all call me in. Birth, where is thy sting? 'Does your mother know you're out?'

I hope that there will be another outbreak of gentility in the Medical School when it comes to Medicine and Surgery. I cannot hope to come across a better sportsman and gentleman than Dr Purefoy. What the hell does it matter if he does operate in a tall hat? It won't harm his patients when he is performing version and bringing down the head. In fact, his hat might have the effect of inductive magic on the child. Anything can happen in Midwifery. And where the head is of so much importance why not a hat? To my mind it introduces a note of tradition and exclusiveness, as do the tall hats in the old photographs of cricketers I have seen. Dr More-Madden always wears his tall hat, and I never heard anything against headgear in Midwifery except it be the doubt cast on paternity in a case where a young mother was questioned about the colour of her husband's hair, and could not tell because he was wearing his hat at the time, a fact which, while it may go a long way to prove the poet's 'saw aright' that 'he never loved who loved not at first sight', is far from suggesting that it could have been a tall hat. I think, on the whole, that we must concede the crown to Dr Purefoy. Anyway, he has provided me with good news for the Master, and the Master is sure to provide the wherewithal for rejoicing to-night.

I knew it! Mahaffy was there. A great figure of a man that the fact of his being seated could not diminish. His auburn cheek whiskers held more colour than his long flat hair, which was brushed straight down the side of his magnificent head. He wore an open collar and a white clerical tie. The effect of his presence on two scholars ranged near the Master's piano was as inducive to conversation as the effect of a merlin on a brace of blackbirds. I too was afraid of him. I had heard so many stories of his sarcasm – for instance, his question to the man who called himself Swift-Delaney on the plea that he was descended from Dean Swift, 'By whom? Stella or Vanessa?'

But that master of the art of conversation was not going to leave them long on tenterhooks. He was about to put them at their ease. He believed (what he had written) that 'the *sine qua non* of good conversation is to establish equality, at least momentarily, if you like fictitious, but at all costs equality among members of the company who make up the party.' He was most tactfully doing that when I arrived. The Master met me at the door and drew me into the room on the opposite side of his little hall. Forests of hock skirted the wall. Darker and bulkier bottles of claret formed as it were a copse. His favourite Chateau d'Yquem was ranged on the window-sill. An open bottle awaited me – perhaps I should say, us. 'Quickly, taste that and get ready to come; the Vice-Provost is with us. We spoke about you.' It did me good – not the news, but the drink. I tried to recall some advice from the *Art of Conversation* regarding the behaviour of inferiors in the presence of the great, but I was too diffident and confused. Yet I knew that the company might be more than five but that it would not exceed eight, 'a form of society the best and most suitable for talk.' What, how would he receive me? He was getting others out of an embarrassment similar to mine.

'Weally, gentlemen [either he could not, like a few I have met, pronounce his *r*'s or he affected to be unable

187

to do so; the fact that a well-known Earl is similarly afflicted may be a contributory cause], you are hardly fair to me, nor indeed to yourselves. Our good friend here might imagine I was the Tywant of Antioch.' A transient smile fled from his lips. 'You remember, of course, how Antiochus Epiphanes would come and sit and drink and joke with his subjects as if to share their amusements. Let me tell you that he was disappointed, and they were far from being amused by his vagaries. His subjects mistrusted his familiarity. That conduct is wather out of date : none of us is subject to another, so let us keep the λεγόμενον ἐς μέσον, as the Greeks say. Pull your chairs closer to the fire. After all we must remember that conversation means a feast to which all must contribute, an *eranos*, a contributory feast. Therefore let us help our host.

'I was asking these young people not to treat me as if being a Don meant being excluded from their conversation. I spoke of the habit of the Tyrant of Antiochus of entering into the houses of recreation of his subjects with the most disappointing results. He, poor man, wanted to join in their conversation, they withheld through embarrassment the one thing, I will venture to say, that would have delighted and flattered him – their society : but they refused to exchange opinions, they refused to let him enter into their discourse. What do you think of that?'

No one replied. He looked from face to face in vain. He was nettled at his own want of success in 'drawing' his audience.

The Master egged me on just as the Vice-Provost repeated the question in another form. 'What do you think he was seeking?' I remembered it, the quotation! In the manner of the Master I quoted it up towards the ceiling.

'Goodly discourse is more hidden than the precious green stone, yet it is found with the slave girls over the mill stones.'

Probably because he did not know where I got it, he ignored my effort and went on as if I had not made a remarkable contribution to the conversation.

'But there is nowadays no such profound gulf as that fixed. On the contrary, we can enjoy each other's society because a University, if it means anything, means the intellectual meeting-place for those who are capable of an universal outlook. Where did you get this claret, if it is not an impertinent question, McGurk?'

The Master said that he had bought it at an auction.

'Ah, another of the great houses sold, and its precious treasures distributed.' Then, with a suggestion of concern in his voice, 'You do not remember whose place it was? I hope it was not the house of some close friend of ours.'

The Master said that one of the scholars, Yourell, came from beside Banbridge.

'Ah, how is my very good friend Sir Harrington McCutcheon? Is he as good a gun as ever? I remember a bag which was quite remarkable: an hundred brace of partridge. His pointers are excellent.'

Yourell was about to stutter a reply when I was introduced.

'A medical student. The bi-centenary of your School will, I hope, be celebrated. It should be only a few years from now. Let me see. It was founded by a clergyman. The Rev. John Sterne. A remarkable fellow. An extraordinary divine who was in the habit of quoting Scripture frequently without a word which reveals the Christian. He takes no account of the work of any church, he never even preaches about the doctrines of the Church of England: it is Chrysippus, it is Marcus Aurelius, it is Seneca, it is Epictetus above all who are his spiritual masters; never once, I think, does he speak of the life and death of Jesus Christ as the source of the soul's enduring happiness.' Then with a faint but charming smile, as the thought about to come to be expressed amused him, 'But he never says one word against it!'

He turned, still smiling, as if to say, 'What will you?' I thought to myself, here was another 'extraordinary divine', greater than Sterne, and more a citizen of that city which is the spirit's capital for so many cultivated men – Athens. By his own words he is exemplifying 'the importance given to social talents over morals and religion – a truly Irish feature.'

What an effect, far greater than anyone knows, must this kind of bright cynicism have had on the young Oscar Wilde twenty-five years ago!

'By the way, Fotheringham, that was an excellent Greek note you made about Chrysippus. I read it with great pleasure. It was amusing to find you quoting Diogenes Laertius, "If the gods are dialectic they can use none other than Chrysippus." ' Then to the servant, 'You will boil that claret if you put it so near the grate. Leave it there; leave it where it is, can't you?'

The Master filled Fotheringham's glass to make him talk, and he was thawing as pleasantly as the claret, after the warm appreciation of his Greek prose.

'When you mentioned the Tyrant of Antioch, it made me think of Nero, who also wished to go about disguised among the people in the taverns and other places.'

'Nero had the artistic temperament. Perhaps more temperament than he could manage. Indeed, a little more than his artistic output could possibly justify. But then we must remember, if the last words attributed to him are not supplied by someone as a critical epitaph, he never claimed to be an artist, but an artifex, which is quite a different thing! *Qualis artifex pereo.* One might almost say a 'producer' or a playboy. For the first five years of his reign he was quite a gentleman and extremely popular. We must not permit ourselves to forget that the golden *Quinquennium Neronis* was one of the most fortunate phases of human history. You see, he had worked under a master. But once he got beyond Seneca's influence, well, he rusticated himself, so to speak.' With his claret-coloured lips he savoured the purpler vintage, and, looking about him, smiled. I was inwardly amused by the phrase 'worked under a master'. It was a favourite one of Mahaffy. It meant that you should work under a don in either Trinity, Dublin, or Oxford University. He had returned an excellent essay, 'Pencraft', by the great poet William Watson, to George Wilkins, the lecturer in classics, with the remark, 'The whole thing is perfectly true; but I am afraid that the fellow has not worked under a master.' He hadn't paid his fees and disciplined his mind in T.C.D. or Oxford.

'Was not Seneca's brother that Gallio, Proconsul of Achaia, who tried St. Paul and "cared for none of these things"?' Fotheringham asked with befitting diffidence. And well it was that for him diffidence was expressed in his voice. It softened what was tantamount to a rebuke.

'Now let us be very careful. Let us tread warily. We must use our knowledge of the exact position. First of all – yes, you are quite right – Gallio was a brother of Seneca. He was called Junius Annæus Novatus Gallio because his father's friend, Junius Gallio, adopted him, educated him. In fact it was adoption. He was a man of a most amiable nature. Statius, you remember, calls him "sweet". Now, as I said, let us be very careful. St. Paul's appearance before Gallio hardly amounted to a trial. His case was dismissed. It should never have been brought to the notice of the Proconsul. No race is more litigious than the Jewish race once they quarrel among themselves. "What, another Jewish quarrel!" you can hear Gallio exclaiming, followed of course by a riot. Well, he left them to their hysterical brawling. He probably was not displeased when he heard that the Corinthians mobbed the head of the synagogue. It was for Jewish squabbles and their rights or wrongs and things of that sort he did not care, in fact he must have been extremely bored by the Jews; but for the things that really mattered, the things of abiding worth – ah, that was different! For these things he did care. We must remember that it was a rhetorician by whom he was adopted. He was a highly cultivated man, probably a Stoic – most of the gentlemen in Rome were Stoics.'

As the lecture was sinking into Fotheringham, I heard a stick tapping on the stairs. Someone was arriving.

The Master, who was growing mellow and sentimental, said: 'I have a warm corner in my heart for Nero. He liked music. He did a lot for the Greeks.'

'And Plutarch put him, for the sake of his voice, with the frogs in the underworld.' My effort passed ignored.

'On my last visit to Greece and the Islands I passed through the Corinthian canal, which was begun by Nero. It was interesting to see a bust of the Emperor set into the cliff side of brown stone, among the nests of the little brown hawks which are the only representatives of bird-life in Greece, for they do not eat grapes.'

Now I had heard a lot about that trip to Greece. I heard that when cruising among the Isles Mahaffy knocked, about two o'clock in the ambrosial night, loudly on the cabin door of the bishop of Thasos: 'Get up! Get up! You are passing your diocese! Thasos!'

But no one was talking to me. I gazed about the room until my eye caught a plaster copy of a plaque with his portrait in relief which some admirer had presented to the Vice-Provost. It was a poor likeness because it made his nose too heavy.

I heard a pleasant voice in the Hall. The Master went out to receive its owner. In a minute the door opened and with a bright face the Benign Doctor entered, warbling little greetings as he made his way in. He got a curt nod from Mahaffy. They were not exactly boon companions. But I got from the Doctor a very gracious hand-shake. The Master followed him with a syphon and a decanter of Jameson. Soon he found an armchair.

'Ah, my friend, you may fill it up. Thanks. Well, now, I fear that I am a little late, a little breathless. It is not easy to get away from Ranelagh nor to return to that delectable retreat.' He gazed graciously round the room, as amiable, as charming, and as sweet a man as Gallio was said to have been. He sipped his whiskey-and-soda. Had George Wyndham continued in office until a vacancy occurred the Benign Doctor would have been Provost.

'We were just discussing the predilection of Nero for tavern company,' the Master explained, 'and we put it down to his artistic temperament.'

Now an awful suspicion clouded up in my mind. The conversation had grown out of Nero's desire for low company and it had, as all good conversation should, put out branches with more and more delightful blooms. We had got from his tutor, Seneca, to the brother of that tutor, Gallio. Why, then, this harping back to the tavern part and the low company? I would be slow to believe that the Master would lend himself to such a thing, but it looked remarkably like an attempt to influence me by Mahaffy's authority and disdain of common people. He knew that I was afraid of Mahaffy. A letter from my aunt would have done the trick, not to mention my mother. They did not like some of my haunts. The artistic temperament was 'suspect', for that had been frequently employed as an excuse on my behalf by the Master himself when wrangling with McNought.

Mahaffy said : 'I am afraid that the artistic temperament is no excuse for being attracted by low life to the detriment of duty. Mark Antony had no artistic temperament, yet we find him very frequently among the sons of Belial.'

The Benign Doctor, holding his tumbler in his hand, said in a high-pitched tone : 'Well now, Mahaffy, I am not quite so sure. Of course Marcus Antonius may not have appreciated the best society, but before he was so warmly received by royalty we find him in Athens assuming to himself all the attributes of the god Dionysus. That looks rather like the temperament of an artist to me. "His delights were Dolphin-like, they showed his back above The Element they lived in." So Cleopatra defended him.'

How the Citizen would agree, I thought: 'a great Artist!' Yes, Nero was more of an 'artist' in the Citizen's sense than Mahaffy's.

With the Benign Doctor to take my part, I ventured: 'Dionysus affords the only example of a member of the vegetable kingdom becoming a god. The apotheosis of the vine.'

'On the other hand, we are not without examples of what we might call a de-deification or a contra-apotheosis when a god turns, or rather nymph or demi-goddess turns, into a vegetable. Let me see. Syrinx when pursued by Pan turns into a reed; and then, of course, there was Daphne, who became a laurel.'

'Apollo must have had a pretty knowledge of landscape gardening before the end of his escapades,' I ventured.

On my right hand came a rumble. 'You dirty brute. Is nothing sacred to you? Not even poor Daphne?' With his great head rolling on his chest, he quoted sentimentally:

' "Like Phoebus thus acquiring unsought praise
He catch'd at Love and filled his arm with bays," '

extending his own arms as he did so and grasping an imaginary tree. He was about to repeat it in a lower tone, muttering it to himself, when the Doctor asked, with a lighted, smiling face:

'Now, my friend, where did you get that? One of the Elizabethans?'

'You are nearly right. Yes; you are quite right, sir,' said the Master, bridging sixty years. 'It is from Waller, who published it about 1670 – he may have written it much earlier, but, of course, he was born within the spacious days.' Then, as if overcome by the sentiment, he muttered, 'Everything goes indirectly in this world : seeking Love he gets Fame. He got fame when all he wanted on this earth was a little fondness.' Self-pity stopped the rest.

The Doctor committed to memory, smiling gently to himself as he repeated it.

'An excellent image,' Mahaffy averred as he too repeated it.

Yes, I thought, a lovely image : the poet, singing his heart out to his elusive love, fails to win her but finds the unfading laurel on his brow. It is the pursuit of the fleeting image, the Eternal Feminine in Nature that brings us any immortality we can earn and not the direct pursuit of Fame.

As I say, they were not boon companions, and my intervention did not alter the fact that for one who had been dominating the evening to be corrected on a point of scholarship or on any point at all before younger men, was uncomfortable. It was as if Dr Johnson had been answered back. But the great Mahaffy –

'Yclept Mahoof by those of heavenly birth,
But plain Mahaffy by the race of earth' –

said, unkindly as I thought : 'No ostentation of scholarship can hide from us the fact that Mark Antony, though he was loyal to his friend Cæsar, rather flaunted his love affairs, and therefore cannot be considered to have been a gentleman.'

'Ostentation' was distinctly uncalled for; besides, it was a quotation from Goldsmith. In a way the Benign One asked for it, for there were phrases, such as 'best society' and 'received by royalty', which might be taken to glance at certain noble infirmities in Mahaffy.

The piano sounded, gently at first. The Master was casting about in his mind what to play. He was an accomplished pianist.

'A lyric of Chopin would not be unwelcome to you gentlemen,' the Vice-Provost suggested. We accepted in silence, only broken by little humming sounds from the Doctor, who wanted to talk to me and to quote. The conversation, instead of being kept in the middle owing to the effect of it on him who recommended that treatment, was now divided up. The Doctor used the music for a background much in the same way as we used Lame Murta in Holles Street.

'Masterful or rather mothering women like George Sand discovered the fact that a croquet-playing little curate can be far more devoted to the Cyprian exercises than a bearded Hercules. She carried Chopin, than whom she was five years older, to an empty monastery in Majorca and "mothered him so assiduously that he died probably of devotion, though nominally of tuberculosis".'

'Tuberculosis seems to accentuate libido or sexual passion,' I remarked. 'There is a tuberculous tailor in the Whitworth Hospital who is the father of nine children.'

'As it takes nine tailors to make a man,' the Doctor quoted, 'he is only reproducing himself once. Talking about medical terms – you have just mentioned "tuberculosis". I wish you would ask your professors and other members of your learned profession not to mispronounce such words as paresis (the "e" is short), angina, elephantiasis, and even enema.'

The wine was beginning to give me courage. I had been a student of Mahaffy's works, so I risked this : 'Had there been any night life in Athens Alcibiades might not have proved himself a gentleman. In fact, he can hardly be regarded as such by us from the way he treated his dogs.'

It went down well with the second bottle of claret.

'You are quite right.' He turned with a swimming smile to the company. 'He cut off the tail of his dog. It is usually a gentleman who possesses a good dog, but to maltreat one!' He gestured with his hand impatiently.

I must be a gentleman, I thought, for I have a good dog with a finely feathered tail. The thought gave me a feeling of equality. It is a pity that I cannot bring it into College – no dogs admitted except Mahaffy's dog.

'Dwellingcourt, you must drink something,' the Master said to the scholar who sat uncomfortably by the piano. Without waiting for an answer he bent his head over the keyboard and sang –

'We were young, we were merry, we were very, very wise
    And the door stood open at our feast.
And there passed by a woman with the West in her eyes
    And a man with his back to the East.'

He muttered to himself, then looked reproachfully at Dwellingcourt. Dwellingcourt muttered an excuse with a Northern accent. It occurred to me that with the exception of the Benign Doctor and myself all were from the North. The Master certainly; Mahaffy was a Monaghan man. I was not too exempt, for I had a Monaghan grandmother. The Doctor was a Tipperary man and came from Ballingarry, a son of the resident gentleman of the parish of Kinnity. Is the whole College composed of Northerners?

I cannot say if it was because Dwellingcourt 'sat in a corner' and had the Doctor's attention drawn to him unsympathetically by his teetotalism, but the Doctor began moaning musically, for he was about to give birth to something rich and rare. At last he recited against the background of the empty monastery in Majorca which was echoing on the piano:

'Little Jack Horner.'
'Cornuti proles petiit penetralia tecti
Scriblitam referunt quam Saturnalia rodens:
Extrahit inde puer prunum dum pollice clamat,
"Non Numa non Tatius prunum me castior edit."'

I knew that a speculative inquiry into the subject of

Jack Horner was expected of me. He took pleasure in investigating with me and in giving exaggerated consideration and attaching preposterous importance to such trifles. Maybe he did it as a parody on more speculative and less resolvable questions.

I led off: 'As a son of a cornucated father I wonder how little Jack came to be so self-assertive. He did not get it from his father, for one would imagine that in that household his mother would have been the dominating partner. I will admit, of course, that he may have been a mother's darling, and so a spoilt child.'

The Doctor smiled; and, with his face lighting said: 'If we take Shakespeare's view,

> ' "The horn, the horn, the lusty horn
> Isn't a thing to laugh to scorn,
> For your father wore it,
> Your father's father bore it." '

the name "Horner" would perpetuate a long descent.'

'Of course! Sir, I should have thought of that. The Cornuti must have been an old Roman family. There is mention of one Cornutus in Tibullus whom the poet does not doubt but that he will ask for a wife's true love when he is praying the gods for favours on his birthday. That would lead me to suspect . . .'

'A moment now . . . Let me see how is this it goes. Oh, yes!

> ' "Auguror, uxoris fidos optabis amores."

There I do not think arises any question of her infidelity. That Cornutus was not troubled by "A word of fear, Unpleasing to a married ear," as Shakespeare appears to have been. For the sake of the integrity of the House of Horner, I prefer to think that it was owing to paternal prowess that the patronymic was conferred. Could you not turn the theme into verse, presuming that all we have before us of the famous family is my little composition? I know that it is not easy to collect one's wits with all the results of the George Sand menage reverberating in our ears.'

It certainly was not. But in quieter circumstances the Doctor and I often exchanged alternate verses : my English for his Latin or Greek. I must not fail him now. The moment was unpropitious. The atmosphere was charged and my head . . . but let that pass.

'I must tell you that, as there is no suitable word in Latin for pie, I use "Scriblitam", a tart or a cake like those we see at Christmas with "For a good boy" or some such nonsense written on it in sugar . . .'

'Impossible at the moment, Sir?' I said.

Seeing Dwellingcourt refusing wine, Mahaffy said : 'Good gracious, Dwellingcourt, surely you are not one of that unsocial sect, a teetotaller? It is the height of folly apart from its being bad – well, rather an unusual phenomenon. How do you toast the Royal Family? In water? Phocylides recommended light and good-humoured banter over the wine cup. Come, now, drink wine and answer me back.'

I pitied the struggling Dwellingcourt. I was beyond the suspicion of being bigoted in that way. But he should have said something – that is, he should have brought something to the contributory feast. Then I should not have had to take his place in the gap, as I had to do when the Master, despairing of Dwellingcourt, called on me. 'Tell the Vice-Provost your couplet on Dawson.'

'Dawson?' Mahaffy asked. 'Let me get it quite clear. Who is Dawson?'

'Oh, he is one of those pernicious little fellows who have never been to a University and yet who set themselves up to pass judgment on things they do not and cannot understand. They have never worked under——' I was afraid to risk it, so I amended it into, 'They have never worked under conditions which would assure a liberal outlook, and yet they sneer at those who have an Athenian view of life.'

'Quite, quite. But the couplet. An epigram, I trust.'

'Dawson had a father who, if not worse, was just as self-assured. He imagined that he could be all things to all men, and, wishing to patronise me, he assured me one evening that he never went to sleep without reading a few chapters of Sappho. Here is the couplet upon Dawson :

' "No need to boast yourself well-read, the gift's hereditary rather,
I read before I go to bed *chapters* of Sappho. Thus your father." '

The sarcasm of the thing attracted Mahaffy. But he did not laugh. The Benign Doctor suggested that Dawson's father was to be envied, for he must be in possession of an unknown papyrus which would be extremely valuable if it were genuine. 'But it is probably a palimpsest.'

'I never take more than two bottles of claret, thanks. Now I will smoke. I cannot understand people who drink wine while smoking. It is a barbarism. How can the palate appreciate wine when fumigated by tobacco? But having taken as much wine as one can relish, a cigar is an excellent entertainment. Thank you, McGurk.' The Master helped Mahaffy.

The Doctor, who never smoked, took a loud helping of snuff. If the Master gives me a cigar, it will mean that it will put an end to my drinking. I perceived Mahaffy watching me, so I could not swallow hurriedly what was left in the glass. I thought of the boys in hospital who never imagined that tobacco should set a period to their drinking. But it was not wine they drank. I sipped my glass delicately, and banished from my mind all memories or imaginations of bottles of stout.

'Talking of Sappho,' the Doctor warbled, 'it was the

custom for the boys of noblest birth to pour out the wine. The beautiful Sappho often sings of her brother Laricus as serving the wine in the town hall of Mytilene.'

'I am afraid that we have lost many of the noble customs which were associated with drinking,' the Master observed, and sighed sentimentally. I hope that he won't break out with, 'Fasolt, you dirty brute!' or some such friendly epithet.

'In all the centuries since history began we know of no woman who could be said with any approach to the truth to have rivalled her as a poet, so Strabo says. And I like to think that she was not above permitting her brother to persuade her to take a glass or two. "Just try this, a little Lesbian,"' said the Doctor, dramatising his idea. 'Then after a few glasses she could say, "Up, my lute divine and make thyself a thing of speech." And they sang till dawn. It is extraordinary when we consider the freedom of refined women as early as the sixth century.'

'Particularly when we think that they lived so close to Asia. Why, even at the present time there is no such freedom, no such use of the night. Of course, I am not forgetting the excellence of their climate,' Mahaffy said; 'no such freedom, no such freedom at all.'

'Our friend here would cure that by Home Rule,' said the Master, indicating me.

It was a shame. I saw the whole thing now. My suspicions were well-founded. He had promised that he would get the Vice-Provost 'to talk to me' so that I would be cured of being *cupidus rerum novarum*, as Mahaffy would say. And he did say it the very next minute.

'So you are *cupidus rerum novarum*, my good friend?'

It was more embarrassing to be his good friend, for I would be expected not to disappoint his confidence in me. It is a damned shame for the Master to let me in for this.

'Well, sir, I thought that this College, which has

produced all the Irish patriots with the exception of one or two, would not find it amiss in me if I interested myself in modern political thinking.'

'Well?'

'The Irish people would advance to – Well, they'd be better off if governed by themselves than – '

What are the seven pillars of Sinn Fein? I couldn't remember. I was putting up an unconvincing show.

'Get this clearly into your head. There is no greater freedom on earth than that of Great Britain. Would you impose that constitution on the Irish people? If it is not in them it will not suit them. And it cannot be super-imposed. A constitution is the self-expression of a people. Surely you would not impose English freedom on the "oppressed" Irish? Any other constitution would be per-fectly worthless without competent public opinion. Where is it? Competent public opinion? Not in pot-houses or disloyal societies or leagues.' I saw Michael Cusack's obtrusive calves diminishing rapidly before the inner eye.

It will be some time before I will come to one of Fafnir's wine parties, after being let in for this, I re-solved. He can drink by himself so far as I am con-cerned. The lecture was going on. I was missing it, thinking of Fafnir.

'Why, only the other day,' I heard, 'only the other day, in the backwoods of King's County, in some out-landish and backward village, a poor woman was buried alive as a witch. Probably she was doubled up with rheumatism. But some cows died in the vicinity and they buried her alive. I forget the name of the parish. It will come to me in a moment. A perfectly backward and benighted and ignorant place. Oh, yes, Kinnity. What do you think of that, Tyrrell?'

I might have guessed that he did not like the Benign Doctor. But this was more than 'the light and good-humoured banter' that Phocylides, or whoever he said it was, recommends.

'Kinnity, Tyrrell, where they buried the old woman alive. What do you think of that?'

Slowly the Doctor, who had been enjoying his glass, laid it down, and, placing the tips of his shapely fingers together, pretended to give the question deep consideration. At length he said cheerfully: 'Well, after all, it is only a case of premature burial, which is not so bad a thing as delayed burial which you so grievously exemplify, Mahaffy.'

'Good God!'

And we could not get out until our seniors went first. Magnificently the Master came to the rescue. 'Surr!' he muttered, letting it be presumed that he was drunk. He took the arrows that thronged the air into his own breast. 'Surr, we all want to hear of your meeting with the lunatic when you went to call on Connolly Norman.'

'Ah, my good friend, it is not necessary to go so far to meet with such folk. Now that you remind me, this is what occurred. I was going to pay a long-delayed visit to my old friend that remarkable psychologist, when an irascible fellow' (I thought that he emphasised 'irascible' somewhat) 'jumped out from behind a bush and accosted me with "You don't know who I am."

' "I am afraid that I have not that pleasure," I said. "Who might you be?"

' "Oh, I might be anybody," he said in quite an offhand manner. "But the fact is that I am Julius Cæsar."

' "I am charmed. Good morning, Cæsar!"

'On my way back the same fellow accosted me again. "You do not know who I am?"

' "On the contrary, my friend, I do. You are Julius Cæsar."

' "Wrong! I am Napoleon."

' "But ten minutes ago you told me you were Julius Cæsar. How can you be Napoleon?"

' "Same father, different mothers." '

We laughed so long with glee, both genuine and

counterfeited, that the Vice-Provost was led to think that the Doctor's shaft had found no mark.

I must have guffawed as loudly as Kinch can, for the Vice-Provost singled me out, but though it was an honour, it was not altogether to my credit.

'Can you recollect any more of the Proverbs of Ptah-Hotep, one of which you quoted so happily?' And I thought that he had not heard me!

To the Master, who was seeking to improvise something on the piano, he said sharply as if to steady him, 'Play that touching andante from Brahms's symphony in E minor.' This was merely an aside. He turned to me again. 'Can you recollect any more of those excellent proverbs of Ptah-Hotep from the Old Kingdom 2980 and so on for about 500 years B.C.? What a civilisation they had even then! They kept the ball in the middle, they respected conversation and held it, and not its enemy, wit, which is explosive, in high regard.' (He was coming back steadily.) 'They considered it an art. How is this it goes?' He bent his great memory to it. 'Oh, yes: *He who giveth good counsel is an artist, for speech is more difficult than any craft.*' And I thought that he didn't know where I got the quotation. My God! is there anything he doesn't know? Now I hoped that he never would know because I read it in *Answers* – one morning. I never heard of the Old Kingdom. The only kingdom I had heard of was the Middle Kingdom, but that was in China.

I felt like a man imprisoned in a surrounded house. There was no escape from knowledge. If I tried Greek – but who would have that audacity in Trinity College? The Doctor knew as much Greek as Plato – almost. If I tried Philosophy, what a hope! Antiquities, Egyptian, Greek, Chinese? I was rounded up in the Old Kingdom a minute ago. Music? the Master and Mahaffy had, what is extremely rare in a generation, perfect musical ears. Politics? I had already let Arthur down. English, even if

204

I slipped a rare quotation past the Master there was always Dowden out in the Front Square. I couldn't even try drinking, fearing that I might be described as 'in my cups'. I was trapped. I know that I should be feeling very glad to be 'trapped'; for that my mother was paying. But it is sometimes painful to feel like a goldfish surrounded by the crystal sphere of knowledge in which all I could do was to go round and round in a circle and gape. I know what is wrong with me. Whenever I feel like this my mind is being formed! 'Bear it, father! Bear it! It will be the making of the pup,' as the boy said to his sire when the bulldog seized his nose. I should be proud to be with the gods. So I am!

'An artist, mark you, for speech is more difficult than any craft,' the greatest talker in Europe continued. He shot a glance at the Doctor, who had silently sunk into his chest.

To the Master he said, 'Tut, Tut!' for the Master was banging at the piano and, overcome by sentiment, was singing, 'They were young, and they were merry.'

Rising he smiled, restored to humour, and surveyed the scene.

'My dear friends,' said Mahaffy, 'I must be getting home.'

Chapter XIX

COUNSEL SAVES THE CORONER

Lad Lane and Bumleigh were drawn together by a great bond of sympathy: they were married to sisters. They were left without illusions about each other; and their regard for each was more equable than high. It is not surprising, therefore, to find them changing sides, exchanging briefs, and slanging each other with all the gusto that advocates can assume when they are paid for being sincere. When the bond is remembered we can forget what might need explanation, the reversal of their rôles. When Friery emerges from the cynically named Mountjoy he finds that he is being prosecuted by his former Counsel and defended by his former prosecutor, Lad Lane. I was on the point of being surprised myself until I realised that it would reveal an ignorance of forensic procedure. Who or what is a prisoner, to set a bound to the march of a great advocate? Friery was not surprised.

Bumleigh rose to his full height. He looked pale and dishevelled, like a vulture moulting. His solemn agony had not yet faded from him. He remembered the pill. He opened for the plaintiff in the tones of one weighed down by a sense of injustice done. He suggested by his appearance that all the world's injustice had afflicted himself.

'We have here a poor woman who is the sister of the dead Duff. She went to live with him on the death of her older sister. Your Worship has before you the spectacle of Miss Duff, a woman twice bereaved.'

'Mrs Aggie Durkin, saving yer presence, a decent married woman, even though I am a widow and all that.'

'Aggie Durkin?'

'Short for Antoinette, me Lordship.'

'A woman thrice bereaved,' Bumleigh continued. When he had recovered from the shock of the plaintiff's recognising Counsel without the mediation of a solicitor, he accepted it was a breach of etiquette, instructions from the plaintiff on the field, as it were. 'She entrusts her little legacy to the City Coroner, who, taking advantage of his high office and of the confidence implied by it, squanders on the fortuitous fields of Baldoyle the hard-earned money of this widow and thrice-bereaved worker. I do not know, nay, I would not care to know that infamy could go deeper. I would not care to know,' he repeated, wagging his head, 'lest my faith in the truth and goodness of human nature be destroyed. There is at root true worth in all men, even in some criminals. That worth is hard to find and is, if present at all, at a low level in the Coroner.'

Lad Lane interrupted with, 'My dear brethren, – '

'This was the manner of the distribution of the lady's savings. It was – you have heard the word "invested" in four ponies – that is, to use racing parlance, until the monkey was exhausted by other pony transactions.'

'There is a society – I believe there is a society in this town, Mr Bumleigh,' said the Recorder, 'known as the Society for the Prevention of Cruelty to Animals. I fail to see why it should permit such an exhibition in such a public place. I hope the monkey has recovered.'

'If the monkey could be recovered, your Worship, we wouldn't be here at all,' Lad Lane informed the Recorder.

Bumleigh in affected despair sat down.

'Get up,' said Lad Lane, 'and go on with your menagger-ey.'

'The *g* is soft in "menagerie", Mr Lane, soft,' said the Recorder. 'Was it at a circus, was it at a circus that the money was lost?'

'No, at Baldoyle races. He put the monkey on in a series of ponies. No bookmaker would deal directly with the Coroner. He had difficulty in investing it.'

'It is very all confusing. Where is the money now?'

'Lost,' moaned Bumleigh, 'through a betrayal of trust.'

'How much is lost?'

'The whole monkey.'

'But a monkey is not money?' the Recorder roared.

'I said I thought that I had made it clear,' said Bumleigh penitentially, 'that I spoke in racing parlance : a monkey is five hundred pounds.'

The Recorder jerked himself high on his seat. 'And have I been kept for two days listening to a case over which I have no jurisdiction? You know well, or you ought to know well, that I cannot – this court cannot deal with sums in excess of fifty pounds. The case should never have been brought before me at all. Take it where you like, Mr Bumleigh. But take it out of my court. And when you appear before me again I will request you not to use horse copers' slang. Dismissed !'

That is how Counsel saved Friery the Coroner. And Friery was grateful to him, for, as he explained afterwards to his friends who were congratulating him, 'It's better not to have Bumleigh with you, but against you, if he is to do you any good.'

An attack of virtuous indignation afflicted Friery :

'I'd rather be a whore any day of the week than one of those barristers. A whore sells her body; but a barrister sells his bloody mind to the highest bidder. A whore can call her soul her own.' The idea of Friery as a whore was overwhelming. Falstaff as the Witch of Brentford ! But Old Friery ! Why, he couldn't get a fidelity guarantee to set up even as the Whores' Bank.

Chapter XX

SURGERY

Romantically the Richmond Hospital stands at the head of Red Cow Lane and gazes down that lane at Smithfield, with its red haycarts, and over them at the Dublin hills. It is a dreadful reminder of the eighteenth century; ghosts of cripples like those that Hogarth drew haunt its wards. But while the new hospital is being built we have to reside in the residents' dormitory, a great loft that runs the whole length of the building. Black curtains sliding on rods wall the beds.

One morning Birrell shouted, 'Up! Begin the happy day. It is time we did something for Medicine and the general public. Bright gave them kidney disease, Graves gave them goitre, Hunter gave the world a syphilitic sore, and Cheynes-Stokes described the last rhythms with which the death rattle rises and falls. We are failing the public : what have we done? I alone stand out in this decadent age. I have invented – '

'What?' I asked eagerly.

'A new disease. It has first to be described. That is our way of patenting it, and making it our own. Then it makes me immortal. Wait till I come back from the bath.'

'Can't you tell me now?'

'Oh, I have no intention of telling you until I first stake my claim by describing it. Many people suffer from it without knowing from what they are suffering, but once it is *described,* then they are diagnosed and, as you know, diagnosis is half the cure.'

'Well, tell it to Tom Myles.'

'Blast you, pair of bastards, can't you let me sleep?' yelled Lumm, the House Physician. Confidence in our parents' probity encouraged us to ignore him and to treat the appellation as a term of endearment, because it suggested that our forebears were in a position to ignore the *convenances*, and therefore it implied in some measure an inherited liberality in ourselves.

'It would not apply to Myles, who is married. It is a disease to which bachelors mostly are exposed. At present it is Birrell's disease and bad enough; and the remedy is desperate.'

Sir Thomas Myles was about to take the class when we got down. He had shaved off his beard and was the best-looking man in Dublin, with his cavalry moustache and his Herculean frame. He was a great Shakespearean. In his youth he was a great boxer, second in strength only to his brother, who on occasions of joviality could take an unsympathetic policeman in each hand and use them for cymbals as he led the chorus back to Stevens Hospital. There were giants in those days.

Birrell and I were lucky to be his clinical clerks. It did you good to be near the man even if he did spar up to you, hit you on the chest, and draw attention to you, saying, 'Come on, now. Expand that bonnie brisket!'

He patrolled the wards in his white coat, while we in our white coats followed, one on each side, like two acolytes. At the last bed near the window at the end of the ward he paused, and, taking down the patient's chart which we had written up, read aloud the following notes to his class, which consisted of about twenty medicals and a strange, gigantic doctor from Cripple Creek in a dickey and top boots under his trousers, who was over here in order to do some post-graduate work:

Name	Sam Simmons.
Age	Fifty-two.

Occupation	Sailor.
Address	Whaling ship *Spitzbergen*.
Diagnosis	Tertiary syphilis : aneurysm right pop-
	liteal space; gumma of nasal septum.

This unfortunate mariner in the last bed by the window was the butt of the cruel wit of Dublin. Patients take a pleasure in chaffing each other, but the chaff can be deadly on occasion. It was our duty to stop it, but unless one slept in the patients' ward there was no way of putting an end to it. And we were uncomfortably enough housed where we were without sleeping with the diseased. Thoughtlessness can give rise to cowardly and cruel jokes. One morning when I came in unexpectedly I heard a muffled shout from under the bedclothes :

> 'Eh, Sindbad,
> Was the last hatch you were in bad?'

Gross guffaws hailed the sally with delight.

I spoke out. 'If this goes on I will read out aloud the diseases from which every man in this ward is suffering and we shall see who will be much better or worse than the sailor.' It would have availed little to ask the sailor who were his persecutors. The sailor with false loyalty to blackguardism would not give them away.

Sir Thomas was beginning :

'We have here a distinguished citizen who went down to the sea in ships and faced the watery wastes in pursuit of his business, which was the pursuit of whales. Many of us have pursued game of one kind or another, but who of us can say that he has hunted a larger or more dangerous quarry? And yet, gentlemen, this man here before us has faced the roaring seas and the biting blast. He has heard the thunder of the breaking ice and he has braved the terrors of the Arctic night. Perched aloft in his cockpit, those eyes have scanned vaster horizons than we have scanned, while he described an arc with his body as the heaving waters swung the ship with him in his precarious position. Picture him to yourselves, gentlemen, as he watched and waited until at last the monster, the physeter, Nature's largest living thing, appeared. He has seen the great whale shouldering off the seas as he comes to the surface; and, regardless of the inappropriateness, perhaps, of the epithet to the gentler sex, he shouts, "Thar she blows!"

'Is not that right, Sam?' Sir Thomas inquired not unkindly of the fascinated able-bodied seaman, who was cheered to find himself the object of so much interest and to see his profession placed in such romantic light.

'All hands on deck! And then, gentlemen, Samuel comes sliding down from the cockpit in his haste to stand to the great sea-beast. Ah, but, gentlemen, the shore has its dangers as great as, if not greater than, the deep. Deadly are the ways of the deep, but the ways of women can be deadlier than the sea: some visit to the docks of a coastwise city, some dalliance, some little sport with Amaryllis in the shade, some entanglement with Neæra's hair, and the harm was done, and the lurking principle entered in then that appears on the surface twenty years later. Show us that right knee of yours, laddie!' Turning him on his face, Sir Thomas delicately felt the aneurysm. ' "Thar she blows!" ' He made a warning grimace. The case was beyond hope. 'Sliding down a rope, gentlemen, or climbing up one will, when the sheaths of the blood-vessel are atheromatous – you perceive what atheroma means, doctor?' he asked amid much laughter, turning to the enormous man from Cripple Creek, ' – cause this distension and thinning of the arterial wall which we call an aneurysm.' The sunny-headed, dusty giant blushed, nodded his head, and drove his dickey out over his low waistcoat. More laughter. So much for that. But we didn't laugh long. At least Birrell didn't. 'The history of this case is perhaps best expressed as my distinguished clinical clerk has expressed it, in lofty rhyme.' Sir Thomas produced – where he got them from no one could tell, but they were undoubtedly Birrell's – a piece of paper with these verses:

> 'O what a wondrous paradox!
> A sailor who escaped the rocks
> Was wrecked by going down the docks
>   When safe ashore;
> And brought to light a hidden pox
>   And Hunter's sore.
> Ah, did he, when he weighed his anchor,
> Weigh all the consequence of chancre?
> For if he did he would not hanker . . .
> . . . . '

'You gave him those verses,' Birrell growled at me.

'I did not, I assure you,' I whispered back.

'The diagnosis here is not in doubt, nor the ætiology, as it might have been in Falstaff's case, when he invoked "A gout on this pox, or a pox on this gout." We may exclude the gout. Now the question is, what to do for this poor fellow who has got what is known in Dublin as "the bad disorder". He makes no bones about telling us that he got it. He cannot remember where. "A little unremembered act of kindness and of love." He is more straightforward than the clerical gentleman who asked me, "Could you get this in a water-closet?" "You could, my friend, but it's a damn dirty place to take a lady."

'It is astonishing how accurately Shakespeare enumerated the signs and symptoms – there is a difference between signs and symptoms – of syphilis. You remember in *Timon of Athens*, when Timon is addressing those two pieces of light flesh, Phrynia and Timandra, his direction to them,

> ' "Consumption sow
> In hollow bones of men; strike their sharp shins
> And mar men's spurring. Crack the lawyer's voice,
> That he may never more false titles plead,
> Nor sound his quillets shrilly: hoar the flamen,

213

That scolds against the quality of flesh
And not believes himself: down with the nose,
Down with it flat; take the bridge quite away
Of him that, his particular to foresee,
Smells from the general weal: make curl'd-pate ruffians bald;
And let the unscarred braggarts of the war
Derive some pain from you: plague all;
That your activity may defeat and quell
The source of all erections."

Strike their sharp shins. Shakespeare must have known that the nodes on the front of the shins are a tertiary phenomenon. They say that he had it himself and that he was fumigated for it in London. It might explain his early death at fifty-two, and the hemiplegic handwriting of his signatures.'

To some whose faces looked shocked, he said: 'There was never a good man yet who hadn't a touch of the pox or of tuberculosis. There's damn little harm in an old Dublin pox.' The effect of this on the patient was instantaneous. His swollen face gleamed, and an icy light like winter sunshine enlivened for a second his bleak eyes.

'Now as regards treatment: our gifted friend here has composed a mnemonic:

' "Rub in blue butter;
And drink the mercury in bumpers
Until you stutter."

Now blue butter, which is mercurial ointment, might easily be found too strong for some skins. I would suggest the oleate of mercury.'

Again he consulted his bit of paper —

' "The glands adjoining your masseter
Are salivating by the litre;
And when you sail your love to meet her,
In boat or barge,
Your sheets will do for the Blue Peter:
Unguent. Hydrarg.!" '

Sir Thomas put his arm on Birrell's shoulder, and with, 'Keep merrie, laddie, as long as you can,' left the ward.

Now I knew that nothing would convince Birrell that I hadn't given him and his mnemonics away. I couldn't have done so, as I told him, even had I wished, for the parts of 'Sindbad the Sailor' which he showed me did not contain any prescriptions, but were directed to certain phenomena of the sea, and to certain hallucinations of the whaler's crew,

> 'Where weighted Atlantics lift and pour
> In thunder down on Labrador,
> They heard, beyond a din and roar
>   Like Thor's great mallet,
> The calling of the Coal Quay Whore
>   Which has no palate.'

There were reference to certain symptoms that were experienced by the whale who thoughtlessly swallowed the sailor. As far as I remember, they referred to the colouring effect of calomel on infants' stools, which turn green, and a suggested origin for Greenland from the effect of the mercury in Sindbad's system on the innocent cetacean.

> 'Where that cetacean defaecated
> A continent was concentrated
> From all the food evacuated,
>   Which made no mean land;
> And from its colour, when located,
>   They called it Greenland.'

After all, you cannot memorise a whole poem when you have only been allowed to see part of it. I remember his comment on the side of the page, about the sailors hearing the calling of the lady who had no palate. It was written as a parody on the marginal glosses on the 'Ancient Mariner'. 'The sailors hear the Siren voices.'

And I remember his description of the storm, which seems to have been pretty bad.

> 'The sea rose up, the South Wind snorted,
> The ship by Davy Jones was courted;
> Rolled she to starboard, then she ported
>   With many a shudder,
> And, when the waters broke, aborted
>   And dropped her rudder.'

He was in a bit of a wax after the ironical cheers he got from the class, and particularly from the hardly suppressed titters of the nurses. It was by no means a time to strike a bargain, but I am such a bad business man that even a favourable opportunity could not outweigh my inability and distaste for bargaining.

'I'll tell you what I will do, Birrell. If you tell me what the disease is that you have invented, I will tell you an invention of my own for which it only needs a little more science in the outlook of this city to earn for me its Freedom. If the town only knew what I have discovered, and from what I can give them freedom, it would be falling over itself to give the Freedom of the City to me.'

'You can keep your bloody discovery.'

'But I can't. What doctor deserving of the traditions of this long-descended profession of ours would keep to himself, or for his own emolument, anything that could be of the least benefit to mankind? I see the medical profession at the prow in all weathers, sailing in the darkness, searching here and there plumbing the depths, but turning back never, in a combined and unremitting effort to rid humanity of the floundering mistakes of that monster which we call Nature, which works regardless of Man.

' "Takes at the mother's breast suck and the babe full of benignitie," and dims with consumption the blue eyes and bright hair. I am ashamed of you, Birrell.'

Birrell got red in the face. Then airily he tried to turn the subject off.

'My disease is only a joke. I thought it out just for fun. I was not serious when I suggested giving the public a disease. What I meant was to describe a disease in the exact sense of the word, a state of being ill at ease. I will tell you if you like, but tell me your discovery first.'

'Simply this. It is not a discovery, but rather, what often amounts to a discovery, the application of one thing to another. It came to me thus. Why, thought I, not rub in the blue butter first instead of trying to overtake the client once it gets into your blood stream? I gave the idea to Medlicott, who won't report results. It takes about forty days to have clinical evidence for or against. But Vincent has been using it, and other fellows you have not met, and they have plucked of the ripest and have escaped while they saw friends of theirs like Clonfeenish, who did not use it, go down from the same distributing centre with the bad disorder. It is a watertight invention, if you can make an invention out of prevention being better than cure.'

'Is there anyone I know who has risked it?'

'That would be tellin' ye,' said I.

'Did you experiment with it yourself?'

'But do you, who have known me all these years, think that I would ask my friends to take risks that I would not be prepared to take? Come and meet Medlicott and the Citizen this evening.'

Birrell looked as if curiosity was getting the better of him. I might as well introduce him to Barney, Weary and the rest now that we are nearing the end of our industrious journey. But we have yet to get Medicine, so an attendance in the Whitworth may not be inadvisable seeing that the lecturer is also an examiner. We went.

I did not want to go. I had a far better place to go to, but, fearing that Birrell would follow me if I went there, I accompanied him to the Whitworth, resolving to get away as soon as I could. My secret was the Ear, Throat and Nose dispensary on Fridays. Sir Robert Woods worked there, and there was a liberal education going in his speciality if anyone had the sense to avail himself of it. But because it was a speciality, a part and not the whole, and because Sir Thornley used to tell the students how he hated the word 'specialist', I was left undiscovered. And I gained knowledge on all subjects medical, surgical and general and, what was more than knowledge, a fast and reliable friend.

Sir Robert worked under the most wretched conditions of anyone in the Old Richmond. A damp room with a little square window about fourteen feet up in the wall was the Otological, Rhinological and Laryngological Department. The place had evidently been a gaol or a padded room. Under the damp floor ran a tributary of the Liffey which flowed down to us from the Grangegorman lunatic asylum. Once during floods we heard a strange series of knockings under the floor. Pebbles cast up perhaps. But it was just as probably minnow with G.P.I. that, thinking they were salmon, were leaping up and striking their heads under the floor.

Remote from the classes he did his godly work. How charitable it was I alone know. What a fool I would be to bring Birrell along when even the nature of the work precluded more than one at a time from seeing the larynx or the nose? So I had the greatest of them all, all to myself. And no one was the wiser but I.

Chapter XXI

MEDICINE

A small figure of a man was lecturing on Medicine. Small as he was he bulked very largely, even bigger than Tom Myles, because he was also an examiner, and one has to respect an examiner even when you feel more like giving him the 'Postman's Knock'.

'Emphysema,' said the little man, 'is derived from the Greek, *en* in; *phusao*, I blow. If you remember the derivation you will get a good inkling of the cause of the trouble which is found chiefly in those who "blow in". Now who are those who "blow in"?' We were just entering the ward as he asked the question; and though some of the class looked at us and grinned, it only showed their ignorance, for the little man did not mean that we "blew in", because he deprecated slang and derived everything from the Greek instead.

'So nobody knows,' he said resignedly. It seemed that he had to add this example of lack of education to the many examples he collected from his class every morning.

'Let me tell you. May I help you? Would glass-blowers be fairly said to be among those who "blow in"?' All agreed with avidity. 'And now what others can we include among those who are by their vocation exposed to this disease?'

We were not having any. Which of us would be fool enough to deprive him of the satisfaction of rubbing it in?

'Users of wind instruments.'

It appeared to come as a revelation to the class.

'You will find that this man, though I have purposely refrained from inquiring what is his history, is a musician.'

The red-faced fellow nodded from the bed, where he had been kept for weeks malingering as he thought, but really preserved as a subject for lecture.

Elated by his display of observation the Professor went on, 'The resistance to the expired air as the player blows into a wind instrument produces a backward pressure, which in the course of time has the effect of dilating first and finally destroying the alveolar passages and infundibula of the lungs. Hence it is qualified in cases such as this by the term *alveolar emphysema* to distinguish it from . . . From what, doctor?' suddenly he asked, turning to someone who had been whispering behind his back. It was Weary. 'You do not know, and yet you can afford to be inattentive.' He shook his head. That meant that Weary was down in his next attempt to get Medicine.

'For non-pulmonary emphysema, air in the tissues, is a very different thing from this *alveolar emphysema* or, as it also called, *alveolar ectasia*, which as you know, or should know if you have been attending to the winter lectures, means a stretching out. Get your Greek right and you have learned half Medicine. We will now proceed to examine this patient's chest. No, no, doctor! Put up your stethoscope. What is the classical procedure for an examination? Inspection, Palpation, Percussion. Now what does Inspection bring to light? Use your eyes, gentlemen, use your eyes. Observe the great barrel-shaped, useless chest. Picture to yourselves the "stretching out" of the alveolæ within until its surface for internal respiration is reduced. And listen to its hyper-resonance as I percuss.'

With a stethoscope of white wood which might have been the caduceus of the Conductor of the Dead he hit the loudly resounding chest. 'That is what comes from playing a wind instrument. Overstrain in the athletic field may be considered as another of the predisposing factors in *Alveolar ectasia*. Now tell the class, my good man, what kind of a wind instrument did you play?'

'A concertina!'

The atmosphere was awkward to say the least about it. But what sort of an ungrateful fool was the patient? One of those who could not co-operate with his physician and therefore precluded cure. 'Blow, blow, thou winter wind!'

I tried to escape from the uncomfortable atmosphere. Not wishing to be seen and possibly connected with the Professor's débâcle, I wandered into the Women's Ward. But I was trapped as I lingered by the bed of a good-looking young girl, wondering what was wrong with her.

'Nurse, take up those bed-clothes.' A sharp command! 'There is a right way and a wrong way of exposing a female patient for examination. You can have the clothes turned down from the top or raised from below. It is neither necessary nor decent to expose a young woman to the gaze of twenty men.' He consulted the chart.

'Let me see her knees, nurse.'

The knees were duly exposed by using the right way.

'Ah, here it is!' A small patch of pink was apparent on the inside of either knee.

'Now, gentlemen, Inspection!'

Of a lout who was gazing unseeingly at a patch of red, he asked, 'What do you see?' After a while he elicited the fact that the uncouth student saw a bit of red.

'Now we are getting on. What is the Greek for "red"? Of course no one knows. Where is Dr Lumm? He is a highly cultivated man. He could tell you.'

We had other uses for Lumm than getting Greek lessons. His principal function was to send us out a list of the cases in the ward when an exam was on, with the diagnoses and the treatment.

'Of course, no one knows. Let me tell you it is erythema. That "bit of red" observed accurately but described unscientifically by our friend here is "erythema". Now for Palpation. Will you, or you, palpate this girl's knee?'

From the volunteers which were the class, he selected one.

'No, no, doctor, never palpate with one hand. Use both hands. Palpate comes from the Latin this time, and it means to stroke or to touch lightly. Now will you touch that patch of erythema lightly and tell me what you observe?'

The pink spot whitened and disappeared under the light pressure, but it reappeared quickly again. The student did not notice that. Therefore there was need for more teaching.

'Observation is one of the most important adjuvants to Medicine. Without it no one can have any success. Now you failed to catch a very significant fact : namely, that the patch for a moment disappeared. Ah, I grant you it reappeared shortly. Let us now translate into scientific parlance the result of that observation. What is the Latin for "fleeting"? *Fugax.* Very well then. We are confronted here with an erythema fugax, or fleeting erythema. Every doctor over the globe will understand you if you say "fugax", for it is the universal language which we use. In the course of your examination or palpation did your sensitive touch tell you anything else?' The student did not see what he meant.

'Was the erythema rough or smooth? I am entitled to ask you that if I am corresponding with you from, shall we say, Paris, and you are describing the case to me from Dublin.'

'It was smooth.'

'*Non nodosum, non nodosum. Erythema fugax, non nodosum.* We are painting the picture for the Parisian authority on diseases of the skin. Let us ask her how long she has had this disease. Have you had this long?'

The girl in the bed, who exhibited considerable agitation, was understood to aver that she only noticed it when the nurse pulled up her clothes.

'Ah, *recens* erythema. Now let us put the results of our diagnosis in order. How shall we phrase the description to the great specialist who is anxiously waiting in Paris? Would you be prepared, in the light of our observations this morning, to send it in this way:

'*Erythema recens fugax non nodosum*'?

Agreement was unanimous.

'But the great man in Paris is not to be put off like that. He will want to hear something of the history, the age, sex, and so on of the patient. Tell me, my good girl, have you had this *recens erythema fugax non nodosum* before?'

The girl, who was by this time sobbing violently, blurted out that she got it every morning, from one knee lying over the other. She did not mean it. She could not help it. It was not her fault.

'Which goes to prove,' said the little man, unembarrassed, 'that this case requires to be treated for – What do you think?' turning suddenly on the Doctor from the Digs, for that was what we called the big fellow from Cripple Creek.

'Narves,' was all he said.

'You have made the one intelligent contribution to this morning's round of diagnosis and treatment. I thank you,' said the little man. 'Now, as it is not my intention to cross the avenue to the Fever Wing, I will lecture you gentlemen on fevers from here. To those of you whose knowledge of medicine is kept well within bounds, it may not be out of place to announce that we are in the Whitworth Hospital. Do not forget the address. If you are examined on fevers you can inform the examiners, among whom I shall *not* be, that you had a lecture on fevers, not in the Fever Wing of the Hardwicke Hospital, but in the Medical Wing of the Whitworth Hospital. The reason for that will be apparent to them.'

Once we heard that we wouldn't be examined by the little man we permitted our minds to wander from the subject. He was telling of a great doctor, Graves of the Meath Hospital, whose dying boast was 'I fed fevers'. Before his time fever cases had their strength reduced by starvation as well as by bleeding and the disease.

'Give me an idea of the diet suitable to a fever patient. Will no one help me? Will you, sir, you who have just come in?'

It was Barney.

'I am anxious to learn what diet is safe in a case of fever.'

It sounded very strange, coming as it did from Barney in his solemn black clerical clothes. He must have had a rozener on his way up, for I don't believe he could have passed Davey Kiernan's, which by deed must be kept as it was in the eighteenth century, without a quick one to blunt the slings and arrows.

Addressing the room from where he was, he recited, glaring from under his brows:

> 'Fluid, farinaceous, fish;
> Then a chicken in a dish;
> Then to mutton, then to beef;
> Then from all rules there is relief!'

He threw up his arm in a liberating gesture. His appearance suggested that he was on no particularly rigorous regimen at the moment, or that if he had had a fever, it was one of those fitful ones which are called false fevers and cured, strangely enough, by the cause. I suffer from that sort at times myself. The little man repressed a smile. I looked at Birrell as who should say, 'Another bard appears'. The town runs with song. I saw Birrell pricking up his ears. Nevertheless I refrained from telling who the sombre-suited nightingale was. He would meet him in due course.

'Perfectly correct; but may I ask, doctor, why the dish?'

Barney was nonplussed, but we who knew the little man knew that he had to reinstate himself in our opinion, and that meant that we had to linger on until he prepared and delivered a few nasty ones.

'There has been, one might almost say, a good deal of merriment, suppressed and expressed, this morning. That is no harm; it is better, I must admit, than profound gloom. It is easy to strike a mean, to acquire a bedside manner. As a rule a student's manners may be taken to be an accurate reflex of the kind of house from which he comes and of the social status of his parents. If he comes from a good house he will need no tips from me. But there are instances which may be used after the fashion of the Spartans, who exhibited a Helot drunk as a warning to their young folk. Now we, at this time of the morning, are unlikely to find such a deterrent spectacle.' I thought he looked at Barney, who of course was sure he did. 'But there is a worse fault, so I will proceed to narrate an example of what must be avoided at all costs, and that is, lack of sympathy with the patient. There was a black-avised practitioner of my acquaintance who practised on the south edge of this city. He was attending a case of consumption. Well, gentlemen, you all know – I sincerely hope that you all know what the *spes phthisica* is – "the consumptive's hope". Listen now how this unfeeling fool treated his patient.

'One sunny morning the patient, on looking out on the strand and seeing the waters coming in from the bay, said, "Well, doctor, it's a fine day to get up and go out!"

' "And do you expect ever to get up again?" Lack of

sympathy with the afflicted is the worst trait the character of a medical man can exhibit. The lack of sympathy need not be always as pronounced and, I will use the word, as murderous as that. The same doctor, if he deserves the name, having spent some time examining the breadwinner of a young family who was dangerously ill, came downstairs to the room where the patient's wife was anxiously awaiting his verdict. What do you think he did? – he was, I should have said, a connoisseur in antiques – he went slowly over to the mantelpiece without replying to her trembling question, "How do you think he is?" He went over to the mantelpiece and nosed among some ornaments that were lying on it, and said, as if to himself, "I suppose there'll be an auction here soon." Now, gentlemen, that is no subject for levity. It shows an innate and indelible stain of inhumanity – and that in spite of the awful and overwhelming knowledge we doctors have of all the woes that flesh is heir to, the suffering of widows and the sufferings of little children, the branch of Youth lopped off. Better far at this moment for you and for all concerned to turn back, if you cannot feel that your profession is dedicated to delaying Death and relieving pain, than which, be it corporal or mental, there is no greater evil on this earth. Turn back now if you are not prepared and resigned to devote your lives to the contemplation of pain, suffering and squalor. For realise that it is not with athletes that you will be consorting – '

I heard it: 'Ha! Helix!' distinctly.

' – but with the dying and the diseased. The sunny days will not be yours any longer but days in the crowded dispensaries, the camp of the miner or of the soldier where, unarmed, you must render service in the very foremost positions. It is in the darkened pathological department of some institution that you, some of you, will spend your lives in tireless investigation of that micro-

226

cosmic world which holds more numerous and more dangerous enemies of man than the deep. Your faces will alter. You will lose your youthful smirks; for, in the end, your ceaseless traffic with suffering will reflect itself in grave lines upon your countenance. Your outlook on life will have none of the deception that is the unconscious support of the layman : to you all life will appear in transit, and you will see with clear and undeceived vision the different stages of its devolution and its undivertible path to the grave. You will see the bouncing child and the young girl free in her stride and "fancy free", as the great Shakespeare has it, and the stripling, lose gradually their freedom and desire for motion and gradually slow down. You will see that sightless forces, the pull of gravity, the pull of the grave that never lets up for one moment, draw down the cheeks and the corners of the mouth and bend the back until you behold beauty abashed and life itself caricatured in the spectacle of the living looking down on the sod as if to find a grave. These are no delightful thoughts, but they will inevitably be yours, and your recompense for them is that your work for a short space may ease pain and baulk, if only for a year or two, the forces of annihilation and decay. You may be able to avert the greatest tragedy in the world – the death of the young mother; you may be able to bring back from the lonely valley of the shadow the babe, and set it again smiling upon its mother's knee.

'Perhaps it is this knowledge that produces that sympathy, let me call it (to be nearer to the Greek) "charity", which radically means loving kindness, which works the most amazing transformations in medical students. Of that merry mob I will not say that all are deliberately debauched, but I shall say to those who are, or rather to those who are inclined to thoughtlessness and frivolity, "Beware lest chambering and wantonness become habitual!" ' He paused and repeated, 'Become habitual'. Then,

'I have seen as the years of experience progress the wildest medicos, the greatest rapscallions, turn themselves into good, sober and sound physicians. It is by Charity that this miracle is wrought. By Charity. You know too much. You have seen too much. You know what suffering means. You have seen it perhaps at the acutest and most pitiable stage of all when it turns delirious in its attempts at wild delight. You have seen what the wages of sin are.

'To shun these things the recluse forsakes the world and retires to his cell. You can never remain in solitude or find leisure for contemplation. You can never retreat from the world, which is for you a battlefield on which you must engage in a relentless and unceasing war from which you know that you can never emerge victorious. You must confront the sightless myriads of the air in the invisible battle from which no medical man turns back. For this you must be prepared to sacrifice more than your lives. You must sacrifice your delight in Beauty; for, as you gaze on it, your knowledge tempts you to see beneath its bloom the intimations of decay. That is the price that you must pay for this knowledge. That is the sacrifice you must make. Your joy in life must be exchanged for devotion to the service of mankind; sometimes, as in those who are psychotherapists, they lose more than life, they lose their reason. Unselfishly to make this sacrifice is the long-descended tradition and prerogative of our profession.

'That is why, gentlemen, I ignore many, very many manifestations of ill-manners and bad breeding, because these are to me but indications of ignorance and lack of experience, and I know that these are but transitory manifestations in any man who at heart is sound. On this transition I base my hope, and on your charity, without which nothing is of any avail to mortal men. Good-morning.'

'Phew-heu!' said Birrell. 'What about that? For whom do you think that was meant?'

'It was meant for all of us. He let us away with the impression that he was an old cod this morning, so as to fix the cases all the better in our minds. He had a lot of leeway to make up, and by George he did it! You should have seen the face of the bard of the diet for fevers. He gave us what was our due. He is a conscientious and learned little man; and, even if his smile does prophesy moonlight on a tombstone, he knows his work.'

With the final exams. next week there is not a moment to be lost. 'Transformation' may get us any time now. So while we may – !

'That is a most consoling theory of his that the bigger the blackguard the better the doctor. There is a strong dialectic of good doctoring in divilment. And Tom Myles says that any man who is worth his salt must have a touch of the pox or of tuberculosis. We poor medicals have to sound the depths.'

'Speak for yourself,' said Yandell Birrell.

'I am going to think over it in a place apart where I am not likely to be followed,' I said as nonchalantly as I could, because it was just the time when Nurse Darling, the Sister in the Fever Wing, had an hour off in her kitchen for lunch.

'I think I'll look into the Hardwicke,' said Birrell.

'Oh, will you! And get scarlatina maybe or spotted fever, or small-pox or diphtheria,' I said, trying to put him off. But he was sweet on Nurse Darling, and he said, 'Oh, those are things "from which no medical man turns back".'

'That decides me, then,' I said; for if he could spoil my little plan I could spoil his. 'I think I'll chuck meditating on the harangue to doctors and go to see how Nurse Darling is getting along in the Fever Wing.' I made the remark as if it was he gave me the idea. It was a case of when two were not company.

Birrell pretended not to be disappointed. He didn't want to give himself and his liking for the nurse away. After a moment he changed the subject.

'It's a wonder he didn't call it the Reformation.'

'He didn't want to hurt the feelings of some of the class. That by bringing up a controversial and religious subject. He wanted to stick solely to the moral side and avoid pathology.'

'Pathology?'

'Luther had a discharging ear and he suffered from subjective noises, one of which he thought was the voice of the Devil. Hence the Reformation. Now anything founded on a pathological condition needs itself to be reformed.'

'Reform the Reformation?'

'What is it but a subjective noise?'

'Sorry!' I said, seeing the effect of my remark on my Protestant friend, who looked aggrieved and pained, pained when he thought that the Freedom of Conscience, for which his forebears had fought so manfully and had given the dullest martyrs to the Church, that the 'still small voice of conscience' appeared to me to be nothing more than a 'subjective noise'.

Sir William, and not Sir Thomas, was in the ward when Sindbad's aneurysm burst. His assistant, seeing the dripping bed, exclaimed, 'God help us!'

Sir William said, 'Before calling in your unqualified assistant, will you kindly proceed professionally and attend to hæmostasis?' Sir William was a precise man.

But the sailor had sailed afar into the Arctic night.

Chapter XXII

OLD MANNERS GONE

'I don't know what things is coming to at all,' said Mrs
Mack. "Lookit that now.' I followed the direction of her
bedizened arm, which pointed, as it seemed, to the centre
of a bare floor covered with oilcloth which had been
newly waxed. The room was empty save for two forms or
benches on either side, and a pianist who sat with his face
turned to the wall in front of a cottage piano on which
stood a half-empty pint measure of stout. He sat on a
revolving stool with his toes turned like the toes of an
organist; and, judging from his inept legs and inturned
toes, he was an advanced case of locomotor ataxia. But
the poor are kind to one another; so are the whores.
Doubtless in his day he had gone 'into the breach bravely
with his pike bent bravely', and had come 'halting off'.
But he got a job as pianist at Mrs Mack's. Over the
mantelpiece two gas jets lowered economically illuminated
an oleograph of Dante meeting Beatrice by the bridge of
the Arno and gripping his left infra-costal space.

'Lookit that!'

Surely it is not for traces of confetti she wants me to
look? A wedding in the Kips is as rare as a christening,
and who ever heard of either one or the other taking
place therein?

'There ye are now, the ballroom's empty and all the
bitches gone to bed.'

'But it's early yet.' It was hardly midnight.

She gazed at a grandfather clock, the face of which

was blank. Possibly some exultant Shakespearean had broken off the bawdy hand of the dial.

'Early or not, ye would think that there was no decency left in the town. I mind the time that the house was swimming in champagne before a gentleman could get a move out of wan of them, what with all their self-respect, and sittin' out, and dancin' and all the rest of it. They had to be floated up to bed in the best of bubbly. Look at it now. There's Lar in an empty room playin' paralytic to half a pint.'

I lamented the decay of manners with Mrs Mack. Her face was brick-red. Seen sideways, her straight forehead and nose were outraged by the line of her chin, which was undershot and outthrust, with an extra projection on it like the under-jaw of an old pike. There is a lot of rot talked about the effect of vice on the countenance. It gives some faces, if anything, a liberal look, but it largely depends on the kind of vice. Avarice was written by Nature's hieroglyphic on the face of Mrs Mack. I thought of the grasping ways of her and of her like, which led to the establishment of the 'Whores' Bank' so that the little starveling street-walkers might preserve a few shillings from the inquisition and the search to which they would be subjected on their return to the Kips.

'Ye can't dance be yerself. And there's nothing doing till wan of them hussies is disengaged.'

I tried to explain that I was seeking sanctuary, as it were, from the stresses of the street until John and Vincent should have been located. She regarded me as a customer afflicted by the precipitancy of her hetairi, and that angered her against them for having dispensed with sweet reluctance all the more.

'Go into the office. I'll be back in a jiff, Aida!'

As Mack flung the door open a jittering sandy fellow who had evidently been hiding somewhere behind it appeared. 'Oh, yes. Ye've come to read the gas meter, I suppose,' jeered Mack. 'You'd be better with your mother in the Hay.' To me she confided, 'He never comes here decent and honest, but always with excuses as if he was afraid to go upstairs. Them incorporated accountants makes me sick.'

The room I entered had, opposite to the door, a large washstand containing two jugs in bright-yellow basins. The basins were of the same pattern, the jugs were different, one of them being made of enamelled tin. A large bed hammocked with age occupied the space behind the door. Open trunks lay on the floor beside a mirror. A sewing machine, spools of silk, slippers, cigarettes, empty cigarette tins, greasy curl papers, a broken alarm clock and one that was busily ticking, together with half-a-hundred odds and ends of gauzy female gear lay in old chocolate boxes or on the table in littered heaps. On the mantelshelf, mottled by the marks made through the years by numerous cigarettes, were several rancid tumblers and a photograph of a smart trap full of girls and another of Kit Malcomson's coach. A candle was stuck in the neck of an empty Guinness bottle to give light. A fly-blown mirror still held the decorations of a vanished Christmas – pink tissue paper and a card stating that Christmas comes but once a year. An empty matchbox lay in two halves in the empty grate. But magnificent on the dirty coverlet lay the satin nightdress case of Mrs Mack.

I looked around for a seat. At last I found a chair, on the back of which stockings were drying behind the muslin curtains of the window. I dragged it into the room, placed my elbow on the side of the washstand and waited an opportunity to explain that 'I was only waiting' to Mrs Mack.

After the second or third cigarette, the door opened softly and a most extraordinary apparition in a white robe or nightdress slowly entered and advanced in dramatic fashion into the room. She held out her hands with one arm raised before her face.

'Jayshus, Lady Macbeth?' I did not say it aloud. Surprised, I said it to myself. It was a new one on me, if you see what I mean. I wondered, was it a joke of Mrs Mack? But then she did not know me well enough for such entertainment, and when I thought of her jowl I knew that a joke was completely out of character with her spiritual make-up.

Meanwhile the white-robed figure was passing diagonally beyond the foot of the bed. She seemed a woman in the early forties. Her profile was almost classic in its dark beauty, though her head was rather flat-topped and large. She advanced on tiptoe, step by step.

It certainly was a new one on me. What is the idea? Is she a somnambulist or what? Mack should have warned me that she had a queer one on the premises. Maybe she wanted to frighten the life out of me, but she forgot that it is not easy for a woman, ghost or no ghost, dead or alive, to frighten a medical Dick.

What is going to happen next? I can't very well run out of the place and chance the enmity of Mack, who, for all I know, may know who I am. And the boys will miss me when they come here if the messenger finds them, for I told at least half-a-dozen brats and an old woman where I would be found.

'It's a shame for ye and the likes of ye,' the old woman had shouted. I had to put up with that. Even when I explained the errand of my friends she was more incredulous. 'A whore's christening!' And then the corner boys began to give me advice – partisan advice, it is true; but they enumerated many houses of joy as I ran the gauntlet between jeering laughter from above the sheets that hung from the windowsills of the street.

My lady of the nightdress had gone as close to the candle as she could. She could not be altogether daft, I thought. She wants as much light as she can get on her face. She stooped forward and drew with her arms the attention of an imaginary audience. What a change! When I saw her full face the beauty of her profile was derided by her mouth and nose. I saw strong square jaws below, more than matching her ample forehead and making an oblong of her face. A tiny, inadequate nose failed to confirm the promise of self-control and character in her jaws and brows. A little petulant rosebud of a mouth hung half open and showed strong, brown, tobacco-stained teeth which were slightly gapped in the middle. It was alarming : it was as if a child's nose and mouth had been inlaid on a strong square face. The skin of her thin neck, on the side towards the light, looked muddy. What was more disconcerting was the hard, dry look in her eyes. This is no fool, thought I. But what can such a finicking nose and weak child's mouth connote in character but vanity and wilfulness? I hope Mack has not codded her that she is an actress, an entertainer, or a 'receptionist'. It would be easy to play on her vanity and to make a complete cod of that poor creature. If that is so, she ought to be protected by the police. What can it mean?

'Dementia præcox,' said my brain; and I felt sure that my diagnosis would be expanded and confirmed by Connolly Norman. She had nothing on under that nightie or Greek robe, or whatever she called it, for I could see her leg when the light went through the fabric.

'Am I in the way?' I asked after some gesticulating business 'up stage'.

She took no notice, but came out suddenly with a whole lot out of Shakespeare. It was easy to see that she was so absorbed in getting the delivery right that it would be time enough to explain what the hell it all meant afterwards.

' "How comes it now, my Husband, oh, how comes it," '

235

I spoke too soon when I said that no woman could make a medical student afraid.

' "That thou art then estranged from thyself? . . ." '

But this is a well-bred woman, a lady, as we say — I realised the moment she opened her baby mouth. What the hell is she doing in this galère?

> ' "The self I call it, being strange to me:
> The undividable incorporate
> Am better than thy deereself's better part.
> Ah, doe not tear away thyself from me;
> For know my love: as easie maist thou fall
> A drop of water in the breaking gulfe,
> And take unmingled thence that drop againe
> Without addition or diminishing,
> As take from me thyself and not me too.
> How deerly would it touche thee to the quicke,
> Shouldst thou but heare I were licentious?
> And that this body, consecrate to thee,
> By Ruffian Lust should be contaminate?
> Wouldst thou not spit at me, and spurne at me,
> And hurl the name of husband in my face,
> And tear the stained skin off my Harlot brow,
> And from my false hand cut the wedding ring
> And breake it with a deep divorcing vow?
> I know thou canst and therefore see thou do it,
> I am possessed with an adulterate blot,
> My blood is mingled with the crime of lust." '

The skin on her brow was stained right enough with what looked like a patch of chronic weeping eczema. Our professor might have diagnosed it as psoriasis, for he is very precise, but—— Her voice rose to a scream. She pulled up her skirt and gathered it about her with the modesty of middle age. I'm in a tight corner right enough, thought I. If she demonstrates any more dramatic power, or goes on with any more recitations or whatever they are meant to be, Mack will be down on me like a hundred ton of bricks, or, what would be worse, on her for compromising the respectability of the house.

> ' "Being strumpeted by thy contagion," '

she shrieked.

If this is intended for me, my good lady, let me inform you that my Wassermann is negative, or words to that effect.

'But your cue would be :

> ' "Plead you to me, fair dame? I know you not!" '

But then you know nothing about the stage or Shakespeare. That was Adriana's speech from "The Comedy of Errors." '

She said this in such a surprising, gentle and sensible tone of voice, full of the most pleasant intonations after all her histrionics, which were to my mind a bit overacted and hysterical, that I fell down flat. I was, if you follow me, greatly surprised to realise of what sudden transitions from the heights of excitement and yelling to the plains of sense are women capable. What an hysterical show she could put up if anyone crossed her! She would be a match for Mack, for she would be quite capable of running half naked into the street and of getting Mack in badly with the police. Perhaps Mack is not the worst, I thought.

'If you could appreciate art, you would see with what feeling I have interpreted that passage.'

'I heard it,' I said.

'Heard it. Of course you heard it. I enunciate perfectly.' She gesticulated daintily with tobacco-stained fingers. 'But that is as nothing compared to the interpretation. Duse treats it differently.'

'I know all about the drama,' I assured her. After all, she was talking to a B.A., T.C.D. who had to know all about Thespis and his wagon and the beginning of drama.

'How did it begin?' she asked me with suspicious meekness.

'Oh, it began in a wagon all right. Thespis and the boys went round giving shows in the different places in Greece.' She frightened me by the contemptuousness of her sneer. When she turned her head sideways her short upper lip came back from her out-slanting teeth in a grimace.

This might be a case of schizophrenia, I thought. She has certainly got a double kind of countenance even if she hasn't got a divided individuality or a double character. She has determination, impatience, and an uncontrollable nervous system :

'How comes it now, my Husband, oh, how comes it,
That thou art then estranged from thyself?'

Well, I like that. It is she that is estranged from herself, as well as from the decent family from which she has probably run away. It is just as well that it is make-believe she is acting. I wouldn't be her husband for more than ten minutes, and that would be risking an hysterical fit.

'Wagons, indeed! Do you seriously think that any play could be presented from a wagon – from the rather primate vehicles that must have belonged to ancient Greece? There would have been no room. How can you be so absurd? There would have been no room for movement. Could a chorus dance in a wagon? You are perfectly ridiculous.'

'Who is perfectly ridiculous? I spoke of the beginning of drama, before there were choruses or that sort of thing.'

'And what other "sort of thing" constituted the early plays?'

'Tragedies and comedies.'

'It would have been both a tragedy and a comedy to attempt to play from a cart.'

Her gesticulations were too dainty for her fingers or the argument. They suggested signals from a child imprisoned in a middle-aged frame.

'I will grant you that there were huge cars called *carroccios* in the Middle Ages which carried altars and priests that went into battle when the borough was at war.'

I thought that I heard sounds of a bit of revelry from the hall. Had the boys arrived? I made as if to go. With an imperious gesture that was rather too stagey, as was most of her style, she willed me back into my seat, which nearly collapsed.

'What about a Punch and Judy show?' I interjected, almost as irrelevant as the Citizen himself.

'Punchinello is said by some people to have been Pontius Pilate in the miracle plays.'

'But, my dear, the club?'

'Don't interrupt me, "my dear". It is not my theory. I was going on to say, until you interrupted me, that it was taking the vocationalists in that put the drama *outside* the church.'

'What do you mean?'

'Don't you see that when the clergy allowed the shepherd to act the shepherd and the merchant the merchant, these introduced the bawdy (just to get their own back). Players then journeyed from church to church, playing outside (in the church enclosure) after religious service – property being transferred by wagon. That is how the idea of the wagon came into the evolution of drama. But these were not your carts.' She gave a little sniff and blew her nose, which remained red and amorphous. She was a bit too contemptuous with 'your carts'.

'But, damn it all, I am not as ignorant as you think. You see, my dear, I am a B.A., T.C.D.'

Suddenly she turned upon me like a harridan. 'How dare you "dear" me, when you are ignorant of the first principles of dramatic art?'

She laughed so long and piercingly that I could not hear what was going on in the front room. Is she on for making a scene, I wonder? This kind of thing will bring down Mrs Mack.

I had an inspiration. 'Can you sing as well as you recite?'

She steadied and regarded me for a moment, an anxious moment for me. At last she decided that, poor creature though I was, I would be worse if I were to go through the world unaware of her beautiful voice.

'Of course I can sing, and I would have won at the Welsh Festival at Carnarvon last week, in fact I had won. It's a tragedy. I would have won again had I gone by an earlier train.'

'Yes, a morning train.'

'But, don't you see, I went by the four forty-five.'

'I don't see.'

'No, no, you don't, for you are always thinking of yourself. You are one of those who are so self-centred and selfish that he can only think of himself. I took the four forty-five thinking that I would have time to meet my accompanist and get him to run over the part for fifteen minutes. I left out a meal, and I found myself on the steps of the place with the door locked and a note pinned on it from him saying that he would be back at seven forty-five. That was no use to me. I knew my part perfectly well, of course, and we ran over it in ten minutes when he did arrive.'

'Splendid! Saved!'

'No. Can't you wait! If I had only that time to spare to sit in the audience and see what was expected of me and how the presentation worked, I would have been all right; but he left me no time.'

'And you were starving?'

'I would have got over the starvation, but another thing happened when I was on the stage.'

'What?'

'Can't you listen? I never sang so well.'

'Bravo!'

'But the judge. I lost only by one mark.'

'Yes.'

'Wait! By two marks, because he said I fell away in the last minute in the dramatic closure.'

'Dramatic closure?'

'Can't you understand? Listen! Can't you even listen? A bucket had been left in one of the wings through which I might have made my exit. I saw at a glance that I couldn't cross over the bucket, and I had to cast about in my mind for a dignified exit.'

'Damned difficult over the bucket.'

'Wait, won't you! And keep singing all the time.'

'Perfectly awful!' This was a case wherewith you could not be too sympathetic.

'Wasn't it?'

'Of course. But you got second.'

'No, you fool. You have forgotten the whole thing. Because – don't you remember? – I won it the year before.'

Ignoring me, she started an aria grande that quavered with hysteria.

I knew it would happen. In came Mack.

'How often have I told you to stop that yodelling! Ye'd think ye was one of them gladiators gliding down an Alp. Isn't it enough for ye that I was fined last week for a misdemeanour? How the hell can I run a decent house with all this bloody Art about the place? Ye'd think this was one of them disorderly shanties up the street. There'll be no recitations or rehearsals to-night. At least none that would suit your style. The few that's come in is mouldy. So you may as well dress and forget *Cavalleria Rusticana*.'

Tears welled in her hard, dry eyes. They softened and were for a moment beautiful, until they reddened with her nose and she went out on a heavy tragic turn.

'Who is that?'

'Whist, will ye? If she thinks we're talking she'll come back and yell you and I into Store Street.'

Mack opened the door and looked out.

'I couldn't let her give her show before them bowsies to-night.'

'But what the hell?'

'She ran away from her husband——'

'What's her name?' I interrupted, bursting with curiosity.

'A minute now and I'll ask Lar. Blast me, if I can ever remember proper names – Lar!'

She returned saying:

'I believe it is Maypother, Minnie Maypother, but she calls herself Mercédès for the stage. As I was saying, she run away to take up slumming and to do good for the poor Magdalens, as she calls them. Her sister goes round the slums in England in a coach and four. When she seen Lar playing the piano – them sort is daft for adjewlation – she said she would give dramatic recitations to improve the tone of the place, and I let her carry on. I let her do it, though she's "rescuing" us, and all that sort of a thing, for it does give a bit of tone to the place right enough. In spite of me kindness she'd drive you daft. She expects the whole place to be given up to her operatics, and she goes mad and then bursts out weeping if she finds any wan inattentive. And I need not tell *you* that their minds is often wandering here,' said Mrs Mack, with a laugh like someone guffawing in hell.

I laughed too.

'Ye'd laugh at the other side of your gue if ye seen the company she keeps. She likes them long and lathey and black-haired. I can never let her out of me sight. She only seen Jack Lalor the barber once when she began calling him "Jack". She wanted to congratulate him on the way he done his sleek black hair. "Rescue" me neck! I'd like to know which of us is doing the rescuing! She's in a huff now, and gone off to peel potatoes for the poor cabbies in The Hay. It'll be Liberty Hall next, and then——' Mack jerked her thumb over her shoulder, put back her head, and, turning up her eyes, said solemnly in

242

her best French, 'Chantez, ma belle!'

So Jack Lalor the barber is lathey and black.

From the street at that moment an uproarious earth-quake sounded. And in the middle of the shouting, scream-ing and yelling a horse neighed. It sounded uncanny in the echoing street. Windows were thrown up, new shrieks added themselves to the growling roars of the bullies and the curses of the auld wans below. Mack dashed into the hall to lock the door. As she did so I caught sight of Vincent's Mephistophelean grin in the ballroom. Behind him, the Citizen and a cattle-dealer he called Dumnorix were standing. Apparently they had been chaffing Lar, the pianist, for I heard him acknowledge fretfully: 'It was because I had no innuendo that I was a failure in life.'

'You must have had an insinuating way about you for all that,' the cynical Vincent said.

Suddenly down the stairs behind us poured half-a-dozen females in different degrees of undress. One who was naked was screaming to be let out.

'Shifts that pass in the night,' said Vincent, enjoying the row.

'A breach,' said the Citizen, 'in the dull routine.'

I marvelled at the pair of them, the Citizen and Vin-cent. They were enjoying a *mêlée* in the Kips.

'Phantom pregnancy,' said the Citizen in his puzzling way, *à propos* of nothing.

'What has happened?'

'Ye bloody well know what's happened. Tiger Roche has been knocked out.'

'And the devil mend him,' said Mrs Mack.

The lady who had answered my question, albeit it was not addressed to her, burst into a storm of tears. It seems that the Tiger was her fancy man. Judging by the 'tur-bido' it further appeared that Roche was every girl's fancy man.

'They're takin' him into Teasy's! Let him in!' The naked girl yelled.

Mack shouted to the nude to get to hell into the office, and, in spite of what I took to be expostulations, went to her assistance.

'Why did ye run out of the room like that?'

'You would if ye were in it with an incorporated accountant.'

Another voice chanted, 'Wan, two, three, four, five, six – buzz!'

Returning, Mack lamented the decay of manners once more.

'I declare to Jayshus, the language of some of them doxies would make me want to puke. Answering me back indeed! Some of them would have the last word with their own echo. It makes me sick.'

It was consoling to find such a delicate reaction against vulgarity in Mrs Mack. I inquired into the significance of 'One, two, three, four, five, six – Buzz!'

'It's a bit personal,' she explained. Apparently it referred to the number of steps climbed and to the electric bell that had to be rung by the candidate who sought admission to the Locke or Westmoreland Hospital. 'It's a bit personal, they're always joking me about that, and I wouldn't mind, but she only just out of it herself.' That apparently made the reference worse. My impression was that it was not in good taste, and that this too incurred the disapprobation of Mrs Mack. Again, reflexly, she shouted 'Aida!'

An iron hoop hit the window and wedged itself between the sill and the lower part of the frame. There was a final stampede in the street.

'The police?'

'It sounds more like soldiers,' said the pianist, who had a good ear.

Looking out I saw a tall figure in a bright waistcoat lying on his back and looking horribly pallid in the greenish light from the lamp. Several women were mourning him. 'Ah, glory be! Doesn't he look terribly like himself? God help us!'

I became greatly concerned for poor Mercédès, led by her craze for adulation to seek any audience that would listen to her and give her praise. Would she ever make The Hay? There would not have been such a row, Vincent said, if a man his own size had knocked the Tiger out. But when a little Seventeenth Lancer that wasn't even welter weight stiffened him under the lamp-post to which he had tethered his horse before absenting himself on felicity in Hell's Gates, it was a bit too much. It was Mother Maher who said that, as far as she could see, he was only a light weight. To those around the prostrate Tiger she shrieked, 'Take him into Teasy Ward's, and that will bring him to.' So the issue had been joined, while the police remained Olympianly aloof until the body was rescued and revived and half-a-dozen Lancers regained for their comrade his tethered charger.

'Is any of yez a medical here?' a hoarse voice shouted through the closed door.

'Aida!' yelled Mrs Mack.

'Come out! There's a bit of a window stuck in Fresh Nelly's eye!'

Vincent volunteered to render first aid. The Citizen had disappeared!

I was left alone with the paralytic pianist and Dumnorix the cattle-dealer. It must have been the Citizen who had named him Dumnorix, who is, I think, if my memory holds, a character out of Cæsar's *Gallic War*. It could not have been his name. He looked hardly Irish, much less Continental. A large loaf-like bald forehead bulged in meaningless massif like that of a hammer-headed whale over his dull suspicious eyes. Long black-sided teeth made his mouth look like a grating in hell when he smiled over his fat, doughy paunch. Damn it all, the Citizen has a gift for, not onomatopœic, but – what do you call it? – onomatideas. I must ask the Benign One. What I am trying to say is that by the word 'Dumnorix' he gave you the idea of dull negative bulk with ikeyness at the end, and suggested the obscene bulk of the cast-up, gas-inflated carcass of a whale. Most of the ominous words in the language are built about the vowel lowest in the scale, U. Dung, Numa, lump, turgescent, bum, rum, slum. He had a large fob of seals. Disraeli? What the hell was he doing in this place, he who was one of those whose mistress was a menu? What did he want?

I looked over my shoulder in the direction of his heavy gaze. A tall, faded charmer with two triangles of raddle on her cheeks stood in the doorway. The triangles brought to my mind the make-up of Joey the clown in Hengler's circus, or the labels on bottles of Bass. She turned her head from side to side, commending herself to Dumnorix the cattle-dealer. She had a pointed chin like a faun, and there was still something faun-like about her. Suddenly I thought – Was this one of the Citizen's jokes: the cattle he dealt in? Dissatisfied, he gazed at his large shapeless boots. The lady advanced on feet nearly as large as his. Otherwise, she was the remains of a beautiful woman. It is something to have an anatomical eye, even though you have dearly to pay for it. You can see beauty in a limb, a movement, a glance, or in the way the teeth are set, just as Homer could see beauty in 'the fair tusked swine'. There was a time, O boy, when this must have been an astoundingly handsome woman; even her enormous feet could hardly have cancelled her attraction in her youth. The cattle-dealer emitted a grunt.

'Kiddie, are you weak? You must be suffering from flatulence. Let me order you a large brandy.' This brought him to his senses. But not before she had beckoned down the back hall.

'I am quite able to order what I want.'

It was too late!

'Don't trouble, Dearie, I've done it for you. And one for little me.'

Dumnorix shook himself and tried to rise by means of a gold-headed cane which suddenly appeared in front of his paunch. It was useless. Mack herself appeared ('It's the maid's night off') with a tray on which there were three large brandies. The dealer in cattle groaned. He was in for it. With the utmost reluctance, incommoded by his girth, he produced a golden sovereign. Mack whisked it away! 'There's no change in a decent house. Them's old liqueur brandies. Who expects it? Aida!' Who indeed?

But I wish that Vincent would return. It is time I was out of the Kip. I should never have landed myself in it but for the Citizen's night call.

When the discussion relative to the cost of the upkeep of such a respectable establishment and the cost of Cupid was over, he rose, poisoning my sight, and took his belly for a personally conducted tour of the house.

I realised I was not alone when suddenly the pianist swinging round on his pivot, said, 'Once the horizontal ridge makes its appearance under your navel, goodbye!' He said it with satisfaction, for he was thin. 'Good-bye.' He blew imaginary kisses left and right as if retiring from an encore and leaving the amorous scene. 'O'Connor of Celbridge told me that, and he is one of the leading doctors of our time. Farewell and Adieu!' He revolved back suddenly and softly strummed a sea shanty. I took the opportunity in all modesty to withdraw.

Vincent was coming up the steps. I turned him back: 'A bit of glass in the cornea. I took it out with my tongue.' That was a good tip. When a doctor is far from help and the requisite instruments, before the conjunctiva swells, lick the foreign body out with your tongue. Vincent was such a long time at medicine, 'taking the long course,' as it appeared to Golly, that he had picked up a good deal of disconnected knowledge.

As Vincent and I walked through the sourly stinking street, I thought of Barney's lines, which in their testimony to a certain decadence threw a light on the bewilderment of Mrs Mack, and her difficulty in accounting for the trend of things.

Across the street I saw two of our well-known athletes. I began to think how unconvincing the words of the apostle, when he wanted to get the 'boys' of Greece, who were all athletic fans, would be to us or to some of our champions at all events. Though they too strove for the mastery they refrained from very little.

> 'Refraining not for any prize
> I saw our young men play with punks,
> The speedy lads with twinkling thighs
> Who beat the world between their drunks:
> Long Irvine trained by Tommy Monks,
> And Purdy Clegg and Windy Way:
> The best who wrinkled running trunks
> Of all the patrons of The Hay.'

(Some things, by God, are better 'unencored' and they'll be unencored if I can help it.) But I said that to myself as we walked through the long rancid hell, the frowsy pores of whose awful denizens tainted even its polluted air.

Chapter XXIII

TUMBLING IN THE HAY

'There is a window stuffed with hay,
Like herbage in an oven cast;
And there we came at break of day
To soothe ourselves with light repast:
And men who worked before the mast,
And drunken girls delectable—
A future symbol of our past
You'll, maybe, find the Hay Hotel.'

With regard to The Hay Hotel I ought to dwell on its antecedents.

'Stephen,' said my Father, angrily it would seem, though the scene is almost forgotten, 'don't you think a man in your position is compromising Maria?' The evidence was what the lawyers call circumstantial. Stephen in dishonour stood and muttered something. 'You will both leave my employment in the morning.' Thus it came about that Maria, the cook, who was so skilled at making those entrées called *Maddeleines en surprise*, owed her exit to her entrée, or rather to her being taken *en surprise* in the house. I always felt proud when I heard that almost unremembered act of love recounted, that my Father did not ask, 'What are you two doing?' It would have been banal, and, coming from a doctor, not to be excused.

So they retired to the mews and acquired the premises which, from the load of hay constantly replenished in one of its windows for the refreshment of night-weary cab-horses, was called The Hay Hotel. Barney, who is a bit of a bard, made this lay:

'Though it is "hotel" all right,
No one ever stayed the night,
For we always came so late
That the night was out of date,
When the sun indecent lit
Summerhill and Britain Street.'

No one took the slightest notice of the excellent belly-
fodder which filled the other window on the opposite of
the entrance door. It was the long table (at the end of a
long passage) full of boiling coffee, hot tripe and onions,
skate (on Fridays) and crubeens that attracted the weary
nightfarer. We were seldom weary, for as Barney says,
'We have Weary with us to provide any weariness we
require.' But it was a welcome haven in the small hours
when, as Vincent says, the soul is apt to shuffle off, etc.
You could stay it with hot coffee and line the stomach
protectively with a gelatinous crubeen.

I could hear a horse sucking water from a barrel at the
corner of the house under the down-pipe in the darkness
as we went in. Right enough, there was Mercédès by the
fire, peeling potatoes that were mostly peeled already.
She took no notice of us. Maria winked. So she was left
alone. She didn't seem to be enjoying her new act as
much as the speech from Shakespeare and the scene
with me. Two of Wauchope's coal porters, with their
peaked caps with the little blue cloth buttons on top,
sat with their backs to the passage sipping tea from a
tin cup. I stole a glance at Mercédès and ordered a
helping of collared head. Where was John? Vincent
didn't know. He was all right, he was paying off a cabby
at the door. In he came with Old Friery and a young
brunette.

'I declare to God,' said Old Friery, 'you're talking like
Rasher Doyle.'

What led up to the discussion I could not ascertain.
Maybe it was the result of John trying to prescribe for

Old Friery's alcoholism. 'Like Rasher Doyle.' I knew the Rasher was so-called because of his preference in the morning for a rasher to a pig's ear. The long passage from the front door was crowded by them a long time. I heard a Cockney voice, that of a girl, asking, 'Where do you think you are gettin' orf?'

The Citizen was the first to come into the light. He was followed by Old Friery, who was already too sleepy to benefit by the hospitality of The Hay, a young girl and Rasher Doyle the greengrocer, with his slanting eyes.

'Tripe and onions for the Coroner,' the Citizen shouted. 'Skate's roe for meself!'

Maria, the cook, scrutinised him curiously, looking at him with her abrupt black eyebrows more than with her eyes. Maria, the cook, with her oblong red face and flat-topped head, made you think of Easter Island or something painted on a post. Her spiritual life expressed itself in Art, in which she was an authority – hence the two delf poodles on the mantel and a statue of Robin Hood.

'Skate's roe!'

Hearing the shouts, Stephen put his head down from the top of the stairs to the right. I had seen Stephen lifting by an axle a brougham with one hand when washing it. He was a good man to fall back upon when in an unclarified situation. He had a great grah for me and I for him, for he often stood me when I was quite a chiseller a glass of raspberry cordial. I delighted in bringing custom to Maria and to Stephen in The Hay.

Mercédès, who was sitting with the muddy side of her neck towards the fire, gave a little scream and shuddered out of the room. Maria turned round with the ladle in her hand to look after her in surprise.

'I wish she'd pare her potatoes somewhere else,' the mild Maria said.

'Leave her aisy now,' from one of the coal porters, preparing if the need arose to fight.

John's new-come lady friend, or Old Friery's, merely said, 'Wotto!' and balanced herself upside-down amongst the crockery on the table. Maria, still holding the hot ladle, hastened to gather up the contortionist's petticoats, which fell like the petals of a time-expired tulip about her wrists.

'Yez, I'd think it was Hengler's,' said Maria the cook. Maria was not too far out. By her eyelashes growing in bundles of three, which made her eyes so starry, I recognised Jenny Greeks.

The place began to settle down now like the Women's Ward in Grangegorman after the Inspector's visit, when the air was shaken with sudden sobs. Some soul was in agony, either in the lavatory or in the kitchen at the back.

'Let me go,' said Jenny, and she threw a hand-spring and righted herself. Rasher Doyle the greengrocer consulted the ceiling and asked : 'Can you beat that?'

Naturally enough, Old Friery did not take the question as applying to himself. The Citizen looked restless and embarrassed. Another labour-like sob shook the place. 'Come to hell out of this, Jenny,' he said, and took the lady acrobat by the arm.

'Arf a mo! Can ye get a grip on yerself and brace yer shoulders till I show them something, Rasher – look!' She turned herself upside-down over the greengrocer, whose face and shoulders were draped by her skirts. I noticed that she preferred to get a grip on the back of the chair than on the Rasher's sloping shoulders.

The coal porters were visibly divided between modesty and chivalry, for Jenny's drawers were short. But she had nothing to be ashamed of – I speak as an anatomist more than as a moralist, and Anatomy gives you a trained eye for a pair of likely legs and pretty hips.

Another thumping fine sob from off stage throbbed upon the air.

'Jayshus, ye'd think I came home without me wages,' one of the coal porters remarked.

Distracted, Maria toddled to the rescue. The sobs were turning into screams and choking tears.

Maria emerged alarmed up to the eyebrows. Her black hair, which was even blacker than her black eyebrows, was stiff and disarrayed. I noticed that it was so black that it became blue at the back of her head, like the middle of a magpie's wing.

'She's put her head in the gas oven! Will some of yez come quick?'

'Is the gas on?' the Citizen inquired, and was off down the passage like a faun, leaving his distracted friends. Suddenly he fell over something in the dark. We heard him swear, gather himself and strike a light. 'Mrs Adrian,' was all he said. He was gone.

We followed Maria into the kitchen, Vincent and I. Mercédès lay snoring beside an open oven.

Vincent opened her corsage. Her clothes were dainty and her body well kept.

'It wasn't from peeling potatoes she got that,' Maria volunteered, not so much to aid the diagnosis as to exonerate the house.

The patient looked anything but pleasant as she lay on her side with her teeth showing in a fixed grin.

'Have ye a jug of water, Maria?'

'What's wrong?' I asked Vincent. 'She hasn't got a fit?'

'For God's sake don't be talking,' said Vincent scornfully. 'Did you never see them hysterical before?'

'What will you do?'

'Give her a dash of this,' said Vincent, lowering the jug, 'and leave her to dry herself when she wakens up.'

'It seems a bit heartless.'

'Heartless? It's the Weir Mitchell treatment. If it wasn't heartless it would only make them worse.'

'Worse?'

'Yes, she might wake up with a fixation.'

'Fixation?'

'Yes; an amorous fixation on you or me.'

'Are you quite sure you have enough water in that jug?' I asked Vincent, for I was full of solicitude for poor Minnie Maypother.

'Glory be to God,' Maria exclaimed, 'the skate's roe will be fried to a cinder!'

There must have been a lot of fun going on when we were curing Mercédès, for when we got back to the dining-room a very tall, grey-haired woman was asking for a bit of string.

A porter held out his belt. She fastened it above her knees to tighten her skirts, and before you could say 'knife' she was on the table standing on her head. What a supple frame for so big a woman, and how deceptive those few streaks of grey! Not satisfied with tumbling upside-down she began slowly to revolve on the crown of her head. She pointed at the ceiling with the toes of her elastic-sided boots. Long white cotton stockings outlined her shapely limbs.

'She's a revolving beauty, all right,' the grim Vincent confessed.

'There's no beatin' the auld town,' said a porter, who took a more patriotic and therefore a less personal view.

Jenny must have had a few jars in her for she was evidently roused to rivalry. She approached Old Friery. 'It's a pity that ye haven't enough 'air on yer 'ead to give me a grip. I'd show them something if you had.' 'It has been a dungeon's spoil,' Vincent sneered, but it was lost on Friery. 'Did you ever see a one-arm planch?' There is no doubt about it, Friery looked extremely alarmed. Jenny turned round and spotted the tumbler's gentleman friend. ''Ere, up on the table with you and give us a hold on yer hands.'

The tall lady fell backwards among the plates of tripe. 'Two coffees and a collared head!' Maria announced emerging from the kitchen before she saw the long-drawn-out sweetness on the tripe. 'The tripe and onions is off!'

As Stephen was remarking that this kind of thing should stop, Jenny leapt into the air, and with her hands on his reliable shoulders, turned herself upside-down. She slowly bent her knees and straightened them again in the evolutions of the feat. Suddenly I began to feel elated. Her agility gave the sordid place the atmosphere of a little village in France where one might see balancing women and contortionists in the booth of a travelling circus. I felt transformed out of place and time. The abandon and élan of mediæval life filled me full. Jenny Greeks flooded the place with the simple gaiety of a long vanished and innocent world where all our artificialities and constraints and conditions of happiness went by the board. Absurdity and simplicity there was, but where was the bad conscience or the 'harm' in these balancing women? 'Even without a few jars he can get drunk on good company alone,' Barney often said. This must be what is happening to me now, I thought, because for a moment I was back in a braver and more gallows world. Back in the Citizen's world through a gap in the 'dull Routine'.

This must be the explanation of my desire for 'low company' — one gets away from sophistications, one savours life nearer to the bone. It is only by placing living above moralising that we can become innocent enough to enjoy Life.

In a way I regretted that the ascetic Kinch was not here. This would be the very place for him to indulge his astringent joy and his delight in the incongruous.

What would he quote in the Hay Hotel? He kept Paracelsus for pubs. Maria was worthy of Novalis. She too
was a mystic. Yes; Kinch would have revelled cynically
in The Hay. I can hear him agreeing gravely with Maria
when she pointed out the symbolism of the ornaments on
the mantelshelf:

'In the spiritual Kingdom man must everywhere seek
his peculiar territory and climate, his particular neigh-
bourhood, in order to cultivate his Paradise in idea, that
Paradise which is scattered over the whole earth, that is
why it is so unrecognisable.' He would have defended
Maria with her statue of Robin Hood.

Stephen was still hidden in skirts while Jenny twinkled
her toes on high. Maria opined that there was time and
place for everything but that those favouring conditions
were not at that moment combined in her home. Stephen
inclined himself forward and Jenny jumped down. Mercédès came rushing out from the kitchen and bolted
down the passage with her handkerchief to her nose, all
signs of suicide gone. Suddenly she tripped where John
Elwood fell. Her scream of terror reached us from the
long dark hall. Stephen went to investigate with a lamp.
A woman about forty years of age lay on her back, foam
was forming at the corner of her mouth. Mercédès, who
had tripped over her body, lay farther on with her brainy
head lying on her slender arms.

'It's Mrs Adrian,' Stephen said.

We raised the well-known and popular epileptic and
carried her into the room. Vincent started a dissertation
on epilepsy. Friery the Coroner pulled himself together
when he heard of the contingencies that made for death.

'She'll look better when she wakens up,' the Coroner
opined.

She had the makings of a good-looking, well-preserved
woman of forty. Her features were straight, regular and
nicely proportioned. She had a compact and shapely

English skull. Her hips were pretty and compact = the English are a compact people. But her countenance was still distorted with spasms or grimaces. Hundreds of dilated capillaries showed like daggers in pale gules on the shield of her face. I could not help comparing that compact, shapely English head with the large Irish head of Mercédès, though Maypother was no Irish name.

'She's looking better already,' affirmed the Coroner, who, in spite of his days among the dead, was full of solicitude for the living.

As no one seemed to be taking any notice of the tumble of Mercédès, I, being a humanitarian at heart, went to see what I could do. I searched with a match the dark passage, felt along a door stuffed with hay, but I could find her nowhere. She was gone.

A coal porter would thank the lady for his belt. Having strapped this about him, he informed the company, unnecessarily I thought, that he was nineteen inches from diddy to diddy and that the hair between was like catgut. His butty drew him away. The Rasher suggested that he should chaperone Jenny home. But Jenny wasn't 'having any', leaving you in doubt whether she referred to the chaperone or to her home. Mrs Adrian woke up and announced in an English accent 'This here ain't Faithful Place.' She fell back swooning. 'Oh, where is he?'

'Take her upstairs?' Vincent inquired.

But Maria was not prepared to extend her hospitality to the people from Faithful Place. 'You'll do nothing of the kind,' she asserted. 'I've had my bedroom papered by a *most* respectable man.' Little did she think that her rusty son was shivering with lust in Mrs Mack's.

'Some day for sure them chaneys will be smashed,' Maria continued. 'And them dogs is for luck, and that fellow stands for wisdom or health or something like that. Ye can see the feather in his cap. They all stand for something or other,' she ended with pride.

'Here everything stands for something else!' the tall woman commented in a cultivated voice.

Vincent said grimly, 'And isn't it just as well?'

I was endeavouring to get her line of thought when a cabby entered with the question, 'Who goes home?'

Seeing that no one wanted it, we engaged the cab.

From the east down Summerhill a shaft of gold lit the great tenements of crumbling rose.

Chapter XXIV

GOLLY CONSULTS THE FACULTY

As we were going down Red Cow Lane a band of small boys came along drumming on empty tins.

'Where are yez going with the band?' some larger corner boys inquired. Instantaneously came the answer: 'To play yer old fellows out of jail.'

How biting is the wit of the kindly Irish, with its assumptions of scandal and hardship for a background! I much preferred Birrell's more genial British cynicism.

When we arrived Golly was in a profoundly mysterious consultation with Barney and Weary. We were sorry to break it, but I had to introduce Birrell. This was done accordingly. Mr Golly with a gesture of hospitality pushed a basket of dry toast and biscuits towards his last acquaintance. 'Sod the lark with that, till I get you a ball of malt.' It was the height of Mr Golly's hospitality since the morning that the drinks, immediately after his *secondes noces*, were 'on the house'.

The metaphor took my fancy. The lark apparently was the alcohol which soared up into your brain and set your imagination singing while the food beneath acted as a sod for the ascending bird. The Halogens sat silently. But I did not look in their direction long.

In came the Citizen; and I was well pleased. He would keep Birrell in talk while I was being called into consultation. My colleagues in their best professional manner explained the position to me and asked me to suggest a remedy.

'There is a mushroom,' I said, 'which if given to women – '

'Whist, for God's sake,' exclaimed Golly, looking about him as was his wont when genuinely alarmed. 'Go aisy on that mushroom. I never heard of it and I don't want anyone else in this place to get to hear tell of it.'

The remedy was, as Weary explained, required by Mr Golly and *not* by his spouse.

When the terror of being overheard died out of his eyes Golly tried to set us on the train of thought.

'Jack Lalor the Barber recommends a skate's roe. He takes one occasionally, not that he wants it. Ye know what a warty fellow Jack Lalor is?' I did not; but even if I did, I refused to call in, or to have Golly call in for me, an 'unqualified assistant'.

'What about a few dozen oysters?' I suggested.

'No use,' Golly said excitedly. 'She'd see me eating them and maybe order herself another dozen, and where would I be then?'

Evidently, I thought, Mrs Golly secunda is no wappened widow. Then, just to show these merchants' sons that there was medicine in the blood, 'My father,' I said solemnly, 'on one occasion prescribed mulled Burgundy, a dozen oysters and a mattress in front of the fire. "And if that fails," asked the patient, "what will I do then?" "Then send for me." I don't suppose my father, who was a serious man, saw the joke.'

'Serious or not, there's no joke when it comes to that.'

Weary asked, 'Do you know Ringsend?' Golly nodded, hoping for a good augury in his intimacy with the place.

'Well, go down to Ringsend, and when the fishing boats come in get yourself a young skate; don't mind the roe, it'll be right enough if it is a kind of cockerel skate with the virtue still in it. The fishermen themselves prefer them even to a black sole, and there's no place fuller of fine children than Ringsend. A young skate.'

'But Holy Heaven!' Golly exclaimed. 'She'd catch me cooking it. How could I cook it?'

'What he wants is a secret love-philtre,' Barney said. 'There's a tailor up in the Whitworth Hospital who has nine children – I'll ask him what he takes.'

'Ask him nothing,' Golly prayed, fearing for the secret. 'Ask that fellow nothing. He's as wide across the chest as a herring is between the eyes. Who cares what he takes? He squats on his hunkers all day and he has nothing to do but stitch. It's the rest he gets does the trick. He used to live in Crampton Court.'

I failed to see the relevance of the last remark. It may have been a spark from the anvil of his mind which was under stress. It may have been the cramped space that led to overcrowding and not the nine children that overcrowded the space – the dialectic here is reciprocal.

Being thoroughly trained in medical methods, I began to get down to first principles. Golly's infirmity might arise from emphysema. 'Have you ever been in the band?' If he said that he had, I intended to ask at once what he blew into, warned as I was by what happened to the Professor after he had lectured for half an hour.

'I was a Forester once, but I only played in practice, not in costume in processions.'

'Ah, what did you play?'

'A bit of a drum the size of a tambourine.'

Wasn't it well I inquired? You see how thorough I am; even the Professor might have been caught out. A tambourine or timbrel. 'Players upon the timbrel.'

'I gave it up as soon as they brought in the pipes.'

('I saw Calliope wyth Muses moe,

No, it wasn't emphysema. I must try other first principles. I tried. Golly did not know his wife's first husband nor the cause of his death. This latter question
threw him into a meditation. After giving the question
considerable consideration : 'I wouldn't put it past her,'
he conceded, almost to himself. But he opined 'from all
accounts' and from her outlook on life, that she must
have had 'one of them sousing husbands'.

There is no knowing what was in the love-philtre that
her nurse gave Iseult. There is a love-philtre described
in *The Midnight Court* which consisted of the wings
of dung-flies and water-beetles soaked in beer. After all,
there is cantharides, which is a green Spanish beetle, in
the British Pharmacopæia. But it was not a love-philtre
which might have a bilateral action that was required
here, and when he would not let me name the mushroom, fearing that it might be overheard, where its
effects would have been superfluous, I realised that what
Golly wanted was something 'For Men Only', like ser-
mons to which Mr Beddy never goes. Something almost
magical in effect. There was an advertisement in the
Whitworth of a German discovery, a circular which in
an idle hour I perused. It described a West African
bark, and a sample specimen was enclosed.

Weary mischievously broke in : 'The Chinese – '

'Aw, my God!' said Golly. 'Don't mention them!
I'd be afraid of them fellows.'

The interruption did it. I resolved to tell no one, but
to give it to Golly myself. Well, not exactly tell no one,
for then I wouldn't have had a witness to attest my
success if it came off.

A loud shout from Elwood startled the room, and
the Halogens at their table were surprised that it was

not directed at them. It was a shout of appraisement, of victory.

'A great huer! Here's a great artist entirely,' said the Citizen, acclaiming Birrell. They had been getting on nicely, it seems. Had their 'balls of malt' been made of ivory they could have played snooker.

'A great artist: he has invented a new disease!' So he told the Citizen before telling me. Was that the effect of 'low company' on an 'artist'? Perhaps this *sacra fames,* this holy hunger for fame, made him more at home in a pub with the Citizen than with me.

'Tension on the tunica, pain along the cord,' the Citizen continued triumphantly. 'A new disease, and our friend's name is immortal! "Engaged Man's Gonad," or Birrell's Disease. What's this it is? *Alpha,* not; *gameo,* to marry; and *algia,* pain. *Agamalgia,* "Engaged Man's Gonad," or Birrell's Disease. Hurrah for Birrell!' Evidently they were drunk, disgustingly so. Their language would have disgusted Mrs Mack and upset the very delicate sympathetic and vagal enervations of her stomach. It would have 'almost made her want . . .'

It didn't take long to tell the Citizen anything. He jumped to conclusions even before he had the data on which to come to a conclusion. This swiftness of mind made a coherent conversation with him impossible, so I talked to Weary and left Birrell to Barney, whom he had heard in song with his 'fluid, farinaceous' effort.

'Did he tell you about the lady that fell for him?' Weary asked, knowing that I was in the mood to hear any scandal about the Citizen.

'Fell for him?'

'Got madly in love with him and his social theories and went peeling potatoes for the poor and downtrodden until she found that me bould Citizen was going about with a lassie that couldn't be kept down.'

'Do you mean the acrobat from Hengler's with the broken nose?'

Weary whispered that he did, the very one. 'And it set the actress frantic. She commits suicide every time she sees him. She has him frightened out of his wits with her hysterics. He skips off the very minute he catches sight of her. She is overdoing the rescue work now to heap coals of fire on his head.'

'Do you by any chance know if she was in The Hay early the other morning?'

'No,' said Weary, 'but he came into the dormitory about half-past two and started to test his knee-jerks with the edge of a candlestick. "Reflexes exaggerated," said he, and went to bed. We guessed there was something up. Early to bed, don't you know?'

'Well,' I said, 'if it was the Citizen's Socialist, it wasn't coals of fire that she was heaping on his head but a gas oven on her own.'

'Was the gas on?' asked Weary Mac. It was the very question that I thought so heartless that the Citizen asked when he heard of the exciting incident. So that explained Minnie Maypother's extraordinary behaviour. I don't wonder at her falling in love with the Citizen, who was a swift, good-looking fellow and mad enough to attract any woman whose own reason was a bit harum-scarum; but to think that she could keep the gamesome Citizen from tumbling in The Hay, so to speak, with the first attractive wench he met, that was sheer conceit, and showed a swelled head. Both of them 'tumbled' literally enough over Mrs Adrian in the long passage to the street.

'He fell over a woman as he left us about one o'clock, who had an epileptic fit in the passage. "Mrs Adrian," was all he said.'

Weary smiled maliciously. 'Mrs Adrian, commonly known as Liverpool Kate, is another flame of his. She sends to Holles Street for him as if she were a midwifery case, and when he comes she throws an epileptic fit. You'll find she was on his trail the other night.' So that is what he meant by 'phantom pregnancy'!

A vengeful thought seized me. How would it be to get Mrs Adrian into the Whitworth where the Citizen goes, so that the Professor could lecture on her and explain to the class what makes her foam at the mouth? Then some fine morning when the Citizen would reach her bedside – Damn it, no! We'll get her taken in somewhere else. But isn't he a caution, with one woman peeling potatoes and the other throwing fits for love of him when she is not pretending to be pregnant. Comfort me with *pommes de terre*!

I was afraid that Golly might think that one who knew so much about that part of the human anatomy – or, rather, that part of the body, for anatomy means a skeleton – might be able to help him, drunk or sober. I must say that Birrell can hold his drink as well as any Englishman, and that is saying a great deal, because I have never seen an Englishman drunk in my life; they eat too much to achieve the Term. But drink makes the Citizen shout. I did not want to have Golly my only patient snatched away – that is, Mac's and Barney's and my only patient. It was exceedingly unprofessional of Birrell, and being unqualified only made it worse. We couldn't have him up before the General Medical Council. We had no redress. That is what made it worse still.

Golly was shocked out of concentration by the savage glee with which the Citizen announced that he had passed his exam in Pathology thanks to recognising Garratty. 'How is Garratty?' Mr Golly, who had missed him for months, inquired with avidity. But it was his liver that the Citizen recognised – 'and a more hobnailed one I never saw in all my life.'

When the full purport of the remark dawned on

Golly, he gasped and asked, 'Is Garratty dead?' Then he said, half to himself, 'That accounts for it.'

'What accounts for it,' the Citizen informed him, 'was the way he used to strain the alcohol off the specimens through his set teeth.'

'But you couldn't tell a fellow by his liver?' Golly asked with a ray of hope.

'A scientist like myself can, of course! Why should a fellow depend for recognition on the morphology of the last few vertebræ of his spine, which we call his face, and not be equally identifiable by a much more important organ, his liver? It doesn't matter what kind of a face you have, but you must have a sound liver.'

Golly was struggling between the humane and the scientific outlook.

'I heard old Friery telling Bumleigh that he had a liver on him like a forty shilling pot,' Golly contributed hopefully.

'What's a forty shilling pot?'

'One of them round ones that holds four gallons and hangs on a pot-hook when the bonhams are weaned and have to be fed. It has legs sticking out.'

'Jayshus, the hobnails!' the Citizen acquiesced.

Chapter XXV

TRANSITION

Beddy's success in disentangling at last, just as he became a qualified solicitor, our involved affairs and the subsequent business in which it involved me, put out of my mind the possible results of the final examinations. Now he would be able to give his professional and undivided attention to the estate. This advantage outweighed the complications that, while waiting for Mr Beddy to become a solicitor, were caused by my having long passed my majority. The fact that he was a qualified solicitor, and as such entitled to charge fees, even though they were merely token fees, would relieve my mother from any embarrassment that might arise from taking such valuable services as his for nothing. As for the years he had worked under great difficulties and after office hours, a little clause enabling him to charge – in the unlikely event of his doing so – the estate retrospectively for his devoted work while he was emerging from the solicitor's clerk stage to the greater executive power of a fully-fledged solicitor; a little clause could be put into my mother's will, a little clause concerning the disposition of an estate for which he was willing to act not only as trustee but as residuary legatee as well; but this would be more than offset by the fact that he was able to give his personal opinion independent of the office and to give first hand his whole-time professional advice.

It appeared that as my father had died intestate I was

the sole heir of the real estate. But my mother had been administering it in the interests of my brothers and sister without putting it into Chancery. This was a very grave offence in the eyes of the Law, and only for the influence and resource of Mr Beddy my mother might find herself in the very serious position of having not only to account for but to make good any deficit during the nine years of my minority. It was a most alarming position and one which my aunt told me gave my mother many a sleepless night. What did the knowledge avail that my father never intended one of his children to inherit all his property at the expense of the rest of his family, not to mention his widow? Mr Beddy lamented that he could not find the will. He also lamented the inhumanity of the Law. It turned a deaf ear to the cry of the orphan and regarded unmercifully the defalcations of the widow. To put the estate into Chancery now would not improve matters. On the contrary, she would have to render an account of her usurped stewardship; and, by the time everything was gone into, the estate would be frittered away in lawyers' costs and still remain in Chancery. What was she to do? She went nearly every night to the church with Mr Beddy to pray for enlightenment and to find a way out that would not leave her children destitute. While she was making a novena, guidance came suddenly to Mr Beddy. If her son made a deed of gift waiving all claim, retrospective and otherwise, the estate would be saved and my mother be no longer liable to a lawsuit from her eldest son, who had no aptitude for business and might find himself under the influence of bad and unscrupulous companions. How simple it was! But Mr Beddy was a devout man and his mind was on his business which he attended as regularly as he did the sacraments; or almost as regularly – you cannot compare the two. He even saw great, if not greater, advantages if he were given a free hand concerning the development of the property. It seems that many fields had to be built on within a limited time. Meanwhile, the existing houses had to be let and kept tenanted. Agreements had to be drawn up, leases granted and rents collected. Thirty hall doors had to be varnished at least once a year. Mr Beddy could not find time to do all the managing. Happily he had a brother who could do the varnishing at half the cost of a varnisher, who would not be such a friend of the family as Mr Beddy was or as pliable as his brother. It was a pity that he could not interest a third brother of his who was a builder, but the fact of the matter was that with the rapid development of the suburbs and the demand for honest and efficient building within reasonable costs, Mr Beddy's builder brother had not a moment to himself. If he paused for a moment it might mean that jerry-built houses would spring up around the splendid mansions he was erecting at half the usual cost and so reduce the value of his own houses. But he might manage to sublet the contract to some person almost as reliable as his own brother, provided that a fourth brother who worked in a well-known builders' provider's office could influence his boss to supply materials at cost price, or nearly so.

There was no time to be lost. Interest was mounting up in the bank, and only for Mr Beddy being put in a position to stave off and to reassure the bankers that the leases would not fall in until the property was developed in accordance with the terms of the said leases, there might be a foreclosure or some move in the banks which enabled them to take over the property of widows who had no friend at need, such as Mr Beddy, to advise them. And remember – all the time the interest was mounting up in the banks.

But there was one negotiation in which even the resourceful Mr Beddy could not act for vendor or purchaser, or relinquisher and recipient, for two sides at once, if you know what I mean. I had to consult another solicitor. This advice on Mr Beddy's part added another to the long list of incontestable proofs of his solicitude and kindness to our family. So I saw 'my' solicitor. Now when a solicitor feels it his duty to make the situation 'quite clear' and to show you 'exactly how you stand', prepare for bankruptcy. In fact, when they are kind to you look out for a crash. But my solicitor – or, to put it in legal parlance, the solicitor who was acting for me, as if I were a playwright – was different, because my position was a different one from the usual: instead of asking for money or money's worth I was about to give away property. Now if I were making my will, he would have been on accustomed ground, but to be confronted without warning by a man who wanted to make a deed of gift that had a retrospective bearing as far as it was necessary, or would or might be necessary, was another matter. I must say that he stood up to it well. He began a little unprofessionally, as I thought. He warned me against a colleague, against none other than the admirable and self-immolating widows' friend and orphans' aid, Mr Beddy.

'Has it occurred to you that in the unlikely event of your mother's death – that is, I trust it will be long delayed – neither you nor your brothers and sister, but your mother's solicitor would own this estate which is increasing rapidly in value? Suppose, on application for a few hundred pounds to set yourself up in practice, you get a letter like this from your trustee and the residuary legatee of what is at the moment your estate.

' "I may further mention that I paid a fee of £111 which, owing to the circumstances and to the drastic taxation, I paid and lose personally. And, in addition, I suffered the loss of having undertaken a considerable amount of work, nearly one quarter of the bill, without any remuneration whatever, the Taxing Master taking the view that I as an executor ought to do a great deal of work for nothing, although that view was contrary to that expressed by your mother and others and contrary to that set forth in her will, etc." '

I recognised the signature with the initials which stood for Ignatius James Xavier Berchmans Beddy, evidently post-baptismal Christian names.

'Could you reply to that or untangle it? Yet I have a letter in those exact terms on my desk from an orphan whose estate Mr Beddy is at present administering. You will find yourself lucky if, not only not owning your estate, you do not owe Mr Beddy money for taking it from you and for having attended your mother while she carried out her religious duties. If a solicitor can charge for attending at a bedside while a will is being made, Mr Beddy can charge for attending at the altar rails while your mother was preparing her soul to detach itself from all earthly considerations. Think it over before making a deed of gift to Mr Beddy, disguised for the moment as your mother.'

Fair enough! But what a bloody lot of twisters most of them are. Even their kindness is more costly than their antipathy. My solicitor was an exception.

'Give me the pen.'

After all, no matter how it got into her head, it is my mother's wish. If I refuse she will only see ingratitude in her beloved son. While she is alive she will realise that I played up. It is to her I owe that extra energy which unfortunately makes it so difficult for me to sit long in one place if there is a textbook in the vicinity and not a barrel. She could have given me a watery cow for a mother. Instead of that she suckled me and, when I asked for more, turned me on to Mrs Wiseman – hence my teeth that can crack a Brazil nut and my love of movement and for charioteering round corners on two

271

wheels. After all, she was my mother, and what son can ever compensate a mother for all her anxieties? She got little joy out of me at best. So here's to her and all of it. I signed.

I had a profession, or I was being endowed with one, that dealt with the forces of life and death and scorned the kind of thing that bred solicitors. Who would compare a pursuit in which money was not the be-all with a profession that fostered Mr Beddy's close designs?

I must get down to see the results. Five of us were qualified. Strange to say the knowledgeable Vincent was not. Maybe the examiners thought him too cynical. Maybe he wanted to live irresponsibly for another half-year, doing locums for residents in different hospitals. Barney again got honours. This time in the theory of Medicine. He was great on theories. Weary did not do so badly 'when all is considered', Barney confided in me and, what is worse, in him.

What were we to do before the Conferring of Degrees, before Transformation determined our freedom?

Barney could not send a wire just yet to his mother announcing his success, lest it would bring that good lady to town before or during the celebrations. Birrell had to go home to England for a rest. He was suffering from an attack of agamalgia contracted from Nurse Darling, which is an example of one of those miracles in Medicine making those give that which they have not got. The whole of England, he said could be regarded as an immense Sanatorium for the cure of his disease. So familiar were the inhabitants with its treatment that 'even the nurses' . . . You had not to consult a doctor at all. What was I to do? Obviously the first thing to do was to get some cash. If I could find Stoddard he could have my bicycle for the nine pounds that was always ready whenever I made up my mind. The next thing to do was to go down behind the Bank to thank Jimmy for aiding and abetting me in getting qualified. Incidentally I might unload a few books and a microscope on that worthy for the use of the next generation of his pupils. Then to Golly's to reveal myself to him on the eve of the Transition, and to ascertain what effect the little tube of tablets, which I took care to send him before Birrell found them, had on his way of life. Then we might collect a few friends and include the Citizen, for since Birrell had gone home he was not so objectionable in his admiration of Birrell.

I sold the trusty bicycle that has a grass track record for a mile in T.C.D. to its credit. I sold it, for it would be hardly becoming to a doctor to take the corners on his ear at Ballsbridge before the assembled multitudes in the halfpenny place on August Bank Holiday. I sold it, but – as Golly reports Jack Lalor as saying when he sold a running dog – 'I didn't get as much as I expected, but, then, I didn't expect I would.'

Jimmy would listen to no thanks. He had too much experience. 'That's all right. That's all right. I don't think. Just so. And what will you be doing with yourself now? Cutting people up and sewing them together again? You won't sew me, I'm telling you. No bloody fear!' He turned about as if to change the scene, then asked :

'And what do you want now?'

'There are many very valuable books——' I began.

'Oh, I know all about them – and a microscope?'

I confessed that there was a microscope.

'Worn out to hell after all these years!'

'On the contrary, very carefully preserved.'

'Who did most of the preserving?'

I admitted that it owed its pristine condition to his care, yet I tried to point out, without seeming to be didactic, that you cannot wear out a valuable lens.

'No, but you can scratch it. And shove it bloody well too far down on the slides. I know all about that kind of thing: Histology and Pathology! Oil-immersion me——! Who got it for you?' Then, shouting even louder than his usual conversational tone: 'Come here, Larry, and give us a quid on all this junk. You can shove the ticket up.'

Suddenly he vaulted over the counter, and, seizing me by the arm, rushed me out into the lane. 'Come on now, and I'll stand you a bottle of stout. Ye got in first, anyway.'

The kind-hearted little man was referring, not to any academical distinction of mine in the examination results, but to the fact that I was the first to bring back the tackle of a medical student to his academy, whence it would be issued in due course to the next generation of his alumni.

It was the first evidence of Transition. I enjoyed that bottle of stout.

With Golly the reception was different, but in its way none the less warm. He was alone in the shop humming to himself:

'"And the ramble through new-mown hay."'

When he saw me his face beamed. 'You heard the good news?' he asked. It dawned on me that it was not to my good news that he was alluding but to something that touched himself. Illumination! The little tablets.

'Did it work?'

'Work! If ye'd seen me this morning you'd think I was camping out.' With a damp glass-cloth which cracked like a whip he demolished a blue-bottle which was lingering too long on a tea-chest thinking of old times. 'We're not hearing much about the late lamented these mornings, I'm telling ye. Not by any means. No, nor about the Knockbock farm either.'

'Knockbock?'

'Yes; me Mother-in-law's. Everything grew there, I don't think, from a potato to a Derby winner.'

'Was it a good farm?'

'I never seen it. And I never want to see it. But if it was as mean and meagre as the auld wan herself, a blackbird would have to go down on his knees to get a bit out of it.'

With a martial air Mr Golly shouldered the wet glass-cloth and marched defiantly along the gangway behind the counter.

'First tremor recorded at Kew, as the bank manager said to his morning signature.'

Golly continued to strut up and down the quarter deck behind the counter.

'And the ramble through the new-mown hay, Titti fol lol!'

I told him my good news. He recovered his thought before it had time to mark a faint qualification of his pleasure on his face. He might be my first patient, after all. Perhaps the medical virtue had no more gone out of me than out of Weary's young skate.

'And you're a doctor now, fully fledged and qualified? Well, well, can you beat that? And I suppose it's the same way with the other boys? Comin' and goin', comin' and goin'; and what's to prevent it?' he inquired of himself. 'Well, it's me that wishes you well!'

The till caught his eye; he went to it and from an interior drawer drew out something wrapped in tissue paper. He undid it and pressed it into my palm and shook my hand with both of his.

'I hope it's your first fee. It will bring you luck. It's a spade guinea.'

Hastily I assured him that it was my first fee and that he was my first patient. He seemed gratified and relieved.

'Talking of fees, did ye ever hear what Surgeon McArdle said to the millionaire? He had been attending him for a broken thigh for three months when the millionaire, a hunting man near Mullingar, put his hand under the pillow and handed the surgeon a cheque for 75 guineas. Mac looks at it. "I'd smoke it before breakfast," sez he. "Make it a monkey!"' We laughed at the magnificence of Surgeon McArdle.

'I seen your father,' he confided. 'Jack Lalor sez it was he was the great gentleman for dogs. Just this little one between ourselves on the house.'

He had to gulp his, for in came the Citizen, singing. Barney and Weary let him enter first. Weary smiled quietly as the Citizen called for drinks all round – quick before the advent of the equally successful Halogens made him sick. The Citizen sized up the situation at a glance.

> 'Yo, yo, ho, Yohimbim,
> Sang the Cherubimbim'

he sang.

Served, we seated ourselves about round the corner.

'And what will ye be doing with yourselves at all, at all?' Mr Golly inquired.

Asked all at once, uncertainty seemed to rule. We looked at one another. None of us like to acknowledge that his qualification came as a surprise, that he was taken aback. It was time I stood a round. Golly must come into this, though he never drank during drinking hours. But he accepted a bottle of Guinness with, 'Well, here's hair on your chest!'

Barney was not sure whether he'd go on as he came in, that is with a few pints in him, or if he'd have a small whiskey. Weary was equally between two minds.

That reminded Golly: 'Did you hear this one? Jack Lalor the Barber took a pint and then a small one, and then another pint and then another small one. Gibney of the Ninth Lock asked him what was the idea. "Well," sez Jack, "if I took nothing but pints, I'd be full before I was half drunk; and if I took nothing but small whiskies, I'd be drunk before I was full." '

'So he sandwiched them?' Weary caught the idea.

'You took the words out of my mouth,' Mr Golly informed him.

One of those strange silences which often fall on festive occasions descended on the company. They are easy to break if you are sitting at dinner with a lady on your left. You can always inquire cheerfully, 'Would you prefer to be eaten by a crocodile or an alligator?' That opens endless vistas of natural history. But it is different in a pub, with medicals to whom nothing could come as a surprise. I make bold to say that if you asked Barney that question he would consider it in terms of the mobility of the upper or lower maxillæ.

It was Golly who helped us out by repeating his inquiry : 'And what are yez going to do with yerselves at all, at all?'

Barney thought that he would devote his life to research. In quest of what he forbore to say. Weary thought that a job in an institution, where you would have free service, your breakfast brought up, and your washing free, was the highest ideal of medical life.

The Citizen emitted a protesting shout; the Citizen, the traveller : 'The Navy for me, boys!'

The Citizen certainly was elated. It would be no use trying to find out what he had been drinking or where he had been. There were times when he required no alcohol. He could get drunk, like myself, merely on good company. 'A life on the ocean wave!' he sang. He stopped suddenly and, turning to the company, said, with some of his old enigmatical manner returning : 'The great tradition! The Nelson touch! The grandest thing in history: the great signal run up!

"England expects every man to commit adultery."

'The battle was joined. The sea dogs snarled. The guns were rammed. The powder-monkeys turned black!' He worked frantically, as if he were sweeping out a muzzle loader with a long brush. He threw down the imaginary brush and, raising his arm, announced: 'And victory was won for the long week-end! Hurru! Rake her, boys!' He ran up an imaginary message. 'We won't be home till morning!'

'The extent of the week-end,' Weary explained seriously, 'is the measure of the civilisation of any country. On the Continent they are back at work at eight on Monday morning. Do you call that civilised? But in England, if Tuesday sees them, and it's time enough, they must thank——'

'Lady Hamilton,' the Citizen shouted. 'Double tots all round; and mine's a large rum!' He was already in the casemate of a ship of the line.

During our conversation he kept up a nagging bombardment of, 'Nelson! Nelson!' No matter what we were discussing we had nothing from the Citizen but, 'Nelson! Nelson!' When we turned on him indignantly, he said smilingly, 'He was a great hu – hero, wasn't he?' The sparkling eyes smiled quizzically. But when the Citizen changed from 'huer' to 'hero' it was more than evident that Transmission had caught him too.

'To have been qualified is only just to have had leave to learn. To read for oneself in the Book of Life whose hieroglyphics are human beings.'

I thought that would dampen the Citizen. Not a bit. So I continued: 'Before we were qualified we were taught, now we have to teach ourselves. I'll put in six months as a house surgeon in the biggest hospital that will take me, then to Vienna and to the United States.'

'Buenos Aires is the place for all that kind of thing. Buenos Aires.' Kinch, who smelt the bottle from afar, appeared. It was hard lines on Weary, but it was his round and he had to include Kinch. We stopped the Citizen from repeating all that stuff about the signal. But Kinch heard enough to learn that the Citizen had the ambition to serve at sea.

Kinch took his pint quietly. We all waited until he sipped it. He stared at us in a half-circle with unseeing eyes and said, waving a finger with absurd solemnity:

'The boat *rocks* at the pier o' Leith.'

'Fu' loud the wind blaws frae the ferry,' I added, not wishing to be outdone.

Kinch stopped in disapproval of my interruption. 'Rocks,' he said. We got the picture in our different ways according to the receptivity of our mind's eye.

'Terrific!' said the Citizen.

Kinch dominated the party, and he would have continued to do so in its semi-sober state, had Mr Golly not asked foolishly, 'Where is it going to?'

Kinch guffawed rudely in poor Golly's face.

'To the islands of Langerhans!' the Citizen said.

Then Weary, to help Golly, suggested: 'A job like the Registrar's at the bottom of the street and a nice house in Ballsbridge. Is there a better life than that?'

' "I doubt it, said Croker of Ballinagarde," ' Golly quoted. It appeared from his explanation that Croker of Ballinagarde, who took pride in his estate and his broad, fertile, horse-raising acres, was somewhat sceptical of there being an improvement on it in the world to come. 'That's what he told the parson, and he dying, anyhow,' Golly assured us, and relished the telling. He was back in countenance.

That was the worst thing about Kinch, his rudeness. It may have been caused by shyness, but whatever caused it, it would have been better than the effect.

'Where is Lettice Lydon playing to-night?' I asked our host.

Barney grunted and looked alarmed. I had forgotten that he had a queer strain of modesty or timidity which, in spite of Mac's theory, could not have altogether been caused by his black clerical clothes.

'That wan? She's corrupting the town. Leave her alone, in the name of God. If ye must go to the the-ater go and see Mai More du Pres dance in clogs.'

But Weary, who recoiled from actresses, reminded us that we were all invited to dine with Sir Thomas to-morrow night. I hoped that it would not be a big dinner. I remembered one to which my mother and aunt were asked, to a house of equal proportions but somewhat more pretentious. My aunt, coming somewhat early, returned 'mortified' because the family butler hesitated when they reached the great lobby on which three doors gave, so he was asked by my aunt, 'which door?' He replied, 'I'm a stranger here myself!'

I couldn't and wouldn't tell them that. That would be Trinity swank and no mistake. I hoped that on this occasion Sir Thomas's household would not require extra help, at a dinner given doubtless to confirm in us the Transition. It would be just like Sir Thomas – no pi-jaw, just a dinner.

'Nelson, Nelson, Nelson,' the Citizen reiterated irritatingly.

'Damn it, that's not fellowly of you, John. Can't you join in the conversation? We all know about Nelson.'

'A great hero, Nelson!' It was useless.

'I have the profoundest bloody respect for Nelson, with his one eye and his one arm – I agree with the doctor – he must have fought something terrible with his sword in the other hand. You can always get a tram at the butt of his Pillar.' Golly said this to ensure peace.

'A job in the Navy would suit John. It would provide a life of perpetual departure,' Barney said, and laughed irritatingly to himself.

The Citizen was about to go in a sulky mood. I laid a hand on his shoulder. 'Before the epaulettes break out on you, can't you stick it out with your friends? There will be no escaping from the mess-room of a battleship.'

'He means that the round's on me.'

'I do not. But I thought that as we have to be in good form to-morrow night, it would be more in accordance with our dignity to go back early to hospital so that those brats of medical students would not think that we were completely knocked off our balance by becoming doctors.'

'Let us start now!' The Citizen picked up his hat.

It seemed incredible, but we were not home yet, that is, back to hospital. Carefully I separated my spade guinea from the other coins and stuck it in a waistcoat pocket. We filed out after the Citizen.

'I'll bet you one thing,' he said, turning to us, 'Lettice Lydon is not as good-looking as Phœbe Hilton!'

'Who cares?' asked Weary Mac.

'I care. I wouldn't have an Englishwoman coming over here and beating one of the trimmest figures and most distinguished faces in our city. In order to re-assure myself. Come on!' He pointed to the lights on his right, where old Dan Lowry's had given place to the Empire. 'The box is on me.'

'A very quiet night indeed,' Barney prophesied. But it was not every night one gets qualified or that one of us could put up a box in a theatre.

We went in, the five of us. The Citizen met with much attention. We were the only occupants of a box. That is, to be exact, Kinch and I were. For the Citizen had to wander about the back of the stalls to find Phœbe Hilton, failing, of course, he had an excellent excuse of searching in the bar. While the quest of beauty was thus in progress,

Kinch and I were left alone to gaze at a ballet of Cockney girls who were singing and dancing on the stage.

'If you understand drama, or rather tragedy——' Kinch began.

Good Lord! I thought. Am I to have it all over again? What is this it is, anyway? Oh yes. 'I will grant you that there were huge cars called *carraccios*——' I countered.

But it was one thing to take it lying down from Minnie Maypother – who would be mad enough to argue with a woman anyway, especially in a kip? Kinch was an entirely different proposition. I knew that he intended to lead up to the Origin of Tragedy (Nietzsche's 'Birth of Tragedy' had just reached the Library on my recommendation) and that he would begin with Comedy, making the pantomime his text. I anticipated him.

'If you are going to ask me who invented pantomime, I'll tell you – and you would never have guessed – a fellow called Agathon who gave, by the way, the best drunk that was ever recorded. He introduced irrelevant choruses. That started it.'

It was all in the little book that the Rev Mr Roberts was reading on the morning when we explained our difficulties to each other. But of the Symposium Kinch had never heard.

'That is how the detachment of comedy from tragedy began.'

Kinch fixed me with his smoke-blue eyes. The fine, long, curved eyelashes conveyed contempt. 'You would realise that a satire or comedy unconnected to a preceding tragedy involving catharsis, is spurious as this is spurious. Without the tragedy, without its purgation through pity and terror, there is no need for relief or comic relief. Therefore, to have these charwomen's callisthenic daughters dancing is meaningless, unless we take it that the tragedy which is presumed to have preceded their appearance is the tragedy of the everyday life of those who have come to find relief in this stupid display of expressionless legs. In the ballet proper—— Excuse me.' He opened the door in answer to an almost inaudible knock. A girl selling programmes had touched it. 'Will Madame excuse me?' He was in that mood of his in which he exaggerated his idea of gallantry absurdly. 'Madame', not knowing what to make of him, giggled in confusion. Our friends wanted us in the bar. I slipped the bolt on the door.

It is strange that it should require some lively, uninteresting scene to enable one to be thoroughly reminiscent and introspective: that is the effect the swaying ladies had on me, and it was not interrupted by the appearance of a music-hall soprano, once I got over the momentary shock that it might be Mercédès in another rôle. The uncultivated voice of the poor creature put that beyond doubt. I went over the years I spent in college. My injustice to McNought in the days when I believed the fault was in my stars, in him and hoodoos like McConkey and the rusty-faced Virgin Queen, instead of my own distaste for anything that did not interest me. The bad luck I had in many of my teachers, the good luck I had in finding Sir Robert Woods, my private University who made up for all my idleness had lost. And now there had to be an end to folly:

'We have to take upon ourselves the mystery of things,
  As if we were God's spies.'

The world was open to me now as it never was before. I could sail with the Citizen over the seas as a ship's surgeon or devote my time to 'research', as Barney intended, or seek a job in an institution, School of Medicine or dispensary, as Weary said he would. But none of these things was sufficient. Freedom was the chief advantage; whatever knowledge I possessed I could give. I could afford to be no man's man. But to achieve that independence I had to go out and work for myself – a proceeding that required self-confidence or courage, they are much the same.

I began to feel tired. The encore was insufferable. It drew my attention to the screaming woman on the stage. Women should be forbidden by law to sing, also forbidden to act before doctors, at least. Doctors, trained as they are, can only see how acting to hysteria 'sure is near allied' and thin partitions, etc. It was rather disheartening. But it was part of the price we paid for knowledge, for knowing what should not be known – for wearing thin the Great Illusion, as Vincent would say. It would never do to throw my gloom over the last night together. If the boys wanted to drink, what pretensions had I to teetotalism? I would see what was going on in the bar.

There was no enthusiasm for sobriety in the bar. It was thick with smoke and the confused sound of many conversations. The thin figure crowned with the protruding forehead of Kinch leant over the form of the seated Rasher. Kinch was admonishing with a finger. That meant that he was reciting something from Ben Jonson or one of his own Limericks:

'Have you heard of old Admiral Togo,
Who said to the girls, "It is no go"?
But won't there be sport
When we come back to port.
Yo ko go, yo ko go, yo ko go.'

He altered the stress on the last two syllables to destroy the rhythm.

The Rasher looked completely bemused, which is what he was literally. Kinch loved to deal out the pearls of the poets to the most unreceptive sorts of people. He probably enjoyed his preposterous and ill-placed accuracy

284

as much as Rabelais did when he detailed precisely the genitalia of Gayoffo.

Where were the boys? I caught sight of Weary and Barney together at the end of the counter. That meant that the Citizen had picked something up who met with the disapproval of the non-philandering pair. A trim figure in a dark blue tailor-made was talking rapidly to the Citizen. I could only see her side-face, which was pale and aquiline. She had a proud profile that could easily convey scorn. Her white teeth flashed in a smile. She must be a quick and witty woman to match the Citizen's machine-gun mind. Leaning with her back against the counter, surveying him seriously, wide-eyed, stood Jenny Greeks. That is why the Rasher looked so lumpish. Jenny has fallen under the spell: physical, not mental in her case of that pard-like spirit. I went over to the boys.

'Kinch says that this pub is too clean. He wants to go to Fumbally Alley.'

'And drop out on the way,' Weary opined.

'Well, that is his own affair, but I am either going back to Richmond now or to the Coombe to hear what happened to Vincent.'

Barney laughed uproariously at Vincent's discomfiture. I promised to bring the Citizen along. The Citizen introduced me to the piece of animated ivory to whom he was speaking. She extended a queenly hand from her chair: 'Excuse me glove' – no; she was waiting for a friend. She was very sorry indeed. She had another engagement.

'Right, right,' said the Citizen. 'I can understand that.' He smiled so tantalisingly that I thought the Phœbe would forget that she was a lady in public and give him a clatter.

'Come on, Jenny. Slip down your drink and come along!'

Jenny tried 'another engagement', but her attempts

to be staid failed to impress.

The Citizen brushed them aside with, 'Let the Rasher fry, he's learning Literature.'

Yes; Kinch was emphasising, finger in air in front of the Rasher, slumped in a chair. Jenny slipped away. She would meet us at the door when we had secured a cab. The Rasher, seeing us still in the bar, never suspected that Jenny was gone or going. It was not so easy to detach the pair who had forgotten all about the dangerous charms of Lettice Lydon, who was at that moment bringing down the house with *double entendres*. From what I saw of her she couldn't compare in face or figure with Phœbe Hilton – and what a splendid name is Phœbe Hilton, with a figure like Phryne's in it! The worst that even the Vice-Provost would say about her, had he emulated some of his emperors and visited our low haunts, would be, 'An interesting type.'

'It's a great thing to get rid of Kinch,' said John with a muffled voice, from the back of the cab, and from behind Jenny who was balancing on his knee.

'He is frying the Rasher,' Barney suggested, forgetting that we had that pun before.

'Wotto, when he finds me gone,' said Jenny, wriggling in search of a comfortable posture.

I could imagine the Rasher's position. His illiteracy attracted Kinch, who at the moment had probably got as far as 'The soul has an ineffable love and permeating yearning for the body, and the body envelops with mortal warmth and love the soul,' or something to that effect out of Paracelsus. It was about time for it now. It came out as a rule after a quarter of an hour when he had his victim well mesmerised, and it was a prelude to 'The Green Cuffs'.

'Dolly Coxon's pawned her shirt, to ride upon the baggage cart.'

We were lurching happily, in spite of the squeeze, along through the teeming Liberties, and coming into the majestic gloom of St Patrick's Cathedral, wherein lay the discontented Dean. I wondered, was that mind at last at rest? He died because his love outran his patience, and because his vision of what was due to human dignity was outraged more in this country than it would have been in any part of contemporary Europe. Over-zealous, he grew to hate those he helped. If you take life too seriously it will break your heart through your own estimate of it. Being an Englishman he could never understand that misery was a *modus vivendi* in Ireland.

I may have had a few drinks. I will admit that, but they did not blind me to the fact that it was no way for Jenny, with a foot, no matter how shapely, out of each window, to pass a sacred fane. I said so and requested her to behave in a more ladylike fashion. I did it with such dignity that Barney said I was drunk.

'A modest proposal! Jayshus, the terrible Dean!' the Citizen shouted. His mind was like lightning. I thought he could not have seen St Patrick's from his position, much less that he could have read the savage essay by Dean Swift.

My remarks anent propriety had the effect of making Jenny swing about and put her two feet out of the left window. She was balanced on the Citizen's knees. Her head was on Barney's thigh and her skirts were all over Weary's lap.

Uneasily that embarrassed traveller inquired if we were anywhere near Fumbally Alley.

'Quite,' said I, and I gazed at the moon. It was certainly there a moment ago, like a chariot wheel rounding the spire. That was a moment ago, but now it seems to be between me and the gloomy black door of the place; and it is not round; it's gibbous, if you see what I mean; and it's more white than bright, and, what's very strange, it seems to be coming along with us in the cab. It's gone! Weary made a movement that put it out. But who could see clearly in a dark cab, with people tumbling and balancing all over the place? And we're not in Fumbally Alley yet.

Suddenly a voice from the sky inquired, 'Are yez lookin' for Clonfeenish's?'

'Why should we pay for a shebeen when we can call on Vincent in the Coombe?' said the economically-minded Mac.

'Go on to the Coombe,' we yelled from the cab.

'We can send out for the stuff,' Weary said.

'I am afraid,' said Barney, 'that we cannot bring this young lady in.'

'Why not?' asked the Citizen sharply.

'Well, just at present she is not eligible.'

It was all lost on Jenny, who did not know that we were bringing her to a lying-in hospital.

'If the Matron hears of it there is sure to be trouble, and Vincent will be put out.'

'Whenever did a Matron hear of anything that there was not trouble? She ought to be in her bed at this hour of the night.'

Nevertheless when the cab stopped at the Coombe door I thought it wise to go ahead and prepare Vincent.

Vincent was sitting in front of the fire, alone, in the students' room. He was smoking quietly, and when I entered he did not look round. On the table beside him were a bottle of stout and several yellow-backed novels. But the sideboard was enriched by a ham, a turkey and a magnum of champagne. No wonder he did not want to transfer to another hospital or to tempt Transition. When I told him my difficulty, he leaped up: 'Jayshus, bring her in. What's the place for if it isn't for women? There's nothing worth looking at here just now, not even nurses.' His outlook was obviously influenced by his want of success.

'But she is hardly a patient.'

'That's all right. She might be tubal or ectopic. Leave her to me.'

'She will be out of place all right!'

I gazed in wonder at the ham as I went out with the good news. It was fresh and there was but a slight concavity in its side, revealing the fine pink meat and the soft white fat. There are mysteries connected with Medicine, I realised for the thousandth time.

The boys poured out of the cab, keeping Jenny in the middle of the huddle, for who knew what the Matron might be up to if she heard a crowd coming in.

Vincent needed no introduction; Jenny recognised his Mephistophelean countenance at once, and – blushed! Did she remember her exhibitionism in The Hay? Or what? Blushed? Exactly! And it was most becoming. It made her look as ruddy as a pippin and quite countrified and unsophisticated. It was impossible to imagine her with her nose before it was broken. But even the broken nose, retroussé as it was, suited her : she benefited by the allowance one made for it – a quite unnecessary allowance, for with her bright, wide-apart eyes she looked like one of those girls who stare from the black frescoes of Pompeii, in whose eyes was nothing but the light of day. I was glad of the blush, for I took it as an earnest that there would be no tumbling in the Coombe. I sent the cabby to Fumbally Alley for five dozen and a few bottles of J.J. It would never do to exploit Vincent's hospitality, stuck as he was, and all of us through.

'Gentlemen,' said Vincent, with extraordinary good humour seeing that he had the exam in Medicine before him again, 'on this occasion, unique in a hospital such as this, you will agree with me that it calls for the best response of your host. I have had the good fortune to receive a hamper from "a grateful patient" who once had a housemaid's knee, and would have had a stiff joint for life had I not sat up with her morning, noon and night for a week as dresser to Sir Thomas Myles. There are some – and I regret to say that Sir Thomas himself figures prominently among them – who question my treatment. But who will question the results?' He waved his hand at the sideboard. We applauded guardedly but sincerely. 'Thank you, gentlemen – and you, Madam. The end justifies the means.'

'Tell us about the means,' said Silly Barney.

'Ah, my friends, the means consisted of a square of lint saturated in tincture of iodine, a useful drug, but one that badly brooks imprisonment. I regret to say, that when I applied it to the lady's knee, I covered it with oiled silk before bandaging. Three days later, on opening my dressing before Sir Thomas, I opened the bursa : the iodine had burned its way through everything, including the bursa, which, when enlarged, as you know, makes what the uninitiated public are satisfied to call "housemaid's knee". The lady was no housemaid but a most respectable citizen – citizeness,' he corrected before the avid, dancing eyes of the Citizen. 'She probably got her bursa from devotion. However, it was cured. Fearing death through infection of the joint, my devotion to her balanced the devotion that preceded her trouble. In two months the skin grew again and the joint remained unaffected. Not so the lady. She assured me that she was very greatly affected by my unremitting solicitude and care. That, and a slight distrust of the security of victuals and champagne in the students' room of the Richmond, cause this embellishment of my sideboard. We will proceed to test the vintage. Some of you – but not you, Jenny – will have to drink from cups.'

'You'd think he had passed,' said Weary, when Vincent left the room for cups and cutlery.

'He's a great h—— Boyo! Nearly killing the poor woman and getting thanked for it !'

Whether he heard the Citizen's remark or not, Vincent

continued his discourse as he laid the table.

'Suppose I had left the knee untreated, what fountains of gratitude would have been dammed up from the world! What grace would the donor not have missed! She has laid up for herself almost as much reward as will compensate her for being unable to kneel in prayer for, possibly, the rest of her life.'

I heard the returning cab. That had to be met and paid off in silence and the dozens carried in, but not, of course, until the cabby got a few bottles for his share.

'Madam, to your bright eyes!' Jenny looked at home for the first time in such puzzling company. Try as hard as she could she could never place us, though one would have thought that a comparison with circus life would have brought her near to an understanding.

We drank the toast to Jenny's eyes, greatly to that lady's embarrassment before Vincent.

'Tell us, Vincent, did you get stuck on purpose?'

'I did and I didn't.'

'What happened?'

'The little fellow was in his full examining robes when he took me to the bed for the first of the three clinicals. He pointed gravely to the patient, who was unconscious and lying snoring.

' "I have called you into consultation, doctor, to see if you can help me with this case" – you know his usual form. I took one look at the bird in the bed and thought a bit. "Well?" he said, growing impatient. "I asked for your opinion." "All he wants is a long sleep," I said. He nearly jumped over the recumbent form. Suddenly it dawned on me that he thought I was being flippant. If so, goodbye to this exam and many unhappy returns of the next ones. "Inspection," he shouted. "Use your eyes, man! The patient is comatose!" Now I would not have minded so much if I had not happened to know exactly what was wrong with the fellow in the bed, for Lumm came up to scratch like a man and slipped me, before I went in, a note with the diagnosis of the three I was to get. No 1: Diabetic coma. No 2: Tricuspid murmur. No 3: Paralysis agitans, intentional tremor and all the rest of it. I had them by heart. And now in order to placate the little cock I had to let him think that I missed the principal case. It is a rare experience for me to pretend not to know. I usually can honestly dispense with all pretence. It seemed such an awful waste of information straight from the House Physician's mouth. "What is wrong?" "I give it up," said I, and I looked at the next bed. There was no No 2. "You could not be more informative if you yourself were suffering from diabetic coma," he said. "I have others to examine. I cannot waste their time and mine." So I'm up again in November. But just now I am too lazy to open a book. Well, well!' He looked at the date, which reads backwards on the label.

'This lethargy must have his quiet course,' said Vincent quietly, smiling as he twisted a corkscrew into a bottle of stout.

'I thought he said that he would not be examining?'

'So did I. That is why I went up. But he was only codding. He would probably tell you, if you reminded him, that he was referring to fevers or to the case with the blown-up chest.'

I was told off to dispense the turkey and ham. There were about fifty bottles of stout in attendance. As I looked at them ranked, I wondered which one would be my last. I passed the turkey and ham.

Weary said as he faced his plateful, 'She had a recovery for which to be grateful, at all events.'

Barney lifted his cup with 'Here's to iodine, the first of the halogens,' but he refused food. 'One thing at a time with all this drink about.'

'But the ham will improve your thirst.'

'Ah, that,' said Barney, 'is like perfection, which does not admit of improvement. It is the only perfect thing I possess. And while it is with me I share in its virtue. "Oh God, our help in ages past," [2] he said irrelevantly, as he raised his bottle of stout.

'A little more turkey, Jenny?'

'Take it in your hand, Mrs Murphy,' sang the Citizen, as he held a drum-stick up.

'Come on, Barney, half a plate of ham?'

'Full many a glorious midnight have I seen,' Barney assured us who needed no assuring. 'But the morning will leave me to wrestle unsupported and alone with a plate of ham and eggs. And the landlady has no dog.'

We left him to prescribe for himself.

Jenny grew chatty after the fourth bottle of Guinness. Yes, she was born in Bradford, and her job was laying mosaics at five pounds a week on the floors of banks: fishes and things; and the way they decorate public lavatories.

Fishes on the floors of banks! Surely not commemorating the miracle of the loaves? No; more probably a sly suggestion from the architect to the rate at which they multiply, only equalled by compound interest.

'Then the strong man comes along. It's easy to get out of Bradford.' None of us caught the English humour of the saying, or rather of the way she said it.

'I was a bit too old for real circus work; but old enough to get married. Then, as you might say, the circus work began in earnest.' She suppressed a smile. I saw it! Where was the Citizen's sense of humour? Nowhere. The Irish have wit but little humour. They cannot laugh at the battle while they are involved in the broil of life.

'How old were you, Jenny?'

'Seventeen.'

But surely——?

'No, for the circus work you has to begin at four or

five to get the backbone supple. I could never do a back balance, I could get no equilibrium nohow. You has to be like a horseshoe hanging down. I done trapezes but no contortionist turns.'

'Did you hear about the fellow who was engaged to a contortionist?' the Citizen interrupted, spluttering out his words so as to be in on Jenny's sentence.

'Well?'

'She broke it off!'

'Sorry, Jenny. Go on. We won't interrupt.'

'That is all about it,' Jenny said, and, conscious that she was addressing the company, she retired into herself. I wished that the Citizen hadn't butted in with a joke that no one could see but himself.

'How long were you married?' Vincent, who wanted to do a little arithmetic, inquired.

'A year and a half. Then he burst a blood vessel.'

'She's not nineteen yet,' the Citizen informed us with a hint of proprietorship.

With one admirer peeling potatoes and another throwing fits for love, you would have imagined that the Citizen would have had his hands full.

'By the way,' I asked, 'who is Dumnorix, whom you left me with the other night?' He thought that I was going to give him away, which I was not. He forgot that Jenny knew nothing of the Kips.

'Oh,' said he hastily, much relieved, 'that old blackguard out of Kraft Ebing is one of those old lechers with one foot in the grave and the other in the housemaid's bedroom. How did I come to know him? I met him in Buenos Aires and he was with me coming home on the boat.'

'Ah, the cattle-dealer exporting them to Buenos Aires!'

'Tom Myles has a finger-nail that would just suit his prostate,' said Vincent.

We all agreed that it ought to be out. 'Medical Juris-

'prudence dictates it,' I said, rather authoritatively, for I had got good marks in that subject.

'Wot goes on in here?' Jenny asked suddenly.

'If you fellows don't stop laughing you'll have the Matron down on top of us.' I had to remind them of that for Vincent's sake.

'We can always fix you up whenever you decide,' Vincent told Jenny.

'Oh, could you, could you? It would take more than you to do that.'

I thought of the strong man dead.

'Burst blood vessels!' the Citizen exclaimed.

'If you could catch me,' said Jenny.

The stout was gone, the champagne was gone, the turkey and ham were finished. It was time to go. I suggested that we might move on.

'Not yet, my liege!' said Barney, quoting Davis on Fontenoy. 'The Irish yet remain.' I had forgotten the two bottles of Irish.

'Those are for Vincent,' I explained. I had bought them and should have had a word to say as to their destination.

'It will do us no harm to open one,' said Vincent as he unpacked a pint of the 'Best Irish'. Vincent refused to mix. He was on duty.

'Whiskey!' Barney began, his smiling muzzle glowing as pleasantly as a copper heater on a breakfast table, 'Whiskey!' He threw his arms abroad and recited, 'Being moderalle taken it sloweth Age, it strengtheneth youth, it helpeth digestion, it cutteth flegme, it lighteneth the mind, it quickeneth the spirits, it cureth hydropsie.' He struck the yielding air as he brought his fist down with emphasis. 'It pounceth the stone, *pounceth* . . . !' He jumped up and stretching his arms in front of him was ready to pounce as he groped with his hands for an imaginary patient. 'It expelleth gravel, it puffeth away all ventositie, Hah, Golly! Why didn't we think of that? All ventositie! It keepeth the weason from stifling, the stomach from wambling. . . .'

'Isn't he the great . . .' the Citizen began.

But Vincent took the bottle and began to open it. 'The heart from swelling, the bile from wirching, the guts from numbling.'

'There is a lady present,' Weary remarked.

'The hands from shivering, the bones from aking and the marrow from soaking.' Barney in his confusion hurriedly gabbled to the end of his piece from Holinshed.

'Was you ever in the rats?' Jenny asked suddenly, looking at no one in particular.

Barney immediately credited the question to Weary and answered for him.

'Oh, no! Ho, ho, no! Weary is too careful. He never gets beyond the mice.'

Weary smiled wanly and enjoying Barney's turn, inquired, 'Can you give us the "Dies Suprema"?'

Barney was ready to oblige, well pleased at having his flair for poetry recognised even by his best friend.

'Ah, the Last Day! Our last day, last night . . . !' Well.

On John Kidney who died of acute nephritis.

'You know the beginning, but this is the important part :

> ° "From the walls of the flesh which immure in
>   The spirit, as tubes do their lumen,
> Came urine, and, mixed with the urine,
>   Were clouds of albumen.
> And, though by the doctors unbidden, he
>   Passed out through these clouds to his goal:
> Albumen and coma and Kidney
>   Secreted his soul.
> And there came on the Dies Suprema
>   That comes unto all who draw breath,

Death, ushered in by œdema,
   Œdema and Death." '

We applauded as well as we could, handicapped by the thought of a wakeful Matron.

Vincent pretended to be shocked by its religious sentiments or the lack of them. 'That's the kind of thing that gets us Medicals a bad name. Is the immortal soul in the human body to be compared to the lumen of a tube which is nothing?'

The Bard was almost sobered by the interpretation Vincent put on his poem. He feared that it might give disedification. He had never thought of that.

I hastened to point out that a sober man is no judge of poetry. And how could Vincent judge until he was off duty? All agreed; and Barney's conscience was relieved.

Glory be, if Birrell were here we could get the whole Rhyme of the Morbid Mariner on a night like this. He would have enjoyed our 'social'. But on the other hand, he might have had an extinguishing effect on Jenny, who would not have expanded before a fellow-countryman as she did with us. But what would I not give to hear Sindbad's adventures in the Underworld before he was blown back to life by the fulmination of the mercury in his system. And spirits he encountered down below.

> 'There was a soul of each old hero,
> From Artaxerxes down to Nero,
> Who liked the bitches with his beer, Oh !'

And then Birrell's lofty moral adjuration to the Godless who live loose lives :

> 'Hydrarg. perchlor. and Pot. iod.
> For those who don't believe in God.'

Yes; if Birrell were here. But Barney was beginning to hum :

'Thou fairer than ever, first flush of the morning,
Thou softer than snowflake when kissing the sheen
Of dawn on the white earth in cold winter gleaming . . .'

'Dawn it is !' the Citizen said.

'And there's no cab between this and College Green,' Weary remarked, who was always practical.

'Pardon me,' Vincent said, 'if you gentlemen, and this lady, do not object to travelling in a vehicle with opaque windows, I think that, aided by her presence here, I shall be in a position to oblige you with conveyance to your different destinations. Excuse me while I telephone.'

'Isn't he the great — Boyo ! He's ringing up the Small-pox Cab.' The Citizen guessed it.

'No,' Weary said, 'but I'll tell you what he is doing. He's reporting that there is a case of scarlatina among us that has to be removed at once.'

'That will be Jenny, then,' I said, 'for it was evident that he couldn't have the cab come to the Coombe to carry off a male patient. But it will only take us as far as Cork Street Fever Hospital, up the road.'

'He is sure to report that Cork Street is full. Haven't we a magnificent Fever Hospital in the Hardwicke, which is home?'

We will be crossing Smithfield about four-thirty, I realised. The Rasher will be there, staying himself with a few pints in the pubs that are privileged to open at four a.m. and waiting for the vegetable carts to come in from Crumlin and Santry.

The cabby who drove the archetypal ambulance which was called the Small-pox Cab did not care which of us was the patient after three balls of malt. Instead of a critical scrutiny, he asked : 'Are yez ready for the road ? Well, then, one for the road.'

We helped him again and helped him into position. Jenny was on the roof, head over heels, trying to kick herself on the back. But she should have begun that difficult feat fifteen years ago.

So that explains it, I thought, as I gazed up at Jenny. That explains what I took for the moon. She always wears them short.

> 'Such sweet neglect more taketh me.'

And she has double garters: the ballet girls started that idea long, long ago. All sense of danger was gone, nearly gone. Yet I dimly felt that if the cab started forward there would be an accident. But I didn't know how agile Jenny was. Gradually she lowered her head until it touched the cab roof. Then she played a tattoo with her feet on the cabman's hat. He didn't seem to mind. It was all in the night's work. It took the Citizen to persuade her to come down. We started, but we had to stop. The wooden windows were closed and could not be opened from inside; neither could the doors of the cab. The cabbie drove relentlessly on. We would be suffocated soon. Barney had to stop singing in the thick air. Banging threatened to break the precious cab. At last it halted. 'What is it yez want?'

'Air, air, air.'

'Air ye are,' he said, as he sarcastically swung open the door. I had sense enough to push the windows down. Off we went.

Barney resumed his song:

> 'Too-looral, Too-looral, Too-looral lay eh!
> We're happy and merry, contented and gay;
> We spit on your coat while we fill out your tay,
> That's humour – real Irish. Just wipe it away!
> Too-looral, Too-looral, Too-looral lay eh!'

I thought of the first cab-drive six years ago, and of

299

this preposterous journey at the end. It began in a cab and it ends, appropriately enough, in a pathological cab. To-morrow to fresh Woods—— How far have I travelled in all these years from cab to cab! All I have learned! All that stuff about philosophy – that there is a dialectic of death in life and a dialectic of life in death. I would like to believe that, even though, if I did believe it, I wouldn't know exactly what it meant. An Irishman believes best in what he knows to be untrue.

There is a dialectic – there is a woman in every man, and so on; and a woman in every cab: the whole world is a cab with opaque windows and I don't know where it is going. Wiseman; Stephen and Maria in The Hay. I should have gone to her to announce my success; poor old Maria! It was too late now. No more tumbling. I can only pray that she, preoccupied by symbols, may have reached some inward truth.

'You were with Piano Mary the other night,' the Citizen said maliciously.

'Piano Mary?'

'Yes; she was singing to you – you know where : better heard than seen!'

And so that was Piano Mary who had been so enigmatically in my mind! Mercédès, nicknamed Piano Mary by the irrepressible Citizen. 'Summer songs for me and my aunts.' Piano Mary! I wish I had known. Jack Lalor is all that remains unmet. But he will for ever be unmet, fresh, brushing through the grass behind his dog before the dew has lifted in the morning air. And so that was Piano Mary tumbling in The Hay. And she calls him Jack and she likes them lathey.

If you were in the Small-pox Cab driving through the dark, with all the instruments lost and the moon obscured, you might not know your way either. I didn't know where we were, but then observations were hard to take, for Jenny's feet were dancing gently on my midriff and Barney's head was on my shoulder as he sang. Weary was leaning out of the window searching for air.

Though no one whom I could hear had inquired, Jenny suddenly announced, 'If you do want to know, I'm dying for a drink!'

'Ha, Helix!' Barney shouted. 'It's up to you!'

'Up to me?'

'What is the use of a profession if you cannot turn it to account?'

'What is the use of all his marks in Jurisprudence, if he doesn't know that a doctor can knock up any hotel and ask for stimulants in a case of emergency?' Weary added.

It was true enough, but what we all ignored at the moment was that you had to do it with a policeman at hand.

My blood was bubbling very pleasantly – not, of course, with nitrogen, which even Vincent could tell you would give you the bends – but with *joie de vivre*; the four o'clock in the morning courage. I was on for anything.

'We have a lady's word for it that she is dying,' Weary reiterated.

Barney said, 'A matter of life and death.'

Instead of pointing out pedantically, as the Professor would, that everything, so far as we are concerned, is a matter of life or death, I shouted: 'Game! Where's the hotel?'

'We're at it.' Weary pointed to a dark door.

Out I got. I groped for the knocker. When I found it I struck a match. It was a fistful and of an unusual shape.

'A dolphin, begob!' The good old Dolphin Hotel! I beat a tattoo on the mahogany door.

'Bravo Helix!' came from the cab. 'That knock was loud enough to bring Michael Nugent out of bed.'

Again I hammered at the door. Again and again, encouraged by the cabful.

I began to wonder whether ten or forty years on there would be anyone left to say in my defence:

> 'His delights
> Were Dolphin-like, they shewed his back above
> The Element they liv'd in.'

' "I doubt it," said Croker of Ballinagarde.'

Light glimmers in the fan-light.

'Is she still alive?' Laughter from the cab.

The door is unchained and a surly porter puts out a dishevelled head.

'Quick! A bottle of brandy! There's a woman dying. Quick!'

It may have been the company I was keeping. It may have been the vehicle in which I was conveyed. It may have been something lacking in myself. What he said was: 'All that's on the night landing is a dozen of stout.'

'That will do!' the Citizen yelled from the cab.

Which goes to show that a substitute may be found for everything almost, except Life itself.

AUTHOR'S NOTE

The time of this book is approximately the beginning of the present century, and all the characters are fictitious.

The story of a lifetime

Ingrid Bergman

My Story

by *Ingrid Bergman*
and
Alan Burgess

(illus.)

Taken to see her first-ever theatrical production at the age of eleven, the young Ingrid Bergman had there and then set her heart on a career on the stage. But little could she have guessed that that childhood dream would one day sweep her to the very pinnacle of public success, and the utmost depths of private torment. Because for Ingrid Bergman, a very special kind of future lay in store. She was to become a legend in her own time, the subject – by turns – of almost fanatical adoration, and almost unprecedented condemnation. Now in paperback, MY STORY – her own account of a rich and varied life – is a very special, very different kind of book. A book that stands apart from all others, because, with a rare warmth and honesty, it tells one of the most captivating and moving stories of our time. MY STORY, by Ingrid Bergman. A remarkable life – A remarkable story.

'Her story has love, passion, despair, great names, exotic locations, bizarre scenarios, and a lot of laughs'
Observer

AUTOBIOGRAPHY   0 7221 1631 4   £1.95

THE HEARTWARMING TRUE STORY
OF A VERY SPECIAL DOG
AND HER VERY SPECIAL OWNER

SHEILA HOCKEN

EMMA V.I.P.

(Illus)

Everyone knows the inspiring story of Sheila Hocken and her wonderful guide-dog Emma, and of the miracle operation which enabled her to see for the first time in her life.

Now, Sheila describes her life since the incredible moment when she opened her eyes and saw the beautiful world we all take for granted. With freshness and humour, Sheila tells how each day brought new joys, new challenges and new surprises.

Emma's life, too, has undergone dramatic changes. She was no longer needed as a guide-dog but her retirement has been far from idle. She is now a celebrity and receives her own fan mail; she has made several television appearances; she was Personality Dog of the Year at Crufts and is greeted in the street more often than Sheila is.

'Writing simply, with innate ability to externalise thought, feeling, experience, she again achieves a lovable intimacy'
Daily Telegraph

AUTOBIOGRAPHY   0 7221 4601 9   £1.25

Also by Sheila Hocken in Sphere Books:
EMMA AND I